THE DARK SIDE OF LOVE

THE DARK SIDE
OF LOVE

Elizabeth Warne

HEADLINE

First published in 1995 by
HEADLINE BOOK PUBLISHING

10 9 8 7 6 5 4 3 2 1

British Library Cataloguing in Publication Data
Warne, Elizabeth
    Dark Side of Love
    I. Title
    823.914 [F]

ISBN 0–7472–1296–1

Phototypeset by Intype, London

Printed and bound in Great Britain by
Mackays of Chatham PLC, Chatham, Kent

HEADLINE BOOK PUBLISHING
A division of Hodder Headline PLC
338 Euston Road
London NW1 3BH

My warmest thanks to the ladies of Buchanan Orthotics Ltd, Kilmarnock, who shared with me their day-to-day experiences of working in corsetry and gave me access to notes taken during training.

Chapter One

'*He's* here!' squeaked the little runabout to Isobel. Her face was flushed and she had scarcely enough breath to speak.

'Get back to your work,' snapped Miss Jolly, the floor supervisor. 'They're waiting for those corsets on the boning tables.'

All three knew that this was an exaggeration. The boning tables in Bennyson's Corset Factory were as everlastingly supplied with corsets as the sewing machines. The runabout – she was just fourteen and looked younger – stuck out her tongue at the retreating back of the supervisor, but she made haste to obey her.

Most of the women who toiled on the machines, sewing the endless yards of tough pink material, enjoyed the visits of Lawrence Dane, the boss's stepson. Isobel considered she had far too much sense to go moony-eyed over a young man whose glance swept over the factory and its inmates with obvious indifference. She wondered why he came with Mr Bennyson. Presumably to please his stepfather, of whom he was reputed to be very fond. This was thought odd because everyone knew that he despised his mother, who had married Ralph Bennyson after her disgraceful divorce in which he had been co-respondent.

Nevertheless, Isobel found it difficult to keep her eyes on her work when she knew that Lawrence Dane was in the department. Whatever you thought of him he was arresting. His tall figure, broad shoulders and slim hips were enough to turn most girls' heads. She couldn't even fault him for being too handsome. His face was thin and the fashionable cream which kept his hair slicked back couldn't hide the reddish tinge which almost overcame the brown, while his jutting nose and chin gave him a predatory look. His eyes were a clear hazel, sometimes green, sometimes blue, but whichever colour they were they looked through the factory girls rather than at them. He's like a man from one of Mum's magazines, Isobel thought, but not the hero. More like the villain who attempted the seduction of the innocent heroine. But many women were drawn to him, as Isobel knew from gossip in the cloakroom and the bits of social news carried by the papers.

The younger girls imagined being swept up by this sophisticated male and carried off excitingly to a sumptuous mansion to live happily ever after. They knew that this was nonsense. Life wasn't like that, but dreams made their lives easier.

Isobel didn't dream of him. He was far too proud ever to descend to one of the lower orders. She wondered if he would prove a faithful husband if ever he married. He looked as if he could devour young innocents. Perhaps he took after his scandalous mother.

On one of his visits Isobel had glanced up as he passed and by chance he was looking in her direction. For an instant their eyes had met. She was annoyed that her heart had begun to beat faster. She might tell herself not to be such a fool, but he definitely had magnetism, charm even. She had wanted to look again but didn't dare. Miss Jolly's watchful eyes became needle-sharp when any of her employers were visiting. Unemployment was rising. There were a million out of work and no one's job was safe, even hers.

Isobel was being extra careful lately. She was eighteen and had begun to receive training which would enable her to work upstairs in 'specials', ready to take the place of the girl who was leaving to get married. On the top floor they made luxury corsetry and underwear but, more interesting to Isobel, they fashioned garments for ladies who needed surgical supports. The machinists actually met clients, who were transported upwards by a creaky lift to be measured by Miss Trefusis, their top corsetière. Some came on crutches, others in wheelchairs. Bennyson's supply of expertly fitted support corsets was crucial to these customers' well-being and there were curtained-off couches where they could rest if necessary, or even be fitted if they could not easily stand.

Ralph Bennyson also brought his daughter, Felice, with him on his excursions to the factory. Mr Bennyson behaved in the same way as Lawrence Dane and never really looked at the women or the hundreds of pairs of corsets turned out by the machinists for wickedly low wages. He paid them; they repaid him by producing the goods which made his money. Presumably he came to gloat over his possessions and the wealth they brought him which enabled his family to live in their large house in Clifton.

The progress of the visitors to the factory continued to be relayed in a series of messages by the runabouts. When the party finally

2

came by Isobel's machine she took a quick look and was as usual struck by Felice Bennyson's pale beauty and even more by her slender figure, so different from her own.

Felice looked like someone who should live in a castle of grey stone, with minarets and cupolas, turrets and bastions, as depicted in storybooks. Of medium height, her clear blue-grey eyes, soft skin and light silken hair peeping out from beneath her fashionable hat turned her, in Isobel's eyes, into a fairy-tale princess. Isobel wondered what it must be like to be so dainty and well dressed, so pampered and adored by her father. Ralph Bennyson could pass as a prince. Or maybe, since he was well over forty, a king. Above all, Isobel envied the gentle courtesy with which he treated Felice. He behaved as if she actually were royalty, opening doors for her, making sure there was a chair if she wanted to sit, ushering her about with soft pressure beneath her elbow. Felice was free to go at any time to her father's exclusive shop in Park Row not far from the centre of Bristol and buy as much as she wished of the beautiful, intimate undergarments, or be measured for the light elastic corsets and brassières worn these days under the more shapely garments which had come into fashion since the tubular look of the 1920s had been abandoned.

Today Felice wore a small hat over her carefully marcelled waves. In this year, 1930, a Frenchman called Patou had dropped an haute-couture bombshell. Hemlines had fallen to mid-calf, waists were creeping back and cloche hats were fast being replaced by little creations which gave an opportunity for thankful milliners to make something different. Felice's tweeds of soft heather shades were ideal for the cool, damp weather of this so-called summer, her hat, perched so far on the side of her head that it seemed it must be clinging to her hair, matched her costume. Its sole decoration was a navy quill. Her heels gave her five-foot-six-inches added height and she clutched a tiny navy handbag in her gloved hands. Isobel risked a longer than usual look and went back to her sewing with increased frustration.

Why should one girl be born so pretty and into such luxury, without having to do a hand's turn, while others must work themselves into the ground to make enough money for food? And why, she had wondered hundreds of times, had she been born with a short strong body which would never be slim? Her legs were good, her hair fair, her complexion better than Felice's and her eyes a luminous blue, but she longed to be tall and as softly rounded as fashion decreed, and not have to make do with her robust shape.

The last time Isobel visited Mum's mother, Granny Shaw, she had raved over Felice's luck, but Granny had said, 'Well, however she looks, she'll not be received at court. Mr Bennyson, her father, was the co-respondent in Mrs Bennyson's scandalous divorce.' Granny Shaw had been working in the factory when the scandal broke. Isobel had to lean forward to hear her further whispers. Granny always lowered her voice when speaking of intimate matters, saying, 'Walls have ears.' Of course, they hadn't, but the walls of her small house admittedly were thin. Granny continued. 'Ralph's wife, Sylvia, was divorced by her first husband, Harry Dane. Poor man. He worshipped her. She was *seduced* by Ralph Bennyson and had to leave her baby son, Lawrence, when she ran away. Then, a year or so later, Harry killed himself because she had broken his heart and he couldn't live with his misery. Naturally the court gave custody of the boy to old Mrs Dane because of Sylvia's sinful behaviour. I don't know how she could bring herself to risk losing her child, but there's no accounting for folks. It's a strange thing how Lawrence is friends with his stepfather, who was the one who brought his mother down, yet hates her. He blames her for everything.'

'Typical,' said Isobel angrily. 'It's always the woman who gets the blame.'

'And the men get the fun,' said Granny Shaw. She became a little bawdy at times, feeling free to behave how she liked because not only had Grandad Shaw left her a nice nest egg, but she'd already got some money of her own. Isobel's parents were vague about where it came from.

'It's a pity she didn't take her baby with her when she left her husband,' said Isobel.

'The courts would have made her give him back. They'd have said that her house was a dwelling of shame. She knew that. Some people don't even consider she's properly married to Ralph Bennyson. She took her vows to Harry and promised "till death us do part" and the second marriage was only in a registry office.'

'Couldn't she have got her son when his father died?'

'Good gracious me, no! His suicide made things worse than ever. Mrs Dane will have fed Mr Lawrence's mind with poison about his mother since he was small. No doubt he keeps in with Ralph Bennyson because there's the factory and shop and the money to be considered. Maybe Lawrence hopes to get it all one day.'

'Won't it go to Felice?'

'Not many men leave their business to a woman,' said Granny Shaw, 'especially a man like Ralph Bennyson. Some say he's unkind to his wife. Some say she's lucky he married her at all. After all, he'd had her in his bed already.' Granny Shaw's voice dropped to a hiss. 'I heard it said at the time that she was expecting, but it came to nothing. I suppose her monthlies stopped with all the worry. That can happen.'

The story shocked Isobel but interested her too. Beauty, riches, a runaway wife, a child, disgrace. It was the kind of stuff in Dad's *News of the World*.

Today, in the light of her grandmother's revelations, she had a closer look at Lawrence Dane. He wore a dark suit and plain shirt. Not at all noticeable, yet Isobel knew that his clothes had been fashioned by a master. Mr Bennyson's, too, though she didn't feel inclined to spend much time on him. She went back to stitching, wondering if Lawrence suffered much over his mother's behaviour and the horrible death of his father. He must do, she supposed, else why would he hate his mother? She found herself feeling sorry for him.

'They've gone upstairs,' sighed the first runabout, who had returned to collect another bundle of the unbecoming garments.

'I've spoken to you once,' said Miss Jolly, her voice raised against the clattering and whirring of the machines.

'Sorry,' said the girl. 'I'm only passing. I haven't stopped, honestly.'

'She'll have to go,' said Miss Jolly. 'She can't seem to keep her mind on the job more than five minutes.'

'She's the only one in work in her family,' said Isobel, her needle not faltering for a second.

'I know. But she'll need to pull up her socks.'

Isobel was anxious for the girl, but sympathised with Miss Jolly. If she wasn't hard on the machinists the manager would come down on her and she'd be out. There was no room for sentiment in Bennyson's Corset Factory. Orders from the top said, 'Work and only work,' and nothing was permitted to interfere.

Not long after she had started in the factory at fourteen, four years ago, Isobel, consumed with curiosity, had gone to look at the Bennysons' house. Mum was ill with one of her Sunday ailments and Isobel had taken her younger brother and sisters for an outing on the Downs. She had left them with strict instructions to obey their elder brother, Desmond, and then slipped through the streets. She knew that Desmond, though a year younger than her, would keep the others under control. No easy task, but he was level-headed and tactful beyond his age.

Bennyson House had been in the family for generations. It was uncompromisingly plain, a square brick building, its window frames and doors painted dark green. Isobel had been disappointed. She had expected a mansion to match the glamorous owners. The bricks weren't even new, but so old they had faded to pink.

'It's probably draughty and terribly hard for the servants to keep clean,' Granny Shaw had said, looking with satisfaction round her cosy room in Two Mile Hill. She lived only a few streets away from her family and Isobel saw her often, taking a penny tram ride if she was short of time. Time was always a scarce commodity for her, Mum being poorly so often.

'It doesn't seem fair that Felice should have so much and girls like me so little,' sighed Isobel, then snapped out of her self-pitying mood because it reminded her of her father and she was careful to ensure that she did not resemble him in any way.

The question of unfairness in life was one which her father, Amos Kingston, frequently propounded. It was his constant theme when he couldn't find the unskilled work which was all he was capable of. This was happening more and more often. He complained that everyone was against him; he resorted to petty thieving for which he had been to prison several times.

Isobel had once said to Desmond in a fit of exasperation when Amos was once again behind bars, 'If he had to turn to crime, why couldn't he pinch something worthwhile? Why can't he be clever about *something* for once? All we ever get from him is a few shillings. Then it's months of making do as best we can. I'm sure you'd manage much better.'

Desmond had smiled and said in his measured way, 'You don't mean that, sis. You can't approve of stealing.'

'No, of course not,' she sighed, 'but if only he could be successful at just one thing!'

Her ludicrous protest had made them both laugh. Desmond looked even more handsome when he laughed. He was tall and well built and worked in Bennyson's as assistant manager. He was impossibly young for the job, but he had impressed the manager.

He attracted the attention of many girls, though so far he hadn't singled one out. 'Time enough for romance,' he said. 'I want to make my way first.' He was the one the family turned to when Dad was in

6

trouble. From an early age he had dealt with the police and was always at the prison gates to bring Dad home when he was released. His good sense and excellent manners had shielded the family from much unpleasantness. The neighbours respected him deeply and for his sake tried to ignore the fact that Amos Kingston was an unrepentant jailbird.

The Bennysons went to the top floor as usual and into the manager's office, a wood and glassed enclosure at one end, where they were served refreshments in delicate porcelain before they returned to their chauffeur-driven car. Desmond said it was a Phantom Rolls-Royce, though he was more interested in Lawrence Dane's car, a French two-seater Bugatti. He had tried to explain to Isobel a few of the mechanical facts, talking about valves and cylinders, but she neither understood nor was interested. She saw the cars in a personal light, trying to picture herself behind a steering wheel, driving, as Felice probably did, her own sporty little vehicle. The Bennysons left the factory, presumably to go to lunch, and Isobel's imagination, as always, saw them sitting at a long dining table in a friend's house, like they showed in films, or in a restaurant, eating highly priced food to the sound of an orchestra.

Once she had told Granny Shaw about her fantasies and was warned, 'Keep your mind on your work, my girl. It's dangerous to dream in a factory and if you get hurt badly that Ralph Bennyson will sack you as soon as look at you.'

Isobel knew she was right. She had seen more than one woman sent off to hospital with a long machine needle right through her fingernail. She was impatient to work upstairs where her brain would be better occupied.

She stayed on the premises for her dinner break, eating her sandwiches with a cup of tea. The staff were allowed the use of a basement room where they could heat water on an elderly gas stove. Many of the women, the married ones with families, had to rush home in their short break to feed schoolchildren and out-of-work husbands, most of whom, thought Isobel disgustedly, did little or nothing to help.

Desmond wasn't the only one in the family wary of marriage. When – if – she married she'd sure as hell pick a proper partner and not some lazy devil who expected to be waited on no matter how tired his wife was. As far as she could see, marriage for women meant the rough end of life, constantly slaving at home and bearing children and, if their husbands couldn't earn enough, going out to work as well. Isobel had ambitions. Some day she was going to be somebody special.

As she made her way home after work, she could hear her father yelling from the end of the street. Neighbours hovered on their doorsteps, or pretended to pull a couple of weeds in the small patch of front garden, listening to the row intently.

She sighed. Hadn't they heard enough by now? Dad's shouting was practically an everyday occurrence, except during his spells behind bars, which Isobel had actually come to look forward to for the respite they afforded the family. Other women's husbands had fits of anger too and yelled, but Dad was the only jailbird in the street. He was recently home again from his latest incarceration and finding fault with everything. She wished that Desmond was with her. He had stayed behind to help solve a problem with the power plant which drove the sewing machines. If the women lost time their wages were docked and most of them were already living on the edge of financial disaster. The workers thought the world of him. There had been times, when trade was slack, when he could have left repairs until the following day, times when the boss would have been delighted not to pay full piece-work wages, but Desmond, choosing to ignore strong hints, would carry on assisting the mechanic until everything was repaired.

'Those girls need every penny they can get,' was his only comment.

Isobel wondered if he might be putting his future with the factory at risk, but he was as determined in his resolution to do what he considered right as Dad was in his determination to lead as lazy and feckless a life as possible.

Isobel hung her coat and hat in the hall and stopped in the open door of the kitchen. Her father was sprawled in the only easy chair. He glared at her. The reason for his fury was immediately evident. The fire had been allowed to die back.

He gestured towards her mother, Grace, who knelt in front of the range. 'She knew I'd be cold. Bloody cold! I need looking after, considering where I've been. She knows that.' He yelled at Grace. 'I'm cold, you stupid fool!'

Grace was on her knees, blowing on the smouldering newspaper. 'Sorry, love, I fell asleep. I was awful tired . . .'

'You're always tired, you lazy bitch.'

'Not always,' muttered Grace.

8

He hadn't quite heard. 'What did you say?'

'Nothing.'

Amos jumped up from his chair and hurled himself across the kitchen towards his wife. He stood over her menacingly. 'I asked you what you said. I know you said something.' He lifted his bunched fist over her head, then, hearing Isobel gasp, remembered that she was watching. She remained very still. Amos had never struck his wife in front of anyone, preferring to keep his brutal bullying out of sight.

'What are you staring at?' he bawled.

'She said she's not always tired,' said Isobel.

'Who asked you?' Amos gave her a look of fury and she caught her breath. She had seen that look many times before, but she had never got used to the knowledge that her father hated her. Hatred! It was written in his eyes, in the twist of his mouth, in the loathing in his voice. Well, what of it? She hated him.

The sight of her mother on her knees, terrified, choking back tears, gave rise to a surge of mingled pity and fury towards Grace. Fury at her brutal father, at Grace because she was so submissive, and inward anger because her reaction to Mum was unworthy. She loved Grace, but if only her mother would stand up to Dad! When anyone showed weakness his bullying grew stronger until it erupted into physical violence. The whole family, with the exception of young Kathy, knew that Mum's 'Sunday ailments' stemmed from the cruelties practised upon her by their father. He always went to bed drunk in the early hours of Sunday mornings. Grace, who seldom drank anything stronger than tea, exhausted after the labours of her day, was forced to stay up to attend to Amos and his disgusting friends for half the night until she was almost broken by fatigue. Isobel and Desmond had both volunteered to take her place and stay with him but the suggestion sent Dad into such a furious rage that Grace begged them to leave things as they were.

Isobel's imagination was fertile, and although she tried to suppress it she could picture scenes behind their closed bedroom door after the drunken guests had left. Grace cowering, sickened by her husband's stinking breath, terrified by his red-eyed fury, driving him by her fear almost to madness.

'Who asked you to interfere?' he shouted at Isobel now, but he retreated before her contemptuous stare and flung himself back into his chair.

'I could hear you right down the street,' said Isobel, going to the range. 'So could the neighbours.'

'Bugger the street! And bugger the neighbours!' He glared in his wife's direction and aimed a futile kick at Isobel. 'And bugger you both, you stupid cows.'

Isobel, driven to reckless anger, took a step towards him, returning his look of hate with one of her own. He rose from his chair, hesitated, and slouched off to the front room. 'It's a damn disgrace when a man can't get a cup of tea in his own kitchen,' he snarled from where he lay on the ancient creaking horsehair sofa.

'Get up, Mum,' said Isobel, forcing herself to sound gentle. Her mother looked up at her, fear lingering in her soft, pale eyes. 'Sit down, Mum, and I'll get things going.'

'You've just done a day's work . . .' protested Grace.

'That she has!' shouted Dad, overhearing them. 'You should have something ready for her as well.'

Ignoring him, Isobel asked, 'Where are Ivor and Olive? Am I first home?'

'Ivor's been to the labour exchange today and they sent him to a place the other side of Bristol. I hope he gets a job soon,' she added. 'Olive's not home from work yet. I suppose they had some last-minute customers.'

Isobel frowned. 'I wish people would give shop assistants more consideration.'

'Well, at least the Park Street shops get Saturday afternoon off.'

'And Kathy?'

'She's at her friend's for tea.'

Their voices were tender when they spoke of Kathy. She was ten and still at school, clever, the headmistress said. She and Desmond were the two people Isobel loved best. The paper leapt into flame and the few sticks of wood crackled as the fire caught hold.

'About bloody time,' shouted Dad. 'Get the tea ready.'

Isobel's abhorrence of this man who dominated and spoiled their lives welled up into a suffocating band around her heart. Her horrified memories of his past evil towards her never really left her. She could now just about have afforded to leave home and keep herself in a modest way in a bed-sitter. She dreamed of solitary tranquillity, but by staying at home she was able to alleviate some of the miseries Amos caused. When he threw one of his savage tantrums she frequently stepped between him and the others and sometimes with a murderous glare that matched his own she could tame him.

Desmond was the only other member of the family who could keep Amos under a measure of control. When Desmond had been younger Amos had whipped him with the buckle end of his leather belt and the boy's body bore the scars from it, but he had grown tall and muscular and his father dared not touch him now.

But Isobel was the one who must protect Kathy against the worst of Amos's wickedness, of which the others were not aware. She watched her father closely when her youngest sister was present.

Fourteen-year-old Olive, with her dark hair and eyes, was very pretty, but she was self-possessed, tough, and had always gone her own way. She stayed out as much as possible. Isobel could picture Olive's retaliation if any man gave her unwanted caresses. Especially her father. Isobel was sickened by her memories. They were ones she could never discuss with anyone. The sense of shame from which she still suffered because of her father's assaults was too painful to speak about; shame haunted her. Kathy must never suffer as she had. Kathy was tender, sweet, innocent and Isobel intended she should remain that way until the day she met the right man. When she thought of her sister at Amos's mercy her blood curdled. There were worse things than a beating. She had taken Kathy into her boxroom bed years ago. In there she was safe.

The following day was Saturday. Ivor had taken himself off, still without a job. He resembled Amos in looks and disposition and Isobel found it difficult to like him.

Amos collected money from all the workers in the family. They handed it over reluctantly, resentful at this plundering of their wages and his wanton spending of them, yet pleased that for a few hours at least they could buy immunity from his presence. He spent his time in the pub or hanging around street corners with his cronies, studying the sports papers to see if his horse or dog had won.

Desmond and Isobel took Kathy to the pictures where along with many others she still marvelled at hearing actual voices coming from the screen.

'That was lovely,' Kathy sighed as they walked home. 'Being a film actress must be wonderful. I suppose Dad will still be out?' she added.

Poor kid, thought Isobel. She's afraid her day will be spoilt.

'By the time he comes in you'll be tucked up in the land of dreams,' said Desmond.

'I hope so, but . . .'

Both her elders knew she'd be lying awake, just as they had lain awake in their turn, waiting for the sound of drunken singing which heralded Amos's homecoming, often with his equally drunken friends, making the night hideous.

'He's not really bad,' Mum would plead. 'It's the drink. He was driven to it. He had a rotten time when he was a boy. His father drank. And there are other things, too. Dad can be kind. He was kind to me once. He will be again one day, I expect.'

When asked what she meant by 'other things' Mum was vague and unresponsive.

Isobel saw her sister into bed and went downstairs. Mum had given up attempting to darn a pile of socks and sat staring into the glowing range, hands clasped to prevent their shaking. Isobel took over the darning, Desmond read the evening paper and they waited.

'A wireless would be nice,' said Desmond. He had broken the silence so abruptly that Grace and Isobel jumped.

'A wireless?' Mum was bemused.

'We could have music. You'd like that, wouldn't you, Mum? You used to dance, remember?'

'A long time ago.'

Her smile encouraged Desmond to go on. 'You used to pick me up and dance round with me in your arms, singing songs until you got breathless.'

'I couldn't do it now,' said Mum, smiling. 'Not now you've got such a big fellow.'

'In fact,' said Desmond, getting up, 'I reckon it could be the other way round. Come on, Mum, show us what you're made of.' Grace made a token protest, then surrendered herself to her son. She was pathetically light and he held her beneath her arms, lifted her a few inches from the floor and waltzed her round the room, singing loudly. She laughed and sang with him. Her voice still retained some of its sweetness. Desmond allowed her feet to touch the floor and she danced round joyfully.

Isobel joined in the song, her body swaying to the rhythm of the waltz. ' "I'll see you again, Whenever spring breaks through again . . ." '

'What in hell's going on here?' Amos's bellow cut across the fun. He was standing in the kitchen doorway, his usual bad humour worsened by drink. 'You were making such a racket you never heard me and my friends come in. Disgraceful, I call it. Can't a man bring his mates home to a place got ready for them? It's bloody cold in the front room.'

The dancing and singing stopped abruptly. 'You're a bit earlier than usual,' gasped Grace. 'And it's still summer.'

'A bit early! Still summer!' Amos mocked. 'It's past ten, the pub's shut and I've known winters warmer than this. And it's started to rain again.'

'I'll make a fire,' said Grace, 'and I expect you'd like tea.'

'Tea? Tea? Did I ask for bloody tea? Bring the beer mugs.'

'I'll make the fire,' said Desmond.

'It's your mother's place to do the housework,' snarled Amos.

'She's tired. I'll do it.'

'I'll not have a son of mine showing me up doing woman's work in front of my mates!'

Desmond moved towards his father, glaring belligerently, and Grace put a trembling hand on his arm. 'Don't, son. It's all right. It is woman's work.'

'I said I'd make the fire and I will,' said Desmond through gritted teeth.

'I'll do it,' cried Isobel.

Desmond would have argued further, but she shook her head at him and gestured towards Grace. Tears were raining down her face and Desmond subsided. 'I'll fetch more coal,' he muttered furiously.

Ivor and Olive arrived home, expressed their usual disgust at the noise coming from the front room and went to bed. Desmond and Isobel, their self-imposed tasks completed, sat in the kitchen, unable to put their minds to anything constructive as Grace made frequent visits to the card-players, carrying trays of tea or coffee which they demanded between swilling down beer. Isobel, tight-lipped, washed cups and glasses, tipping tea-sodden cigarette butts into the waste bin. The men cleared their throats noisily and spat on the floor and Grace wiped up their spittle.

'Bastards,' Desmond ground out to his sister as Grace left with a tray of sandwiches. 'I'd like to shoot the lot of them. Why does Mum do it? Why can't she stand up to him? *You* wouldn't give in to a man like that. He's a bully. Bullies never respect weakness. I'd leave home if it weren't for the others.'

'I know.'

'I'm surprised you don't go. I'd stay and let you have your freedom.'

'I know you would, Desmond, but I'll stay. Kathy likes to have me with her.'

She shivered, her memory dark again. She could never talk to anyone about the time Dad had slipped into the boxroom where she

13

had slept alone and climbed into bed with her. She had been thirteen. She tried to turn the memories aside, but tonight they came flooding back. She remembered how his tongue, wet and stinking from beer and tobacco, was shoved into her mouth and his body weighed her down as his hands groped beneath the bedclothes and pulled up her nightdress. She had only recently started her woman's monthlies and learned of the things which went on between husbands and wives, and even in the midst of her struggles she couldn't believe what was happening. He was drunk. He surely must think he was in Mum's bed.

When he removed his tongue she gasped, 'Dad, don't. It's me. It's Isobel.'

'And a tasty bit you are, too,' was his reply.

Then fear had coursed through her and she fought until sweat poured from her body, fought unrelentingly until her healthy strength and well-developed muscles had tired him before he could penetrate her and he had rolled off her, cursing. 'Bloody hellcat!' She had heard him go to his own bed, the creak as he climbed in, more creaks as he took his fill of his wife, and Isobel covered her ears against her mother's muffled cries of distress.

On the following day Mum had had one of her ailments. It kept her bent over as she cooked the Sunday dinner, made her wince when Isobel hugged her before running off to Sunday School. Amos insisted on all the children attending Sunday School. When they returned he was usually back in bed and Mum was white-faced and dishevelled.

'You know he hits her,' said Desmond now. He sounded almost dispassionate. 'He beats her. Sunday ailments be damned!'

Desmond seldom swore. That was twice in one evening and Isobel was startled. He had never alluded to Dad's cruelty before. And she had never heard that particular note in his voice. It scared her.

By now, Grace was grey with fatigue. 'Go to bed, Mum,' Isobel said. 'I'll wait up.'

'No, I can't do that,' said Grace. 'He'd be so angry. You two should go to bed. You need your sleep.'

'I'll not leave you,' said Isobel.

'I'm the one to stay with Mum,' said Desmond. 'Who knows what they may get up to? Dad sounds really vicious tonight.'

Isobel felt her brother's deep and bitter anger. 'Go to bed,' he said again. 'Tomorrow Mum will need a lot of help and I'm not much of a hand at cooking.'

14

'How do you know? You've never tried very hard.'

'My boiled eggs are fine.' Desmond smiled and so did she, but their smiles were forced.

In the end she was persuaded to go upstairs where she snuggled up to Kathy who murmured, 'I'm glad you've come. I can sleep now.'

Isobel kissed the child's smooth cheek. 'Haven't you slept at all?'

'I can't. Why do we have to have him as a father? Why can't we have someone nice and kind? I've been to my friends' houses and their dads are different. I wish he'd go away and never come back.'

Isobel smoothed Kathy's soft fair hair from her face and realised she was crying. She sat up and lit the candle. Kathy sat up, too, and Isobel put her arms round her and hugged her close. 'Don't cry, my darling. I wish Dad was different, but at least we've got Mum and the others.'

'The others?' sobbed Kathy. 'Desmond is brave, but Mum's frightened to say a word and Ivor and Olive hardly seem to be in our family. They go out all the time and I don't like Ivor at all. He reminds me of Dad.'

'Hush, darling, it won't always be like this.'

'How can it change? Only if Dad gets put in prison for a long time. Is it wicked to wish your father would go to prison for years and years?'

'You wouldn't know how to be wicked, darling.'

'At Sunday School they say if you think bad thoughts it's the same as if you do bad things.'

Isobel suppressed the tart reply on the tip of her tongue. 'Thoughts just slip into your head.'

'They do, don't they?' said Kathy. 'I do try to think good things, but I can't help thinking how nice it is when Dad's in prison. Oh, Isobel, Olive told me you'd be getting married one day and I'd have to stick up for myself.'

Isobel promised herself she'd have a word with Olive. 'I'll always look after you,' she said. 'I won't desert you. And one day you'll have your own home with a good husband and babies.'

'I shan't get married if I have to put up with a man like Dad.'

'Desmond isn't like Dad.'

'No, but I can't marry him.' Kathy gave a little chuckle and Isobel wiped away her tears with a corner of the sheet.

'That's better. There are plenty of boys as nice as Desmond.'

'But Mum must have thought Dad was all right once. How do you know which the nice ones are?'

15

It was a question which frequently troubled Isobel. Just how did you know?

She blew out the candle and the girls lay down again; they were drifting into sleep when a commotion downstairs brought them sitting up once more. Shouting in the night was not unknown, for Dad often quarrelled with his cronies over their card games, but this sounded different. Then Isobel knew why. The loudest voice was Desmond's.

'It's our Desmond. What are they doing to him?' gasped Kathy.

'Stay where you are.' Isobel slid out of bed and pulled on her knickers, dress and shoes and ran downstairs. She found her mother crouching by the kitchen fire, her whole body trembling. The front of her dress was wet and water dripped from her hair.

'Whatever's going on, Mum?'

Grace's teeth were chattering so hard she could hardly get out the words. 'One of them vomited all over the couch and your father called me to clean up. I would have done it, I got a bucket of water and a cloth to do it, but Desmond said I shouldn't. I begged him to let me, but he went in and told Dad that the pig who made the mess could clean it up.

'Your father yelled so loud I took the bucket in. Desmond was kneeling over the man who'd been sick and was trying to rub his face in the mess. Your father was furious. He and his mate jumped on Desmond. The man who was sick was too far gone to move. Our Desmond is strong and managed to shake them off a couple of times, but it was two against one and then the other man joined in and they began to get Desmond down and were going to rub his face in the horrible mess and I couldn't stand it and I began hitting out with the bucket. Everyone got soaked and one of them fell down. Oh, Isobel, I think I might have killed him. I landed him an awful crack, and then Desmond knocked the other one out and the sick man was still too dopey to move and that left just Dad – and Desmond began shaking him so hard I thought his teeth would fall out. Then I ran away.'

Grace finished her recital and Isobel realised that the shouting had stopped. She went to the front room. Dad's three cronies were stretched out. They lay still. She wondered if they were unconscious from drink, if Desmond had given them all a knockout punch, if Mum really had killed one. Dad lay on the floor groaning. Desmond was dusting off his hands, a look of infinite satisfaction on his face.

16

'My God,' she whispered. 'It looks like a battlefield. Mum thinks she's killed someone.'

'Killed be damned. The swine got up again and jumped me. What a scene! And that filthy devil on the couch is so drunk he can't lift himself out of his own vomit. Go and see to Mum, sis. I don't think she ought to go to her own bed tonight.'

Isobel stared for a moment longer. She stared hardest at her father, whose eyes were dark pools of malevolence as he glared at his eldest son. Then she returned to the kitchen. 'Come on, Mum, it's bed for you.'

'The mess in there.' Grace waved feebly in the direction of the front room.

'We'll see to it. You must go to bed now.'

Isobel guided her exhausted mother upstairs and Grace made only a token protest when she was undressed and her nightgown slipped over her thin body. Isobel tucked her up with Kathy. 'But where will you go? And what about those men? And Dad – what will he say?'

'Stop worrying.' But Grace fell asleep before Isobel could say more.

Kathy whispered, 'What's happened? And where will you sleep?'

'Our Desmond got fed up with Dad and his mates and gave them what for but not until after Mum hit one of them with her bucket. It was full of water, too.'

'What?' Kathy squeaked, then gave a nervous giggle. 'Fancy Mum doing that! Fancy Desmond! I wish I'd seen. I suppose you wouldn't let me go and have a look.'

'No fear. It's revolting down there. You'd hate it. Now take care of Mum.'

'I will, I will.' Kathy was proud of being given such an assignment. 'I'll take good care of her.'

Isobel went back to the front room where the casualties were moaning and beginning to move. Olive and Ivor, now that the commotion was stilled, came downstairs.

Olive yawned, raising her arms above her head so that the silken sleeves of her peignoir fell back revealing her white-skinned, rounded flesh. She spent most of her money on clothes and make-up and gave reluctantly to the family housekeeping, and even more reluctantly to her father, and often swore she had only a sixpence or two to hand over.

17

'What's been happening? God, what a mess and what a row! The neighbours will have a field day tomorrow.'

'The neighbours can go to hell,' said Isobel angrily. 'Look at you, neither of you tried to help. For all you knew Dad might have been murdering Mum.'

'He hasn't done it yet,' said Ivor, in an uninterested tone which further infuriated Isobel. 'So what did happen?'

'One of Dad's friends behaved even more disgustingly than usual and Mum hit out with a bucket. Then Desmond joined in . . .'

'What? Well, good for Mum,' laughed Olive. 'That's the best thing I've heard about her yet.'

Ivor said, 'I'm going back to bed.' He returned to the room he shared with his brother.

'I may as well go, too,' said Olive.

Desmond had dragged the sick man from the couch, dumped him on the floor and cleaned the obnoxious mess he had left on the couch. He stepped over the others, who were recovering with groans. 'I'll empty the bucket and come back,' he said. 'Don't try to do anything on your own.'

Isobel had no difficulty in obeying. The men, their stench, their drunken impotence, their degenerate behaviour, appalled her.

Desmond returned and shook each man in turn. 'Get up and get out,' he grated.

They cast appealing looks at their host who had seated himself on a hardbacked chair, but Amos ignored them as they slunk away, two supporting one too far gone to walk, muttering about the bitch with the bucket and bad sons and a man having no control over his family.

'And you'd better go upstairs,' said Desmond, turning to Amos. 'We've all had enough for one day.'

'I'll do what I like in my own house.' Amos's words were slurred. 'And I'll have something to say to your mother. She could have killed my mate. Did you see him? He was bleeding.'

'Nonsense. She didn't even dent the drunken sot.'

Amos looked at Isobel and said, 'As for you . . .'

'I'm not interested,' she said. 'Go on up. And try for once to be quiet.'

'I'll make as much noise as I bloody well like!' He stamped upstairs.

Isobel and Desmond waited until the expected roar of rage came. He stumbled down the uncarpeted steep and narrow staircase so fast he nearly fell and burst into the room. 'Where is she?' Where's the stupid cow I married?'

'I suppose you mean Mum,' said Isobel coldly. 'She's asleep unless you woke her with your clumsy feet. In *my* bed and you are not to go there.'

Amos's eyes met Isobel's and his flushed face went a deeper red. He opened his mouth to argue, then turned and went back upstairs.

'I thought he'd have put up a bigger fight,' said Desmond.

Isobel didn't reply and brother and sister worked in silence to make the room neat.

When they said goodnight, Isobel fetched cushions and blankets and slept on the floor of her bedroom, effectively blocking the door.

Chapter Two

Felice Bennyson stared unseeingly from the comfort of her father's Rolls-Royce, driven by Stratton, the chauffeur. She resented the fact that Lawrence, her half-brother, was able to escape from her father, driving away in his own car to continue his own life. He hardly ever visited her home, unwilling to see their mother. Felice knew the story of Mother's disgrace and surmised that Lawrence could not have escaped being hurt, but she couldn't understand how he could cherish such an unrelenting, intense loathing for so many years. Or why he blamed his mother entirely for the long-ago scandal and appeared to be uncritical of Ralph.

Mrs Dawson, the housekeeper, who had been with the Bennysons since she was twelve and knew everything about the family, had thrown some light on the past when at eleven Felice had begged for enlightenment. She was well aware that she shouldn't gossip with a servant, but she suffered from her tormenting curiosity. Why, if Lawrence was her brother, had he a different surname from hers? Why did he avoid the gentle, nervous woman who was their mother? Mrs Dawson had explained the puzzle as tactfully as possible, making allowances for the innocence of the child.

'Penny for them, darling,' said her father softly.

'I'm not thinking of anything in particular, Father.'

Ralph sighed in a martyred way. 'You must have been thinking of something. A mind as lively as yours cannot remain wholly empty.' Although his voice was tender, his manner pleasant, the familiar air of domination made her uneasy. Father allowed her physical freedom within his strict boundaries, but tried to probe her mind. Mother was usually silent and brooding, often scarcely seeming to notice her.

This year, since Felice had returned for good from the expensive boarding school where she had been educated from eight to eighteen, she had begun to sense the extreme width of the barrier between her parents. During her school years she had visited friends' homes where there was harmony and love and realised that her own was exceedingly short of both. Friends had come to stay with her, but in spite of all that Father could do to make them welcome, and despite Sylvia's struggles, for her daughter's sake, to come out of her shell, they never accepted a second invitation. She had hidden the hurt this gave her. Now she was beginning to comprehend what they found repellent about the atmosphere surrounding her parents. She had begun to feel uncomfortable in Father's presence. She wished there was someone who could discuss the problem with her. Mother was not someone to whom you could confide emotional troubles and the older, more sophisticated Felice had never turned to Mrs Dawson again.

'Felice, you have been ignoring me for several moments,' said Ralph. 'I said, "penny for them".'

'Sorry, Father.'

'Darling, you must curb your tendency to drift off into a dreamy state. It was quite amusing when you were a child, but it is different now you are a young lady about to make her mark in society.'

Or as much of it as I shall be admitted to, thought Felice. She said: 'I was actually wondering why you bought Lawrence that lovely car and yet you won't buy me even a little Austin Seven. They don't cost much.'

'Cost has nothing to do with it,' said Ralph irritably. 'I prefer to have you driven by an expert. How can you think I would permit you to go to parties and dances in your own car? I shouldn't have a moment's peace of mind.'

'I needn't use it for evenings. I could take Mother shopping. She enjoys an outing. Well, she used to when I was very small, before she was ill. Perhaps I could help her to feel better.'

'There is no reason for her to feel unwell and she can go out whenever she wishes. She brings her nervous debility upon herself. Felice, you must allow me to guide you. If the Rolls is not available you can always call a taxi.'

'Other girls drive. Quite a lot of them these days.'

Ralph frowned. 'I am aware of it. I have not yet forgotten the one who drank too much and crashed into a lamp post on her way home. She was lucky she wasn't killed. As it is, she'll always have a limp. I couldn't bear such a disaster happening to you. I don't approve of her kind and do not wish you to become intimate with such girls. One day we shall be looking for a suitable husband for you and your reputation must be above suspicion.'

Felice felt a surge of angry rebellion. *We* shall look for a husband? She would choose her own mate, if ever she felt drawn to marriage. At present she was disinclined even to contemplate putting herself in the power of any man who might rule her as her father did. She might be leaving one tyrant for another. Tyrant? That was a shocking thing to think about your father.

She said, 'It was Marjorie Allenby who crashed her car. She often has a fall when she's riding because she takes foolish chances. I wouldn't do that. Actually, she still has plenty of men friends even if she does have a limp.'

'Friends, perhaps. A future husband? Perhaps, though I doubt it. I have no guarantee that you would be safe to drive. You would mean to be circumspect, but the atmosphere at parties and dances can become very convivial. You would be considered eccentric if you refused alcohol altogether and although you may not *intend* to over-indulge it can have an insidious effect.'

'But, Father – '

'My child, please do not argue, I am sure you would mean to be careful, but you might meet the wrong sort of young man who would entice you into excesses. Some of them nowadays are so wild. I could not risk you in such a way. You are far too precious to me.'

'Father, please – '

'Felice, you are hurting me very much by your insistence. You must know how I look forward to our outings.'

'I could drive you,' said Felice eagerly.

'Will you stop harping on the subject!' Ralph drew a deep breath and said in a gentler tone, 'Really, my darling, can you see me curled into an Austin Seven?'

'Buy me a bigger car then,' said Felice. She felt suddenly desperate, seeing her future only as a series of outings with her father.

He laughed loudly. 'Now I know you must be joking.'

Felice could almost taste her impotent fury. There was an old song, how did it go? 'She was only a bird in a gilded cage . . .' Something like that. She knew the feeling. She was imprisoned in a gilded cage without a clue as to how to escape.

She cared for her mother in spite of the fact that Sylvia had retreated more and more into herself as the years passed until she seemed like a shadow in the house, while only Father had substance. She wished she could discuss her dilemma with Lawrence. At boarding school she had met girls whose brothers had given them guidance, making them aware of the perils which lay in wait for the innocents at the hands of unscrupulous men, telling them in semi-

23

humorous ways which both warned and amused them. At school, when they were supposed to be sleeping, the girls had giggled over some of the revelations. No one had ever mentioned how to deal with an overbearing father whose love was growing suffocating.

Stratton pulled up in front of the house and the front door was opened by Murray, the butler. As usual Ralph climbed out of the car first and offered his hand to his daughter. Felice was startled by so intense a spasm of dislike for him it made her gasp.

'What is it, my love?' asked Ralph.

'Nothing.'

'That can't be true, dear. I distinctly heard you gasp.'

'It was just a minor bump on my ankle.'

'How did that happen?'

Felice wanted to scream at his perpetual digging into her. 'I kicked myself.'

'Really, dearest, how silly.' Ralph smiled indulgently. 'All the same we must get Janet to look at it. She will have suitable medicaments in her first-aid box. Your mother is always ailing and needing some kind of treatment.'

Sylvia's maid, Janet, had been with her since both women were young girls and Sylvia trusted her. Janet was so much in and out of the bedrooms she couldn't have failed to pick up the bad atmosphere, but she was totally discreet.

'Ask Janet to come down and look at Miss Felice's ankle,' said Ralph to Murray. 'Tell her to bring something for a bruise. Miss Felice will be in the morning room. There is no reason for you to go all the way upstairs, darling.'

'Father, really . . .' But Felice, knowing Murray's eyes were upon her, smiled to prove she was only voicing a token protest.

Janet brought arnica and, having closed the door, removed Felice's cobweb-thin stocking to tend her ankle, which showed no sign of a bruise.

'There isn't much to see, Miss Felice.'

'I know, Janet, I'm not really hurt, but you know Father – '

'I know him all right.' Janet's tone was grim and Felice fell silent. Janet performed her task efficiently, rubbing balm on a perfectly white ankle and waiting until Felice had pulled on her stocking and fastened the suspenders.

When Felice walked into the drawing room, Ralph said, 'Ah, I see Janet has decided a bandage was necessary. You must never treat an injury lightly. One thing can lead to another.'

24

Sylvia had been making a handkerchief, sewing a dainty piece of lace round a square of lawn, but now she was dozing in front of the fire that was needed this summer and the sewing had slid from her lap to the floor. Felice bent to pick it up. She felt pity for her mother. Even sleep failed to eliminate her tired look.

'She'll sleep her life away,' rasped Ralph. 'Bed at ten, even sooner, if I did not protest, and then she's asleep again. It isn't as if she ever does anything worthwhile. Making handkerchiefs! She could buy as many as she liked of the very best craftsmanship.'

Sylvia's eyes flew open and she sprang to her feet. 'I'm so sorry, I didn't hear you come in.' She put a long thin hand to her white forehead. 'I must have dozed.'

'As usual!' said Ralph.

Sylvia sank back into her chair and Felice saw that her hands were trembling. She had seen pictures of her mother in old photographs, many taken for the society pages of magazines. She had been a beauty, but now she was thin and pale, her eyes without lustre.

'Here's your sewing, Mother,' she said gently. She had to suppress her anger at Sylvia for showing fear, for taking all Ralph's ill-treatment without protest. Why couldn't she stand up to him? No wonder he bullied her. His cruelty took the form of mental and emotional harassment. The word 'cruelty' had slid past her guard and it startled her.

Ralph walked out of the room; they heard the library door slam and Felice knew she had annoyed him by treating her mother gently. The women breathed sighs of relief and Felice sat by Sylvia as her feelings underwent another abrupt change. 'Shall I ring for tea?' she asked softly.

'Would you, dear? Did you enjoy your visit to the factory?'

'It was the same as always.'

'Was anyone else there?'

Felice knew her mother was referring indirectly to Lawrence. She hardly ever spoke his name.

'Lawrence came.'

Sylvia's pale skin was suffused with a flush. 'Did he? How did he look?' She tried to keep the eagerness from her voice, glancing fearfully at the door in case Ralph had entered quietly. He did so sometimes and made them feel threatened.

'As well as he always does. I don't know why he bothers. He takes as little notice of the work or the women as Father.'

'You can't expect anything else,' said Sylvia. 'It wouldn't be possible for a man to get enthusiastic over the making of corsets.'

Felice remembered her late grandfather, Ralph's father, with his warm interest in all that happened in his factory, his concern for the women. He had installed a stove in the basement so that they might heat their drinks. He held jobs open for those who fell ill or had to stay at home to give birth or look after a sick child. He had introduced a nurse who took care of many of their medical problems and he paid for a doctor when one was needed. Since his death the nurse had retired and had not been replaced and the doctor was only called in if a woman received a serious injury. And that was only so that Ralph couldn't be criticised if the injury led to permanent damage.

'Lawrence has a splendid new car,' said Felice. 'A Bugatti.'

'I suppose your father bought it for him.'

'Yes, yet he won't let me have even a cheap one.'

Sylvia put out her hand to touch her daughter's shoulder. 'He has your welfare in mind, darling.'

'Has he, really?'

'But of course. How can you doubt it?'

'Oh, Mother! Sometimes I think he simply wants to be master. Master of us all!'

Sylvia was startled. 'Master? But that is exactly what a man is in his house and among his family.'

'I wonder he doesn't try to dominate Lawrence but of course he isn't part of our household.'

Sylvia paled and Felice cursed her quick tongue. 'I'm so sorry, I didn't think – '

'It's all right. I know you didn't mean to hurt me. I am thankful that your father and Lawrence care for each other. If they didn't I might never see my son at all.'

'Why is Lawrence so nice to Father, yet horrid to you?'

'He can't forgive me because he believes I never wished to see him as a child. He is regarded by everyone as the innocent son who was badly treated by the woman who should have loved him above all others. That's what he believes. And I did treat him horribly badly, though not intentionally.'

'Why don't you tell him the truth? That you hated losing him. That you still suffer.'

Sylvia bent her head so that her silvery blonde hair concealed her face. 'He would never believe me. Too many years have gone by and I haven't had the courage to speak – ' She stopped, her hand to

26

her mouth, then said, 'Father treats Lawrence well and buys him expensive gifts and I'm grateful for it. Perhaps it makes up a little for my neglect as well as the loss of his father.'

'I still wish you could tell Lawrence how much you always wanted him.'

'No, I won't resurrect the past. It is a mistake to do so. It can do more harm than good. No, I'll leave matters as they are. Father enjoys seeing Lawrence take his place in society, helping him now and then. He wanted a son, you know – ' Again Sylvia stopped speaking.

Felice was appalled by the pain in her mother's voice. But she was still chagrined. 'My dear brother might be improved by having to work at something,' she said. 'He's so stand-offish, even with Frank Bagley who has perfect manners even if he is only the factory manager. And he's cool to me! His own sister! You'd never think we were related.'

'Half-sister, dear.'

'There were a couple of girls at school with half-brothers and they were as close as could be.'

Sylvia sighed and Felice went on, 'Sometimes I think Father denies us pleasure simply to show his power over us. I've visited places where the wives were respected and allowed full control of the house.'

'I should not care for that. I am hopeless with money, you know it – '

'I know that Father says it often enough. What about your previous marriage? Did *he* treat you well? Did *he* not permit you to take charge?'

'Harry was all that was good. I was wicked – ' Sylvia began to stammer and her colour faded to a deadly white.

Felice was frightened. She regretted allowing her indignation to run away with her. 'You aren't going to faint, are you?'

'No,' gasped Sylvia. 'But you should not mention ... you should not talk of my former husband.'

'Please forgive me, Mother.'

Sylvia took a couple of breaths. 'Father is never unkind to you, is he?'

Felice, still struggling with unfamiliar rebellion, said, 'He's unkind to you and too damned kind to me.'

Sylvia's eyes opened wide. 'How can that be? Ring the bell, please,' she said without waiting for a reply and, after a moment's reflection, Felice allowed the subject to drop.

Shortly afterwards Murray entered, accompanied by a parlour maid, both carrying laden trays which they slotted on to the special stands. 'Do you wish me to pour, madam?' asked Murray.

'No, thank you,' said Sylvia. 'You may go.' She glanced at the trays and called him back. 'Murray, I asked Mrs Dawson to be sure that Cook made macaroons for tea today. There are none here.'

'No, madam. Cook did make the macaroons, but Mr Bennyson decided to have a rich fruit cake.'

'I see,' said Sylvia, almost choking over her words.

'Do you require anything else, madam?'

'Nothing.'

When Murray had closed the door behind him, Sylvia said miserably, 'Your father knows that fruit cake is too heavy for my digestion. If I eat it I will be in pain for hours.'

'Never mind. There's bread and butter, cut as thinly as you like it. You needn't eat the cake.'

'Is there jam?' asked Sylvia hopefully.

'I'm afraid not, but the butter is spread generously.'

The door opened and Ralph stood for a moment on the threshold, staring at his womenfolk. 'Ah, tea.' He advanced and stared at the trays. 'Good, my orders have been followed. Splendid. A rich fruit cake. And bread and butter?' He frowned and reached for the bell. Sylvia poured, nervously slopping tea into the saucers while Ralph stood gazing through a window at the trees and shrubs, their leaves dripping after a heavy shower. When Murray appeared he gestured towards the trolley. 'I asked Mrs Dawson to make sure that butter is always spread thinly. There is far too much on this bread for Mrs Bennyson's health. Remove it.'

'Yes, sir.' The butler stooped to pick up the plate of bread and butter and Sylvia watched its departure with hungry eyes.

'Tell Mrs Dawson that we do not need bread and butter today,' said Ralph.

'Very good, sir.'

When the door had closed behind Murray, Sylvia said, 'I was looking forward to the bread and butter. I prefer it to cake. To heavy cake, that is. I enjoy macaroons or fairy cakes and am fond of scones – ' Her voice dwindled as Ralph waited impassively for her to stop, his features expressing no emotion.

'The fruit cake is made in our own kitchen and cannot fail to please,' he said. 'Cook has a light hand in all she does.'

28

'But fruit cake is not meant to be light. It is supposed to be rich and heavy. At school I was taught a little cookery. They said we should know something of what transpired in our kitchens so that we would make good mistresses of our marital homes.'

'So you have told me. On several occasions.'

Sylvia said, 'I think I will just take a cup of tea.'

'I would prefer it if you ate a slice of cake. You need sustenance. You are far too thin.'

'I would so much rather not . . . Very well . . . if you think . . . just a little then . . .'

Already, inexorably, Ralph had picked up the silver cake knife with which he cut three large wedges. He placed one on a plate and handed it to his wife. She looked at it despairingly and took a small bite.

Ralph lifted his teacup and deliberately watched the drips plopping into the saucer. 'You have spilled the tea again.'

'I am sorry,' muttered Sylvia.

'I beg your pardon. I didn't quite catch . . .'

'She said she's sorry,' blurted Felice, then shrank back as her father turned cold eyes upon her before ringing the bell once more.

When Murray appeared he showed no surprise at being ordered to bring more cups and saucers. It had become almost a daily occurrence. 'And renew the tea,' said Ralph. 'This must be cool by now.'

'Yes, sir.' The butler left.

Felice was angry with her father. He had always maintained that Sylvia had a weak personality and needed guidance, but Felice was finding this increasingly difficult to believe. Sylvia was weak, to be sure, but he had loved her even when she was married to Harry Dane, Lawrence's father; loved her enough to court the censure of society by actually making love to her and, when her husband had taken them to the divorce court in a scandal which rocked society, to marry her. Felice was the child of their union, the daughter of Ralph Bennyson, born a couple of years later.

From the time she could reason she had watched her mother trying to win her husband's approval. Sylvia had persisted until his constant indifference to her sensitivity, his endless pinpricks, his determination to thwart her every wish, had defeated her.

The clean china was brought and a fresh pot of tea. 'You had better pour, Felice,' said Ralph. 'Your mother is evidently incapable of even so simple an act today. Are your nerves upset, my love?' he asked, his voice mockingly soft. 'Perhaps we should see the doctor again and ask him to engage a room in the nursing home.'

'No, please,' burst out Sylvia. A nursing home was, in this case, a euphemism for mental home. Not a public ward: naturally he would put her in a luxurious place which offered every care that money could buy, but she would be surrounded by nurses assigned to watch her day and night, held in captivity by a series of locked doors. He had done it twice before, the first time soon after Felice's birth, an extremely difficult one which had left Sylvia deeply exhausted and in pain. Longing for the small son she had abandoned, she became increasingly distressed until she was a shaking mass of nerves.

'How typically illogical of you,' Ralph had said. 'You have lost a child; I have given you another. True, it is a girl and I suppose you wanted a boy, as I most certainly did, but next time we'll have a son. Can't you be satisfied for now?'

'You don't understand,' Sylvia had moaned weakly. 'I want them both. I want to be able to put my arms around them and give my Lawrence some of the love I have for him, as well as for this little one. I want him to know his sister. Please, Ralph, speak to Mrs Dane once more. I'm sure she would be merciful if she knew how I am suffering. She would surely allow him to visit me and his little sister.'

'She would not!'

'How can you know that without asking her?'

'You are well aware that I asked more than once. Many times, in fact. She declared that you will never, under any circumstances, be permitted to have contact with the boy, and one can hardly blame her after having to suffer the shame of her son's divorce and the horror of his dreadful suicide.'

'I suffered it, too.'

'Indeed! You were married to me at the time.'

'I still cared enough for Harry to grieve.'

'How touching.'

Sylvia had wept. 'You took Lawrence from me!' she sobbed.

'*I* took him from you? You left him.'

'What else could I do after you had broken my marriage?'

'*I* broke your marriage? I flirted with you and you fell into my arms without a single protest. I was amazed at how easy it was.'

'That isn't true. I tried to resist you, you know I did, but you kept on and on at me. No matter where I went you were there – '

'For God's sake, it's past and done with. We are married, though why I bothered I don't know. I need not have done so. Who would have blamed me?'

'Society would have blamed you.'

'They blame me now. The best houses are closed to me because of you.'

Sylvia's bitter weeping had been prolonged until finally her milk had dried up and Ralph had engaged a nurse to bottle-feed Felice. Sylvia had been removed to the nursing home from which she had returned with her spirit even more damaged.

The second incarceration occurred when the doctor informed them that she could never bear another child. Ralph had been merciless in his angry taunting until she attacked him physically, screaming, fists flailing. She returned that time utterly subdued, her spirit broken, and since then he had held the threat of further restraint over her cowed head.

The anguished thoughts sped through her mind as she sipped her tea without tasting it while Ralph sank his strong white teeth into his cake. 'Eat up, ladies, this is truly delicious. I must compliment Mrs Whatsername, the cook.'

'Mrs Rose,' supplied Felice.

'Ah, you know. Good girl. It is up to the woman of the house to remember the servants by name. One gets so much more co-operation from them if they believe you care about them. Your poor mother forgets.'

'I know Cook's name is Mrs Rose,' protested Sylvia. 'And I know the housekeeper's name and there's Janet and – '

'Spare me,' begged Ralph and she fell silent. Ralph confused her, sent her mind spinning out of control.

Felice ate her way through the cake. She did not care for its richness but her digestion would cope. She pitied Sylvia and then was angry again because her mother induced such negative emotions in her. She wanted to love her, but she felt the oppression of her father's will bearing down upon both of them and for the thousandth time told herself that she must find a way out. She had a small private income, but needed to enlarge it if she were to be free. How? What did she know? How to jump over a tennis net and give a sporting handshake when she lost, which was often because she wasn't aggressive enough. How to play a round of golf and smile when she was beaten, as she usually was. How to swim, to sail a small boat, how to walk and sit in a graceful manner, how to address persons of importance. How to curtsey at her court presentation. Some hopes of court for her, the daughter of a disgraceful union. Of what use was her education to a girl who needed to work? What

31

was there which a gently bred female could manage? 'Gently bred females' was what the schoolmistresses had called the girls in their care. To Felice it had sounded nineteenth-century. Most of the pupils had laughed at their mentors behind their backs, but they accepted the fact that they were ladies of whom certain things were expected and assumed that their lives would consist of the luxury of leisure, money and a 'good' marriage, followed by the pains and pleasures of childbirth. They looked forward without rebellion. Felice had felt alien in their company.

Lawrence Dane parked his car in the old stables and went into the house, where his hat, coat and gloves were taken by a maid. The old butler had retired to a cottage on the estate and they had not engaged another. The Dane fortune had been depleted by his grandfather and great-grandfather, both men being overfond of gambling and prone to losing. Their portraits hung on the dining-room wall and Lawrence had studied them long and hard. They looked austere and dignified and it was difficult to comprehend the stories he had learned of their excesses and their riotous behaviour. Apparently, it had been accepted that the gentlemen of a family played hard and if they came off the worst for it they smiled.

'That's all very well,' Lawrence had argued when he was about sixteen, listening to their philosophy expounded by Grandmother, 'but if they leave their families without the means to live a proper sort of life surely they are to blame.'

Grandmother had tapped him gently on his head with her silver-topped ebony cane. 'Enough! Such disrespect. It is not seemly to criticise the dead and we are not exactly paupers.'

But neither were they as wealthy as they should be and Grandmother had been hard put sometimes to find the money to keep up appearances in the society to which they belonged as well as to find fees and extras for school and university. Lawrence was not academic and had protested she was wasting her money in giving him a classical education.

He had been far more enthusiastic about aspects of his life in their country manor a few miles from Bristol. He loved his horses and dogs, he revelled in manly sports, going out with the guns whenever possible, fishing in the small stretch of river they owned, visiting like-minded friends, meeting their sisters and dancing with them.

'You really needn't worry, Grandmother,' he had explained, his narrow boyish face intent, trying to get her to see things his way. 'I

32

get all the tuition I need from our own library. Grandfather's collection is wonderful.'

'Grandfather's collection,' retorted Grandmother, 'consists mainly of tomes on sport. He was no academic. Nor were your ancestors who began to build the library.'

'Exactly, and neither am I. I love the manor. I want to devote my life to it. I believe one day I could make it pay. Think of the farms, two besides the home farm, and I can tell from the stewards' books that none of them is as productive as it should be.'

'Oh? When did you see the books?'

'Ages ago. Sanderson showed them to me.' Sanderson was the head gamekeeper.

Grandmother had nodded. 'Well, that was wise of him. You need to learn about your inheritance. Sanderson is a good man. Trustworthy.'

'The stables could be made to pay, I'm sure. They're almost empty. I should like to introduce horse breeding.'

'Good God! You sound like a stud farmer.'

'And why not! It's a splendid occupation.'

'Maybe when you have enjoyed the company of your peers at Oxford you will change your mind.'

'Oxford! That's two years away and I shall have to kick my heels there for at least another three. I want to begin work now.'

But, of course, Grandmother had had her way, as he had known she would. Eton and Oxford were the accepted destinations of his contemporaries in like position and he must have those advantages. He had unexpectedly enjoyed Oxford, and although he had left knowing almost as little about the classics as when he arrived, he had gained many friends. He was good company and highly presentable and invitations always crowded the mantelpiece of the drawing room.

Lawrence was bitter at the break-up of his father's home. He had been too young at the time of his death to be able to comprehend it, understanding only that a beloved father was seen no more. He had been told the truth since and there were terrifying memories locked in his mind which, occasionally, without warning, would spring at him. Then he would be standing once more at an open grave, his hand filled with dark earth to throw on to the coffin. He would remember the sound of its soft falling which seemed to echo in his head like drums. And he had always been aware that something had happened before that moment which had marked him.

He had misty dreams of his mother as she had been, young, beautiful, scented like a flower, bending over his bed to press gentle kisses to his lips before going out with his father to some grand party. He woke from these dreams elated and heavy with love for her before consciousness returned. Then reality would break over his head like a wave and he cursed his mother and renewed his hatred. For years he had nursed these bitter emotions, especially at school when other fellows' mothers had visited to watch their sons taking part in sports. Grandmother came, of course, but it was not the same. He barely acknowledged Felice's existence and then only because Ralph was her father.

It was for his stepfather's sake that he visited the factory, not really seeing the rows of white-aproned, white-capped common women who bent over the sewing machines.

Grandmother was waiting for him now in her drawing room. She smiled as he entered. 'A successful visit, Lawrence?'

He bent and kissed the cheek she held towards him. 'It went as usual. Filthy smells of cheap cotton and machine oil, crowds of women, men standing around in brown coats. It's an unpleasant place. Every inch of it.'

'The top storey is different. Friends of mine have been impressed by the comfort of the fitting room and the courteous, expert service they receive.'

'I know,' said Lawrence in resigned tones. 'Ralph insists on our walking through the public part of the upper department and taking refreshment in the office beyond. I don't know why he does it. I'm sure he never notices much.'

Mrs Dane rang the bell and ordered tea. 'I dare say he sees the important things.'

'Maybe. But he leaves a lot to his manager and office staff. He trusts them. The girls in the office are chosen for their respectability, mostly churchgoers, I believe. The manager, Frank Bagley, is an upright man. Ralph has empowered him to dismiss any dishonest person instantly and without references.'

'That is a big responsibility. No one is infallible. Has Mr Bagley never made a mistake?'

'I shouldn't think so. Even if he had they couldn't protest.'

'Aren't the unions supposed to look after workers' rights?'

'Have you forgotten? Ralph refuses to allow the union to gain a foothold.'

'I wonder he is able to do that?'

'He does what he pleases. Joining a union is a reason for dismissing a worker and their biggest fear is of unemployment. All the newspapers say the figures are rising.' Lawrence accepted a small sandwich. He had lost interest in the subject. 'I've been invited to the Havergills' dance. Shall I go?'

'My dear boy, that is for you to decide. For my part, I've found the Havergills pleasant enough people. They are wealthy and still have a couple of pretty daughters to dispose of. The three eldest girls were given huge marriage settlements. Money is always useful, especially when a man has plans to expand his business.'

'I know. I shall go then.'

In Bennyson's exclusive shop in Park Row and in the upper workroom at the factory the workers knew only too well that there was to be a grand dance given by a leading family. For weeks clients had been attending for fittings of corsetry designed to show off their new gowns.

'We're rushed off our feet,' said Isobel to her mother. 'We've had to take work from the shop. They can't cope there with all the orders.'

'I can vouch for that,' said Desmond. 'I've been ferrying bundles from one place to the other.'

Dad was at the pub so the house was peaceful and everyone but Kathy was gathered in the kitchen enjoying a cup of tea. She was in bed. She should be asleep, but it was likely that she was reading by the light of a candle.

'Did you think the work would be easier when you were moved upstairs?' asked Olive.

'I thought it was supposed to be a promotion,' said Mum. She looked flushed in the light of the fire which had been lit on this cold August night. 'Such a summer we're having,' she sighed.

'Or not having,' said Olive.

'Where's Ivor tonight?' asked Desmond.

Grace said nervously, 'I don't know. He seems to mix with some very odd folk.'

'They just enjoy a good time,' said Olive. 'Nothing wrong in that, is there?'

'It depends what they call a good time,' said Desmond.

'You're just a stick-in-the-mud,' Olive jeered.

'Better a stick-in-the-mud than a convict,' said Desmond.

'A convict!' cried Grace. 'What do you mean? Our Ivor isn't going to land in prison, is he?'

Desmond wished he hadn't said so much. 'No, but a couple of the

35

lads he meets are sticky-fingered. Still, Ivor's seen enough of the trouble Dad's caused not to follow their ways.'

Grace's hand went to her mouth and she bit her knuckles. 'I couldn't bear more disgrace. Do your best to get Ivor away from bad company, Desmond. See if there's a job for him locally. Ask in the factory. If he had a job he wouldn't have time to get up to mischief.'

Olive waited impatiently for them to finish. She had no interest in Ivor. 'It was a promotion being moved upstairs, wasn't it?' she asked Isobel.

'Yes.'

'Do you get paid more?'

'Half a crown a week.'

'Not much, is it?'

'No, but everything helps.'

'I would have thought they'd pay her more than that for the extra responsibility,' said Olive. 'You have to get the fittings perfect, don't you, Isobel? It's no off-the-peg or out-of-the box affair when you work on the top floor.'

'They will pay me more when I've learned more of the trade. Meanwhile the work is very interesting. Custom-made corsetry is so different. It fits exactly and hides clients' bad points and shows up their good ones. Not that anyone tells the customers they have bad points. We have to be very discreet. And the top-floor clients pay a lot so a mistake could be costly and you might lose a customer. I've been told that a hundred times in the time I've been there.'

'Do the Bennysons still visit the office?' asked Grace. 'When I worked there the boss always used to. It was their last call.'

'It's the same now.'

'Do they get tea or coffee, and biscuits and little cakes all served on china so delicate you can see through it?'

'They do.'

'I had a set of bone china once,' said Grace. 'Granny Shaw gave it to us for a wedding present, but it all got broken.'

There was a silence. No one wanted to ask how. It was most likely that Dad had hurled it about in a temper, or thrown it at his wife.

'That Miss Bennyson looks a stuck-up piece,' said Olive.

'When did you see her?' asked Grace.

'Oh, I was in a shop in town the other day and she came in. She could hardly bring herself to speak to the assistants.'

'What shop?' asked Isobel. 'It must have been posh if she was there.'

'It was. I bought myself some extra-special stockings. Silk ones.'

'What?' Grace was astonished. 'Real silk?'

'Yes.' Olive was prepared to be sulky, but the atmosphere was so unusually pleasant she decided instead to confide. 'I've met a really nice boy. He works in a boot factory and makes good money. He says he likes girls in silk stockings.'

'Olive, I'm surprised at you!' cried Grace. 'What kind of boy talks to a girl about her stockings?'

'Just a normal boy,' said Olive cheekily. 'There's nothing wrong in it. Stockings are advertised all over the place.'

'You're only fourteen,' said Desmond. 'Too young to let a boy make free with his speech. Mum, I'm surprised you let her have a boyfriend already. Our Isobel had to wait till she was sixteen.'

'I was stricter with her. I think you are with the first child, then you learn to be a bit more trusting.'

'Didn't you trust Isobel?' asked Olive.

'It wasn't a case of not trusting,' said Grace. She was beginning to get flustered and Isobel frowned at her sister.

'You'd best not develop expensive tastes, Olive,' said Desmond. 'I doubt a boot factory worker earns enough to dress you in silk.'

'For goodness' sake!' Olive went red with anger. 'He's taking me to a dance at the church hall, that's all, and I just fancied wearing something grand. When I marry I'll choose a man who makes really good money and can give me a big house and a car of my own and a maid and all the silk and satin I want.'

'You don't ask for much, do you?' said Desmond.

Olive leaned forward and tried to box his ears, but he dodged, upsetting a cup which fortunately was empty.

'That's enough,' said Grace. But she had relaxed and was enjoying the banter.

Then they lifted their heads and listened, like a group of wary animals alerted by the approach of an enemy. Dad was singing as he walked down the road.

'He's had more to drink than usual on a weekday,' said Olive. 'Where did he get the money?'

'He took the extra half-crown Isobel earns,' confessed Grace. 'He says he's going to have it every week.'

Isobel frowned. 'What an idiot I was to let him know about it. I was so excited and proud I told you while he was there.'

'A mistake,' said Desmond grimly.

'Pride goeth before a fall,' said Olive. She could be very irritating.

Later, when they were alone, Isobel said to Desmond, 'I have a horrible fear that Ivor will end up like Dad.'

'Maybe. No one can control him. I can't tell Mum, but I shan't try to get him taken on at Bennyson's. Our reputation there is good and he could wreck it. Our money is what keeps this family going.'

'I know. Desmond, this is an awful thing to say, but I don't much like Ivor.'

Brother and sister fell silent, then Desmond said, 'If you meet a nice bloke and want to get married, I'll stay on here and do my best. Frank Bagley likes you, doesn't he?'

'How do you know?'

'I've seen him watching you. Has he ever asked you for a date?'

'Once. I turned him down.'

'Whatever for? He's a good chap and makes enough to give you security.'

'I haven't got marriage on my mind. But I might go out with him. I'll make it clear that I'm only looking for friendship.'

Desmond smiled at her. Frank Bagley was a widower fifteen years older than Isobel with two young sons, but he was an attractive man in many ways and a real catch. He owned his house, had a good reputation, was well-spoken and enjoyed books, music and the kind of films that Isobel liked. Desmond loved his sister dearly. He decided to point her in Bagley's direction as powerfully as he could without actually interfering.

Isobel asked, 'What about you, Desmond? Have you got a girl in mind?'

'A man has to make his living before he can think of girls.'

'Not even think of them?'

'Stop teasing, sis. I'm normal. I like girls, but they'll just have to wait until I'm ready.'

'Poor dears,' said Isobel.

Desmond threw a cushion at her.

Chapter Three

Ralph Bennyson read his newspaper then returned to an article on the unemployment figures. When Ramsay MacDonald's Labour Party had won the last election the figures had fallen slightly and businessmen, although detesting the idea of being ruled by Socialists, began to hope that the worst was over. The General Strike of 1926, when the workers had brought the entire country to a standstill, was still a vivid horror in employers' minds. The bosses had beaten the men in the end, even the coalminers whose insurrection had lasted longest, but the memories were clear. Now the unemployment figures were rising again, fast, and trade was suffering. Women would always need corsetry, but takings were down. Even the clients of the Park Row shop, My Lady's Bower, must be keeping their body armour for longer periods before replacing it. He wondered what he could do to entice the customers. Bennyson's had made it a policy to advertise only in genteel terms in women's magazines. So genteel and discreet indeed that Ralph had wondered in his younger years if the women had understood them at all. There were references to the beauty of ladies, the necessity for control, the expertise of fitters. The word corsets was never mentioned. He remembered his father's scorn at the blatant advertising methods of other corsetmakers and wondered now if he would find it necessary to compete on similar terms.

'Not while I can prevent it,' he muttered, lighting his second cigarette of the day.

'More coffee?' Sylvia spoke softly.

Occasionally she took it into her head to come down to breakfast and he had forgotten she was there. He handed her his cup without lowering the paper.

'I thought I heard you speak,' said Sylvia, handing back a full cup with cream and brown sugar just the way he liked it. 'Did you ask me something?'

'No!'

Ralph shook the paper shut and slapped it on to the table. 'Damn government! If women hadn't been given the vote I doubt if we would have the Socialists in power.'

'I thought you were pleased with the government,' ventured Sylvia.

'*Pleased* with them! *Pleased?* I tolerated them. I was prepared to put up with them if they kept their election promises. Of course, they did not.'

'Is business poor?'

Ralph glared at her. She had aged faster than he had expected. That was the worst of women with delicately fair complexions, and though he knew of many such who spent a great deal of time and money in beauty parlours, endeavouring to keep their youthful looks, Sylvia was not one of them, though it would have given her something to do as well as improving her. A man liked to have a pretty woman at his table. He lifted his paper in front of him again, but he did not see the words. His mind slipped back to the time when he had coveted her, when she had represented all that he desired in a woman, beauty, an excellent taste in clothes and jewels, intelligence enough to converse interestingly. She was well-bred and her appearance of delicate fragility had fascinated him. The fact that she was another man's wife bothered him not at all. He had gloated over the number of women he had seduced and felt contempt for husbands who were so easily deceived. Sylvia had proved more difficult to conquer than he had expected. At first he had scared her, which only increased her desirability. Then she spoke of her love for her husband. Ralph had seen Harry Dane as a weakling and her strong attachment to him made him the more determined to score over him. He had eventually worn Sylvia down, but not until he had lied to her, telling her that he had seen Harry embracing another woman.

'I don't believe you!' had been her expected reaction.

'It is quite true.'

'No one has ever seen such a thing.'

'No one else has the courage to tell you.'

He worked on her feelings skilfully, employing a deceit she was too naive to suspect him of, even using a faked photograph of Harry and a half-clothed woman, and the rest had been simple. He groaned inwardly. If he had known the result his lust would bring he would have run a mile before he touched her. He had been astonished to realise that he was a little in love with her, and the novelty intrigued him, though he had no intention of instigating a permanent relationship. For one thing she wasn't rich enough, but, more than that, the thought of getting mixed up in an unsavoury divorce that might destroy his social life brought him out in a cold sweat. So he took what she gave him discreetly until she began to bore him. He was about to break off the connection when she told him that she loved him and that she was pregnant with his child. That hadn't bothered him. He instantly assumed that she would behave as other women did, present the child to her husband as his and keep the marriage intact. But to his horror she told him that she had confessed their affair to Harry and asked for her freedom.

'How can you be sure it's mine?' he had demanded. 'Harry is your husband. Presumably you and he have ...'

Sylvia had laid her long cool fingers over his lips. 'Oh, no! How could you think I would allow him such intimacy when I care for you?'

'But it's been months ...'

'He's a kind and patient man. I told him I was unwell.'

'And he never once ...?'

'Never. Besides, if he has been seeing another woman, as you told me, it would not be difficult for him to refrain, would it?'

He was hoist with his own petard! She was obviously telling the truth. He had tried to deflect her, describing vividly the inevitable scandal that would ensue if the newspapers got hold of the story.

'Harry will be discreet,' was her unbelievably naive answer.

'Darling, you can't keep something like this discreet.'

'Harry will.'

That was the first time he had encountered Sylvia's unexpectedly stubborn streak. She had proceeded with incredible tenacity along the lines she had mapped out and was actually amazed by the furore that ensued. Inevitably he had found himself named in divorce proceedings and, naturally, all the sympathy had been with Harry and his poor little abandoned son. Ralph had writhed in frustrated humiliation, especially when it turned out that Sylvia's pregnancy had been a mistake, an honest one on her part, but their union was looked upon as a foregone conclusion by everyone and he had surrendered. By that time neither he nor Sylvia were deeply in love, probably not in love at all, and she had begun to suffer the agony of guilt which hadn't left her since. Their marriage was damned from its beginning. The only good thing to come out of it was Felice. He had wanted a son, Sylvia had failed in that, but he clung to Felice with overbearing love. He had jealously watched her progress from the day of her birth. He supposed that Sylvia loved her daughter, but she gave little outward sign. At first she'd been happy to bear the child, but she wanted her son back, and when she finally understood that it would not be permitted, that she was to have no contact, she was devastated. Then had come Harry's suicide, dealing her a further appalling wound and loading her with so much heavy guilt that she had been useless to Ralph ever since.

He lowered his paper. 'Where is Felice?'

'Felice?'

'Our daughter. You remember her? Is she still in bed?'

'Of course I remember Felice! You need not be so . . . She has gone riding with the Havergills.'

'What?' His eyes bulged slightly in temper. 'Why didn't you stop her?'

'I? Stop Felice? How? She never listens to me.'

'You could have referred her to me.'

'I could have, but I didn't. She begged me not to.'

Ralph was overcome by fury. 'Begged you not to? Felice trusts me.'

'She knew you would try to stop her.'

'I would definitely have stopped her. I would have pointed out all the reasons why I am not in favour of her riding.'

'So she said. She likened it to your refusal to allow her to drive.'

Ralph felt frustrated. 'She hasn't had a riding lesson in her life. She may fall.'

'She has been taking lessons with the Havergills' groom.'

'You knew! And you did not tell me!'

'Riding is a healthy pursuit. I once enjoyed it.'

Ralph glared at her. She so seldom had the spirit to defy him he was at a loss to know how to deal with her sudden insurrection.

'I suppose it gives you some kind of satisfaction to go against me,' he said angrily.

'No. In fact, I would much prefer not to, but Felice can be very—'

'She has no riding gear!'

'The Havergills will lend her some.'

'I abominate the idea of her borrowing clothes!'

'If you allowed her to ride she wouldn't need to.'

Ralph glared at her. 'So it's all my fault!'

'No. I don't know. What is your fault? I don't understand.'

'You never do. I shall speak to her tonight. I shall make her see how displeased I am.'

'And forbid her to ride again?'

'Of course.'

'But she has disobeyed you today.'

'Not only today, it seems, if she has been taking lessons, aided and abetted by her mother.'

Ralph felt anger rolling over him. Sometimes Sylvia was like a ferret, sinking her teeth into him and hanging on. 'I suppose you encouraged her to defy me. You know I fear for her safety. But you never did care for your children or you wouldn't have left your son.'

His cruel barb went home. Her eyes revealed her suffering. He knew he had gone too far, but he refused to recant. It served her right.

'I did not encourage her,' she said, her voice shaking. 'I simply didn't interfere.'

'You knew I should be displeased and worried.'

'She likes riding. She's always wanted a pony.'

'You stupid woman! I don't want her to have an accident. She is my only child.'

Sylvia subsided. That was the statement which always defeated her. She wondered, as she did so often, if Ralph would have loved her if she had given him a son. Not that it mattered any more. It hadn't for a long time. When Harry had been buried she felt the best part of her had been buried with him, and Ralph had not attempted to make love to her for years.

He pushed his chair back. 'I shall visit the factory.'

'Again? So soon? Is there something wrong?'

Ralph walked out, banging the door behind him, and Sylvia felt immense relief. He was bad enough when she pursued her usual course of avoiding trouble, but if she ever dared to defy him in the smallest particular it left her quaking inside. To take her mind from him she reached for the newspaper and read the article on unemployment. It mentioned loans to Germany – how odd to be lending Germany money when not so long ago they had been enemies – payment of war debts, financiers' profits. She didn't really understand. Ralph was right, she had never been much good with figures, but she could have run his home efficiently if he had allowed it. She'd run her former husband's home to the satisfaction of them both. Memories of Harry Dane seeped into her mind. Usually she thrust them away, unable to bear the torment, but last night she had scarcely slept and she was so tired, too tired to control her thoughts. How happy she and Harry had been. She cursed herself, as she had done a thousand times, for her stupidity in yielding to Ralph Bennyson's advances. If only he hadn't told her those lies! Of course Harry hadn't been seeing another woman. She'd long known the truth.

She jumped to her feet, the chair falling back, and without stopping to right it hurried to the small drawing room where she felt happiest. A fire had been burning there since six o'clock and it was cosy. The decor had been selected by her in shades of softest blue and rose. It was like a bower, and here she could sit over her sewing and think only pleasant thoughts. She had a wireless which played the music she enjoyed, light classical pieces, popular tunes, songs sung by men and women with attractive voices, and there was a gramophone and a neat pile of records. Some of them had been chosen by Felice, who seemed to know what her mother would like. Sylvia didn't spend much time thinking of Felice because if she did she knew she would begin to weep, and the weeping would weaken her and she would remember her son, taken from her by the events that had steam-rollered her inexorably from the time she had cheated her husband.

Isobel soon grew accustomed to the more delicate work required in the exclusive department of Bennyson's and began to enjoy it. She liked seeing the women who would be wearing the custom-made corsetry, she enjoyed the pleasure in the improvement of their figures, in their comfort. One client was a particular favourite. She had borne seven children and had needed a Caesarean operation to save the life of the seventh. Her muscles were slack and her appearance had given her a great deal of unhappiness until a friend had advised her to apply to the specialist shop in Park Row. She was too diffident to encounter the smart women there and had come to Bennyson's Corsets.

Isobel was given the job of measuring her, Miss Trefusis, who was in charge of the specials, popping in and out to check her. Mrs Shelton was shy, but hidden in the curtained cubicle she was more forthcoming.

'You cannot imagine the miseries I went through during the twenties,' she confided. 'To be thin was to be admired and I was so *lumpy*.'

Isobel gave a little laugh at the odd description, then was nervous in case her first client should take offence.

But Mrs Shelton laughed, too. 'I know it sounds funny, though' – she sighed – 'it wasn't funny at the time. Wearing the combined hip confiner and bust bodice which was supposed to flatten you did nothing for me. Then they began to put in those little bulges they called "cups" for the breasts and I was too big for them and they made me look even droopier. Do you really think you can make me look presentable again?'

'I'm certain of it, madam.'

'It's lucky that the new fashion expects a woman to be more rounded. I never did think women who were straight up and down were attractive, though it didn't seem to put the men off. Mind you,' she giggled, 'nothing seems to put men off. Oh, dear, now I *am* blushing. And you a young unmarried girl. I shouldn't say such things.' She sighed. 'I once had a lovely figure. My husband did so admire it,' she went on as Isobel slid the tape measure round her waist. 'And my dear husband still loves me the way I am, so it must be the opinion of others that bothers me. You know, my dear, some women can be so catty, especially those who have borne perhaps only one baby, or even none at all, though how a woman can bear life without having given birth is something I shall never understand.'

Isobel listened, smiled and nodded in appropriate places. She had been warned that the clients' confidences must be as sacred as if they were in a doctor's surgery and that they seldom required much of a reply.

'They like to get it all off their chests,' explained Miss Trefusis. She had an uncanny gift for empathising with the problems presented to her, though she was tall, bony, unmarried and had certainly never been pregnant.

Isobel took careful note of Mrs Shelton's hip measurements.

Before Isobel had moved upstairs Miss Trefusis had had a long interview with her. 'You are quick and intelligent, Miss Kingston, and will learn fast. Some of our customers have sad medical conditions, many of them incurable. We can help these poor ladies. I am thrilled when someone arrives at Bennyson's unhappy and in pain and I am able to assure her that we can deal with her suffering. My greatest joy in life is to watch the transformation when they put on the finished garment and realise that once more they can look forward to some comfort. I have always looked upon that side of the business as a mission.' Her eyes had shone with fervour, her earnestness had coloured her cheeks pink. She had seen Isobel's amazement and her colour had grown deeper. 'I dare say you think me rather foolish.'

Even more astonished by this sign of vulnerability, Isobel had taken a moment to bring her thoughts to order, then she had said with obvious sincerity, 'I think that's marvellous, Miss Trefusis. I'd heard that you did good work but I had no idea – honestly, you make me feel like a crusader. I really would love to learn that side of the business.'

'You'll need patience and you'll have to spend hours in tuition. There's such a lot you need to know.'

'I'll do anything you say,' promised Isobel. She had kept her promise.

'Do each measurement twice on the specials,' Miss Trefusis had taught her. 'There is nothing worse than to have a client return full of expectation to try on their precious garment, then discover that we have made her something which doesn't fit.'

Isobel had heard about a disaster once perpetrated by a careless girl. Everyone in the factory knew that a titled lady had swept out of Bennyson's in a fury, never to return, and had adversely influenced other potential customers. The story was told in whispers of how the unfortunate client had gone all the way to London to a rival establishment and still spent her money there.

Mrs Shelton lifted her arms obediently for Isobel to begin the breast measurements. 'What does the tape say?' she asked.

Isobel carefully wrote down the figures in her notebook, which was scanned constantly by Miss Trefusis, and thought about her answer.

'It doesn't do to always tell a client exactly what they measure,' Miss Trefusis had said. 'A little white lie is sometimes called for.'

'But don't they go home and get their maids to do it and find out we haven't been telling the truth?' Isobel had asked.

'Not if we give them the information they want to hear,' said Miss Trefusis firmly, and as Bennyson's special department was so well patronised Isobel concluded she must be right.

Mrs Shelton's breasts were large and drooping after breastfeeding all seven of her babies. 'I wanted to feed them myself,' she told Isobel. 'Dear little creatures. Do you know it's a wonderful part of motherhood, holding your child to your breast and knowing you are giving it all the nourishment it needs for months on end. It makes me sad when I hear that some lady cannot feed her baby. Er, what did you say I measure?'

'Thirty-eight, madam,' said Isobel.

'Why, that's very good, isn't it? I feared I was bigger.'

Actually she was a size forty-two and Isobel hoped that Miss Trefusis was right about their clients' vanity and that she hadn't overdone it.

However, everything proved fine. Mrs Shelton returned and was eased into her corset-brassière combination; she regarded herself in the long mirror, beaming with satisfaction.

'My dear Miss Kingston, you have made me look young again. But what is this? You have given me steels. I thought they were no longer in fashion.'

'We have used flexible ones where we could, and put in short ones which help to define your waist. They shouldn't give you any discomfort.'

'No, I feel no discomfort,' said Mrs Shelton, bending backwards and forwards. 'How splendid! I shall ask for you when I return, Miss Kingston.'

Isobel glanced quickly at Miss Trefusis, who was looking on, worried at being given the fulsome praise she didn't deserve, but the corsetière was smiling contentedly as she wished Mrs Shelton good morning and went into a cubicle where another customer was waiting. She cared too much about her job for petty jealousy.

Mrs Shelton was saying, 'When I remember my youth and the dreadfully long steels and tight lacing! Oh dear! I still can have lacing, I know, if I want it, though I much prefer these hooks and eyes. Fashion is not so cruel as it was – one could scarcely breathe. And we were such an odd shape. But you won't know anything about that.'

'I know a little, madam. We are not allowed to begin work up here before Miss Trefusis has shown us examples of corsetry from several different times.'

'What a clever woman she must be.' Mrs Shelton twisted and turned, gazing at herself from all angles in the double mirrors. 'I shall put on my frock. I can tell then if I am really different.'

'It may not fit on your new figure,' said Isobel nervously, wondering if Mrs Shelton would be displeased.

She helped the client on with her frock and they both viewed the result.

'My goodness,' breathed Mrs Shelton, 'it doesn't fit!' She was ecstatic. 'You have made me look inches slimmer.' She tugged at her clothes and drew them in to reveal her new shape. 'I am curved in all the right places.' She went on turning, gazing, enjoying, and Isobel stood quietly by, relieved and happy that her first special assignment had proved successful.

'I do so wish I had a gown to fit my new figure,' cried Mrs Shelton. 'I would wear it right this minute. I can hardly wait to go shopping.'

Miss Trefusis had come in again to supervise. 'Our Park Row shop sells exclusive gowns,' she murmured, 'and we have an experienced alteration hand there.'

'Really? I thought it only sold underwear.'

'That, too, madam.'

'I have never ventured into it, but now, with my new figure, oh, my goodness, shopping will be a pleasure instead of a worry.'

When Isobel had shown Mrs Shelton out by the side door reserved for such clients she joined Miss Trefusis, who was treating a woman whose pendulous stomach was dragging on the bones of her back, making them ache. Not surprising, thought Isobel when she learned that the woman had given birth to five children and had needed operations for the last three.

'Write down the measurements,' said Miss Trefusis.

Isobel got out the special notebook and Miss Trefusis called out a series of figures to her, measuring the customer, carefully securing her sliding tape measure round the lady's body. She took the top and lower circumference of the abdomen and hips, then she turned her attention to the back, the depth of her upper back from the waist, the lower back, the bottom. Isobel concentrated hard. Surgical corsetry must be fitted precisely for the customer–patient to obtain the fullest relief. She stored everything in her head and later would write it carefully in an exercise book.

When the customer had left Miss Trefusis would cut out the many pieces of coutil which must be sewn together with skill, leaving pockets for the necessary steels.

Isobel was not just doing a job. She was learning how to give a real service, working in conjunction with doctors. The idea had fired her imagination from the start. She wished she could help all women in so special a way.

That night she talked to her mother and sisters about her work. 'It's all confidential,' she said, 'so I can't give you details, names and things.'

'Confidential!' mocked Olive. 'What do you think you are, some kind of medical specialist?'

'In a way, I am,' said Isobel.

'Doctor Isobel,' jeered Olive.

'Don't you go on at her,' cried Kathy. 'She's clever and kind and . . .'

'Calm down,' said Isobel, laughing. 'It is rather funny when you think about it. Spending your life measuring women and trying to give them back a bit of their lost beauty and youth.'

Grace said sadly, 'It's a pity everyone can't have that. Most women have to make do with ready-mades. And some of them really need help. They suffer from' — she looked at Kathy and lowered her voice — 'certain complaints.'

'What kind?' demanded Kathy.

'Run upstairs and bring me a handkerchief, please, Kathy,' said Grace.

'Oh, you just don't want me to hear things. It's not fair!' She raced from the room and up the stairs.

'Some women have dreadful things wrong with them after a bad do at childbirth,' said Grace. 'They really could do with being sewn back – their wombs, that is – but they can't afford it. Special corsets would probably help them.'

Isobel didn't know just what happened to wombs which needed sewing back or how a doctor went about it. It all sounded dreadful. It was enough to put a woman off having children.

Olive looked disgusted. She loathed having anything to do with childhood and insisted that she would never want babies.

Kathy burst back into the kitchen and looked as disappointed as Olive looked relieved at the abrupt end of the conversation.

A few days later Ralph Bennyson and Felice visited the factory again. At the end of their tour they were shown into the office where tea awaited them, and at any pause in the machines Isobel could hear the musical tinkling of porcelain and the murmur of voices. There were only two machinists needed up here. They sat in an alcove right by a window and could be curtained off from clients. They would have had an excellent view to the distant hills if someone had not used frosted glass, presumably to prevent exactly that kind of time-wasting. The other machinist was Ruby Tyndall, a woman of about thirty, of medium height and weight. She had dark hair and eyes, and mobile features which she pulled into contortions that expressed more than speech. When the Bennysons walked by she grimaced after them and Isobel had a job not to laugh aloud. Even Miss Trefusis gave a tiny grin. Frank Bagley, the manager, didn't notice.

49

Isobel tied the thread and took the garment she was making off the machine. Next came the bit she liked best, hand-sewing the decorative lace. It could have been done by a machine, but Bennyson's took pride in telling clients that their garments were hand-finished. She pinned the lace frill to the brassière top and a longer frill to the bottom and began to work in tiny stitches.

This was a time when she could think, a precious rarity in her busy life. She wondered often what kind of home they would have had if Dad had not taken to drink and crime. Mum said he wasn't bad before he went off to the war. He had come back with horror in his eyes and Grace hadn't had the heart to stop him when he said drinking helped the nightmares to go away; she had always put aside money for his visits to the pub. Then the drinking got out of hand.

Isobel stirred restlessly as her mind roamed over events which were clearer to her than to the others. She was the eldest, the one the others looked to for guidance, the one Grace turned to for help. Dad had never possessed any skill and was forced to take labouring work, but jobs were difficult to get and employers would obviously choose a sober industrious man before Amos. When Isobel had time to think, she faced the truth about her parents: Amos beat Grace cruelly and constantly until violence had become as much a way of life as his drinking and thieving.

She was brought back by Frank Bagley coming out of the office. 'How's it going?' Ruby asked him, keeping her voice low.

'They're enjoying their tea and cakes.'

'Did you make them?'

'Certainly not!' Mr Bagley had little sense of humour.

'If I'd made them they'd have arsenic in them.'

'Be quiet, they'll hear you. And remember, Mr Bennyson is your employer.'

Ruby pulled a face which made Isobel smile and even brought a reluctant grin from Mr Bagley.

He bent to look at the work Isobel was doing. 'Such fine stitching,' he complimented.

'Goodness me,' said Ruby, 'I had no notion that a gentleman like you knew so much about ladies' work.'

Mr Bagley straightened. The slight flush on his face might have come from bending over. 'I make it my business to understand each aspect of the manufacture,' he said primly.

The office door opened and Miss Trefusis ushered out the important visitors. 'I'm so glad you enjoyed the cakes.' She sounded rather gushing.

'You must pass the recipe on to our cook,' said Mr Bennyson.

Felice frowned, light creases appearing in her white forehead. 'I think I would prefer to enjoy the cakes here, Father. It will be something different to look forward to.'

'I bet their cook would have forty fits if a mere factory supervisor sent her a recipe,' muttered Ruby, earning herself a glare from Miss Trefusis, who believed that an employee should not speak until spoken to.

'As if he was the king,' Ruby said once when she told Isobel about this rule. 'I've read that if you meet the king you must wait until he speaks first before you can open your mouth.'

'Some hopes you have of meeting royalty,' giggled the runabout who overheard.

Ruby said, 'You never know. Perhaps his wife will need a special corset and I'll make it and get mentioned in the Honours List. OBE, perhaps.'

'What's that?'

'Order of the British Empire.'

'What's that mean?' asked the runabout.

'Don't know,' Ruby had said. 'Maybe I should ask for the Order of the Garter, and before you ask I don't know what that is either but it sounds nearer to corsets. Then Mr Bennyson could put "By Appointment to Her Gracious Majesty the Queen" on his letters. That would put a feather in his cap.'

Felice waited now while her father glanced in a desultory way round the room. 'This is a pleasant place to work,' he said. 'I like it better since we had it painted that pale yellow. It's as if the sun shone.'

Ruby raised her brows and made a long, soundless *Oooooh.*

'They never see the sun in here,' remarked Felice.

'Oh, but we benefit from its light,' assured Miss Trefusis, 'even if we can't see out.'

Felice wandered over to the machinists whose heads went down over their work. She lingered by Isobel. 'You make such tiny stitches. One can scarcely see them.'

Mr Bennyson said, 'We employ only the best here.' He looked at his gold watch. 'Come along, dear, or we shall be late.'

Felice sighed. Lunch with some stuffy friends of Father's. She'd wanted to get out of it, but he'd been so angry at her riding that she'd given in to put him back into a good mood, though she still intended to ride whenever she could. Father might dominate Mother, but he would find her more difficult to subdue. She thought rebelliously: I'll never be bossed by a man in my own home.

Isobel watched Felice's departure. It was the first time she had seen her so close and there was something about her . . . She felt almost sorry for her and that was ludicrous. The girl had everything.

At the end of the day Frank Bagley asked Isobel to stay behind for a moment as he had something to say.

'Shall I wait?' asked Ruby. 'He might try something on.'

'I'm sure he won't, a respectable widower like him.'

'You never know. And his wife's been dead a couple of years now. He might be wanting a wife to be a mother to his sons and a bed-mate to him.'

'Honestly, Ruby, you do talk twaddle sometimes.'

'Twaddle? A man needs a woman, especially when he's been used to it.'

'Don't talk like that. Go on home,' said Isobel, giving her friend a little push.

'Tell me what he says, won't you?'

'That depends.'

Since the Bennysons left Frank Bagley and Miss Trefusis had spent the afternoon going through papers and both looked worried. Ruby had decided that someone was going to get sacked. 'Business is down,' she'd said, 'and they'll never keep on girls to idle by their machines. Well, I don't suppose it'll be us. They'll just pick the least skilled.'

'Some of those are women who need money most.'

'I dare say, but Bennyson won't care about that.'

Miss Trefusis left on time and Mr Bagley looked pleased when he saw Isobel waiting. 'Miss Kingston. I'm so glad . . . Thank you for staying on. I'll just lock up and we'll be out.'

'What do you want to see me about? Can't you tell me here?'

'It's nothing to do with work.'

She followed him as he locked the series of doors until they got outside. 'There now, we are free from our working environment. I have been wanting to speak to you for weeks, but it didn't seem feasible to ask for a date when you worked in the factory. Now you have been promoted. Miss Kingston, would you give me the pleasure of accompanying me to the pictures?'

The final words came out so neatly Isobel decided he had been rehearsing them. He sounded very stilted, not at all a man with a sense of fun.

She gave him her full consideration. She liked him, but had simply regarded him as the manager, never as a man. She knew he was a widower with two small sons and that many girls had set their caps at him without success. Now here he was, a man of position and good wages, asking her for a date.

'It sounds tempting,' she said, smiling.

'Then you'll come?'

'Not tonight. I'll think about it. Perhaps tomorrow.'

'Sorry, I can't, tomorrow. The boys have their Cub Scout meeting and I always take them and bring them home. They're so young, you see. You do know I have sons, Miss Kingston?'

'Two, I believe.'

'And that I'm a widower. I wouldn't be asking for a date if I weren't.'

'I'm sure you wouldn't.'

'Why not give me a try? We could just go for a meal and chat, if you'd rather, and I'll bring you back home as early as you like.'

'It sounds lovely. Could we postpone it until Saturday?'

Mr Bagley thought for a moment. 'I'm sure that will be fine. My mother will care for the boys.'

The work on the top floor had grown more interesting by the day, especially when local doctors sent women with misshapen bodies for help. There were those whose bones had shortened and whose elderly flesh hung loose and heavy, others whom arthritis had twisted brutally. Miss Trefusis knew exactly how to measure them and fit them with a comforting corset. She could not effect cures, but she could and did alleviate symptoms and enable the clients to gain more confidence. Isobel grew to admire her. Looked at dispassionately she was a dowdy spinster with no dress sense, but Isobel discovered that she had a true and intense desire to help unfortunate women. Deformity was not a prerequisite for her sympathy: she extended it to those who hated their own obesity, or to the overthin. For the latter she prescribed padding – Isobel had begun to think of Miss Trefusis prescribing, like a doctor.

Isobel assisted at the fitting of one such client. She watched admiringly as the corsetière overcame the diffidence of the shy woman who thought such subterfuges were dishonest.

'Not at all, madam, it is up to us to do our best with what the Good Lord has given us,' said Miss Trefusis. 'Our mothers and grandmothers knew this. They had no hesitation in making themselves as attractive as possible. Padding was completely accepted.'

'But what will my husband say? I mean, when I undress.' Here the client was overcome by embarrassment and went a deep shade of crimson.

Miss Trefusis was not in the least put out. 'I am sure he cares far too much for you to worry about such a trifling matter, and you will feel much more confident and therefore happier and he will be cheered by your joy.'

'Do you really think so?'

'I know so. That very thing has happened to other clients. Of course, I cannot betray confidences, but when you go to your next party take a look at some of the ladies and see if you notice any difference from when you last saw them.'

After the woman had gone, having consented to padding on hips and bust, Isobel said, 'You are so kind to the poor things, Miss Trefusis. I never knew corsetry could be so interesting and rewarding.'

The older woman smiled. 'I'm glad you think like that, Miss King-ston. We've tried out girls who could sew beautifully but haven't cared about the women they served, and they've had to go. I believe you'll do well.'

'Will that lady really notice a difference in some of her friends?'

'I'm sure she will. If you look hard enough you can always find differences and people believe what they want to believe. And who knows? – she may spot a friend who looks happier for having visited us.'

Isobel stayed to help Miss Trefusis with a last-minute order. 'You don't have to remain here,' said the supervisor in her prim way. 'You won't get paid overtime.'

'I want to learn as much as I can,' said Isobel. 'Why did a client return her combination corset? Surely it wasn't faulty?'

'Not at all. She discovered she was expecting a baby' – Miss Trefusis dropped her voice on the last words although, apart from them and the night watchman, the place was empty – 'and she wants to go to a grand ball tomorrow. Later she'll come to us for specials to hold her firm without squeezing. You see, if I insert a little elastic gusset here and there, she'll have the room she needs and still con-ceal her condition.'

'Is it important that she conceals it? She is married, isn't she?'

Miss Trefusis was shocked. 'Of course she is! Good heavens! Mr Bagley would not ask me to work with a person who was disgraced.

And Mr Bennyson – what would he say?'

Isobel thought about the matter. Perhaps it was the fact that the two of them were sitting cocooned in silence above a factory which was usually awash with sound or perhaps it was Miss Trefusis's unbending attitude that made Isobel say incautiously, 'Mr Bennyson's no saint. Mrs Bennyson was married to someone else once. My gran said . . .' She got no further.

Miss Trefusis turned to stare, her face grim, her eyes angry. 'Don't dare repeat gossip to me.'

'It's more than gossip,' said Isobel weakly. She felt as if she'd been slapped.

'Nevertheless, I don't want to hear it. Not ever. Such talk! It's outrageous. I think I can manage without you now, Miss Kingston.'

Isobel stared at the angry supervisor, wishing she could think of something to say which would reinstate her, but Miss Trefusis's mouth was set in grim lines.

Isobel said goodnight, but received no reply.

She left the factory feeling very down.

Chapter Four

Isobel hurried home thinking of Mr Bagley's invitation. She had been out with boys and enjoyed their company, but Mr Bagley was a man. He must be over thirty. His sons were about eight and nine years old.

'A nice pair of lads,' Miss Trefusis had said in a confidential moment. When she spoke of them she looked animated, quite unlike her usual stern self. Isobel wondered if she herself had hopes of Mr Bagley. How old was she? Isobel slowed down. She regretted offending her supervisor and wondered what would happen tomorrow.

Dad had finished his latest labouring job – loading lorries in the fruit market – and was at home. Although he was sober he was noisily enraged about something. Isobel sighed resignedly and pushed her way into the kitchen. Amos was ranting and raving at Ivor while Grace clasped her hands so hard her knuckles were white.

'What's up?' asked Isobel loudly.

'Who the hell asked you to interfere?' yelled Amos. But encountering his daughter's hard gaze he said, 'This fiend out of hell has pinched my tobacco money.'

'Haven't!' yelled Ivor.

'Yes, you have,' bawled Amos. 'It's gone.'

'How do you know it's me? It could have been anyone. It could have been her.' He pointed to his mother. 'She's always saying she's short of money.'

Isobel cried, 'Don't dare insult Mum! If you've taken Dad's tobacco money then own up and hand it back.'

'I haven't got it.'

Brother and sister glared at one another. Ivor was short, like his father, but he was wiry and tough. She doubted her ability to hold him and search his pockets as she had done in the past. He gave a sly smile and Amos roared again with rage.

Grace was overcome by the naked anger in the room. 'I'll give you the money for your tobacco, Amos,' she said placatingly. 'I've got some put by for the weekend joint. You can have that.'

'And what meat will we eat on Sunday?'

'Don't worry,' said Grace, 'I'll think of something.'

Isobel opened her purse and handed her father a shilling. 'For heaven's sake take this. You can buy your cigarettes and a beer.'

Amos smiled quite pleasantly. 'That's a good girl. You see how good your sister is, Ivor?'

Ivor slouched out of the room and they heard him running up the street. 'One day I'll swing for the little devil,' snarled Amos.

'Well, I wonder where he gets it from,' said Isobel with heavy irony.

Amos ignored the jibe and walked out. 'I'll be back in a while,' he called. 'I'll bring a jug of beer and you can have some, Grace.'

'Lucky old you,' said Isobel.

'No need for sarcasm,' reproved Grace automatically. 'Thank you for helping out. I don't know what I'd do without you.'

I do, thought Isobel grimly. I know just what would happen to you. And to Kathy. She shuddered. Never would she leave her sister to Amos's merciless behaviour. She decided to lighten the atmosphere. 'Mum, Frank Bagley asked me out on Saturday.'

'Did he?' Grace was thrilled. 'He seems such a nice man, and reliable. His boys are always well dressed and polite. I see them sometimes when I'm shopping. Mr Bagley has to shop for himself and his mother because she's rather weak, though she keeps an eye on the boys.'

'What colour socks does he wear?' asked Isobel.

'What? Oh, I see. You're making fun of me.' Grace laughed. 'That's all I know. Except that he owns his house. Will you go to the pictures? Ask him here for a bite first.'

Isobel was ashamed of the distaste the idea gave her. Mum was used to the tattered furniture, the oilcloth in holes, the threadbare curtains and all the other dilapidations of a house where money was scarce.

'I expect he'll take me for a meal, Mum.'

'In a café? What a treat it will be for you. You deserve it. You work so hard and look after us when you should be out having fun like other girls your age.'

'Well, I'm going out on Saturday. I'm glad you're pleased.'

'I am. And with Frank Bagley, too. He was very good to his first wife and terribly upset by her death. Consumption it was. We must hope the boys haven't been born with a weakness, though the younger one looks very like his mother. Their mother's mum looked after them as long as she could. Poor old soul. She didn't live long after her daughter. He's hardly looked at a woman since. He's a bit old for you, I suppose, but he'd be a good catch.'

'Oh, Mum, don't jump ahead of yourself. I'm only going out with him.'

The next day Miss Trefusis had forgotten her irritation and Isobel was comfortable again.

On Saturday, after her morning's work, she hurried home and spent the afternoon bathing herself with a bowl of water and a flannel. She washed her hair and put it in curlers, then opened the door of the communal wardrobe which was wedged into a corner in the passageway upstairs and extracted her new blouse. She had made it herself after a style she had seen in a magazine. It was floral crepe de Chine with a navy background, simply cut without frills as advised by the magazine for shorter women. Her skirt was plain navy, as were her best shoes. For once, the day was summery and warm and she was able to wear a small blue straw hat with a flower and carry a cardigan. When the time came to leave to meet Frank she peered at herself in the mirror on the inside of the wardrobe door, the only mirror in the house. It didn't go all the way to the floor and it was impossible to stand back far enough for a full view without falling down the stairs. However, she was pleased with what she saw.

Downstairs, she met her father in the narrow corridor and her heart missed a beat. He looked dark with anger.

'I'll do for that brat!' he shouted.

Grace came running out. 'Don't, oh please, don't,' she begged. 'Come on, Amos, I've got a lovely mutton stew, just the way you like it with plenty of potatoes, and there's bread and butter and I've got jam tart for afters . . .'

Amos ignored her.

'What's happened?' asked Isobel. 'Where's your jug of beer?'

'That's what I'm mad about. That bloody son of yours,' he turned to Grace, 'ran out of an alleyway and crashed straight into me. He knocked the jug out of my hand and now I've got no beer and I owe for the jug and the little bugger ran off laughing at me.'

Isobel could have cursed Ivor as heartily as his father did.

Although Ivor was small in stature he had never been beaten. Perhaps because he resembled Dad so closely, or perhaps Amos feared him. Ivor had a dark, secretive nature and Isobel had always wondered just how he would defend himself if attacked. By any means to hand, she decided. She opened her purse. It went against the grain, but she couldn't bear to leave Grace in this situation. She handed her father one and sixpence. 'Pay for the jug and try again.'

He glared at her; his eyes were red-rimmed and Isobel saw with sudden fear that he had already been drinking and was past the point of reason. It seemed as if some devil in him rose up and took over.

'My, aren't we posh tonight? Aren't we *bloody* posh? New hat?'

'No, Dad . . .'

'New blouse?'

'Yes, I made it . . .'

She got no further. He lunged forward, dragged her hat from her head and tore off the flower, splintering the straw and stamping the flower underfoot. Then he reached for her blouse, grabbed it at the throat and ripped it from neck to hem. She listened to the buttons dropping on to the linoleum with small tapping sounds before she choked and ran upstairs, holding her torn blouse over her breasts. This latest outrage devastated her. It reminded her vividly of the time when he had torn and fumbled at her nightgown, when he had tried to thrust himself into her. She hadn't been able to cry then, but she did now, gagging over the bowl on the washstand, her face streaming with tears. She heard Kathy's voice behind her. 'Don't cry, Isobel.'

The child was terrified. She had never known her father mistreat her sister, never seen Isobel give way. 'It's all right, my love,' Isobel managed. 'I'm not feeling very well.'

'Dad looks funny,' said Kathy. 'He hurt you, didn't he? Has he hurt you, Isobel?'

'No, my love. He got cross over something and my blouse got torn somehow.'

'Look, I picked up the buttons. I'll put them on the washstand. You sewed them on yourself, I saw you, and you used lots of cotton like you teach me. How did they all get torn off?'

'It was just a silly accident, darling. Now don't ask any more questions. I just don't feel well. Go downstairs and tell Mum I'll be down directly.' As Kathy left her with a backward, agitated glance, Isobel wondered if she was doing any favours to Kathy by lying to her.

Grace came to her, put her arms around her and sobbed. 'I'm sorry, Isobel. I'm so sorry.'

'It's not your fault, Mum.'

'It is, it is. I should have been stronger. I need never have put you through this. If only I'd been strong. If only . . .' She stopped, then said, 'But the past can never be undone.'

'It's not your fault,' said Isobel. 'I think I'll lie down, Mum. I feel a bit queasy.'

'But what about your date?'

'I can't go now. I must look a sight.'

'No you don't,' said Kathy eagerly from the door. Neither woman had realised she was there and they were startled. 'Just bathe your eyes in cold water, the way you tell me to. You could wear my hat. It's plain straw . . .'

'And I've got a silk flower somewhere,' said Mum. 'I'll sew it on for you. Kathy, run and tell Mr Bagley . . .'

'No, wait!' cried Isobel. She hated the disappointment on their faces, she wished she could remove it, but she knew she was in no state for seeing Frank Bagley, not when memories were tearing at her again, insistent and undeniable.

'I'd like you to take a message to Mr Bagley for me, Kathy. He's waiting for me at the tram stop.'

'I'll tell him you're a bit late then. He won't mind. How can he? You're so nice.'

'No, my love, say I'm not well.'

'Won't he think that's funny?' asked Mum. 'I mean you were all right at work this morning.'

'Oh dear. Kathy, you'll have to tell a tiny white lie. It's true I feel quite ill, but you'd better say it's something I ate.'

'But it isn't, is it?' said Kathy. 'It was Dad, wasn't it?'

'We had a quarrel,' said Isobel. 'It's over now, but I'm still rather upset. Please, dear, do as I ask.'

'All right, Isobel. I'll do anything for you. Even tell lies.' She ran downstairs and they heard her footsteps receding up the street.

'This is dreadful!' said Grace. 'Fancy having to tell a child to be dishonest. And you looked so pretty and you were going to have a lovely time with a very nice man. You never have much pleasure. Oh, Isobel . . .'

'Mum, stop crying, please. It's not the end of the world. He'll probably ask me again.'

'I hope so. Do you feel a bit better now? I mean, you're not going to be sick, are you?'

'No. I'd just like to rest quietly.'

Grace tiptoed out as if her daughter was an invalid, glancing back anxiously before she closed the door.

Kathy came upstairs and crept into the room. 'I told Mr Bagley what you said, Isobel. He looked sad and I said you'd go out with him another time. That was all right, wasn't it?'

'Quite all right,' said Isobel, smiling at the earnest face leaning over her. 'I'm going to rest a while, then I'll come downstairs.'

The door closed and the house was quiet. Isobel didn't notice the sounds that always rose from the street at this time of day, the voices of women, the bulk of their day's work done, chatting with their neighbours; the sounds of men, their steel-tipped boots ringing on the pavement on their way to the pub; the children laughing, crying, arguing; music from gramophones and the occasional wireless. It was a conglomeration of sound, merging into an incoherent whole which allowed her to dissociate herself from it and think. She knew that the only way to ease her torment was to let down her defences and remember. Amos had tried more than once to climb into her bed. Once, she had been heavily asleep after a day at the seaside with the Sunday School and she had woken to find his hand between her legs, touching her. She could almost laugh, if grimly, to remember the consequences. The unaccustomed mix of hot sun, ice cream, fish and chips and chocolate in her insides, the horror of waking up to a nightmarish situation, churned her up, and she had vomited, her stomach seeming to heave inside out as she disgorged its contents in a violent purging which had cascaded down his pyjama jacket.

'You bitch! You filthy bitch! You did that on purpose.' The voice was so clear she turned her head sharply to see if he was in the room.

He had leapt off her, tearing off his jacket and hurling it on top of the trousers, and in the moonlight she had seen him naked, seen a protuberance which she had not understood. Her nude brothers had never displayed such a sight. Mum had bathed as many of her children as possible together in the tin bath to save carrying water, and her brother's parts were small and wrinkled by hot water when she had seen then. She had stared, mesmerised, then her father had stumbled downstairs and she'd heard the rush of water as the cold stream ran into the low, square stone sink in the scullery. He'd have no trouble explaining anything to Mum. He frequently got so drunk he vomited. She would assume he had done so again. Isobel's stomach heaved now as she remembered and she drew deep healing breaths.

When Kathy was born Mum had been ill for a long time afterwards and didn't really recover for several years. She had been able to feed her baby for only a few days and Isobel had taken over Kathy's care. Her tiny cradle had stood beside Isobel's bed; she had bottle-fed her, nursed her at night when she wept with teething pain, watched over her through chickenpox and measles, read to her for hours, and loved her with an endless love. As soon as she had grown too big for the cradle Isobel had taken her into her own bed and guarded her there, never leaving her at night. She had seen her father's eyes devouring Kathy's infant beauty, watched him with a hawklike gaze which he resented. When she had fully understood the reason for a man's extended member the shock quickened her heart in horror. Now she groaned aloud and turned aside from the past, unable to face more, and as if she sensed her sister's need Kathy came in and asked quietly, 'Do you feel like a cup of tea? I'll bring it to you.'

'Is he downstairs?'

'Dad? No, he must be at the pub. Mum's keeping his stew hot.'

'I'll come then.' Isobel swung her legs over the side of the bed and stood up. For a moment the room whirled about her and she put a hand on the wall to steady herself.

'What's the matter, Isobel?'

'Nothing, my love, I got up too quickly. There, I'm well now. Let's go.'

Mum greeted her without looking up from the stew she was checking. Isobel walked over to her and turned her round to face her. A bruise was appearing on Grace's eye.

'He hit you!'

Grace glanced anxiously at Kathy who said, 'Yes, he did.'

Isobel was both puzzled and worried. Dad had always kept his brutality towards his wife hidden, apparently assuming that what no one saw or spoke of would remain a secret. This was a new aspect and a frightening one. If Amos was so lost to shame he had struck his wife in front of Kathy what else might he not do? As always her thoughts turned to her beloved younger sister.

'Did he threaten you, Kathy?' she asked.

'No. He's never hit me.' The child's voice dwindled as if she found difficulty in speaking. 'If he comes near me I always say I'll tell you. He's scared of you.'

'What do you mean, if he comes near you?'

Grace's head jerked round at the alarm in Isobel's voice.

63

'Nothing really, Isobel. If he lifts his hand to me. Why are you so angry? Don't glare at me like that.'

'Sorry, darling. I didn't mean to. I wasn't glaring at you.' Isobel turned to her mother, but Grace had her back to her again and was making a pot of tea.

Since Grace had hit Amos's friend with her bucket she had not suffered from her Sunday ailments. Now it appeared that the brief respite was over and Amos's fists were ready to strike again and to do so without concealment.

Olive came home, glanced at her mother's face and grimaced. Isobel thought she mouthed the word 'bastard'. Olive said she'd eaten with a friend and took a cup of tea upstairs to her bedroom which had originally been intended for a large cupboard. Wilful from childhood, she had demanded a place of her own. It had no windows and Isobel would have found it claustrophobic, but it suited Olive, who lived within her family yet aloof from it. But today she was angry with her father.

'*He* did it,' she said. 'Why do you put up with him? Why not leave him? I would.'

'I couldn't leave your father,' said Grace, her eyes wide and startled.

'Do you mean if you got the chance you'd still stay with the pig?'

Grace sat down, tears near the surface. 'I don't want to talk about it.'

'It's time you did,' said Olive. 'It's time we all did.'

Kathy said, 'Mum says she doesn't want to talk.'

'Shut up,' snapped Olive. 'What do you know? Isobel, say something.'

Isobel stared at them: Olive's face red with fury, Grace white, the delicate skin round her eye purpling fast. She wanted to say so much, yet was inhibited by her mother's reaction.

'Please stop arguing,' begged Kathy.

'She shouldn't be hearing this,' said Olive.

'It's your fault,' said Grace. 'You began it.'

'I would have thought Dad began it,' cried Olive.

Thankfully, Isobel heard Desmond arrive home. He walked in with his usual confident stride, then stopped. 'What's going on?'

'I'm trying to talk about Dad's nasty ways,' said Olive, 'and nobody will back me up. Take a look at Mum.'

Desmond stepped over to Grace who was in the shadows and peered at her. 'I see.'

They all looked at him as if for salvation.

'Will you have a cup of tea?' asked Grace.

'Sit down,' said Isobel. 'I'll make it. We'll all have a cup.'

'There's stew ready,' said Grace.

'And very good it smells,' said Desmond.

He took his tea and put it on the table without tasting it. 'Mum, Olive's right. We have to talk about Dad.' He glanced at Kathy, who shrank against Isobel's side. 'You can't make me go away this time,' she said. 'I know what's happened. I saw it. And he hurt Isobel as well.'

Desmond looked hard at Isobel. 'Hurt you? In what way?'

'He tore my new blouse . . .'

'And ruined her hat,' cried Kathy, 'and she was going to have a lovely time with a nice man. It's no good shutting me out. I've heard things. I know what he does.'

Her elders looked helplessly at her, then Desmond said, 'She's right. She's part of the family and growing up fast. Mum, he's getting worse. He's really dangerous. You shouldn't have to put up with it. We couldn't help it when we were young, but now we could. In fact, I've had this on my mind. I reckon that if we pooled our income we could manage without him.'

'Manage without Amos?' Grace was bewildered.

'We mostly manage without him now. I mean, he's either out of work or drinking away what he earns or . . .'

'– in prison,' finished Olive.

'You should hear the names they call me at school,' said Kathy.

'What?' Isobel turned her round to face her. 'What names?'

'You know,' said Kathy, suddenly tearful. 'They must have said them to you once.'

Isobel held Kathy close. 'All right, my love. I know.'

She had no difficulty in recalling the playground scenes where the words 'jailbird's kid', 'thievin' magpie's girl', and worse, had been hurled at her. One time it had been, 'My dad says hangin's too good for your dad. He steals from old ladies.' That was the time he had robbed a seventy-year-old woman of her old age pension and the neighbours had clubbed together to make sure she didn't go hungry that week. The memories were prolific and shaming.

'They were just as bad in the boys' playground,' said Desmond. 'I've had to fight over Dad many a time.'

Grace opened her mouth to speak, then closed it. She couldn't have failed to notice when her sons came home from school with

65

bloody noses and split lips. She had remained as silent then as she remained now.

'It's a good idea, Mum,' said Isobel. 'I don't suppose he'd leave and let us have the house, but there's nothing to stop us renting a different place.'

Grace looked unbearably sad. 'You're all so good, but you're young. The time will come when you want to marry, and what would happen then? We couldn't all live in the same place, not unless it was a mansion.'

'One of us would always be happy to have you,' said Isobel.

'Shunt me around like a parcel like some women I know? No, thank you very much.'

'Well, all right,' said Desmond, 'you could stay in one place on your own and we'd help with money.'

'I can't leave your father. I took him for better or worse . . .'

'He's always worse,' cried Kathy.

'Not always,' said her mother. 'I know he does some bad things, but he can be nice when he wants to.'

'He doesn't seem to want to very often,' said Olive.

Desmond said, 'He may have been nice once, but he isn't any more. Mum, you have to face reality. You must tell him to go or leave him. We'll solve any problems together and we'd make sure he never came near you again.'

Grace sat twisting her hands. 'I can't. I couldn't do it to him. I know I seem weak to you, but you don't understand. He's not bad. Not really. He knows no better.'

'Any man knows better than to hit a woman,' said Isobel.

Colour flooded into Grace's white face. She was embarrassed and ashamed and Isobel realised her mother was suffering from a humiliated disgust similar to her own.

'He was brought up all wrong,' said Grace. 'His father was harsh always and wicked in drink.'

'I remember Grandpa Kingston made a lot of rules,' said Desmond. 'Grandma was always very quiet when he was around and we had to behave ourselves, but he never raised a finger to us.'

'Because you didn't dare defy him,' said Grace sadly. 'Visiting him was no pleasure, was it?'

The others caught each other's glances. What Grace said was true. They had been fond of their gentle grandmother, but the atmosphere in the house had been cold.

'Your grandpa beat his children much too often and too hard.

And he hit Grandma many a time. I knew, though she never spoke of it. He beat her all the time – even when they were old he used his fists on her. He was cunning. He never touched her where it showed.'

'Women who get ill-treated should speak of it,' said Olive angrily.

'You don't understand, none of you understands, what it's like to love someone. He's my husband. He was good to me, very good, he even . . .' She stopped and they waited, but she said no more.

Isobel said gently, 'So you think Dad was affected by his boyhood?'

'I know he was. Honestly, when we first married he did try to be kind. He hit me once on our honeymoon. He was terribly upset about it, he even cried, but I forgave him.'

'And went on forgiving him,' said Olive.

'I don't want to go on talking about this,' said Grace. 'He loves me, though you might find that hard to understand.'

'I certainly do,' said Isobel, 'and we *must* talk.'

'Do you mean to stay with him all your life and just put up with everything he hands out?' asked Desmond. 'The rest of us won't stand for it. He needs to be taught a lesson.'

'Any lessons he needs are for me to teach,' said Grace.

'But if you won't act he'll never change!'

'I don't suppose he'll change whatever I do. It's been born and bred in him.'

'People can conquer their badness if they want to,' said Desmond.

Kathy said, 'If Dad is bad because Grandpa Kingston hit him won't that make our boys bad, too?'

Desmond put out a hand and smoothed her hair. 'Not necessarily, my love.'

'What about Ivor?'

'I don't know,' said Desmond, 'but I shouldn't think . . .' He stopped. They couldn't be sure of Ivor.

Isobel wondered how difficult it was for Desmond to subdue the antagonism he felt for Amos now that he was big enough to fight back. She wanted to ask if Grandpa Kingston had molested his daughters. She never could. She thought of her father's two sisters. One had married an American and gone abroad and wrote only to her mother. When Grandma Kingston died her letters had stopped. The other, Aunty Martha, had never married. When her father died she sold the house and bought a tiny place in Warmley where she lived alone, apparently content. She was always pleased when her nieces and nephews visited, but never minded them leaving. Grace saw her only occasionally, and Amos never went there.

When Aunty Martha came for Christmas Day she had nothing much to say to her brother. How had she fared at her father's hands, especially after her mother's death? The pictures which were forming in Isobel's mind were added to the horrors already there.

'Mum, no matter what you say,' said Desmond, 'I can't go on living here as if nothing was happening. He's got to be stopped.'

'I don't want him hurt,' cried Grace.

'Not hurt?' Desmond exclaimed angrily. 'After all he's done to you? And I've got scars.'

'Please!' begged Grace.

Desmond stared at her, then his anger died away. 'For your sake, Mum, I'll not give him the hiding he's asking for, but I won't stand for any more of his cruelty to you.'

'Are you sure he isn't stronger than you?' asked Grace with a wan smile. 'He might be small, but he's tough.'

'So am I and I've been taking boxing lessons.'

They all gazed at Desmond. 'Boxing?' said Kathy. 'Where?'

'With Joe Framley in his gym.'

'Joe? He's daft. He got knocked about so much his brain is scrambled,' said Isobel.

'But he remembers the right moves to make,' said Desmond. 'He just never got out of the way of punches. Months ago I made up my mind I wasn't going to put up with Dad's behaviour any longer.'

'He doesn't know how to box,' said Grace.

'I could hit him quite lightly, Mum, stop him without doing too much damage.'

Grace looked desperately at the anxious, angry young faces around her and reached to the dresser for dishes. 'We'll eat our stew now,' she said. Her tone was final, her face expressed nothing. They seated themselves and tried to eat as if everything was normal.

On Morning morning Mr Bagley greeted Isobel with reserve.

'I'm really sorry about Saturday night,' she said quietly so that the others couldn't hear. 'I felt so ill so suddenly. I was looking forward to our evening.'

He gave her a searching look, then said, 'I was disappointed.'

Miss Trefusis arrived and Isobel fell silent, but all through the morning she wondered if she had offended him.

It seemed not. At the dinner break she had to finish off a delicate piece of stitching and was left alone for a short while, but long enough for him to ask again if she would meet him. He suggested going to the pictures on the following Saturday and she agreed. By then she would have repaired the blouse. Her hat was irrecoverable, but she would buy a shape and decorate it.

On Saturday the workers poured out of the factories and the streets were crowded: the men intent on getting to the football, the married women on catching up with their household duties, the girls looking forward to a whole day and a half away from their machines. Isobel left with the others. Amos would already be out drinking with his mates before they went to support their favourite team.

Frank had managed a quiet word with her. 'I'm looking forward to tonight.'

'So am I,' she said with a smile.

Grace set the dinner in front of her family. They were all there, except for Amos, a situation which gave her peace of mind, even if Ivor and Olive scowled at one another in their perpetual feud. Desmond was going to watch local factory teams. Kathy was off with a couple of friends to the afternoon cinema which showed silent movies and cartoons for the children and one talkie.

'They're having a Laurel and Hardy picture today,' she announced ecstatically.

'What's the serial?' asked Desmond solemnly.

'Oh, it's dreadful! There's this cowboy – Gene – who's found an ancient city at the end of a *huge* cave and he's in love with the queen, but they can never marry because she's got to marry a special prince. Last week the prince – he's really nasty – had Gene tied up and was going to throw him to a den of lions. I can't wait to see what happens.'

'I'll lay you a hundred to one he gets free,' muttered Desmond to Ivor.

'What did you say?' demanded Kathy suspiciously.

'Nothing, dear,' smiled Desmond. 'I was being silly.'

Kathy frowned at her grinning brothers.

'Where are you planning to go, Olive?' asked Grace.

Olive looked sullen; she preferred not to talk about her plans.

'Mum asked you a question,' said Desmond, mildly enough, but she scowled at him.

However, she was not quite daring enough yet to defy Desmond openly. He had once discovered that at the age of twelve she had crept out to attend a hop in the local dance hall. Grace had been in tears and he had marched into the hall and detached her from a youth who was holding her close. The youth had squared up for a fight, but after a second look at Desmond, tall, strong and aggressive though only fifteen at the time himself, he had backed down. Once outside, Olive had given her temper full rein and bitten, kicked and scratched her brother, but he had taken her home and ordered her to bed and she had obeyed, almost spitting in her rage.

'I'm going dancing,' she said now.

'Who with?' asked Grace.

'A few of my friends. No one in particular.'

'Anyone we know?' asked Desmond.

She gave the names of a couple of neighbours' daughters and Grace was satisfied. 'If you're to be in this afternoon perhaps you'd give me a hand with some extra washing.'

Olive was horrified. 'Ruin my hands in washing soap and soda? No fear. I'm going to my room,' she said and walked out.

'It's a lovely pudding,' Kathy called after her. 'Treacle tart.'

Olive's voice floated back downstairs. 'Ugh! I've more respect for my figure, thank you very much.'

'Anyone else worried about their figure?' asked Isobel, as she carried the gleaming golden tart to the table, adding a jug of yellow custard.

The eagerness with which they accepted their dishes was answer enough.

'I'll give you a hand, Mum,' said Isobel, 'after I've washed up.'

'I'll wash up before I go out,' said Desmond, who had no inhibitions about helping a woman with the housework.

When the washing was blowing on the line, Isobel sewed the buttons back on her blouse and looked at her hat shape. She had not been able to resist an impractical eau-de-nil millinery velvet which would have to be kept in tissue paper to save it from dust and marks. Now she took a yard of one-inch-wide satin ribbon and pleated it into a rosette, shaped it with pale pink muslin and fine wire, and began to sew it on to the side of her hat which would perch cheekily on the side of her head, the rosette over one eye. The effect, she decided, would be just right.

If Dad's team had won he would come home in a reasonably good mood, ready to go out after tea for an evening in the pub; if his team lost he would arrive in a bitter temper. Isobel always waited to see what mood he was in to alleviate as much as possible her mother's distress, but tonight she desperately wanted to be free and Desmond had promised to be back in time.

He arrived home from the inter-factory match looking pleased. 'My team won,' he said. 'I like what you're doing to your hat. You're really clever. I suppose you helped Mum with the washing.' At Isobel's nod – she was at a tricky part of the rosette – he went on, 'I'll wait for Dad to come home, so you can leave before he gets here.'

She gave him a glance full of gratitude. 'Thanks, Desmond, you're a pal.'

'It's time the rest of us took more of the burden from your shoulders.' He sat beside her and looked down at her busy fingers. 'Do you know, I believe you could set up as a milliner if you wanted.'

'No, that's not what I want.'

'What do you want?'

'I've decided I would like to become a corsetière.'

'I thought you'd have had enough of that after the years you've been on those machines. It's slavery.'

'I never minded. Well, not much. Anyway, it's different now. After seeing what goes on in the specials department I realise you can help women, really help them. Some suffer badly and I'd like to be able to do something for the ones who can't afford Bennyson's specials. Oh, Desmond, it would be wonderful to have a place of my own.'

'How could you possibly compete against Bennyson's?'

'I wouldn't try. I've got in mind the poor women who never get a chance to buy anything that really fits them.'

'It's a good ambition, but you wouldn't make much money. Poor women can't afford to pay.'

'No, I know that, but there are others who can't afford Bennyson's prices, even though their husbands are in full employment. I hope I should attract them.'

'A philanthropic ideal,' said Desmond in mock-despairing tones. 'You want to make everything right for everyone, don't you?'

'I wish I could. I'd make things right for Mum first.'

'You can't help someone who won't let you.'

'Why is she so stubborn? How can she love Dad after the years he's treated her so badly?'

'I've tried to understand myself. Mum's so gentle it wouldn't take much to break her spirit. And she's got so much love to give.'

Isobel stopped her sewing for a moment, then said, 'You're so perceptive, Desmond.'

71

Kathy returned from her picture-house trip full of what she'd seen. 'Laurel and Hardy were ever so funny and Gene got free just in time. A man came in a leopardskin thing – sort of vest – and rescued him. He was right in the lion pit but the man could talk lion language.' She ran to the kitchen for a drink of water.

'She's probably hoarse with yelling all the subtitles aloud,' grinned Desmond. 'Half the kids can't read.'

They heard Amos's uncertain footsteps at the door, which told them he was drunk from the bottled beer he and his mates took to the match.

'Who won?' asked Desmond calmly as his father stumbled into the kitchen.

'Not my bloody team, that's for sure. Grace!' he yelled.

She came running from the scullery. 'You're home early.'

'What if I am? A man's got a right to be early if he likes.'

'Of course, I only meant . . .'

'Get me a cup of tea.'

Grace pushed the kettle over the hob. 'It's nearly boiling. It won't be long.'

Desmond, fuming but unwilling to leave his mother, retired behind Grace's magazine.

'What are you, a pansy?' sneered Amos. 'Reading women's magazines?' Desmond ignored the insult. Amos threw a small log of wood at his son. It landed on the magazine, tearing half the pages out.

'Oh, please, don't,' begged Grace.

'Why not?' demanded Amos.

'I haven't read the stories yet. And you shouldn't throw things at Desmond.'

Desmond put the torn magazine down. 'I'll buy you another, Mum.'

'Got money for rubbish, have you?' said Amos. 'You can give it to me. I'll make good use of it.'

'Pour it into your belly, I suppose,' said Desmond.

Amos went red with fury. He got up and lurched over to Desmond, fist raised. 'Who the hell do you think you are? What happens between man and wife is nobody's business but theirs.'

'It's our business when you hurt Mum.'

Amos brought his fist down, but before it landed Desmond caught his arm in mid-air.

'Damn you!' screeched Amos, 'Let me go! Let me go, I say! I'll bloody pulverise you!'

72

'No you won't,' said Desmond, still sounding calm. 'Nor will you touch anyone in the house. Sit down and I'll make your tea, then you can have a nap and go to the pub.'

'No I can't,' snarled Amos. 'I bet that the City would win and I've got no money.'

Desmond held his father fast and when he tried to lift his other arm he held that too. In the end, glaring hate from red-rimmed eyes, Amos gave up the uneven struggle and sank into his chair in front of the range.

'I'll make tea,' said Desmond, 'and I'll stake you to an evening at the pub.'

'You've certainly got money to spare,' snarled his father.

'I'm saving for something, but you can have a bit. How about half a crown?'

'Half a crown? You've got that much to give away? Well, it's only right you should give it to your father. I'll have to have a word with your mother and get her to ask you for more housekeeping. Where's Isobel?'

'Upstairs, getting ready to go out.'

'Where's she going?'

'To the pictures with a friend.'

'Man or woman?'

'A man.'

Amos half rose in his chair, then sank back as Desmond leaned towards him to give him his tea. He'd put plenty of milk in and Amos drank thirstily. 'I've got a right to know what my own daughter is doing,' he said aggrievedly. 'What man's she seeing?'

'That's for her to tell you if she likes,' said Desmond.

'She'll not go until she tells me. I won't let her. I had to stop her the other night, going out done up like a dog's dinner.'

'You didn't stop to ask where she was going then, or who with,' cried Kathy. 'You just tore her blouse.'

Amos scowled at her. 'Well, I'll ask tonight. She'll have to come down for her tea.'

'She's having tea with her friend,' said Desmond.

'He must be a fool paying for good victuals when a girl can eat at home.'

They heard Isobel's light tread on the stairs and Amos plonked his cup and saucer on the table and got to his feet.

'Isobel, you come in here!'

The footsteps halted and Desmond called, 'Dad's made a mistake, go on out. Have a nice evening.'

Amos tried to push his way to the door, but Desmond stopped him. His father's rage exploded and he attacked his son with whirling fists, whereupon the family was treated to a skilful display of how to control a man with boxing techniques without doing him any injury.

Amos subsided at last and sat down heavily. 'To think my son would fight me like that. My own son. And over Isobel. She'll turn out to be as much a flibbertigibbet as her...' He stopped and looked round, as if puzzled to see where he was, and said no more. Grace had sunk into a chair and her face was buried in her hands.

Chapter Five

Mr Bagley treated Isobel as if she were royalty, just as Mr Bennyson treated Felice. It gave her a warm glow of appreciation towards him as he assisted her on to the tram and stepped off first, giving her his hand. They went to a small but attractive café. As they ate their way through soup followed by beef and vegetables and ice cream they discussed ordinary topics, and Isobel realised that at home all conversation was centred on the family, much of it concerned with the struggle of everyday life with Dad. If Isobel and Desmond ever began to talk about something interesting it would be interrupted. Olive and Ivor were absorbed only in themselves, Mum was too involved with her own unhappiness to say anything constructive and Kathy was young and often bewildered by the hostility that flowed around them. Much as Isobel loved them she found their restricted outlooks tedious. Mr Bagley seemed to know so much about current events.

'They've awarded the Nobel Peace Prize to the Lutheran archbishop, Nathan Söderblom,' he said.

'Have they?' replied Isobel. She had of course heard of the Peace Prize, but that was about all. She wanted to ask about Nobel, who he was, why he had awarded such a handsome prize, but hesitated to show her ignorance.

Mr Bagley went on smoothly. 'Nobel acted wisely but surprisingly for a manufacturer of weapons. I suppose he had a conscience. After what I saw in the last war . . . the number of dead . . . it was horrible.'

'You fought in that?'

'I did. I was conscripted as soon as I was seventeen. A dreadful thing.' He fell into a silence which Isobel found impossible to break. Dad never talked of the war. There was something about the men who had returned, especially those who were unmaimed, which discouraged people from asking questions. 'I don't think anyone who saw service in the trenches will ever be able to forget,' he said finally.

'My father never speaks of his experiences.'

'When was he called up?'

'He volunteered.'

'Did he, by George! What a brave man he must be. I should like to shake his hand.'

Granny Shaw had once said to her, 'Your father's no hero. He enlisted because he had a row with your mother and got blind drunk afterwards. He didn't know what he was doing.' It was not the kind of thing she wanted to tell Frank. Perhaps Dad had been brave once he reached the front line. He surely must have some good quality.

'I read in the newspaper that Amy Johnson has flown from Britain to Australia in only nineteen days,' she said, eventually, trying to keep up.

'A courageous woman, but I'm not sure I would like a daughter of mine to take risks like that.'

'No,' agreed Isobel, though when she had read the account she'd felt envious of such freedom to explore life.

'Do you read much, Mr Bagley?' she asked.

He smiled. 'Look here, I think if we are to be friends you should call me Frank. Outside of working hours, naturally. It wouldn't do to show familiarity at the factory.'

'No, of course not. I'll try to remember.'

'You asked me something. Oh, yes, do I read much? I do. More since my dear wife passed on. When she was with me she would put the boys to bed, then we would talk or play draughts, or a game of cards. And music! She was fond of a good tune. I bought her a wireless and she liked the talks as well.'

'It was a tragedy to lose her,' said Isobel. 'The boys must have been dreadfully unhappy.'

'We all were, but we managed, and we live together well enough.' He gave a small laugh. 'My Annie believed that a man should be able to cope on his own if necessary. It was almost as if she knew she would go young.' He fell into a silence which again Isobel didn't know how to break. Finally he went on, 'She taught me plain cooking, how to keep the place clean so that food never got contaminated, things like that.'

'I wish I could have known her! But if she'd still been here you would never . . .' Isobel broke off feeling unbearably gauche.

But Frank only smiled at her, a warm smile which made her feel special. When had she ever felt special? Certainly not at home. They were all too busy fending off Dad's ill-treatment.

76

'You look pensive,' said Frank.

'Do I? Sorry.'

'No need to be. I read *Angel Pavement* recently, by J. B. Priestley. He's such a good writer.'

'What?' Isobel had forgotten her original question.

'We were speaking of books. What do you like?'

'Any really. I don't get much time for reading. There's always a lot to do at home.'

'Do you ever read in bed? Annie and I used to and quite often we'd go on far too late, but it was fun reading and exchanging opinions.'

Again Isobel was lost in thought. What a wonderful way to be married. Perhaps one day she could enjoy a relationship like that. Poor Mum. She pulled herself back. 'I don't read in bed. I tried it but had to get out to turn off the gas and I find it difficult to read by candlelight. And I'm afraid of disturbing my little sister's sleep.'

'She shares your room, does she? How considerate you are towards her. Life can be somewhat restricted when there are children to consider.'

Isobel had no wish to go deeper into her home arrangements. 'When I do read I enjoy Somerset Maugham and I like a mystery. I read *The Maltese Falcon* not long ago.'

'A good story,' said Frank. 'I bought a copy of *Mein Kampf* and read it with immense interest.'

'That's German, isn't it? Can you read in a foreign language?'

'No, it's been translated from the German.'

'I see.'

'Do you know it?'

She had to confess she did not.

'It was written by a man called Adolf Hitler when he was imprisoned for speaking out against the state. He's a martyr, I suppose, and has some interesting ideas. I'll lend it to you.'

'Thank you.' She tried to imagine her father's reaction if she took a German book home. Since the war he had been prejudiced against anything Teutonic.

Coffee arrived. Isobel had never tasted anything like it. It was strong and fragrant and a little bitter.

'This is delicious!'

'Don't you drink coffee at home?'

'Yes, but it isn't like this. It comes from a bottle and is very sweet. Essence of coffee.'

He handed her the sugar bowl, but she shook her head. 'No thanks. I'm enjoying this.'

'A sophisticated taste.' He smiled approvingly.

Isobel felt unreasonably pleased by his compliment. Sitting there in her pretty outfit, knowing her hat suited her, gave her a splendid feeling of confidence.

The main film was *Anna Christie* with Greta Garbo, who played to a rapt audience marvelling at the miracle of sound. Afterwards Frank suggested a drink.

'In a pub? Mum wouldn't like that.'

'I quite agree with her, but I'll take you to a respectable one. A cocktail lounge in a hotel. Would your mother mind that?' Isobel felt sick at the idea of this man learning just why drink was anathema to her mother.

The cocktail lounge was carpeted and inhabited by well-dressed people who spoke in low voices. She had no idea what to ask for so Frank chose. He bought her a Maiden's Blush. 'I thought it would suit you,' he said, which brought Isobel's colour up. He laughed. 'They serve these in the Savoy.' He settled beside her with a glass of beer.

'That's in London, isn't it? Have you been there?'

'To London? A couple of times. I took the boys. I thought they should know what our capital city is like. The Savoy is above my income.'

'Did your sons enjoy themselves?'

'Very much. And so did I. But we would all have been happier for a woman's company. I said we do well together, but it isn't the same. It's as if the heart has gone out of the house.'

Isobel felt even more nervous than she had at the beginning of the evening. He sounded significant. Did he have her in mind to replace Annie? The idea thrilled and scared her at the same time.

She took a sip of her drink. 'My, that's nice,' she said. Frank laughed. She sipped again. 'It gives me a warm feeling all the way . . .' She paused. Was it polite to say 'stomach' in company? The boys she had gone out with before had been easy to understand. They talked about football and work and her dates had ended with a couple of inexpert kisses. Frank was so different. 'What's it made of?' she asked.

'Absinthe, dry gin, grenadine and lemon juice.'

'Oh.' Mum always said no lady drank gin.

'Are all cocktails made with gin?'

'No, but they usually have something strong to give them a kick. Do you like it?'

'Yes,' she said truthfully. 'And it certainly does have a kick.' Mum bought one bottle of wine at Christmas and Isobel had only ever drunk one glass from it and that was usually diluted with fruit squash.

They sat silently side by side on a red plush seat. Frank was at his ease, but Isobel felt awkward. She tried to think of something interesting to say, but her life, so circumscribed and narrow, held little he would want to hear about. She dug into her memory. 'I read that the former butler of a Mr Hatry has appeared in court on a charge of stealing. A vanity case and some precious cuff links – I forget what the jewels were.'

'Yes, I read it too.'

He was silent again and Isobel said, 'A duchess has been arrested for attempted suicide.'

'I know.' He frowned. 'Some of these wealthy people live disgraceful lives. I read about their exploits, but see no advantage in discussing them.' Isobel felt rather small, but he turned to smile at her. 'There is plenty we can talk about without reverting to gossip. I deplore gossip. Are you happy in your new position at the factory?'

She would have preferred not to think about work, but he was still her boss, even if they were on a date. 'Very happy, thank you. The work is interesting. I had no idea that it could be so interesting fitting. . . .' She stopped. Somehow, sitting here in this hushed, carpeted place, the word 'corsets' seemed to be out of place, almost as vulgar as 'stomach' . . . 'ladies,' she finished.

'Miss Trefusis is pleased with you.'

'Is she? Good.'

'She is most efficient. The kind of woman I like to deal with.'

Isobel wondered what he thought of her. Would he ask her for another date? Had she behaved circumspectly enough? Would he want to kiss her? The idea made her go hot. Kissing boys of her own age was a mild experience, but Frank was a man, an experienced man who had been married.

He glanced at his watch. 'I'm afraid I shall have to escort you home. My mother is caring for the boys and I must see her to her front door too.'

Isobel jumped to her feet so quickly he was startled.

'You needn't be that quick,' he smiled and she felt gauche again.

They walked to her front gate. It was dark now, dark enough

to shield them in shadow where they stood between the flaring gaslamps.

'Thank you for a lovely evening,' said Isobel decorously.

'No, I must thank you for giving me such pleasure. May I kiss you goodnight?'

Isobel was completely thrown. No boy had ever asked her permission. They had just leaned forward and pecked her cheek or taken her in their arms like they'd seen film stars do and landed a kiss on the lips. She had no idea how to answer. If she said no Frank might think she was ungrateful and stand-offish. If she said yes he might think she was forward. A hussy, as Granny Shaw said about a girl who lived near her and who she had heard kissed on first dates.

'You may kiss me,' she gasped.

He held her shoulders and stared at her for a moment. She couldn't read his expression in the gloom and wondered what he could see of her. Then be bent forward and brushed her mouth with his in a kiss which moved her more than any she had ever known.

'Thank you, my dear,' he said. 'Goodnight. Sleep well. I'll see you at work.'

And he was gone. She watched him until he turned the corner. He didn't look back. Then she went into the house.

The runabouts were busy tidying as they scuttled from place to place. The machinists brushed fluff from their sewing machines and folded loose material into neat piles. Mr Bennyson was visiting. He had just handed Felice out of the car.

Miss Trefusis remained calm, but a pulse beat in her neck. She was polite to Isobel but there was no question of friendship. Isobel had been out twice more with Frank Bagley and inevitably they had been seen and gossiped about. Miss Trefusis had been giving Isobel some very odd looks. Isobel suspected that she was attracted to Frank herself. She was slim, too thin, really. Her long neck was always pink as if it had been exposed to the sun. Her complexion was quite good but unremarkable, as were her eyes and mouth. Her brown hair was long and pulled back into a bun. Even in the 1920s she had never had it cut. It was said that she had lived with her mother who was irascible and demanding until the day she died.

A runabout brought news of the entry of the Bennysons.

Isobel got on with her stitching. The workers were more nervy lately when the boss arrived. So many were being laid off in other factories and there were rumours about Bennyson's. Today their employer completed his round quickly and arrived in the top room before Miss Trefusis had finished preparing tea. Her face went an even brighter red than her neck.

Mr Bennyson was gracious. 'Don't give it a mention,' he said. 'We can wait a while.'

But he did mind. Isobel sensed that he did. He expects us to read his thoughts, she decided. What arrogance! Felice came out of the office and wandered aimlessly round the workers.

She stopped by Isobel. 'What do you do?' she asked in her cultured silvery tones.

'I sew, Miss Bennyson,' said Isobel.

'I can see that for myself,' said Felice, tetchily. 'I meant what do you sew?'

'Corsets, miss.'

Felice sighed. 'But you're up here so you must be doing something different from that lot downstairs.'

Isobel resented her allusion to 'that lot'. It lumped all the workers with their separate lives, their problems, their joys, into a homogeneous lump. 'We make special garments here, miss. Ladies come to be measured.'

'I already know that. Is that all?'

Again Isobel was annoyed. What did she mean, *all*? She spent a large part of her life bending over her work and this spoilt and pampered darling of good fortune came along and made her task sound trivial and in doing so degraded her.

'It's not all, miss,' she said, so loudly that Miss Trefusis, hurrying past with a loaded tray too heavy for her, looked at her sharply. I'll get a telling-off, thought Isobel. 'I hand-sew things as well, miss,' she said, but Felice was already drifting towards the office. There was the usual gentle sound of porcelain and quiet talk, then Frank Bagley arrived upstairs with Mr Lawrence Dane, and Mr Bennyson and his daughter emerged from the office with an entourage of employees.

'Mr Bennyson has something to tell us,' said Miss Trefusis importantly.

Work stopped. Isobel was certain he was about to break the news that employees were to be laid off. But when he stepped forward he said, 'I have decided to hold a fashion show. You will be surprised at the idea, I am sure, as it is not usual to display undergarments on mannequins, but I must follow every avenue to keep the factory busy in these difficult times. I know you will do all you can to assist Miss Trefusis and Mr Bagley.'

There were murmurs of astonishment.

'We have engaged some young women as models and need one more to complete our plans.'

Felice turned to her father and said something too quietly for anyone else to hear.

He looked surprised, then gave Isobel a long stare which made her uneasy. Was the spoilt wretch telling him that a mere corset-maker had been brusque with her, or that she was stupid in answering questions about her work?

Then Mr Bennyson nodded slowly and said to Isobel, 'Stand up.' Isobel obeyed, her heart hammering. 'Turn round. Slowly, girl, not like a windmill. I believe you are right, Felice, my dear, she will do very well.' He turned to Miss Trefusis. 'What's her name?'

Isobel was overtaken by rebellion. It was as if she existed only when Mr Bennyson dictated she should.

'I'm Isobel Kingston,' she said loudly.

Miss Trefusis looked cross and even Frank was frowning at her. Lawrence Dane looked faintly amused.

She received the full benefit of Mr Bennyson's glare. 'Are you always so forward?'

Isobel couldn't think of an answer to this one.

'She only told you her name,' said Lawrence Dane. His obvious boredom dissipated any gratitude Isobel might have felt for his intervention.

'Isobel Kingston,' repeated Mr Bennyson.

'She's exactly right for what you want, Father,' said Felice gently.

'That's settled then,' said Mr Bennyson.

They left without addressing another word to Isobel, who was left wondering what plan they had for her.

Miss Trefusis returned after seeing the Bennysons to the big front doors.

'What do they want me to do?' asked Isobel, forestalling the supervisor's rebuke which she knew must be hovering on her lips.

'You are to model.'

'Model? Me? Model what?'

'What do you think? You just heard Mr Bennyson's announcement.'

'Do you mean I'm expected to strut about wearing underwear in front of people? I couldn't! I couldn't possibly.'

'There's no need to make a drama out of it. There will be other models, girls who have done it before. Some make a living out of it.'

82

'I know, but they wear dresses and coats, not underwear. Not *corsets*!'

'Some of them do. In fact, some of them do it all the time for catalogues. Every one of ours is an artiste in displaying lingerie.'

'I don't know how they can.'

'You are being extremely foolish.'

'But why am I wanted if they've got professionals?'

'They didn't confide in me.'

'I won't do it! They can't make me.'

'If you defy Mr Bennyson I can't answer for the consequences.'

'Consequences?' Isobel was dazed. She was being threatened. She might lose her job and the mere thought had the power to weaken her at the knees. Could an employer dismiss a girl because she refused to prance around showing off her body?

'Well?' demanded Miss Trefusis. Ruby had stopped work altogether in contemplation of this absorbing situation. It seemed to Isobel as if the whole factory must be holding its breath, machines stilled, while she hesitated. But only for a moment longer. She really had no choice. They had given her none.

'How much of myself will I show?' asked Isobel.

Miss Trefusis unbent. After all, she was a modest woman herself. 'Not more than you would in a bathing costume,' she assured her. 'You've made the right decision. Mr Bennyson is a fair boss, but he can't abide having his will crossed.'

'He sounds like all the men I've ever known,' muttered Ruby.

Miss Trefusis whirled round, but Ruby had her head bent over the darting needle of her machine and one couldn't be sure if she were smiling or not.

Miss Trefusis turned back to Isobel. 'Oh, and of course, there will be no men present,' she said.

Isobel gave a gusty sigh of relief. If they'd told her that in the first place . . .

Frank came hurrying into the room, rubbing his hands. 'That's settled, then. We are to organise a show. It'll be a new experience for all of us.' He strode over to Isobel. 'You've done well, Miss Kingston. I'm sure you must feel honoured at being the chosen one among so many.'

'You sound a bit biblical,' said Ruby daringly.

Frank frowned. 'No need to mock religion.'

'I wasn't!'

'You will have to stay late *without pay* if you don't get on with your work,' said Frank.

Ruby made a grimace at his retreating back which Miss Trefusis saw. She frowned, then hurried after the manager.

'Damn!' said Ruby. 'That's another black mark against me. I'll be sent downstairs again as sure as fate.'

'No,' exclaimed Isobel. 'After all, they must think a lot of you to have brought you up here in the first place.'

'I know I'm good at my work, but I really think His Majesty Bennyson expects more than that. I'm sure he thinks we ought to get up and curtsey to him. And as for his precious daughter . . .'

'Today was the first time I'd heard her speak. She's usually so quiet.'

'You've got her to thank for suggesting you as a model.'

'I know, and now I've got used to the idea I think it was kind of her. I wonder if I'll get paid extra?'

'They'll expect you to be satisfied with the honour of modelling for wonderful Bennyson's . . .'

Ruby stopped short when Miss Trefusis returned, hurrying as always, her sensibly shod feet carrying her along as urgently as if she were a nurse in a hospital. Perhaps she felt like one, mused Isobel. She ministers to women all the time, often in a sort of medical way. She realised abruptly that she had stitched an inch too far on a long silk petticoat. She'd have to unpick it and the holes would show unless she could get them ironed out. Miss Trefusis left again and Isobel ran the sharp unpicking tool along the seam and hurried over to the ironing table.

'Something wrong?' enquired Ruby.

'Had to unpick. I think the marks are going. Pray Miss T. doesn't inspect this too closely.'

'She will. It's for the Havergills' dance. God, they've been an age planning it. I'll be glad when it's over. And now extra work for us!'

Felice sat gazing into her dressing-table triple mirror. She moved the side pieces so that she could examine every part of her face and hair. She looked insipid, she decided. She took after her mother who was even paler these days and she had the same light blue eyes. Her nose was straight and her mouth well defined, but she had always thought it looked uninteresting. She lacked sparkle. Fat chance she'd had to sparkle. Father ordered her life at every turn, lavishing on her the care and attention he should be giving his wife. Since she had been a

84

child she had taken her cue from Father and treated her mother with a lack of true respect, and even shown contempt for her weak ways.

For the first time Felice wondered if her mother had ever tried to withstand Father's will. It would be difficult to defy him. Her own mild act of rebellion in going riding with the Havergills without his permission and borrowing clothes had proved to be an isolated incident. She had returned home dreading his anger but he had received her with reproachful sorrow which had defeated her utterly.

The face of the girl who worked in the specials department floated into her mind. Isobel Kingston would never look insipid and she would never permit anyone to dominate her. Even when she was old she'd look arresting with those good bones. Where did she get such a fine bone structure? Felice wondered if her whole body was as well formed. From what could be seen under the working overall she was sturdy. Not a fashionable shape these days. She would be perfect for the modelling Father had in mind for her. Felice smiled a little maliciously. She had suggested Isobel Kingston without giving it much thought and was surprised at the girl's dismay. She sighed. Why should she care about a factory girl's humiliation? She began to brush her fine fair hair. That girl's hair was fair, too, as much as could be seen beneath the unbecoming mob cap the women workers wore, and her eyes were blue, but unlike Felice's they were a clear luminous colour, arresting eyes which demanded notice.

Tonight Felice was to attend the Havergills' dance. Father had forbidden her acceptance at first, then capitulated when Sylvia pointed out that the cream of society would be there, including Lawrence. She wished it was over. She would have been amazed had she known that a Bennyson's machinist had expressed a similar wish about the dance. Until today she had never credited the factory women with feelings at all. If she had ever considered them they would have seemed as insentient as the machines they laboured on.

She patted on a delicately scented skin cream. It wasn't that she didn't like dancing. She did, very much, and she especially liked the Havergills, boys and girls equally. There were a lot of them, six or seven, she was never quite sure. She didn't see them often and only in ones or twos, and as they were all ebullient redheads she got confused.

It had been mention of Lawrence that had swayed Father. He always regarded her stepbrother's opinions above those of his own daughter although he professed to love her more than anyone. Not that he ever said so: to speak openly of love was simply not done, but it was implicit in all his actions. 'The Havergills are a good family,' Lawrence had said to Ralph, 'and extremely wealthy.'

'I am aware of it. Much of their money came from profits made during the war.'

'But they made them honestly.'

'It's still tainted money.'

'Tainted or not,' said Lawrence, 'I am going to their dance. I should marry well and the girls are pretty and ladylike.'

'They are not true ladies in my opinion. They're altogether too boisterous, too self-opinionated. In any case, my dear boy, you know you will inherit wealth from me. You have no need to look below you for a wife.'

'I would prefer not to think of your demise, Ralph,' Lawrence said, a remark which pleased his stepfather.

'So you mean to attend the dance?'

'I do and I think you should allow Felice to go. I'll take her and bring her home and keep an eye on her, but honestly I am sure you have no need to worry. Mr and Mrs Havergill may appear slack on the surface but I can assure you they are strict with their daughters and watchful over their sons.'

So Felice was getting ready, resentful that Lawrence had been the one to persuade Father and was, moreover, going to be her escort.

She fastened the new-style light strapless brassière and the dainty corset, neither of which she needed, and slid the petticoat sent yesterday from the shop over her head, watching its shimmering satin folds fall to the carpet. It was so beautifully made it hardly needed a dress over it. In fact, looking now at the dress hanging on the wardrobe door she would have preferred to wear her petticoat.

A tap on the door heralded the arrival of Janet, her mother's maid, who raised her hands in overemphasised wonder at the petticoat. 'That's lovely,' she enthused. 'Really lovely. You hardly need a gown.'

'You would not surely expect me to attend a dance in my lingerie!'

'No, of course not.'

'My new frock is hanging on the wardrobe,' said Felice.

'Yes, miss.' Janet hesitated. 'It's so beautiful. The master has excellent taste.'

'You don't think anything of the sort,' snapped Felice, 'and Father's taste is dreadful.'

Privately, Janet agreed with her. As she clipped the fasteners which held the petticoat's shoulder straps to the gown she decided she had been right in thinking that it would overwhelm Felice's fragile beauty. Mr Bennyson had personally supervised a surprise for his daughter in the shape of a seventy-guinea model gown in orange taffeta with off-the-shoulder sleeves and ribbon shoulder straps. It succeeded in displaying Felice's thin body to its disadvantage and made her finely defined bones look sharp, while the strong colour gave her a washed-out appearance. Felice knew it was wrong for her, she had known when it had been sent home, but Ralph had been so beamingly pleased with himself that she hadn't had the heart – or the courage – to disagree with him. She wriggled her hands into tight white kid gloves and slid her feet into high-heeled white satin shoes, and Janet fastened a necklace of orange beads round her neck and handed her the long earrings to match.

'You look wonderful, miss,' she lied.

Felice stared at her in a way which made Janet uneasy before she surveyed herself in the long wardrobe mirror.

I look awful, she decided; in fact, I look *bloody* awful. She wished she dared swear aloud.

When she went downstairs her father was waiting in the hall. He watched her descent. 'You look simply splendid,' he said, smiling broadly. 'There won't be a frock there to beat yours.'

'No,' agreed Felice dutifully.

'You mother wants to see you.'

Felice walked to the drawing room where Sylvia was dozing over a magazine. She looked at her daughter and her eyes opened wide. 'Darling . . .!' She saw Ralph in the doorway. '. . . You look – magnificent.'

Magnificent! And splendid! Not lovely or pretty. The words they used were grandiloquent and told her with greater emphasis that her looks were overriden by her gown. Even the material – taffeta – was not for her. It needed a presence to wear something which rustled with every movement. She had wild thoughts of returning to her room and changing into one of her other frocks, but Lawrence had arrived. Whatever he thought of her outfit he said nothing, but held her white fur cape for her and said goodnight to his mother in his usual cool way.

'You'll take care of my baby,' said Father.

Felice cringed inwardly. Lawrence smiled. 'Of course.'

'Don't keep her out too late. She must get her beauty sleep. Home by midnight, please.'

Lawrence held his hand beneath Felice's elbow as they walked down the steps to where his car waited. To her disappointment he wasn't driving his sporty two-seater, but a plain black limousine.

'Grandmother's car,' he said laconically. 'I gave the chauffeur the night off.'

Felice was tongue-tied. Her feelings towards her half-brother were ambivalent. She admired his rugged looks, especially so when he wore his handsomely made evening clothes, but she resented his patronising offhand attitude and lack of real interest in her, and she feared and was bewildered by his implacable dislike of their mother. He drove expertly, and all too soon for her they swept up the drive of the Havergills' large country house situated on the Gloucester road.

It seemed as if every light in the house was blazing from the windows. Dance music and the sound of laughter floated across the still air. Felice associated the Havergills with laughter.

In the hall a maid took her cape while the butler removed Lawrence's cloak. He was elegance itself. Two of the Havergill daughters were unashamedly lying in wait for him. They approached him together and in open rivalry began to squabble loudly as to which of them he would dance with first. To extricate himself from the dilemma he laughingly turned to Felice. 'I am promised to my sister,' he said.

She was petrified with embarrassment as he led her on to the floor. The girls pouted and frowned, but it was all in fun and moments later Felice saw them dancing vigorously, one of them with a brother, their red curls bouncing with a life of their own.

'Do you like dancing?' asked Lawrence as politely as if she were a stranger.

'Yes,' she said. Something more was called for. 'Do you?'

'Very much when I have a good partner.'

Was this a reflection on her dancing? At school she had been diligent in her dancing lessons, understanding that it would prove an important part of her future life. But maybe a man expected a girl to behave as uninhibitedly as the Havergill girls. She gave a small experimental bounce which threw them both off-balance. It wasn't etiquette for her to apologise, but she knew she shouldn't have giggled. Lawrence couldn't know that the giggle was a product of nerves and she expected him to be irritable. Instead, he laughed and she was encouraged to try again.

'That's the way,' he said approvingly. He held her tighter and swept her into the rhythms of the dance until she was breathless and her hair flew about her face.

At the end of the dance he bowed and thanked her and, carried away, she gave a little curtsey. Lawrence laughed again. 'You should let your hair down more often,' he said as he escorted her from the floor.

She had time to look around her at the flowers massed between the gilt chairs and tables and she breathed in their scent as she watched a bevy of maids and liveried footmen bring in trays of drinks. She was thirsty and drank two glasses of wine before Mrs Havergill, tall, bony and redheaded, began to introduce her to young men. She was asked for every dance and no one seemed to care that her frock was wrong for her, and for the supper dance she was actually solicited twice and had to choose between partners, something that had never happened to her before.

After supper she went upstairs to the large bedroom allocated for ladies to repair their make-up, ask the maids to attend to tears in their flimsy gowns, or just sit and chat for a few moments with a friend.

There was a bustle as girls entered and left and chattered. Felice slipped into the bathroom and was about to leave when a girl with a voice cultivated on the hunting field said, 'I say, who's that in the ghastly orange frock?'

A chorus of voices responded. 'Felice Bennyson, you mean. *Too, too* awful, isn't it?'

'Quite *utterly* unsuitable. It makes her look as if she's in the last stages of consumption.'

'And the way her bones stick out!'

'She doesn't seem to know anyone. Mrs Havergill had to introduce her to partners.'

'But that's usual,' remarked someone.

'I know, but not after the first hour. By then chaps have chosen for themselves.'

The voices went on. Felice had no idea who was speaking. She felt as if she were suffering slow torture. There were others waiting to come in, but if she left they would see her and know she had heard. The first girl, who had spoken so loudly, banged on the bathroom door. 'I say, will you be in there all night? There's quite a queue out here.'

Chapter Six

Taking a deep breath, Felice unlocked the door and walked out to a sudden appalled silence. The room contained a number of young women but she felt flayed by their eyes. The girl nearest the bathroom door who had led the catty criticisms was extremely tall and when she saw Felice her already rubicund face became a deeper red. Then she fled into the sanctuary of the bathroom and conversation broke out again, animated, false conversation as the girls tried to cover the serious faux pas. Felice walked to the mirror, trying to appear calm though her legs were shaking, and patted her hair into place. She wanted to move, but her legs felt like stone. She wanted to go home. She longed to go to her own room and hide her shame, to tear off the hideous orange frock and rip it to shreds, to weep with frustration and fury, but it was only just after eleven and Lawrence certainly wouldn't leave this early, even if she could bear to tell him the reason. She thought of feigning illness, held a hand to her head as a preliminary, then she heard the bathroom door open and lifted her chin. She'd be damned if she would give in. Without looking at the others she managed to walk to the door, feeling as if her legs were being dragged along the carpet, and returned to the ballroom, but her previous happy mood had been destroyed.

To her horror she saw the tall girl walking towards her and looked round desperately for a partner to make her escape with. Everyone was dancing. She expected the girl to turn back when she saw her, but realised instead that she was actually making for her. Felice stared at her belligerently. She must be almost six foot tall with a windblown complexion. Who was she to talk about someone's appearance! She looked like a beanpole with a red face.

The girl said, 'I'm Betty Westbury and I'm a rotten bitch. A rotten, bloody bitch. I don't usually behave like I did just now. I just want to tell you how sorry I am.'

Felice was at once paralysed with embarrassment and amazed by the girl's colourful language.

'Well, I'm not surprised you can't accept my apology. I'd feel the same in your shoes.'

Felice found her voice. 'Thank you,' she managed.

'What have you to thank me for?'

'For having the goodness to apologise.'

Betty looked relieved and sat down beside Felice. 'I say, you're remarkably forgiving. I didn't think you'd come across, but I had to do it anyway. I'm absolutely furious with myself. Look here, the truth is I'm jealous of you.'

'Jealous? Of *me*?'

'*Absolutely.* You're just the right height, you're petite and dainty and pretty and I'm jealous. *Bloody* jealous. What I said was unforgiveable and I wouldn't blame you if you never spoke to me again, though I hope you will.'

Felice couldn't find words. She wanted to tell this frank girl that she liked her honesty. For the first time it occurred to her that someone who appeared confident could have inner problems. And for the first time, too, it seemed to her that someone was actually talking to her straight from the heart. It was an unnerving experience. She would like to ask the girl a thousand questions, but her thoughts were incoherent so she took a direct course and stuck out her hand.

Betty seized it and shook it enthusiastically, squeezing it so hard that Felice winced.

'Sorry. Don't know my own strength. I think you're an absolute brick and I'd like to be chums. How about it?' Before Felice could answer, Betty continued. 'It isn't true that Mrs Havergill had to persuade men to dance with you. God, how could I have been so ghastly? I say, why are you wearing gloves? No one does nowadays, don't you know? Damn! There I go again. Just ignore me. Mama is always telling me I'm gauche.'

In her intense relief Felice laughed easily and pulled off the gloves which she hadn't wanted to wear anyway. They were too bulky to go in her tiny beaded evening bag and she looked around for somewhere to put them. A potted plant stood beside her and she stuffed them down into the soft loam. Betty laughed with her. 'You're a real good sport. Come on, let's find some chaps to dance with. Easy in your case, old thing.'

'Are you sure Mrs Havergill didn't have to order men to dance with me?'

The colour in Betty's face deepened. 'No such thing, old fruit. At first, yes, but that's the form, isn't it? As a matter of fact, hostesses are usually having to push the chaps at me. I've known most of them since childhood, but I wonder sometimes if they have to be paid to dance with me. Chaps don't like a girl towering over them and I ride such a lot I've got enormous muscles and find myself taking the lead when I can see that a collision is inevitable. Half the time they have to try to steer me the wrong way for them, peering over their shoulders because they can't see over mine. I think that made me most jealous of all of you!'

Betty's conversation was crazy and her laughter infectious and Felice laughed with her, delighted that someone who was sure to be popular would bother with a mouse like her. For all Betty derided her appearance Felice was certain that there were young country squires who would love to marry her.

'One day,' said Betty, 'I'll have to grab someone at least six foot tall or look ridiculous with a dwarf.'

'I'm sure you're joking,' protested Felice. 'You're so . . .'

'I'm so what?' Betty had a habit of cutting off her words sharply, which took some getting used to, and for a moment Felice was discouraged until she saw the mirth in her new friend's eyes.

'You're so jolly and full of life.'

'Is that how you see me? I think it's a good enough foundation for our mateyness, don't you?'

Betty's encouragement, the wine she had drunk at supper, made Felice realise that she was no longer bothered by the opinions of malicious girls who were probably outnumbered by nice ones. It all went to her head and when Lawrence came to her and gravely told her that it was midnight and he must take her home she smiled serenely at him. 'I'm not going. I'm having far too good a time.'

He frowned and turned away, but the youngest sprig of a large family who had been her latest partner shouted with mirth. 'That's the ticket! Who does he think he is, anyway?' he asked, loudly enough for Lawrence to hear, as the music began again and they tripped down the room in a military two-step.

'My brother.'

'Good God, don't tell me that brothers still escort their sisters in these modern times.'

'Don't know,' carolled Felice. 'Mine does, but I'm not going home with him yet.'

Then Lawrence swept past with a very pretty girl in his arms. He looked happy. Perhaps he didn't care for the role of guardian into which Ralph had cast him.

The heavenly ball had to come to an end and Felice went to the bedroom where weary-looking maids helped girls into their cloaks. Several gave Felice shy smiles and she couldn't see the ones who had insulted her, or maybe she had deliberately forgotten their appearance. It had been a glorious evening, the best of her life.

As they drew near Bennyson House Lawrence said, 'Your father will be furious.'

'I suppose he will.'

'Don't you care?'

'I don't know. I expect I'll hate it when he goes on at me. Sometimes he rages and I just wait for the storm to blow itself out, but other times he seems hurt by my actions and I find that very difficult to manage.'

Lawrence gave her a quick sideways glance. 'I hadn't realised you put up any kind of defence. Even a passive one.'

'That's an odd thing to say. It makes Father and me sound as if we were battling in a war.'

'Aren't you?'

Amazement held her silent for a while. 'Is that how you see us. A father and daughter at war?'

'Tonight I do.'

'What did you think before tonight?'

'When I thought about it, which I have to confess was not often, I assumed you mostly knuckled under quite happily. For instance, your frock tonight . . .'

'It's hideous, isn't it?'

'It's beautiful and must have cost the earth, but it doesn't suit you and you obviously know that. Why didn't you refuse to wear it?'

'If you can ask that you still don't understand how much power my father wields over us. That's Mother and me.'

'Your mother!' Lawrence's voice was hard.

'You are not very kind to her. She's your mother, too.'

He swung the car too fast round a bend, jerking her to one side. 'That's my affair.'

'Yes, but I can't help wishing she wasn't so sad. She's always sad.'

'She asked for it and she deserves it.'

Felice wanted desperately to ask why he didn't blame Ralph. He was the one who had stolen his mother from his father, but she was afraid to say more. Harry Dane's suicide stood between them like a thick, unbreachable wall.

Felice expected Lawrence to wait until the front door was opened to her and then drive off. She was sure that in his place she would have done so, but he climbed out of the car and assisted her from the passenger seat. The front door flew open with a crash and Ralph was outlined against the light.

He was ragingly angry. 'Where in hell do you think you've been? Midnight, I said, and *that* was a concession.'

Lawrence held Felice's arm and helped her up the steps and into the hall. She wondered if he knew that her legs had begun to tremble.

'The dance was a good one,' he said calmly. 'Felice wanted to stay on.'

'Did she, indeed? I trusted you to bring her home.'

'I have done so,' said Lawrence.

Felice was astonished at his amiability. It restored her courage. 'If you feel so strongly about it I wonder you didn't telephone the Havergills,' she blurted.

'Telephone? Telephone the Havergills? Allow them to know that you were disobeying my orders? What an infamous suggestion. They would have thought I had no trust in you.'

'You don't seem to have much,' retorted Felice.

Dark red stained Ralph's face. They had been speaking in lowered tones, mindful of the ears of servants. Ralph had sent them to bed but one never knew. 'Come into the library,' he commanded, 'both of you.' He stamped off without looking back.

'You could slip out now,' said Felice to Lawrence.

He looked down at her and his eyes, green in the half-light, were actually showing amusement and admiration. 'Not I! I'll not run away!' His hair, the reddish streaks gleaming in the subdued lighting, was ruffled. She thought: I could like him if only he'd let me.

Ralph paced up and down the library. Felice swayed on her feet with weariness and Lawrence led her to a comfortable chair where she curled into a defensive crouch, wishing she was in bed.

Lawrence waited for Ralph's first fury to subside, his strong jaw thrust forward, his nose appearing particularly beaky, then he said calmly, 'Felice has made friends, one in particular, Lord Westbury's daughter.'

There was a pause, then Ralph said, 'Lord Westbury's daughter?' He could not conceal his gratification. 'He has two or three.' He turned to Felice. 'Which one did you meet?' he asked in much gentler tones. Lawrence knew how to handle him all right, thought Felice. Father was such a snob.

'I don't know,' she said. 'Who are we talking about?'

'The tall girl, Betty,' explained Lawrence.

'I didn't know. She just said she was Betty Westbury.'

'Lady Betty.' Sylvia spoke from the doorway. 'The Westburys are one of the oldest families in Britain.' She wore a silky dressing gown which flowed around her, revealing how thin she had grown. There were dark shadows beneath her eyes.

'There was no need for you to come down,' snapped Ralph.

'Felice is my daughter. I too have been waiting for her to come home.'

'I am capable of caring for my own child.'

'She isn't a child. She's eighteen. You should not hold her on so tight a rein.'

'Are you dictating to me?' Ralph hissed. Felice glanced at Lawrence and saw that he was surprised and displeased by his stepfather's bullying manner towards Sylvia.

Felice said, 'Mother, you should get your rest or you'll feel dreadful tomorrow.'

Sylvia walked forward and seated herself by the dying fire, holding out her thin hands to the tiny flickering flame.

Ralph shrugged, then said, 'The Westburys are from the top drawer, Lawrence. How do they come to know the Havergills? I would have thought they were below their touch.'

'The Havergills have good blood, though you won't admit it,' said Sylvia. 'But the thing is, they all hunt. The hunting field is a great leveller. I should know. I was once friends with Millie Westbury, Betty's mother. Since my retirement from society I miss her friendship, as I miss others.'

'You choose to isolate yourself,' snapped Ralph.

Sylvia nodded, and sighed.

Her air of sadness was quickly glossed over by Ralph who said, 'So Lady Betty made friends with you, Felice? I don't suppose it'll last, though.'

'Why not? I like her very much and she likes me. She's asked me to go for tea tomorrow to talk about the dance.' She glanced at her watch. 'Today now.'

The revelation had knocked all the pomposity out of Ralph. 'You had better get to bed, Felice, my dear. Lord Westbury's daughter, eh?'

'I'll be off, then,' said Lawrence. The evening was full of surprises, but none more than the wink Lawrence gave Felice behind Ralph's back. Over her body a great lassitude was creeping, an amalgam of physical tiredness, happiness at the turn the evening had taken and relief at Father's sudden capitulation. Now everything seemed to be moving slowly. Ralph was lighting a cigarette, his hands scarcely appearing to move, Sylvia was getting out of her seat with slow, languid grace. She smiled at her daughter and wished her goodnight.

'Go to bed, Felice, my dear,' said Ralph. He was prepared to loosen her shackles now she had made a friend with a title. She suddenly felt sorry for him. How irksome he must find the limitations of his social life.

The factory was abuzz with news of the corset show, as the women called it among themselves, in spite of a firm directive that it must be called 'The Ladies' Show'. Underwear was also to be displayed and entry was by ticket only. The younger girls giggled and made jokes of which the older women disapproved as strongly as they did of the idea itself. They expressed themselves forcefully in their dinner break.

'Showing such things off in public!' they muttered.

A woman of about fifty said, 'Even my hubby's never seen me in my corsets. I mean to say, who wants anyone to see how you look all strapped up in whalebone?'

'We use steels now,' said a cheeky runabout.

'I still call 'em whalebone,' was the retort. 'I can't get used to new-fangled ways. Don't want to.'

'Would your hubby rather see you in the flesh?' asked another runabout.

'You're asking for a clip round the ear,' retorted the woman. 'I undress in the dark and always have. So does my hubby.'

'They say no men will be there,' pointed out a younger woman.

'I should think not!' was the chorus which greeted this bit of news.

Then the shrill bell sounded the end of dinnertime and the women trooped back to their machines.

Isobel was torn between gratification and nervousness. She once dreamt she was wearing a corset which enveloped her from nose to knees so that she couldn't walk and she tripped, rolling over and over until she landed at the feet of Lawrence Dane. She woke, sweating.

The time arrived for a first fitting. The professional models came up to the top floor, all well dressed, beautifully made-up, their hair

97

set in perfect waves and curls. When introduced to Isobel they looked amused.

'My dear girl,' said Cecily, a tall slender girl in dark blue. '*You* are to model undergarments?'

'It's an insult to us,' said a second girl who was built a little more heavily than Cecily.

'You're right there,' said Cecily.

Isobel realised that each woman was a different shape, from Cecily to Jess, who was prettily well rounded. If the model thought she was an insult to the others so be it. What did she care for the opinion of a stuck-up girl who had nothing better to do with her life than become an animated clothes'-horse?

Miss Trefusis came hurrying in, not even noticing that Ruby had stopped work and was staring open-mouthed at the elegant visions who had invaded the top floor. 'Here you are, Miss Kingston,' she said. 'I have paid attention to your wishes for concealment and brought these camibockers for you to use.'

Isobel looked at the strange voluminous garment, the like of which she had never seen.

'Well, put them on, girl, don't just stand there.'

Isobel looked round. 'Where do I change? May I use a cubicle?'

'If you wish, though we are all ladies here. Mr Bagley and your brother have been warned not to come in. Take off everything and just come out in the camibockers.'

'Just what in hell is it?' asked Cecily.

Miss Trefusis looked disapprovingly at her. 'An overall garment, combined knickers and knickerbockers with a bodice.'

Isobel saw that Cecily and her companions had trouble in concealing their mirth and marched firmly into the cubicle and removed her clothes. There were three mirrors where she could view her body from all angles. Never before had she seen an all-round view of herself in the nude and she was interested. Her figure wasn't bad; in fact, it was quite good. A little heavy, it was true, but she went in and out where a girl was supposed to go in and out and her breasts were high and firm. It took her a while to sort out just how the camibockers went on, and twice Miss Trefusis called to her to make haste, but she managed it in the end and stood gazing at herself in dismay. The curious garment had ribbon straps which revealed a little of her shoulders; otherwise it covered her from her neck to her knees in billowing white cotton. She felt ridiculous and wished she hadn't placed such emphasis on her modesty.

'Will you be much longer?' called Miss Trefusis irritably.

'I'm ready.' Isobel peered through a crack in the curtain to see the other models were being fitted by Ruby and Miss Trefusis into a variety of corsets and dainty camisoles, managing to look as elegant as if they were fully clothed. She ventured a hesitant step through the curtains and the others took one look at her and exploded in laughter, all but Miss Trefusis, who raised her voice to an unprecedented level to ask them to behave. It was useless. Even Ruby was giggling helplessly. Isobel felt angry, then was suddenly struck by the idiocy of the situation and was herself overtaken by mirth.

When the laughter died away Cecily said, 'You're a real good sport, Isobel. Is she really going to wear that?' she asked Miss Trefusis.

'She is a very modest girl,' said Miss Trefusis primly.

'And we're not?' said Nora, a dignified brunette with a large bust.

'I had no intention of making a critical comment,' said Miss Trefusis in her precise way. 'Isobel is not a professional model and is bound to feel shy.'

As corsets were fitted over Isobel's all-concealing garment, another woman entered the room. Isobel had met her before and knew she was the manageress of Bennyson's shop.

'This is our Miss Prewett from My Lady's Bower,' said Miss Trefusis, introducing everyone with a sweep of her hand. It was rumoured that she was jealous of her colleague whose job was so much more glamorous than hers.

'What in God's name is that girl wearing?' cried Miss Prewett. 'Camibockers? Couldn't you find her something more up to date and flattering?'

'Miss Kingston is not a professional model,' said Miss Trefusis stiffly. 'She is a machinist and wishes to preserve her modesty.'

'She'll protect it to the day she dies if she goes around looking like that,' said Miss Prewett. She gave a frosty smile. 'When you told me you had a girl to model corsets and lingerie for the short, stout figure I wondered where you would find her. I don't know any professional girl with such a shape.'

Isobel stared. Short, yes, but *stout*? She was not stout. She hated the description. How dare they make a guy of her! She had a good mind to refuse to take part. But if she did she'd make things difficult for herself and Desmond. Mr Bennyson struck her as being a ruthless man who wouldn't think twice about sacking someone simply because he was annoyed by his sister. And deep inside her there was a glimmer of pleasure that her routine was broken. What did it matter if a few pampered women thought she looked odd?

'How soon can you be ready?' Miss Prewett asked Miss Trefusis belligerently.

'How soon would you like me to be ready?' replied Miss Trefusis coldly, resenting the critical attitude of the shop manageress.

'Next week?' Miss Prewett was being deliberately malicious. To be ready next week would require more fittings by models who had other assignments, and extra work for Isobel and Ruby who were deputed to make the new garments.

'Very well,' said Miss Trefusis. She had expected Miss Prewett to reply that the room above the shop could not possibly be prepared in so short a time.

The two women stared at one another in a clash of wills, each knowing they had made things difficult for themselves, and Isobel asked innocently, 'May I dress now, Miss Trefusis? I must get back to work and make sure we have the corsets ready for another fitting.'

She was rewarded by an unprecedented look of gratitude. 'Not yet, Miss Kingston. I need to take certain measurements.'

Miss Prewett sighed. 'I must return to the Bower. I am expecting clients.' She departed.

Isobel was attended to first, and was soon back at work on her machine. 'Come in tomorrow afternoon for further fittings,' said Miss Trefusis to Cecily and the others.

But it transpired that two of them had day-long engagements and there was much checking of diaries before times and days were settled.

When Miss Trefusis, Ruby and Isobel were alone Miss Trefusis said, 'I can't understand Mr Bennyson. We have plenty of richer clients who don't need a show to encourage them to shop with us. The greatest profit comes from the hundreds of cheaper garments we sell.'

Ruby and Isobel stared at the angry supervisor. She had never been known to criticise her employer and, as if she realised how indiscreet she had been, she snapped, 'Don't sit there with your mouths agape. Get on with the work. We must clear as many special orders as possible to concentrate on the show. I'm going to the cutting room.' She swept out.

Ruby said, 'Well, did you ever! I actually feel sorry for the old buzzard. I bet she wishes she hadn't said we could hold the show next week.'

100

'Have you ever seen the upstairs room at the Bower?' asked Isobel.

'No, why, have you?'

'Twice when I was sent with specials and I had to go upstairs to the office. The long room there has bare boards, and it's very dusty, except in one curtained-off area where they hang clothes. The clients only ever see the cubicles behind the showroom and it'll take Miss Prewett all her time to make it fit for a show.'

'I've only looked in the windows,' said Ruby. 'Everything seems really posh. Do you think Miss Prewett herself will have to scrub?'

Their machines were stilled as they contemplated the haughty Miss Prewett wearing a sacking apron scrubbing yard after yard of bare boards. Hearing Miss Trefusis's step they hastily began to sew, heads bent as if they hadn't looked up since she left.

'We're having a fashion show next week,' Isobel announced to her family.

Kathy squealed with delight. 'What's a fashion show like?'

Isobel laughed at her. 'You're so excited about something you don't even understand?'

'Well, it sounds nice.'

'Sit down and have a cup of tea,' said Grace.

'No, you sit down and I'll make it,' said Isobel.

'You can both sit down and I'll do it,' said Kathy.

Her mother and sister smiled at her, but Olive scowled. 'Mind you boil the water. I hate tea with leaves floating in it like you brought me in bed last Sunday.'

Kathy had risen early last Sunday morning and tried to give her sisters a morning treat. She said indignantly, 'Mum's shown me how to do it properly.'

'Well, get on with it then. I'm going out soon.'

'Where to, love?' asked Grace.

She wasn't surprised when she received an ambiguous answer. 'Not sure yet. I'm meeting friends.'

Grace asked, 'Have they hired models?'

Desmond said, 'Yes, five professionals and one from the factory.'

'Who have they chosen?' asked Grace.

'Isobel,' said Desmond.

'What?' Everyone but Olive was pleased and impressed. Olive was angry. 'Why you? You've not got a good figure.'

'Don't you say that about my Isobel,' cried Kathy. 'Her figure's lovely, much better than yours.'

Olive laughed scornfully and said, 'Don't be silly, Kathy. You know nothing about it. My measurements are the ideal one for today's fashions. Isobel is short and dumpy.'

'Not dumpy,' said Grace. 'Well-built.'

'And short,' said Olive.

This was undeniable and Kathy returned to making the tea. In her indignation she forgot to let the water boil and Olive made an exclamation of disgust when she saw tea leaves floating in her cup. 'Ugh! I can't drink that! Don't bother to make tea for me again. I'm going upstairs to get ready. I know where I can get a *decent* cuppa.'

Kathy had a job to hold back tears of chagrin. 'Shall I begin again, Mum?'

'Pour off the water and add boiling,' advised Isobel. 'That way we'll have tea without any waste.'

Kathy smiled at her elder sister, her eyes filled with love.

'Tell us more about the show,' said Grace.

Isobel glanced at Desmond. He knew what kind of show it was and had probably heard jokes about his sister's part in it, but he left her to tell as much as she wished.

'We're going to model corsetry and lingerie,' said Isobel.

Grace's mouth dropped open. 'You're doing what?'

Isobel repeated her words, trying to sound casual.

'What's lingerie?' asked Kathy. She pronounced it wrongly.

'You *can't*!' cried Grace, drowning out the child's words.

'It's all perfectly respectable, Mum. You should just see the cami-bockers I'm to wear. They cover me.'

'The what?' asked Kathy.

This time she was heard. 'Camibockers are like a tent with buttons. I show more in my bathing costume.'

'It's true,' said Desmond.

'Have you seen her in them?' asked Grace, shocked.

'Of course not. No men are ever allowed near the cubicles and there won't be any men at the show. It's a ladies-only job. But I know what they are. It's all part of my training.'

'What's lingerie?' asked Kathy again.

'Underwear,' said Isobel.

'Are you going to walk about the factory in your underwear?'

'Of course not, darling. The show is to be held in the Park Row shop, upstairs with ladies only.'

'That's all right then.'

Grace was still dubious. 'I suppose it is all right.'

'What is?' Amos had returned.

'Did you get the job, love?' asked Grace nervously, standing up.

'Sit down, Mum,' said Desmond.

Amos glowered at him. He had grown wary of this big son of his and lately Grace hadn't borne so many signs of her Sunday ailments. He seated himself near the fire. 'It's bloody cold out.' He rubbed his hands vigorously.

'What do you expect?' asked Desmond. 'It's nearly winter.'

'I can remember when autumn used to be warm,' said Amos. 'Indian summers we had when I was a boy.'

'It's true,' said Grace. 'Indian summers. I'd forgotten them. We don't seem to get them now.'

Steam hissed from the kettle spout and Kathy carefully poured boiling water on to the damp tea leaves.

'Why is *she* making tea?' demanded Amos.

'She's giving Mum a sit-down and learning how to be a good housewife,' said Desmond calmly.

Kathy's lips moved in silent prayer that her brother and father wouldn't quarrel.

'What were you talking about when I came in?' asked Amos.

Kathy said eagerly, hoping to placate him, 'Our Isobel's going to be a model in a show. She's going to wear – I've forgotten the word – oh, I remember – lingerie.'

'Lingerie?' said Amos. 'That's underwear. No member of my family is going to show herself off in bloody underwear.'

'It's all perfectly harmless and decorous,' Isobel said, trying to keep her voice even.

'Rubbish! You'll be showing off your body to strangers. I suppose there'll be men there, looking at you and thinking things.'

Coming from him that was rich, thought Isobel. 'There won't be any men there,' she said. She suddenly felt like yelling, And even if there were what do you care, you bastard? You don't care about me and never have, except in your own filthy way. Since her elevation to a better job, and her pleasant relationship with Frank Bagley, her spirit had grown stronger. For a moment she imagined that she had spoken aloud, but the others were still in their places, Mum leaning back in her chair, pale-faced, Kathy perched on the leather fender stool, Dad glaring at her with bloodshot eyes.

'You're not bloody well going to parade around in underwear! I'm surprised your mother didn't tell you so. She can't have brought you up very well to have you turn out so brazen.'

103

Grace said, 'She's wearing a concealing garment underneath the . . .' She stopped.

'Underneath the what?' Amos was in a dangerously ugly mood now.

'Underneath the corsets,' said Isobel.

'Corsets? *Corsets*? You're going to flaunt yourself in corsets? I'll see you dead first.'

Isobel remained outwardly calm. 'Then you'll have to kill me because I'm going to do it.'

Amos went red with fury and opened his mouth, but before he could speak Desmond said, 'The bosses want her in the show. If she refuses she could be sacked.'

Amos glared at him. He wanted to continue the row, but Isobel made a generous contribution to the family finances. Greed won. He got up and said, 'I'm going out.'

'You've only just come in, love. I've got a nice bit of brisket cooking slowly, just the way you like it.'

'Keep it!' snarled Amos, stamping out and banging the door. The front door closed with a crash behind him.

Grace said shakily, 'I'll keep his meal hot. It won't spoil. He's bound to come home hungry.'

Desmond's lips were pressed together to hold back angry protests; Isobel wanted to go to Mum and hold her tight. Kathy was before her. She put her arms round her mother's waist and kissed her cheek.

Felice opened her wardrobe, wondering what to wear to the Ladies' Show. What a bore it was! But then almost everything in her life was boring. Except Betty Westbury. Felice smiled when she thought of her new friend. Betty was almost twenty-one, but still as spontaneous as a puppy, flinging herself into Felice's life, appearing or telephoning at frequent intervals in the belief that she would always be welcome. How very welcome she was she would never understand. Ralph had immediately put her on the list of ladies to be invited to the show and Betty had accepted.

'What a lark!' she had declared. 'Your papa is much more adventurous than mine. When I told him where I was going he roared.'

'Roared?'

'With laughter,' explained Betty. 'Mama said she was great friends with your mama once, years ago. She said that Sylvia was the beauty of her debutante year and married well. Then something went wrong. She didn't say what. Damn! Here I go again, busting in like an idiot. Sorry.'

Felice had said, trying to keep her voice even, 'You had better know the truth at once. Someone is bound to tell you. Mother eloped with Father and left her husband. Lawrence Dane is my half-brother and he was brought up by his grandmother after his father killed himself. He doesn't even like our mother.' She had ended angrily, suddenly hating the adults who had made her life so difficult.

'I say! How awful for everybody. What fools women in love make of themselves. Oh, hell. Sorry. I'm not criticising your mama, or your papa, either. Thanks for telling me. You're a brick, Felice. May I call for you so that we can go to the show together?'

Felice took out her outfit, a new pale blue matching skirt and three-quarter-length jacket. She pulled on a tiny matching blue hat over her newly marcelled waves and slid her feet into navy court shoes. Her gloves and bag were navy. She had chosen the clothes herself and was pleased with her appearance.

When Betty saw her she exclaimed, 'How lovely you look!' She wore a dark costume with a pale blouse and a rather large hat. 'I decided to do you justice by getting my hair waved. You should see it, or rather you shouldn't. It's gone frizzy. God knows what the hairdresser put on it. Mama is in despair! That's why I'm wearing this voluminous hat, *absolutely* out of fashion but what the hell!'

'I love the way you look,' said Felice. And the way you dress and the way you speak and everything about you, she thought.

Betty's smart little car waited in the drive. Betty drove badly, admitting it cheerfully. 'If I was half as handy as I am with my horses I'd be a champion. I'm surprised you don't have your own car, Felice.'

'My father is afraid I'll get roaring drunk at a party and drive up a lamp post.'

Betty laughed loudly. 'What an old fusser he must be. My father expects all his children to cope with everything, bless his cotton socks.' Her love for her father, her belief in his creed and her sureness of his love were implicit.

Felice stared at the passing scenery and Betty, who was far more perceptive than most people believed, was silent. Then she said, 'What a gorgeous day. One doesn't expect so much sun in the autumn.'

'It's lovely,' agreed Felice.

'An Indian summer day,' said Betty. 'Papa says they always had

105

Indian summers when he was young, but I don't expect they did. One remembers the good things more readily than the bad, don't you think?'

'Probably,' murmured Felice, wondering which parts of her life would be prominent in years to come. When Father had told her about the show he had taken it for granted that she would attend, not giving her an opportunity to say whether or not she wanted to. She would have preferred not, deciding immediately that it would be tedious and full of boring, gawping women, but when she understood that Betty was coming she had looked upon the whole thing quite differently.

'A lark,' Betty called it, making Felice see it in a different light, reminding her that rejection was the first emotion which swept over her these days whenever Father proposed anything. The revelation of her growing antagonism was quite frightening. And with it had come more respect for her mother who, although not openly defiant, nevertheless had coped with him for years and remained meticulous about her appearance and gentle in her speech.

They were driving through the town now, round the Centre and up Park Street, taking a somewhat circuitous route because Betty sometimes forgot her way. She disliked negotiating Bristol's steepest hills. 'It terrifies me when the car reaches a part where I have to drop into bottom gear,' she said. 'You have to stop completely and slam it in and hope that you won't roll back into the car behind, then put your foot down and go like crazy.'

Felice laughed. Anything Betty did was fine by her.

Chapter Seven

Isobel was cold with nerves. The past week had been a turmoil of non-stop work and fittings. Once or twice one of the models hadn't turned up, which had thrown Miss Trefusis into a panic of near hysteria. 'Some women think they've no obligations to anyone!' she declared. 'I swear I shall never take part in anything like this again.' Isobel and Ruby felt sorry for her. 'They call themselves professionals, but they act as irresponsibly as children.'

She was being unfair. The five girls had many other commitments and did their best to fit in this unexpected work.

'I bet she's jealous,' muttered Ruby, 'because she's never been as gorgeous as them. If she had she'd be married by now with kids.'

'Not every woman wants that,' protested Isobel.

'*She* does. I've seen her giving cow-eyes to Mr Bagley since his poor wife died. A pretty woman she was.'

'You don't think she's in love with him!'

'I'm not saying that, but I bet she would be if he gave her half a chance. But he likes you so he's not going to make eyes at her, is he?'

Isobel sat for a moment, her hands idle as she contemplated the future. And as she and Ruby worked overtime above the silent factory her thoughts ran on. She and Frank were seeing one another at least once a week now, sometimes more often, and they had taken Frederick and Thomas, his little boys, to the zoo, where they had all got on well together. They never had their names shortened, Frank had told her gravely. 'Neither my wife nor I wished it.' Then the gravity of his countenance had been lightened by his tight smile. 'They like you,' he had said.

'A visit to the zoo isn't a proper way to judge,' she had pointed out. 'Children enjoy outings.'

'They miss their mother. They need a woman in the house.'

A woman? Any woman? Perhaps sensing her doubt, Frank had

said more. 'I have been a widower for four years. At first I couldn't look at anyone else, though I knew the boys needed the touch of a woman. They have my mother, but she is old and not very spry. I am very fond of you, Isobel.'

Isobel had been surprised and gratified. He sounded serious, as if he definitely had her in mind as a wife and as a mother for his boys. Knowing how much he cared for them she was flattered. But she was bothered by his attitude to the show. He disapproved of it and said so repeatedly, but he especially disliked the thought of her appearance in it.

'I think Mr Bennyson is going too far. It may be all right for women who are used to showing off their bodies, though that's bad enough, but to ask a well-brought-up girl like yourself, well, it's not right, it's not correct.' He didn't expect Isobel to refuse because he knew it might threaten her job and he behaved towards the Bennysons in a deeply respectful way. His job was absolutely essential to his family.

She lay awake a lot thinking about Frank. He was a fine man, he owned his own house and earned a good wage, large enough to employ a daily woman to do the housework and keep a friendly eye on the boys. Isobel had no doubt he would make a pleasant and caring husband, but he wasn't exciting. Did she want excitement in her life? Surely her father had given her enough for a lifetime. She stirred restlessly, then lay still again, afraid she would disturb Kathy. Tranquillity was what she had often longed for and Frank would supply it. She wondered how he would react if she asked whether Kathy could live with them. She wondered how Mum would react and how Amos would take it. Sometimes she wondered if she cared for Frank at all in the way she should, or did those stories in which passionate love was the only prelude to marriage paint untrue pictures? Maybe love just grew with the years.

The invitations to the Ladies' Show were to be filled in and sent out by Miss Miller, the office girl in My Lady's Bower, and she had called to fetch the list. Miss Trefusis treated this with contempt. 'As if we couldn't do the job here,' she had sniffed.

'You've already got too much to do,' pointed out Ruby.

'Mr Kingston could have written them out. Your brother has a good hand,' she said to Isobel, a certain mateyness having sprung up between them since she and Miss Prewett had opened hostilities. 'But, no, Mr Bennyson must have them sent from Park Row. He thinks it looks better because that's where the show is, as if anyone will know or care!'

Isobel didn't venture a reply. Miss Trefusis would probably regret her harsh words and it was safer to remain silent.

Miss Miller hurried in again another day to fetch a further list, the one to which Lady Betty Westbury's name had been added. 'You should see them at the Bower,' she giggled. 'Miss Prewett goes stamping around, furious with everybody. She's had to get more women to scrub and clean because the first lot weren't fast enough. Poor things. How can she expect them to wash away all those years of dust in a couple of days? And she's got men wallpapering and painting, you never saw such a mess. I can't think how it'll be ready in time and she's furious because the men are liable to come down to the shop if they want to ask about something, no matter how often she tells them not to, and our clients don't like it when they see workmen in mucky overalls clumping about. One walked out saying she'd come back when things quietened down, or she might go elsewhere.'

This stream of information cheered Miss Trefusis to smiling point, especially when she was able to assure Mr Bennyson, who was beginning to look anxious, that *this* end of the show would certainly be ready.

Amazingly, all was prepared in time. On the great day Miss Trefusis arrived exhausted and cross because once Mr Bennyson understood that everything had gone as planned he took it all for granted.

She said to Isobel when Ruby had gone downstairs for thread, 'I don't mind telling you, Miss Kingston, because I know it won't go any further, that I feel quite annoyed with Mr Bennyson. He does not appreciate all I have done for him.'

Isobel smiled commiseratingly, sticking to her resolve not to be indiscreet. It might be the sort of sneaky behaviour she despised, but she had to keep her job.

Ruby came hurrying back carrying the spools of thread. 'Everyone tried to stop me to ask questions,' she said gleefully.

'I hope you didn't gossip,' snapped Miss Trefusis.

'Of course not. Even if I'd wanted to, which I didn't, Mr Kingston ordered them to get on with their work. Your brother's a proper dictator sometimes, Isobel.'

Miss Trefusis frowned. She had never approved of the casual use of forenames. 'Your brother is an excellent man, Miss Kingston,' she said pointedly. 'I have no doubt that one day he will take over as manager.'

Isobel tried to look gratified. She felt torn. Of course she wanted

Desmond to succeed, but Frank had twenty or more good years of work left in him and she was convinced that her brother would not be content to hang about that long waiting for promotion.

Isobel, Ruby, Miss Trefusis, Desmond and Frank were transported in a fleet of taxis to My Lady's Bower with the boxes of corsetry and underwear. Desmond and Frank were to help carry the boxes. Isobel wondered how much all this cost. Ruby giggled and when Miss Trefusis wasn't looking waved her hand graciously from the window as she had seen the Queen do on newsreels.

Miss Prewett welcomed them with a frosty smile which softened when she saw the men. 'Please go straight upstairs. The room is ready. I'm sure you will like it.'

Miss Trefusis, much as she longed for the show to go smoothly, was nevertheless disconcerted by the results of her colleague's heroic efforts. The long room had been transformed. It was decorated in soft pastel shades, the floor had been carpeted, leaving sanded and polished surrounds, and small chairs were ranged each side of a strip of cream carpet. Electric fires were burning, several along each wall. At the far end curtains were draped from the ceiling to the ground, concealing the office. A side table held porcelain cups and saucers and small plates. 'That cream will show the dirt dreadfully,' she muttered.

'It all looks quite splendid,' said Frank.

'Handsome is as handsome does, Mr Bagley,' said Miss Trefusis. 'I should not be at all surprised if that carpet wears out quickly.'

'You may be right, Miss Trefusis. You have a good eye for such matters.'

Miss Trefusis blushed, Ruby pulled a face at Isobel, then the senior salesgirl came running up the stairs. 'The dressing room is at the end behind the curtains.'

'I guessed that, since there is nowhere else it could be,' said Miss Trefusis coldly.

Ignoring the girl's indignant look, she led her group behind the curtains. It was to be a communal changing room. There were tables holding make-up, brushes and combs, and one was covered with soft shoes in white, pink and ecru. There was a full-length three-way mirror, four smaller ones over the tables, and racks with hangers waited for the corsets and underwear. A small washbasin had been installed and Miss Trefusis glared at it as though it was the last straw.

'Where shall we wait?' she asked the girl, who had followed them.

'Here, of course. You'll be wanting to hang the clothes, won't you? There's an ironing table and irons in case you need them.'

'I can see that for myself,' said the supervisor frostily. 'As it happens we know how to pack and nothing will be creased.'

The girl shrugged, looked sympathetically at Isobel and Ruby and left.

'They have not provided us with chairs,' said Miss Trefusis. 'I dare say they think we can work until we drop.' She glared at Miss Miller who was watching them through the glassed-in office.

The office girl came out. 'Is there anything you need?'

Frank said, 'A chair or two would be acceptable, Miss Miller. Ladies can get tired and these ladies have been working exceedingly hard.'

'Nothing was said about more chairs, but you can have a couple from here, if you like.'

Desmond smiled at Miss Miller, bringing an answering smile to her face. 'That's good of you. I'll carry them through.'

Having no other grumbles, Miss Trefusis said, 'Mr Bagley, place the boxes on the long table, if you please, then you had better leave. No men, remember?' she finished. She actually looked archly at him and dark colour stained her thin neck.

'Good luck to all of you,' said Desmond as they left.

Frank said, 'We'll be back to help later. Can't have ladies lifting those heavy boxes.'

'How very kind he is,' said Miss Trefusis, gazing at the spot in the curtain through which the men had vanished.

Miss Prewett came bustling in. 'You have all you need? Good. Hang the clothes in the order in which they are to be shown. You have no idea how muddled a show can be if the proper precautions are not taken.'

'As no one has troubled to give me a programme,' Miss Trefusis snapped, 'I can't possibly know the order.'

'I have brought one for you,' said Miss Prewett triumphantly. She handed over a large double card. On the outside was printed a line drawing of My Lady's Bower delicately coloured in the pastel shades of the room. Inside was printed the order of the show.

'This *seems* clear enough,' said Miss Trefusis. 'I can describe the garments without a script. I know them so well, you see.'

'Oh, but Mr Bennyson has asked me to give the commentary,' said Miss Prewett.

Isobel thought for a moment that Miss Trefusis would spring upon her rival and demolish her. 'How can you?' she grated. 'You know nothing about my garments.'

'Nonsense!' Miss Prewett sounded as if she were reprimanding a small child. 'I am a trained corsetière. And I know equally as much about lingerie.'

'But I know every single detail,' said Miss Trefusis. 'And you are not qualified to describe the maternity and surgical garments.'

'Good God! Surely you won't be having those modelled. It's an obscene idea.'

Miss Trefusis was so angry by now she could scarcely get the words out. 'Of course not! I shall just walk out and tell the ladies what they can order from me.'

'Mr Bennyson did not mention this. I shall have a word with him. He is coming in soon.'

'Not to watch the show, I hope.'

'Certainly not. Have you no sense of decorum?' And Miss Prewett glided away, satisfied that she had got the last word.

But Miss Trefusis called her back. 'Miss Prewett, I see a washbasin, but no toilet arrangements. There will be eight young ladies and surely . . .'

'If you had troubled to ask Miss Miller she would have informed you that the facilities are through a door in the corner *behind* the curtains.'

Miss Trefusis was too angry to get any words out, and this time Miss Prewett had definitely succeeded in getting the last word.

Isobel and Ruby unpacked the boxes without looking at her or speaking more than a few quiet words concerning their work. Miss Trefusis ostentatiously dusted the rails before hanging the garments in the order according to the programme, muttering the names of the models as she did so. Isobel heard hers several times and her hands shook.

The boxes unpacked, the tissue paper folded ready for reuse, Miss Trefusis said, 'I trust you bathed last night, Miss Kingston.'

Isobel was furious. 'Of course. And this morning.' She was clean because she had washed her body with soap and flannel as she did every night and morning. She would have loved a bath, but how could she tell Miss Trefusis that bathing had been out of the question last night? Dad had come home from a day hanging about with his cronies, seated himself in front of the fire and snarled at anyone who disturbed him, so Isobel had to carry water to her bedroom.

She was getting more and more nervous. Three o'clock was the advertised time of starting and she was one moment wishing the time would come when she could get on with the job, the next that she had never agreed to this idiotic, embarrassing occasion. For a while, as her terror grew greater, she even thought of running away, but sympathy for Miss Trefusis, who now looked distraught, held her, and there was her pride, which wouldn't let her show cowardice. The arrival of the models calmed her a little. They came in together, Cecily, Jess, Nora, Lucy and Hilda, beautifully gowned, behaving as if nothing extraordinary was to happen that afternoon. When they removed their hats their hair was cut and waved to perfection. Isobel had believed hers was pretty enough, styled as it was by a local hairdresser, but now she realised it couldn't hold a candle to the others. What was it about hairdressing that made two apparently similar styles look so different? It was the same with make-up. She had dabbed on powder and lipstick and she watched with fascinated interest as the models sat down before the small mirrors and began to paint their faces.

Cecily smiled at her. 'Nervous?'

'A little.'

'Would you mind terribly if I suggested a little more make-up?'

'I don't mind, but I don't know how to apply it.'

'Will you let me?'

Isobel was delighted. Anything which improved her appearance seemed good to her. She sat still while Cecily's experienced hands patted and creamed and powdered her. 'Now look,' said Cecily.

Isobel obeyed. 'I look pretty,' she said. 'Oh dear, that sounds conceited.'

'Not at all. You *are* pretty. You should do up your face every day.'

'You're very kind.'

'But you're still nervous, aren't you?'

'Yes. Horribly.'

'That's natural. I was terrified when I did my first job.'

'Were you?' Isobel couldn't imagine the sophisticated Cecily being terrified. 'Was it corsets?'

'No, it was hats actually.'

'The other end, in a manner of speaking,' said Jess.

'Ignore her, she's vulgar,' said Cecily.

Isobel glanced to see how Jess would take such an insult but she only laughed.

'We all think you are very brave,' said Nora, removing her jacket to reveal the large bust which was to display brassières and all-in-

113

ones for the big-breasted woman. Her skirt followed.

Miss Trefusis began to bustle about. 'Come along, ladies, we have only a quarter of an hour to the start. Let me see, who is first?'

'It is me,' said Nora. 'Miss Prewett decided that it would be a good idea to say right at the start that the show is not just for young girls with perfect figures.' She smoothed her hands over her bosom in such a self-satisfied way that Isobel almost laughed aloud. Ruby choked, but when Miss Trefusis looked at her she was busy helping Cecily.

'Miss Prewett thinks she knows it all,' muttered Miss Trefusis. 'She does not, of course.'

'She's had some experience with shows, hasn't she?' said Hilda, who was stock size, medium height, bust and hips the same size, slim-waisted but not skinny.

'A little, I believe, but only with frocks and other outerwear and that was some while ago. Bennyson's doesn't usually put on shows. This is their first.'

Cecily and the others began to remove their frocks and shoes, displaying not a sign of embarrassment as they stood naked while they were fitted with undergarments.

Miss Prewett arrived and Isobel could have sworn she caught a look of relief on Miss Trefusis's face before she scowled.

'Getting ready, ladies?' said Miss Prewett briskly. 'Good. Miss Kingston, you haven't begun. Come along, girl, you have to appear with the others.'

They could hear an increasing swell of voices from the long room. Ruby peeped through the curtains. 'It's filling up,' she squeaked excitedly. 'Ladies in their best clothes.'

The scent of cigarettes, Virginian and Turkish, drifted to the waiting girls. Isobel, encouraged by the unselfconscious behaviour of the models, removed her outer garments. 'And your vest and knickers,' said Miss Prewett. 'Oh, for heaven's sake! We are all females here.'

Isobel hesitated. Her shaking hands fumbled with the buttons on her vest. Miss Prewett hastened her, dragging at the buttons fiercely. 'Now your knickers. For heaven's sake, will you take them off?'

'Can't I wear them under the camibockers?'

'Of course you can't. They'll spoil the line, and in any case whoever heard of a model wearing patched cotton knickers? Hurry, girl, they've begun the music.'

The sound of a gramophone floated over with the tobacco smoke. Did they have to play the 'Pagan Love Song'? It made the show seem even more outlandish as Isobel removed the last of her clothes and was handed the camibockers, quite sure she was blushing from head to toe as she was fitted with her first support garment.

'Ready everybody?' Miss Prewett gave them a last critical look-over, her eyes resting for a moment on Isobel, then she stepped through the curtain. 'Good afternoon, ladies.' The chatter gradually stopped, the music was lowered to a muted background level. 'We at My Lady's Bower and at our special department in Bennyson's workshops have long understood the art of corsetry. We know how very important it is to wear a garment which is of an exact fit. It is especially so nowadays when the fashion has altered so drastically. It no longer calls for the boyish figure, but demands gentle, feminine curves and, as we ladies know, we can guide our appearance to fit any fashion ever intended.'

'Clever,' whispered Cecily as she waited. The suspenders which held up her flesh-pink stockings on legs that seemed to Isobel incredibly long nestled like ornaments among the lace of the cami-sole. 'She's flattering them. They'll be in a good mood.'

'Fashion, so arbitrary, ladies, now demands longer hems, a softer line altogether, frequently with the bias cut of the skirt which reveals so much of our figures.'

There was a murmur of agreement from the audience and a few light laughs.

'We at Bennyson's offer a perfect foundation garment to any lady who is desirous of looking her absolute best along with our swift and decorous service.

'And now we have great pleasure in presenting to you our up-to-date designs in corsetry and lingerie.'

Ruby was staring in wide-eyed fascination at the five professional models who abruptly switched on modest smiles, and at Isobel, her co-worker who, unbelievably, had just stripped to her nakedness in front of others and was about to show herself off in bedroom garments. Nora stepped unconcernedly through the curtains.

'Here we have Miss Nora in a beautifully formed all-in-one garment in pink satin. As you can see, it is cut as one would cut a gown, tucked snugly at the waist, swelling at the bosom where it is especially reinforced to accommodate the generous bust and at the hips to give comfort as well as beauty.'

As she spoke Nora walked along the strip of carpet, her bountiful breasts thrust forward. She was given a scattering of applause by ladies who were unaccustomed to a live display of corsetry. As Nora pushed her way back through the curtain, Cecily stepped out and walked with the grace and aplomb to be expected in a professional mannequin. The applause was a little louder and longer this time and by the time it was Jess's turn the girls were being clapped all the way back to the curtain.

'We've got them,' said Miss Trefusis excitedly. 'They're on our side.'

As soon as Cecily was out of sight of the audience she had, like the others, been galvanised into activity. Miss Trefusis unfastened the corset and dainty brassière and helped her into a long-line brassière and high-waisted corset which left two inches of skin showing between the two. Not a vestige of fat bulged; she looked lovely, though Isobel wondered how some of the women she knew would manage to wear such garments. They would undoubtedly have a protruding line of flesh at the midriff.

It was Nora's turn again and Miss Prewett continued. 'Miss Nora is now wearing a foundation garment which partly conceals and partly flatters the heaviness of her upper body . . .'

The show went on, the models changing swiftly from one garment to another, combing their hair to perfect smoothness, wearing the soft shoes to fit the colours, powdering their noses, wiping beneath their arms with a damp flannel – though how anyone could be warm enough to sweat was beyond Isobel. She was icily cold now as she waited for her turn, which seemed long in arriving. One glance at herself in the long mirror had petrified her. She looked absurd, short, stout and ridiculous, with the idiotic camibockers fastened up to her neck and splaying from beneath her corset. She was sure the corset must be a size too small, or she had grown fat since the garments were made, because she found it difficult to breathe.

She heard Miss Prewett's voice: 'And now we have Miss Isobel, who is wearing a garment suitable for the short lady who is blessed with a little more avoirdupois perhaps than she wishes.'

A ripple of laughter ran through the audience at Miss Prewett's mild essay into humour. Isobel felt she had taken root until Miss Trefusis gave her a push to get her moving and then she was stepping through the curtains. Hilda, a girl with a pretty but small bust and generous hips, passed her on the way back and murmured, 'Good luck, kid.'

Isobel had emerged to a blaze of light. There seemed to be a thousand eyes staring at her, the carpet stretched for a mile and she felt she was incapable of further movement. She breathed deeply

116

and, as if taken over by a power beyond her, she was walking along the carpet. She would have closed her eyes if she'd dared, but she needed to see to maintain balance on her wobbly legs. It amazed her that no one burst out laughing at the sight she presented. On the contrary, there were murmurs of appreciation and one voice said quite distinctly. 'That would suit me. A nice short all-in-one, exactly what I've been wanting.' She returned to the changing area to whispered congratulations.

After the corset display had ended, the models showed the lingerie: French knickers, camiknickers, petticoats with lace and smooth unembellished ones to go under smooth gowns, even backless ones for women who dared to wear the new frocks which dipped to the waist and daringly beyond.

Isobel found she was expected to remove the camibockers and put on lingerie, which made her blush at the amount of skin it revealed.

'No one told me about this,' she protested. 'I can't go out there showing this much.'

Miss Trefusis sighed. 'You are wearing concealing French knickers and a lacy petticoat. Look at the others. They know what is expected of them.'

Isobel walked down the carpet strip and again was surprised by a voice which said clearly, 'What *heaven*. I didn't know Bennyson's sold such dainty undergarments for people like me.'

Isobel would like to have seen which discerning customer appreciated her, but had been told not to look at anyone directly. By the time she was ready to model her second set of lingerie her legs were stronger and by the end of the show, when hired waitresses handed round refreshments, she was filled with a deep sense of accomplishment.

'It went well, Miss Trefusis,' said Miss Prewett, relief animating her voice.

'It did indeed, Miss Prewett,' responded Miss Trefusis, accepting the olive branch. Undoubtedly the two would go to war again but at the moment they were in a state of truce. A waitress brought tea and biscuits and small iced cakes to the models. Isobel tucked in hungrily as did Ruby, but the models accepted only tea, shaking their coiffured heads at the food.

'Poor things,' said Ruby, 'They can't let themselves eat much or they'll lose their figures.'

'Glad I'm not a real model,' said Isobel.

'Oh, I don't know, they seem to have a nice life.'

117

'I wouldn't want it. I'm never going to do it again.'

'You looked as if you enjoyed it.'

'I felt better as it went on, yes, but it's not a job I want. Ruby, stand in front of me while I change back into my own things.'

'Still modest,' grinned Ruby. 'We've seen all you've got.' But she obligingly stood as Isobel began to remove the camiknickers she'd just modelled.

'What on earth are you doing, Miss Kingston?' demanded Miss Trefusis, peering round Ruby, her eyes wide with irritation. 'You must wait for the photographer. Mr Bennyson intends to use pictures in his advertisements.'

'What?' Isobel was outraged. 'You said no one would see me except ladies. If they put me in a newspaper everyone will know.'

'Don't worry,' said Lucy, a girl as short as Isobel but with a petite, perfect figure. 'No one ever recognises anybody from a newspaper photo.'

'It will not be in the newspapers,' said Miss Prewett, 'only in a ladies' magazine.'

'And the boys will peep at it when their mothers aren't looking,' laughed Ruby.

Isobel flushed, but Cecily said kindly, 'Don't be a goose, dear, it's done these days. Some stores are having corset weeks and the girls are put on the front pages of the papers.'

Isobel swallowed a lump in her throat, wanting suddenly to cry. For some reason recollection had intruded cruelly and her father's image had risen in her mind, with the memory of his shocking behaviour.

'Come on,' encouraged Ruby.

'Don't be nervous,' said Lucy.

Finally the last woman in the audience left. Many had made appointments for fittings and Miss Trefusis praised Isobel. 'We have gained several customers, one at least who is influential, who were impressed by you,' she said delightedly. 'I knew that your figure must resemble somebody's.'

Isobel wasn't sure if that was a compliment or not.

A photographer arrived with his tripod and camera. He set it up so that the girls could be silhouetted against the curtain. 'Lovely,' he muttered constantly, 'lovely.'

Isobel didn't know if he meant the girls or the underwear. But he seemed to have no interest in the subjects as women, only ordering them to stand this way or that. Once more they changed rapidly and he took more and more pictures until he was satisfied and left. Then

118

at last Isobel was able to put her own clothes on. The factory had closed by now and she went straight home, as exhausted as if she had done a week of sewing in one day.

After the bustle of the show the women in specials felt somewhat dejected. But life had to return to normal and soon it was as if the show had never been, though it continued to rankle with Miss Trefusis that most of the new customers went to My Lady's Bower to purchase their underwear and Miss Prewett would reap all the glory.

In due course Isobel guessed from the whistles and catcalls of the machinists which followed her progress upstairs that the magazine had appeared in the newsagents and they had all seen the photographs.

'You look a treat,' cried one woman.

'Simply adored your French knickers,' called another in a falsetto voice.

Isobel, quite enjoying her fame, turned and dropped a cheeky curtsey before she went into specials.

Miss Trefusis greeted her frostily. 'If I had known there would be this kind of immodesty I would have forbidden your appearance.'

Both knew that Miss Trefusis would never have defied her employers, but Isobel saw that the supervisor was really rattled and she smiled. 'They'll soon forget,' she said soothingly. 'After all, we have you to thank for the extra orders. I know Miss Prewett contributed, but the sewing was done here.'

Ruby, who was setting up her work, stopped to listen and added her bit. 'Everyone's saying you did most of the work, Miss Trefusis. They don't like that stuck-up Miss Prewett. She thinks she knows it all.'

They succeeded in soothing the harassed woman.

Amos was in a filthy temper. Isobel heard him as she turned into the street. One would think the neighbours were weary by now of sticking their heads out to listen to him, but her progress was followed by peering eyes. She kept her head high as she ran the gauntlet of their stares, wondering what had happened to upset him this time.

As soon as she stepped into the kitchen she knew. He was waving a magazine above his head, his fist clenched upon it as if he'd like to crush everything inside.

'There she is!' he yelled. 'There's the bitch who's brought shame to me and mine.'

119

He flung the magazine at her; it fell to the floor, the pages fluttering. Isobel picked it up and glanced with assumed aplomb at the cover. 'Goodness! It cost a whole shilling. That's steep for the likes of us. How did you come to have it, Mum?'

'It was pushed through the bloody door,' yelled Amos. 'Someone wanted us to see that they knew about it. I suppose the whole bloody street's gawped at it. Do you think your mother and me want to see you looking like a . . . like a . . . well, I don't need to spell it out. You know what I mean!' He looked as if he wanted to strike her. She stared calmly back at him, though she felt anything but calm as she wondered just how she was depicted in the magazine.

Grace was looking imploringly at Isobel in an unspoken plea that she wouldn't allow the row to escalate.

Isobel's heart was thumping, more in anger than anything else. How dare he take a holier-than-thou attitude with her? How dare he, after what he had done to her!

'Something upset you, Dad?' she asked, then without waiting said, 'Mum, is there a cuppa in the pot? I'm thirsty.'

'Upset?' screamed Amos. 'Upset? I'm bloody furious. Have you seen the pictures in that filthy rag?'

'No.'

'Open it,' yelled Amos. 'Go on, open it and see what a disgrace you are!'

Isobel's mouth had gone dry and she longed for tea, but her hands shook too much to pour it and the others were mesmerised. She turned the pages slowly, terrified as to what she would find. There they were as clear as daylight. The models, Cecily, Jess, Nora, Lucy and Hilda, displaying to the world the richness of their varying figures, their beauty and composure in their scanty clothes. And there was she! Short, full-bodied – and *pretty*? She stared. She actually looked pretty. Her hair was attractive, she wore the same expression of distant dignity as the others, induced in her case by nerves. Even the camibockers didn't appear outrageous and the lacy underwear transformed her appearance. Her figure wasn't bad, not bad at all. That photographer certainly knew his job. Then the memory of the first time she had tried on the camibockers returned in force and she wanted to laugh. She felt the laughter bubbling inside her until like a spring of clear water it had to be released.

'She's laughing!' Amos was in a screaming rage. 'Laughing! I'll give her laughing. She'll laugh on the other side of her face when I've done with her.'

He sprang at her but, astonishingly, Grace grabbed at his raised arm and hung on.

'Let go, damn you!' cried Amos, trying to shake her off.

'You shan't hit her. I won't let you. I won't have it!'

'You won't have it!' Amos twisted in his wife's frantic grasp and tried to punch her. She ducked. It was far from funny, but still Isobel laughed, until Amos's rage died, cooled by the tears of hysterical mirth which ran down Isobel's face and the tears of anguish shed by his wife.

Grace released his arm. He looked at her and then at Isobel as if bewildered. 'I'll be a laughing stock,' he muttered. 'They'll make sport of me at the pub.'

The laughter died away. 'You bitch,' he said to Isobel. 'You filthy bitch! All the men hereabouts will see these pictures. You won't be safe walking down the street.'

'I'll be as safe as I am in my own home,' said Isobel.

Amos stared at her and messages passed between them, silent messages – hers expressing the full extent of her loathing and her scorching memories. She couldn't read his.

'Don't quarrel,' begged Grace.

'Whose fault is it?' demanded Amos. 'Look at her. See what a daughter you've got. Bad blood! That's what she's inherited! Bad blood!'

'If I have it's from you,' cried Isobel.

'Oh, is it really? I could tell you a thing or two—'

'No!' The anguished cry came from Grace.

Amos looked at his wife and the temper died out of him. He sat down heavily and stared into the fire. 'Let's have a cup of tea,' he said.

Grace, although white-faced, was actually looking at him lovingly and Isobel wondered, as she had so often, how her mother could continue to care for him. Mum had explained once that Dad's family had been quite well-off with a shop in Bath, but his father had squandered his income on gambling.

'You'd think that would make Dad show more sense,' Isobel had said.

'Perhaps.' Mum had sighed, philosophically. 'But it had the opposite effect. His elder brother didn't want any more to do with his father. He left home at sixteen and emigrated and hasn't been heard of since. And his other sister went off as soon as she could and you know what your Auntie Martha is like. Practically a recluse.'

Isobel drank a cup of tea and, as the latest storm seemed to be over, went upstairs to fetch her two best frocks. It was all very well for Miss Prewett to talk about the new longer lines, but some girls could only achieve them by lengthening the frocks they already owned. The articles she had read in Mum's magazine (twopence a week) said that skirts could be made longer by adding a strip of toning material to the previously fashionable low waist, sloping it down to fit the hips and making a belt or tie. Line drawings proved that it could be done and Isobel was striving for the right effect.

When she came downstairs Amos had gone. 'Where is he?' she asked.

'I gave him something for his beer,' explained Grace. 'Enough to treat his friends.'

'Mum! You can't spare it.'

Grace held up her hand. 'Don't be cross with me. I can't bear any more. Besides, our Kathy's due home and we don't want her upset.'

Isobel sat down, her cup warming her hands. She was reminded of the times when she had played in the snow and had run in, aching with cold. She remembered Mum massaging the life back into her hands and feet and how she made her hot sweet cocoa and sat her cosily by the fire. Had she been happy then?

'Mum,' she said abruptly, 'Dad made some odd remarks just now about bad blood. What did he mean?'

Grace jumped up, dropping her cup which shattered on the grate, flinging tea everywhere.

Isobel grabbed a floorcloth and cleaned up the mess.

Felice had agreed to attend the corset show only because her father insisted. Even Sylvia had felt obliged to be there. But for both of them the occasion was made enjoyable by the company of Lady Betty who had become a close friend in a short time. Betty's generously given love disarmed all shyness and Felice looked forward to each day which held an engagement with her.

At first she had resented her father's fulsome praise of her new friend. Perhaps he saw her as the means by which he might re-enter the society he longed for.

Then Father had said, 'I'm so glad for you, Felice, my darling. Lady Betty will be able to introduce you to company from which your mother and I are excluded.' She felt like a prisoner allowed out on parole. After the years of his possessiveness it seemed impossible that he should give her any freedom. She still found it irksome when he insisted on knowing where she was going, whom she had met, was

122

impatient of his insistence that she should be home at certain times, but now his car took her only to functions to which Betty was not driving and he sent the chauffeur to pick them both up afterwards.

'Your papa is a nice man,' said Betty.

Felice was glad she felt that way. Betty was like the sister she had always longed for and she could hardly believe how quickly their friendship had flourished. Betty had so many chums. They were all chums to her, men and women alike. Father said that the Westburys were as rich as Croesus and that Betty had a large personal fortune and could go anywhere she liked, so it was even more flattering to know that she enjoyed spending so much time with her, simply playing records on the gramophone, listening to the wireless or just talking. And there was another advantage. Felice was now permitted to hunt and had the smartest gear that money could buy.

'It all looks too new,' said Ralph, 'especially the boots, but they'll soon be well worn.'

Of course he could have hunted and taken part in other similarly democratic occasions, but pride held him back. If he couldn't have all he would have nothing.

Sylvia came out of her shell when Betty visited and sometimes joined their discussion, talking about current events, fashion, anything of interest to the girls. In Betty's company her pale face took on colour and she gained in animation and Felice realised how much her mother had been damaged by her past.

After the corset show they had gone to Bennyson House to discuss the event over cocktails. Ralph had formerly permitted only the best wine to be served, but this restraint had also been withdrawn and the girls now had their pick of fashionable cocktails which they drank as they discussed the show.

'Did you notice the short, rather tubby girl?' asked Felice.

'I didn't see anyone I'd call tubby,' said Betty. 'Which one exactly?'

'The one with fair hair – the other short girl was dark.'

'Oh, I know who you mean. I thought she looked awfully jolly.'

'Did you? I suggested her. She works on a machine in Father's factory.'

'I say, does she really? How clever of you to choose her. She was perfect for the stuff she was showing.' Felice was gratified. 'It must take some nerve to model such garments.'

'Nerve?' Felice thought about it. 'I suppose so. Most of them were models, of course.'

'Yes, but not the one from the factory. She must be a good sport.'

Before today, Felice had never given the characters of her father's work people any consideration. 'Yes, I dare say she must. I don't really know.'

'You told me you've been visiting the factory since you were small.' Was there an implied criticism in Betty's voice?

Felice frowned. 'I know. Perhaps that's why I've never thought about them. When you're small you don't pay attention and I've taken them for granted. When I was younger I was thrilled when Father took me about, but lately it's got boring. Are you ever bored?'

'Good gracious, yes! Mama makes me attend all sorts of ghastly things. Charity bazaars and garden parties and frightfully stuffy meetings where I have to be polite and listen carefully in case someone asks me a question. The whole family has to take turns. Chaps as well.'

Felice asked timidly, 'Don't you approve of charity work?'

'Not quite the way Mother and her chums do it. I can't see why people with money don't just give some where it's needed.'

'I suppose they feel they're entitled to a little fun and it may make the more stingy open their purses.'

Betty looked at her admiringly. 'Do you know, I had never thought of that. You are clever, Felice.'

Felice glowed with pleasure. She had never in her life been called clever. Father had ensured that her education had concentrated on the social graces. There was no doubt about it; Betty's friendship was transforming her life.

The girls in the special workroom had to work harder than ever because the rush of orders immediately following the display actually increased. Isobel had also to cope with her ambivalent feelings for Frank.

They met regularly outside of work and she was getting to know his sons Frederick and Thomas. They were as solemn as their father, their brown eyes, so like his, gazing at her. It was when the four of them went to a Charlie Chaplin film and she heard them laughing that she realised how seldom they laughed. That afternoon, after hints from Frank, she took them all home for tea. Grace and Kathy had worked wonders. Everything with a shiny surface was brightly polished, everything was splendidly clean, almost hiding the shabbiness which followed Amos's constant demands for money. Amos knew nothing of the proposed visit and had been given enough cash to keep him away.

The two boys unbent with Kathy and chattered so much about the film that she begged to see it, and Olive, who had stayed in, curious to meet her sister's boyfriend and softened by the general atmosphere of goodwill, actually promised to take her. Tea was replete with goodies and the guests ate well. Isobel felt embarrassed when the boys needed the lavatory and came back with eyes rounded by surprise.

'It's outside!' cried Frederick.

'And it doesn't have a flush,' said Thomas.

Frank had hushed them instantly as if the subject was beyond discussion and Isobel felt irritated, though she wasn't sure with whom. She wondered what Felice Bennyson and her haughty brother would make of their sanitary arrangements.

The visit had increased her underlying anxiety about her growing friendship with Frank. He and his sons had suffered terribly from their bereavement and must not be hurt again. At such times she felt a tender regard for them, but then doubt assailed her. Her home was not exactly a palace of mirth, but when Amos wasn't around they laughed quite a lot. Even Ivor was capable of producing some dry, bitter piece of wit about the employers who had turned him down. In fact, if Amos could be made to disappear life would be a good deal better for them all. The idea made her feel guilty and that caused more inward anger until she sometimes couldn't sleep at night for the turmoil of her feelings. Ivor called Frank Pagliacci. He surprised them sometimes with his knowledge. His mind was far too quick, his body far too full of energy, for it to be safe for him to be numbered among the unemployed. Isobel had protested, but he had only grinned, his thin mouth stretched wide. 'He looks sad, just as clowns are supposed to when off duty.'

'He can be good fun,' said Isobel.

'Is that so?' Ivor was sceptical and Isobel had said no more. Ivor had a way of digging under the skin.

Chapter Eight

Amos couldn't let the subject of the corset show go. Isobel tried to ignore him when he referred to it, but one evening when she returned from overtime at work, tired and with a slight headache, he tormented her once too often.

'My mates make fun of me all the time!' he raged. 'One even asked if you ever posed in the nude.'

'I hope you told them I didn't.'

'How could I? What do I know about your carrying-on.'

'Carrying-on? I work, that's all.'

'Some work. Dolling yourself up like a tart . . .'

'Be quiet,' yelled Isobel. 'You're disgusting!'

'Please, don't argue,' begged Grace.

'What do you mean?' blustered Amos, staring at Isobel, his voice cracking as he saw the accusation in her eyes.

Isobel wished she hadn't given way to her temper. What had happened was past. Nothing could change it and she had no wish to add to Grace's burdens.

'You and your friends,' she dissembled. 'They're what I call disgusting. And filthy.'

Amos glared at her, his eyes bloodshot, dribbles of spittle at the corners of his mouth. Unwelcome memory had grasped him, but he struggled on. 'How many men do you think have seen that picture?' His voice was calmer now.

'I don't know and I don't care,' said Isobel, her voice clipped and scornful.

'You don't know what men are like,' began Amos, then stopped.

Grace stood near the range, her head averted, wanting to run away, wanting to be anywhere other than here where the deep, virulent anger of years seemed to be boiling up. Unable to endure the tension any longer she turned a white face to them. 'Don't quarrel. Let's have a nice cup of tea.'

The familiar words dropped into a void, not even reaching the other two, who were glaring at each other, and Grace dropped into a chair, her legs unable to support her.

Amos was the first to look away and soon afterwards Isobel went upstairs. When she came down Amos had gone out.

'Thank God,' said Grace.

'How much did you give him this time, Mum?'

'Only a shilling. It's all I had.'

One afternoon Mr Bennyson, Felice and Lawrence Dane made an unexpected appearance at the factory. Mr Bennyson was looking extremely pleased. He stopped in the workroom, rubbing his hands. 'Orders are coming in. I must thank you, Miss Trefusis, and you, Miss Kingston.' He turned to Ruby, 'And you, Miss, er – I know you helped.' He hurried on. 'I have received many congratulations and orders from our clients. I was right to hold the show. The whole thing was beautifully managed.'

'Miss Prewett assisted,' said Miss Trefusis.

Ruby said later she had almost fallen from her chair in amazement. Isobel knew that the unexpected remark had been born out of the supervisor's inability to cope with the fulsome praise. She would probably regret making it.

'Miss Prewett, too,' said Mr Bennyson. 'And now, Miss Trefusis, let us discuss over tea what further measures we can take to further our business interests.'

He and Miss Trefusis walked into the office. Felice and Lawrence Dane stayed in the workroom. 'You were awfully good,' Felice said to Isobel. 'One would think you had always been a model. In the magazine pictures you look as if you have been doing the job for ever. My chum, Lady Betty Westbury, thinks you're a terrific sport.'

It was the longest speech Isobel and Ruby had ever heard her make, and it was the first occasion she hadn't appeared sulky and bored.

Felice went into the office, but Mr Dane remained. He subjected Isobel to a long stare. At least, it seemed long to her. She glanced at him from the corner of her eye, then stopped work to give him back his stare, holding it although she felt herself blushing. Was he remembering her photograph in pretty, lacy lingerie? 'Can I help you?' she asked.

He strolled across the room and touched a piece of ecru satin which she was working on. 'What is this to be?'

The answer should have been 'French knickers', but Isobel

couldn't bring herself to say it. Ruby was straining her ears to listen.

'It's an undergarment.'

He was amused and she was sure he knew exactly what she was sewing. He had a reputation for being popular with the ladies and the factory women hinted that more than one had succumbed to his love-making. 'Has it been ordered? Is it for a certain lady?'

'Yes, though I can't tell you her name. It wouldn't be proper.' She heard her voice emerge prim and correct.

Lawrence Dane laughed. His laughter softened the hard lines of his face and Isobel thought, He's really not bad-looking. A frisson of excitement coursed through her.

'I think my father may be planning regular corsetry shows. Will you be taking part?'

'That's not for me to decide.' Again she sounded impossibly prudish and it irked her. She would like to show him a less priggish side to her nature. Then she remembered how she had paraded up and down before the curious eyes of many of his acquaintances and, not only that, she had stood brazenly for a man to photograph her in intimate clothing. Overcome by embarrassment, she returned to her sewing and, after watching her bent head for a moment, Lawrence Dane joined the others. Frank came hurrying through, followed by Desmond.

'We're a little late,' Frank was muttering to no one in particular.

Desmond looked unflustered as usual. He smiled at his sister and Ruby.

'God, he's a heartbreaker,' sighed Ruby as the two men entered the office.

'Mr Bagley, do you mean?'

'You know I don't! I mean your gorgeous brother. I wish I was a few years younger.' Remembering belatedly that Isobel and Frank went out together she added quickly, 'Not that Mr Bagley isn't attractive, too. He's very nice, but he's older. I mean, Desmond, I mean Mr Kingston—'

'Do shut up,' said Isobel, laughing.

Frank called for Isobel to take her out. It was the second time he had been asked into the house. Mum was still nervous with him, but she approved of him and cherished the hope that Isobel would hang on to such a desirable man.

'How smart you are,' she said. 'Have you seen the magazine? The one that Isobel's in?'

Isobel glanced at Frank. He disapproved strongly of her appearance

129

in public in underwear but could hardly say so without running down his employer and appearing critical of Isobel. To him, Mr Bennyson, the factory, the work were the major part of his life.

It was too cold and wet to go walking; they didn't always want to visit a picture house and Isobel wondered what Frank had planned. He might appear to those who did not know him to be unassertive, but he was the one who took the lead and made plans. This time he surprised her. He had tickets for the Hippodrome.

'How lovely!' she cried. 'What's on? Not that it matters! I've hardly ever been to a theatre.'

'That's wonderful, Isobel,' breathed Grace.

Olive, who was mending a stocking, her lips moving in what Isobel knew were silent swearwords, was envious. But she would die rather than admit it. 'I've been to the Hippodrome heaps of times.'

'When?' demanded Grace.

'When I've been out with my friends. I love variety shows.'

Grace said, 'Well, to think you've been to the theatre without mentioning a word about it.'

Frank gave Olive a condescending smile. He disliked her. She bridled. 'Variety is the spice of life, they say.'

Frank turned to Isobel. 'What have you seen?'

'Pantomimes.'

'What else?'

'That's all.'

He looked surprised and pleased. 'Then it will give me even greater pleasure to remedy that,' he said in his precise way. 'I am very fond of the theatre and hope that you will share my enthusiasm, as did my dear wife.'

Olive gave a snort of mocking laughter which the others ignored.

Isobel wasn't sure she wanted Frank to bring his wife into the conversation. Was she jealous? She didn't think so. Of course, she understood that it was natural for him to speak readily of her. They had been happy and her two sons had good memories of their mother, but she would prefer to be a twosome. Frank's wife as a shadowy presence made that difficult.

'You asked me what is on? An opera, *Faust*. I hope you enjoy it.'

'Opera? I've never been to an opera. In fact, I've never set foot in the Hippodrome. We've always been to the Prince's.'

'Then my pleasure will be all the greater.'

Arriving at the Hippodrome, Isobel was overawed by the black and white marble vestibule, but that faded into nothingness beside the auditorium. It was a marvel of gold and white with rose-coloured carpets, matching wallpaper and plush seats. There were mirrors set in the walls. Pillars with bronzed figureheads held up the balconies. 'It's wonderful!' she breathed when Frank returned from depositing his coat. She had hung on to hers, not quite certain that it would be safe out of her hands.

'I'm glad you appreciate it. Wait until you hear the singing. That's *really* wonderful.' He sounded as satisfied as if he were personally responsible for the whole thing. Isobel smiled. It was pleasant to be with a man who cared so much for the better things of life and wanted to share them. He had booked seats at the back of the stalls. Good seats, suitable for those who came dressed in ordinary clothes. Isobel was fascinated by the people who arrived in evening dress. They filled the front stalls and the boxes from where ladies glanced down haughtily. It was all so exciting. As she stared up at some glamorously gowned ladies in a stage box Lawrence Dane entered it and gave a small bow to the most beautiful of the women. Her gown of chartreuse crepe with a small coatee was exquisite and she wore diamonds in her hair and round her throat. When she smiled up at him Isobel felt a stab of envy. Just for a moment she wished she were that woman and that Lawrence Dane was bowing to her.

Even the members of the orchestra wore faultless evening dress. The overture began and she was impressed by the beauty of the music. But unfortunately she cared very little for the singing. She admired the costumes, the scenery, the effects and conceded that the voices were grand, but a story in a language she couldn't understand bored her. She did not fidget, keeping her eyes upon the stage, not wanting to let Frank know, dreading his possible scorn. How could she live up to his ideal of a woman? She supposed his wife had enjoyed opera. Perhaps in time she too would like it.

In the interval Frank bought himself a beer and a glass of lemonade for her. It was delicious, but capriciously she felt he should have asked her preference. She knew she was being petty. She wouldn't drink beer if she was paid to, and she didn't want anything stronger. She hoped he wouldn't prove impossibly bossy. But you can't have it all ways, she assured herself. She liked the way he took care of her. Almost paternally. That was an odd thought, especially as Dad had never shown her the slightest hint of conventional paternal behaviour.

After the opera they filed out with the others, Isobel trying to look intelligent and appreciative. She waited while Frank queued for his coat.

'Good evening, Miss Kingston.'

Isobel spun round. Lawrence Dane was standing close. He looked incredibly attractive close up, even if his black opera coat did give him a sinister appearance. Isobel had read *Dracula* and pictured him swooping through her window to her chaste bed. The thought brought colour rushing to her face before she had to suppress a laugh.

'Did you enjoy the opera?' he asked.

'Yes. Some of it, anyway.'

He laughed. 'You don't sound very sure.'

'No, I'm not,' she answered. 'It's the first one I've ever seen.' She wished she didn't feel so gauche.

'You look charming tonight.'

'Do I? Thank you,' she managed. 'It's my best coat and hat.' Why had she said that when she was surrounded by women in lovely outfits? She tried to think of something intelligent, something sophisticated to say, then she remembered the lady who had occupied his box; she surely would never be thrown off balance by a man.

She opened her mouth and blurted, 'Is it true that Mr Bennyson is going to cut down on factory staff?' She had not meant to say it. It was ill-mannered of her to confront him with a work problem in a social situation. It had slipped out and she waited for the blistering retort that he had every right to give.

He said nothing for a moment as the people leaving the auditorium swirled round them like water round a couple of rocks. 'I'm sorry—' she began.

He interrupted her. 'No need to be. I won't lie to you, Miss Kingston. Business is slow and getting worse. It may have to come to that.'

Taking heart, Isobel said, 'I do hope it won't. Perhaps orders will come in. And, after all, Bennyson's things are good.'

'Kind of you to say so,' he smiled.

Frank came to her, pushing his way through the crowds. He was surprised to see Isobel in conversation with his employer's son. 'Good evening, Mr Dane. Did you enjoy the opera?'

'I enjoyed it in parts.' Lawrence gave Isobel a quick, very small, conspiratorial grin.

Frank looked from one to the other, sensing some nuance of meaning. 'I shall take Miss Kingston home,' he said severely.

Lawrence bowed and Isobel felt she should curtsey. The idea amused her.

Outside, Frank asked, 'What were you talking about? You both looked very serious.'

'Factory matters, actually. I was asking if there were to be layoffs.'

'Isobel, you didn't! Fancy doing such a thing. And in the lobby of the Hippodrome. I believed you were more discreet.'

His reprimand irritated her, an irritation mixed with regret. 'I know. I'm sorry.' Why was she apologising to him? The evening was turning into a jungle of pitfalls.

Frank said, 'Well, after all, there's no harm done. Maybe it will do the Bennysons good to understand that those on the factory floor are not entirely ignorant of their employers' plans.' He took a deep breath of pleasure. 'The opera was beautiful! We must come again. They vary the programme. I wonder? *Rigoletto*, perhaps?' It was typical of him to assume that Isobel enjoyed the opera enough to wish to attend another. 'There seems to be no difficulty in obtaining tickets.'

'I noticed that there weren't many people in the upper balconies and even the stalls had empty seats,' she said.

'Yes, it's disgraceful! I dare say if they had been showing some vulgar variety the place would have been filled with catcalling louts. I don't know how they can live without the beauty of true music. I was not referring to your sister. I am sure her behaviour is always decorous. You both come from a good home.'

Had he never heard about Amos? Surely everyone knew that she had a jailbird for a father.

He said, embarrassment tingeing his voice. 'Your mother is a splendid lady.'

He knew about Amos. She felt scorched by the shame her father continually brought upon them. Yet Frank had asked her out. He did not class her with her father. For that she was grateful, but she was glad she hadn't voiced her disappointment about the opera.

She thought about Lawrence Dane's frank reply when asked if he had enjoyed the show. She turned her head from Frank and smiled.

As they waited for a tram Frank said, 'You will know that I have seen the magazine containing pictures of the show.'

His cool voice left Isobel under no illusion that he was speaking of the Hippodrome. 'Did you like them?' she asked nervously.

He said after a moment, 'The photographer did his work well, though that's what one expects from a professional.' He could not help sounding doubtful. 'I can't say I altogether approve of your appearing in undergarments.'

She was suddenly cross. They might be walking out together but that didn't give him the right to criticise her. So far, there was no commitment. 'You knew I was in the show before it happened! I must admit I was surprised when I heard that a photographer was expected, but I could hardly spoil everything by refusing to take part.'

'No, I understand.'

'Do you think I should have refused?'

'There is no need to be belligerent, Isobel. I am at liberty to express an opinion.'

'How was I to know you disapproved? You said nothing before the show.'

'It is not for me to tell my employer what do to.'

'Nor for me!'

'Would you have taken heed of me if I had asked you not to appear?'

'I might, I suppose, though I don't see myself arguing with Mr Bennyson, do you, especially when business is bad.'

'But if I had requested it would you have refused?'

Isobel had thoroughly enjoyed appearing with the professional models. Her appearance in the magazine had been accepted by others, if a little humorously by some, and the experience had broadened her outlook. 'How can I tell? It's all over now.'

'But you may be asked to participate again. What would your answer be if you were?'

'I don't know. There's nothing wrong with modelling. The other girls were all perfectly respectable.'

'Are you positive of that?'

Of course she couldn't be. She was sure that Lawrence Dane would never put a woman through this inquisition. She was startled by the thought. She remembered his humour-filled smile and how it enlivened his serious expression. It had seemed to turn them into conspirators. He was probably fun to be with and that was a new concept.

'Isobel, I have spoken to you twice.'

'What?' She came back to earth to find herself standing at a draughty tram stop on a cold night with a man with whom she had to be careful of her speech, her actions, her thoughts. 'Sorry. Did you ask me something?'

'I wondered which of the singers you thought best?'

'I can't choose. I know so little, nothing really, about opera. Tell me which you thought best.'

Frank was delighted to give his views, which lasted all through the short tram ride home. Isobel felt her attention wandering, but she enjoyed the way he walked her all the way to her door, his arm protectively tucked into hers. Grace must have been listening out for them because she opened the door before they knocked. 'Come in and have a cup of tea, Mr Bagley.'

'Frank, please.'

'Oh yes, I must remember.'

'And I would very much like a cup of tea, though I can't stay long. My mother is looking after the boys. She needs her beauty sleep.' A lightening of his tone told them he had made a joke and Grace smiled nervously.

Isobel glanced anxiously at her mother. When Frank had been escorted into the best room she whispered, 'Dad will be home soon. The pubs will be shutting in a few minutes.'

'He's gone into town with some of his mates. A new pub they're trying out.'

Isobel was still agitated. Dad might suddenly take offence at something said by one of his mates and stamp home early. Frank seemed to take ages sipping his tea and eating one of the biscuits Mum served. He enjoyed talking about the show.

Grace was impressed. 'The Hippodrome to an opera,' she breathed, looking at Frank admiringly.

The flurry of orders activated by the show died away even more quickly than Mr Bennyson had feared and he began touring the factory more often, looking grim. He held long conversations with Miss Trefusis and Frank, who refused to repeat a word to Isobel.

'What is said in that office is confidential,' he explained in what she considered an unnecessarily pompous tone.

'Don't you trust me?' She had been half teasing, but Frank had frowned.

'If you thought I was untrustworthy would you contemplate a deeper association with me?' he asked sternly.

'No,' said Isobel, meek in the light of his incorruptibility. She didn't feel meek. In fact, she wondered increasingly if she could cope with the net which he seemed to be tightening around her. He was taking too much for granted. She felt she should try to make him understand the way she felt. But gradually her uneasiness in his company began to fade and she enjoyed their dates. She admired his measured, educated conversation, his orderly way of conducting his life and the lives of his sons. After living with Dad she appreciated the calm he generated. She contemplated the idea of becoming a mother to Frederick and Thomas. The boys, young as they were, were quiet in their father's presence. Were they always so decorous? Or had Frank the ability to dampen down their childish spirits as he did her turbulent thoughts and worries? She was reassured when they were together, but when they were apart she became confused.

Isobel wasn't anxious on her own behalf about the future of the factory because she was pretty sure that if layoffs came she and Desmond would retain their jobs, as would Ruby and the men from the cutting room and any others who were specialists in their line. She worried about the women on the factory floor. Some of them had never known any workplace but Bennyson's. As the unemployment figures continued to rise and as every year the schools turned out young people who would work for small wages, Bennyson's many employees felt that a sword was hanging over them. They knew that orders were falling off. Some days it was all Desmond could do to make them appear busy and he had to be cunning to spread the work over all the machines.

As brother and sister were walking home from the factory one evening, Desmond said, 'I'm afraid layoffs are inevitable.'

'I've been hoping they wouldn't be. Lots of those women have menfolk out of work. They're supporting their families.'

'I know, but Mr Bennyson can't afford to keep them on if the work isn't there.'

'Are you on the side of the bosses?' flashed Isobel.

'Of course not! You know I'm not!'

'No, I don't!' cried Isobel, unreasonable in her agitation. 'After all, you are almost one of them yourself. You've been called more than once to listen to the discussions going on.'

'That doesn't make me a boss. I have no power at all. If I had, I would suggest that Ralph Bennyson took less money from the business and kept on the whole staff until times got better.'

Desmond's level-headedness cooled her temper. 'Sorry. Do you know which of the women he's thinking about getting rid of?'

'I didn't say it was definite.'

'No, but you think it, don't you?'

'I'm afraid of it.'

'Christmas is almost here. He won't sack them before then, will he?'

'I don't know. He couldn't possibly understand how desperate that would make them.'

'How can anyone be so insensitive?'

'He doesn't realise what a struggle people like us have.'

Christmas brought a flurry of last-minute orders to the factory as women decided they needed firm support for their figures beneath their new party frocks.

Christmas in the Kingston household was dominated by Dad, his drinking, his quarrelsome moods, his bursts of violence, though the latter were growing fewer. Grace seldom came downstairs on Sundays looking white and bruised. In fact, it had last happened three months ago. Desmond had looked grimly at the bruise staining her cheek and asked his father to step into the front room with him. Amos had blustered, not liking the look he saw in his eldest son's eyes, but Desmond had grasped his arm and Amos hadn't the strength to resist. Desmond told no one what had been said. The others had heard Amos's voice rise once or twice in tones of indignation, and Grace had murmured nervously, 'I hope Desmond won't hurt him.'

Olive had given a snort of anger. 'Hurt him? He's too pickled in booze to feel anything and if Desmond knocked him down it would be what he deserves. I don't understand you, Mum.'

'I know you don't. He isn't your husband.'

Olive had left the house, slamming the front door, and for once Isobel had felt like copying her.

But words were all the weapons Desmond had used and Amos had not hurt Grace since. She was safe as long as Desmond was around just as Kathy was safe as long as Isobel remained near her.

In their first wage packets of the new year many of the machinists found the notice they had dreaded. Most of the older women discovered that after long and faithful service they were no longer required. Some were in tears, which were not dried by the extra week's pay Mr Bennyson awarded them.

Mrs Curtis had been with Bennyson's since the age of fourteen with only short breaks for childbearing; she had an unemployed husband and son, and children still at school. She looked so white her mates thought she was about to faint. They fetched a chair for her.

Isobel was on her way through the workroom and stopped. 'Poor Mrs Curtis,' she said. 'She should go home. She's ill.'

'*He'll* only stop her wages if she does. He might even tell her to leave today.'

Isobel ran up to the office for brandy, kept there in case Mr Bennyson felt the need of a nip. She held a cup to the woman's lips. She sipped and some colour returned to her cheeks. By this time Miss Jolly, the floor supervisor, had arrived.

'Exactly *what* is going on here?' she demanded. 'What are you giving her? Is that Mr Bennyson's brandy?'

Isobel turned. 'I thought it would help her. Poor thing, she looks dreadful. She's had news of her dismissal.'

'She has been laid off through lack of business,' said Miss Jolly severely. 'It is not the same thing as dismissal. She will receive an excellent character reference.'

'That won't get her another job,' murmured another of the women who clustered round.

Miss Jolly said angrily, 'Go back to your machines. All of you.'

The woman who had spoken up glared at her. She too had received her notice and had a good mind to give the supervisor a piece of her mind. But she needed a reference, however useless it might prove to be.

Miss Jolly stared at Mrs Curtis. She dared not be lenient. Who could tell who would be next to go? The boss might decide to promote Desmond Kingston into her place. 'Do you feel better now?' she asked.

Mrs Curtis nodded. 'I'll get back to work. It was the shock, you see.'

Miss Jolly nodded and walked away. Over her shoulder she said, 'You had better return the brandy to the office quickly, Miss Kingston. Mr Bennyson may arrive.'

Isobel felt like yelling, 'Damn Mr Bennyson.'

Desmond came hurrying from the cutting room. 'Mrs Curtis, I hear you feel ill. Should you be at work? You still look unwell.'

'I'm fine,' snapped Mrs Curtis. Then tears began to roll down her cheeks. 'Sorry, Mr Kingston. It's not your fault. You've done your best for us. But I don't know where to turn and that's the truth. I had a lot of expense before Christmas with two of the children ill and I hadn't the money to buy presents so I got them from the tallyman.

Now I owe him over five pounds and no way of paying him when I lose my job. Oh, Mr Kingston, if there's any way you could keep me on ... I'll do anything ... sweep up, scrub, anything, only let me keep my job, at least until I've paid my debt.'

Desmond said desperately, 'I'll do what I can.'

He tried. Ralph Bennyson and Lawrence Dane arrived later and Desmond approached his boss. Isobel saw them in the office, Desmond talking fast and gesticulating, Mr Bennyson listening with a slight frown on his handsome face. At the end of Desmond's speech he shook his head. Desmond tried again and Mr Bennyson looked angry. Finally, Desmond left. He gave Isobel a slight shake of the head.

At dinnertime he said, 'Ralph Bennyson is a mean, rotten swine. I told him about Mrs Curtis. He said if he gave way to one all the others would expect the same. I pointed out that Mrs Curtis's position was critical, but it made no difference. When he heard of the tallyman he didn't know what that meant. When I told him Mrs Curtis had bought toys on credit he said, "The woman's extravagant foolishness is not my concern." Bloody bosses. They know little and care less about us.'

'Did Lawrence Dane say something?'

'Yes, he suggested that a job be found for Mrs Curtis in Mr Bennyson's house where they apparently need a housemaid, but it seems that Mrs Bennyson controls the house and he never interferes. From all I've heard, Mr Bennyson is the one who rules at home, but I couldn't say it. Poor Mrs Curtis.'

With terrifying inevitability the day came when women least able to cope with poverty left Bennyson's, along with two trainee juniors from the cutting room. The office staff remained. There were so few of them that not one could be spared. The entire populace of factory and office had clubbed together and Desmond handed each of the redundant workers an envelope containing a ten-shilling note. It meant real sacrifice to most of the contributors and more than one woman's tears were shed from gratitude as well as from dread of the future.

The atmosphere in Bennyson's Corset Factory was subdued. The knowledge that some of their mates had been tossed out on to a job market which had little or nothing to offer affected them all.

Desmond did his best to cope with the fears of those still in work, pretending not to hear their bursts of anger, keeping to himself

139

anything derogatory they said about their bosses.

Miss Jolly took him to task. 'If you side with them you'll not last long here. You're part of the management whether you like it or not, and if Mr Bennyson ever finds out about the way you cosset those women he'll be down on you and you'll be the next to go.'

The threat couldn't fail to impress Desmond but neither could he bring himself to be overstrict with the women and he continued to do his best to help them. He even called on those who had left, giving them an extra reference off his own bat.

One of them smiled. 'Mr Kingston, you're only a lad. How do you think any boss would feel about a reference from you?'

'I don't care what they'd think. As long as I'm a legitimate member of management I reckon they'd take my word. And how will they know how old I am?'

But his efforts were useless. Only a couple of the women found regular employment as cleaners. The others sank further into the mire of unemployment, the dole and debt.

Isobel watched Ralph Bennyson's visits to the factory and wondered how he could sleep at nights when he had plunged so many into poverty.

She said as much to Miss Trefusis, who pursed her lips in disapproval at this criticism of their employer. Then she said, 'They can sleep easy in their beds because they don't have any understanding of what they've done. If you took Mr Bennyson into some of the local homes he'd be amazed, shocked even, by conditions. But he'd think they were primitive people and didn't mind being dirty, never thinking that it's impossible to keep a place spotless and the children clean when you've only a cold-water tap in the kitchen and hardly enough coal to heat water for cooking. How can you expect him to know what difference a few shillings a week means? He spends that on a cigar. He's had it easy all his life. His sort understand nothing. Look at his daughter. Miss Bennyson would be wrapped in cotton wool if her father had the chance. She practically has been. Stuck-up miss!'

Miss Trefusis must have been shaken to unbend so far. Isobel had never before heard so long a speech from her and certainly not one that criticised the bosses. The supervisor walked away quickly. 'I haven't time to gossip,' she flung over her shoulder.

For a few weeks the work continued as before and gradually the women regained their spirits. Then one of them turned dizzy at her machine and only the rapid action of Desmond, who had been passing, saved her from having her hand pierced by the relentless machine-driven needle. Mrs Prentice bent her head to try to gain control over her sick faintness. Someone fetched water. The woman sipped it then declared herself fit for work. But she looked white and drawn and Desmond decided she had better go home.

'I can't, Mr Kingston,' argued the woman. 'I can't afford to lose the money.'

'You can't afford to lose a finger,' said Desmond gently. 'You must rest. I'm sure you'll be well tomorrow.'

'In old Mr Bennyson's day there was a restroom and a nurse,' muttered Nell, one of the machinists who was so skilled at her work she was kept on when younger women were got rid of. 'Fat chance of getting that with the mean bugger we've got now.'

'What's going on here? What's happening?' The clipped tones of Frank Bagley sent the women scuttling back to work Only Nell dared to remain.

'It's Mrs Prentice,' she explained. 'She's been took bad.'

'Return to your machine,' said Frank to Nell. 'What's wrong with you, Mrs Prentice?'

'Nothing, sir. Just a dizzy spell. I think I'm a bit tired.'

Miss Jolly arrived. 'I suppose you've been gadding about instead of getting your rest.'

'No, Miss Jolly, honest I haven't.' Mrs Prentice leaned towards her work, then swayed. She put her hand to her head.

'It's plain to see you'll have to go home,' said Frank. 'Perhaps you should see a doctor.'

'He won't cure what ails her,' muttered the woman on the nearest machine.

Miss Jolly's sharp ears overheard. 'What's that supposed to mean?'

Nell, who had ignored the order to leave, said angrily, 'She's expecting, that's what. She's not been well since her last kid. Seven she's got already. This'll be the eighth and she'd have more to feed if some hadn't been stillborn.'

Miss Jolly looked pointedly at Frank and Desmond, who left her to sort out this woman's problem. 'How far gone is she?'

'She's not gone deaf and dumb, Miss Jolly,' snapped Nell.

Miss Jolly repeated her question and the ashen-faced woman in the chair said, 'I'm not quite sure. The last one's only a baby still. I never saw anything, you know, my monthly between the two.'

Miss Jolly wrinkled her nose disgustedly. 'You shouldn't have so many babies. It's bound to affect your health.'

'I know,' said Mrs Prentice miserably.

'Tell her husband that,' said Nell loudly.

Some of the other women laughed and Miss Jolly turned crimson. 'It's not a laughing matter.'

Nell said boldly, 'You can say that again. Ask any married woman here.'

'And one or two that ain't married,' someone said.

'How dare you!' snapped Miss Jolly. 'I won't have lewd talk. What would Mr Bennyson say if he knew?'

'Are you going to tell him?' asked Nell.

Miss Jolly decided to ignore Nell, who seemed to be not only out of control but influencing the behaviour of the others. 'You must go home,' she said to Mrs Prentice.

Desmond called a taxi for Mrs Prentice and paid for it himself.

As Desmond and Isobel walked home Isobel expressed her anger. 'That poor soul. I suppose they'll lay her off until the baby's born and then she probably won't get her job back. She's one of the best machinists too. Don't these women know anything about preventing babies?'

'Obviously not,' said Desmond, 'and I didn't know you did, sis.'

Isobel faced him steadily. 'Well, I do. I've known about it since I read a book by Marie Stopes. I found out all I could then. I was quite young at the time, but I've seen enough of what happens round here to put me off having too many babies – ' She stopped.

'Maybe you should give a few lessons to the poor women who need them.'

Isobel flushed. 'As a matter of fact I've tried a couple of times. They seemed to think I was asking them to sup with the devil. Some said their men were enraged at the very idea. Even Mum was shocked. After a few rebuffs I gave up. I suppose I should have persisted.'

Desmond looked at her sympathetically. 'You can't force knowledge on people who won't take it.'

The next day the factory was buzzing with the information that Mrs Prentice had had a miscarriage the night before and nearly died. Her husband brought round a note from the doctor saying she was on sick leave.

That night Desmond told Isobel that notice of dismissal had been sent to the sick woman with two weeks' wages in lieu of notice.

'Surely not?' Isobel cried. 'Surely not even Ralph Bennyson would be that awful!'

'He could and is.'

'What did Frank say?'

'I'm afraid he agreed. He said they couldn't afford to employ a woman who's likely to need lots of time off. He went back through the records and discovered that Mrs Prentice has miscarried twice before.'

'Frank did that?' Shock made Isobel feel sick. She respected Frank and trusted him to do the right thing, and sacking Mrs Prentice was definitely not what she considered the right thing. She decided to tackle him, to give him the benefit of the doubt until he had told her the absolute truth. She brought up the subject the next evening when they went walking. They had been getting on well together and she hated to disturb the harmony between them, but she couldn't rest until she had heard his side of the story.

Frank was astonished. 'I can't permit you to question me about a matter of business.'

'It doesn't seem like business when you sack a woman whose only crime was to get herself pregnant.'

'Isobel! That is a term I dislike. I hope you will not use it again.'

'What, pregnant?' asked Isobel, extremely irritated by his reply.

Frank set his lips.

'You could have kept her job open,' said Isobel. 'Mr Bennyson leaves such things to you.'

'Exactly, and that is why I felt it my duty to remove Mrs Prentice. Imagine the trouble we would be in if she fell again. I was told she was lucky that your brother was passing and saved her from what might have been a serious injury. She could have slumped forward and caught her cap in the machine, then her hair. What would have happened then?'

Isobel shuddered. 'I hadn't thought of that. But she wouldn't have fainted again. She's lost her baby.'

'I know, and two others before. She's really not strong enough for the job and as for her losing her baby I can't help thinking it a blessing. Her husband is feckless and lazy. The last thing they want is another mouth to feed and it'll be only a matter of weeks before she's in the same condition again.'

'Surely you could have found something for her away from the machines. Her husband doesn't have a job and not one of her children is old enough to work.'

'Now you are being ridiculous. What else could she do?'

'Sweep up, anything.'

'We already employ a cleaning staff, as you very well know. We can't afford and don't need anyone else. Would you have me dismiss one of those women to keep on another? They rely on their jobs, too.'

'But she needs money desperately.'

'I am aware of it. That is why she's always gone on working no matter how she felt.'

He was right and it annoyed her. 'Pregnancy isn't a crime, you know. Why should a woman be punished for it? Oh, Frank, it's all so heartless!'

'I did my duty which is first of all to my employer and, equally important, to my sons. I must keep a good home for them and maybe one day – '

'Yes?'

'A wife.' He paused. 'You, Isobel. Perhaps?'

She was taken aback. 'Is that supposed to be a proposal?'

'You might call it that. Or a tentative feeler. I am never sure how you look on me.'

'I see. Well, I'm not in the mood to give you any sort of answer. I'm going home.' She turned and walked back to the house, straight through the front door and up the stairs. To her amazement she discovered that Frank had followed her home.

Grace answered his knock and invited him in. 'Good gracious, Frank, I thought Isobel had already gone out to meet you.'

He said solemnly, 'We had a disagreement. I do not wish to let the sun go down on my wrath.'

Grace, always awed by Frank's sombre manner and decisive way of speaking, called Isobel.

She wouldn't reply.

Kathy giggled nervously. 'What's happened, Isobel? You look very cross.'

'Hush, darling. I don't want to see Frank just now.'

'Have you had a row?' whispered Kathy.

'Sort of.'

Grace climbed a couple of stairs, saying over her shoulder, 'I think you must be mistaken, Frank, She isn't here. Isobel?' she called again. 'Kathy, have you seen Isobel?'

'What shall I say?' asked Kathy. 'Shall I tell a fib?'

'No. That won't do.'

They heard Grace ascend further up the stairs. Isobel opened the door to her timid knock.

'Didn't you hear me shout?' her mother hissed. 'I've been calling and calling. Frank wants to see you.'

'Well, I don't want to see him.'

'What?' Grace was shocked. 'Why not?'

'Because I don't.'

'That's no sort of answer,' said Grace, amazed at her reliable daughter's unreasoned response.

'Well, it's the only one I've got for him. Tell him so, if you like.'

'I can't,' wailed Grace. 'Oh, Isobel, don't forget he's your boss.'

Isobel was incensed. 'Not when we're out of the factory.'

'No, no, I didn't mean – ' Grace began to wring her hands.

Isobel's irritation increased. 'Mum, for goodness' sake, just tell him I've got a headache.'

'Have you?' asked Kathy sympathetically.

Isobel sighed. 'Not really, but I soon will have if this goes on much longer.'

Kathy stared at her with great serious eyes, puzzled by her sister's uncharacteristic behaviour, wondering how she dared to repulse a man of Mr Bagley's importance. 'Hadn't you better go down? He'll be cross if you don't.'

Isobel had to smile at Kathy's artless words.

Grace said, 'She's right, Isobel. You ought to speak to him.'

'All right, I'll see him.'

Grace had shown Frank into the front room and Isobel smoothed her hands over her tousled hair and went in.

He was looking out of the window at a rough game of football being played in the street. He turned and smiled.

This irritated Isobel still more. 'Yes?' she said ungraciously.

'We'll get nowhere if you're in a mood,' said Frank.

His suddenly belligerent response startled her, but she liked him better for it. 'Sit down,' she said more calmly.

'Only if you sit with me.'

They sank on to the ancient sofa. Its springs stuck up awkwardly and its rexine covering had grown thin, allowing spiky bits of horse-hair to stick in her legs.

'I'm sorry if I sounded unkind, Isobel – '

'You were unkind to poor Mrs Prentice.'

Frank sighed. 'Must we talk about her? She is gone. The decision is irrevocable. Mr Bennyson won't reverse it.'

'He might if you had argued. But, of course, he thinks only of money.'

145

'He has to. The factory keeps so many homes going.'

Frank's answer cooled Isobel. Logically, Frank was correct. Emotionally, she believed he was wrong. But nothing could be done about it now and she didn't want to put a barrier between herself and a man she had always respected.

'Isobel, I have asked your mother to allow us a little peace. I believe she has guessed how I feel about you and is happy for you. I would very much like to marry you.'

Isobel had no ready answer. If the idea of marriage to Frank had crossed her mind the actual celebration had been set far into the future to a time when she had done something with her life. She didn't know what, but something which would take her out of the common rut and lift her to a position where she had self-respect, an income of her own, a knowledge that she could rely on herself. One day she would like children by a man she loved, but their misty forms were even further in the future than her dream of independence. Now here was Frank thrusting into those dreams, asking her to undertake the part of wife to him and mother to his sons.

Frank said, 'Surely you have realised that I am very fond of you?'

'Yes, I believe I have, but I had no idea you would ask me to marry you after so short an acquaintance.'

'Short? We have known one another for years.'

'You know what I mean. I've always looked upon you as a boss. We haven't been going out together for long. We hardly know each other. Not really *know*.'

Frank sighed. 'Perhaps not. But you aren't turning me down, are you? I do have a chance with you? We will still go out together?'

'Yes, of course. I enjoy your company.'

He looked relieved. 'Good. I'm willing to wait. But don't forget, my dear, that my sons are growing up motherless. They like you very much and I'm sure they would accept you as a mother substitute.'

The word substitute gave Isobel a jolt. Was that what he really wanted? A substitute mother for his children, a homemaker, a substitute woman in his bed. She felt a sudden sense of revulsion. She would never consent to be a replacement for something better. It was all she could do to sit in the kitchen with him long enough to drink a cup of tea, then say a civilised goodbye.

'You were very quiet,' said Mum when he'd gone.

'Was I?'

'You know you were. Have you got anything exciting to tell me?'

'No.'

Grace smiled. 'But he did say something, didn't he? He asked for privacy. I'm sure he meant to propose.'

'He wants to marry me,' said Isobel, 'but it won't be for a while yet.'

'No need to wait, my love. I shall miss you terribly, but I'd be really happy to see you nicely settled. Frank's a good man, a real gentleman. He'd treat you properly.'

Isobel looked at her mother's eager, worn face. 'I believe he would, but I'm not ready to settle down.'

'Don't be too independent. You don't want to lose the chance of a good husband.'

'No, Mum, I suppose not. But I'll be at home a while yet.'

Chapter Nine

The anger of the factory women over the treatment of Mrs Prentice showed no sign of abating. Dark looks and mutterings were directed every day at Frank Bagley.

'What do they expect of me?' he asked, sounding unusually plaintive. 'I'm sympathetic towards Mrs Prentice, of course, but the whole thing is out of my hands.'

'They think you could have let her take sick leave, then come back. They say that Mr Bennyson would never have noticed.'

'But you understand, don't you? I explained my position to you.'

'I understand your position, Frank, but Mrs Prentice is having a dreadful time. I'm beginning to think that an accident which no one can really predict would be less awful than the deprivation she's going through now. She has to hide when the tallyman calls and is terrified that he'll repossess the children's toys. It's so unfair.'

'Life is unfair,' burst out Frank. 'If it weren't, my dear wife wouldn't have died and my boys needn't have suffered.'

Isobel was silent. They were returning from a visit to the local picture house. They had seen a comedy, but neither had been in the right frame of mind to laugh and the evening had fallen flat.

Frank said, 'You're being cold to me. Don't shut me out, Isobel. I hate it when you do that.'

She was startled. 'Do I do it often?'

'Lately you've been unapproachable at times. I feel we are drifting apart.'

'Do you? I would have said we have never been close enough to drift apart.'

'Whose fault is that?'

'You tell me!' She knew she was being unreasonable, but she felt angry with him. His behaviour over Mrs Prentice had been correct in the circumstances, but she couldn't help resenting it and it had done nothing to enhance her feelings towards Frank which, at best, were ambivalent.

Frank sighed in what she felt was a typically masculine way, a sigh that expressed his view of the inconsistency of women.

'Don't sigh at me!' she snapped. She sounded so ridiculous in her own eyes that she suddenly wanted to laugh. If Frank had read her change of mood he might have laughed and their quarrel would have ended.

But he was not sensitive to others' moods. 'You are being exceedingly foolish,' he said.

Exceedingly! Only a man as pedantic as Frank would use such a word in such a conversation. She was afraid to attempt a reply, afraid that she would release all her frustrations at his intractability, his lack of humour, his possessiveness, and she had no wish to hurt him again. He could not help his nature.

'Isobel,' he said solemnly before he said goodnight at her gate. 'I hope you will explain my dilemma to the women. They will surely understand.'

She said, 'I'll try. I owe you that. But they only understand that a friend is in desperate trouble and they see you as being the main cause.'

'I was only obeying the policy of Mr Bennyson. They must see that I can't go against it.'

Isobel said again, 'I'll try.'

She kept her promise. During the lunch break she ate in the basement and listened to the vilification of Mr Bagley and the Bennysons.

She told them of his fears for Mrs Prentice's safety. 'Mr Bagley says he was only doing his duty. Remember, he's got two motherless boys to bring up. He can't afford to lose his job either.'

'He could afford it better than Mrs Prentice,' cried Nell amidst murmurs of assent.

'He must have money in the bank,' stated Mrs Phelps. 'He's earned a good screw for years.'

'He needs all he's got,' said Isobel. 'He has to pay a woman to clean for him and he looks after his mother, too. She's quite frail.'

A short silence fell, broken by Nell. 'We know that and we've always respected him for his duty to his family, but he owes a duty to us as well. Mrs Prentice has given good service to Bennyson's. She even lost her baby because of her work.'

150

'That's not quite true,' said Isobel. 'She's got a history of miscarriages. She must have known the risk she was running, tight-lacing the way she did and working long hours when she should have been resting.'

'Resting!' bawled Nell. 'When she's home she's forever running around after her kids and her good-for-nothing lazy bugger of a husband.'

'I know,' said Isobel, 'but you can't blame Mr Bagley for that. I wish I could help.'

'You could. Why don't you talk to Frank Bagley? Ask him to bring Mrs Prentice back.'

'I did.'

'And?' prompted Mrs Phelps.

'That's when he said she was a danger to herself. Remember, she almost got stuck through by her machine needle. If Desmond hadn't been passing at the time—'

'She's better now,' declared Nell.

'But she'll be carrying again soon. You all know it. If only she'd – I mean no woman need have a baby she doesn't want these days.' Isobel was crimson.

'Now you're talking the dirt that Marie Stopes peddles!' said Mrs Phelps. 'She tries to make women interfere with nature and that's going against God.'

Isobel looked helplessly at the careworn angry faces surrounding her. Except for the younger women who hadn't had time yet to be bent by suffering, they all looked older than their years. Most had lost some or all of their teeth. They put this down to pregnancy. 'Every baby another tooth gone' was an old saying. Some of them never really got enough to eat, giving the food to their children. And their husbands. There was a silent conspiracy which said that husbands must always be fed first with the largest portions. That was all very well when the men were the breadwinners, but nowadays so many brought in nothing.

'The Prentices will get dole money,' said Isobel.

'Dole money!' cried Nell. 'Starvation money, don't you mean?'

'Did you honestly speak to Mr Bagley about Mrs Prentice?' asked Mrs Phelps.

'I don't tell lies,' said Isobel.

'No, we know that,' said Nell. 'Does that mean you're on our side?'

Isobel said nothing for a moment. On their side? Instinct held her fast to the women who were her friends and neighbours. Inevitably, they knew the history of her father, yet it had made no difference to the way they treated her. She was their workmate and that was enough.

'I'm on your side,' she said.

'Good,' said Nell, 'because we need someone with the gift of the gab and clever like you to speak for us.'

'In what way?' asked Isobel.

'We've decided to teach the bosses a lesson,' said Mrs Phelps. 'We're going on strike until Mrs Prentice gets her job back.'

'That's right,' said Nell. 'It's time we made a stand. Bit by bit they're getting rid of all of us. We can't forget the other women who got chucked out with no more than an extra week's wages. Now women who have never owed a penny are in debt, two have been evicted and one family's split up in the workhouse.'

'Oh, no!' Isobel was horrified. 'I hadn't heard.'

'We knew that the work wasn't coming in, but there were other ways the bosses could have handled it.' Nell was in her element now, everyone silent, listening to her intently. 'We could have shared jobs. We could have all taken a bit less. We were willing, but nobody asked us. You can tell the bosses how we feel. If we refuse to work until we get our own way we'll stop production and see how Mr Toffeenose Bennyson likes that.

'Tonight we'll gather down in the playing field and have a proper meeting and tell you exactly what to say. You can put it in the right words.'

Isobel felt as if her world was swaying. She wanted the women to win, but they had no comprehension of the carelessly ruthless people the Bennysons of the world were. She wondered what Frank would say. She was afraid she knew.

'And another thing,' said Nell, 'no one must know what we plan. Don't forget, Isobel. Tell no one until we're ready.'

'And that goes for your brother,' cried a voice from the crowd.

'Desmond will never go against you,' cried Isobel, incensed for him. 'He's as safe as houses.'

It was an unfortunate simile, bringing to mind as it did the memory of the families cruelly evicted.

'We like your Desmond,' said Nell. 'He's the only one who lifts a finger to help us, but he's got his way to make. He might be tempted to side with Bagley and Bennyson.'

Isobel felt miserable when the family sat down to their tea. Waves of fear swept over her. Mr Bennyson would be furious when he heard the verdict of the women and in his anger he could hit out at anyone.

'Are you seeing Frank tonight?' Mum asked.

'No.'

'I thought you had a date,' said Desmond. 'He was saying this afternoon that he was taking you out somewhere special.'

'It's been cancelled.'

'A whole opera's been cancelled?'

'No, of course not. I mean I've cancelled my date.'

Desmond said no more. He knew about the meeting in the playing field. He hadn't been invited, but the news had reached him in a series of whispers. The rebellion worried him. His heart was with the workers, but he was anxious that Isobel should not jeopardise her job or her value to Frank. He would make a good husband.

There was a fine drizzle in the air when Isobel made her way to the playing field of a school about a mile away. A thin mist curled over the grass as the rain met earth warmed by the spring sunshine.

About fifty women, almost the entire complement of the factory floor, were talking in murmurs while several small boys lingered on the outer edges, indignant about their play area being annexed and curious as to what the women were doing.

Nell stood on a soapbox. 'Ladies–' she began rather pompously.

There was good-natured chaff from her audience. 'Ladies, eh? No one's called us that before.'

'Ladies,' said Nell again, smiling a little grimly. 'We are gathered here—'

'In the sight of God,' chanted several voices.

'For goodness' sake shut your mouths,' yelled Nell. 'If you won't be serious how can we make any decisions?'

'Now you sound more like yourself,' cried Mrs Phelps.

'Get on with it. I've left my old man with the kids,' bawled a large woman in a colourfully flowered wrap-around apron. 'He'll go to the pub and leave them if I don't get back.'

'Well, then, pin back your ears and listen,' shouted Nell. 'We're here to talk about our colleague, Mrs Prentice, who's been treated worse than a dog by the bosses. Are we going to stand for it?'

'No!' bawled fifty voices.

'And there's the others who've been sacked. They didn't do a thing wrong.'

'Not a thing,' chanted the crowd.

The small boys cheered and repeated, 'Not a thing.'

153

'You kids get along home,' cried Nell, 'or I'll tell your mothers.'

The boys made faces at her.

One woman ventured to say, 'But if there isn't the work I don't see how Bennyson's can keep us on.'

There were loud jeers of 'traitor'.

'That don't wash,' declared Nell. 'Isobel here will tell the bosses that we're willing to share jobs. It wouldn't cost him much more. And he's rich. If we stick together he's bound to give us what we want. Remember, no one's going to take the food from his children's mouths, only from ours. Who knows who'll be the next to go?'

'That's right,' chorused the women. 'Who knows?'

Isobel felt her nervousness being spirited away by the enthusiasm of her workmates. What good creatures they were to venture into the unknown in aid of their friends.

'Are we going to do something about it?' asked Nell.

'Yes!' The yells were louder as the watching boys added theirs.

'Clear off home,' shouted Nell.

'Clear off yourself,' answered the leader of the boys. 'This is our field.'

Nell addressed her audience solemnly. 'And what are we going to do about it?'

'Strike!' came the reply.

'That's right. All agreed on strike action put up their hands.'

All hands went up.

'Agreed!' pronounced Nell. 'We give him the ultimatum the next time he steps into the factory. Keep your courage going. Don't waver. Always remember your mates out of work. We've got the whip hand. He can't sack us all.'

'There's a few not here,' shouted a voice. 'What do they think? Are they with us?'

'To a woman,' answered Nell. 'I've spoken to all of them. They'd have come along if they could. Solidarity, that's the word, sisters. Solidarity. And now I'd like to introduce our spokesman, Isobel Kingston. Come on, Isobel, let's be hearing you.'

Taken by surprise, Isobel climbed on to the soapbox. 'You've done me the honour of making me your spokesman,' she said. 'I'll do my best for you, I promise.'

'How about Mr Bagley?' someone cried.

'Yes, what'll your sweetheart say?' asked another voice.

There was a general outcry, mostly good-humoured.

'He's not my sweetheart. He's just a friend,' replied Isobel hotly.

154

Nell jumped on the soapbox and clung to her, placing a heavy arm round her shoulders to save them from toppling off. She held up her hand for silence. 'Shut up, the lot of you. Isobel's thrown in her lot with us. What she does in her private life is no business of ours.'

'It is if she's mixing with one of the bosses. How do we know she's loyal to us?'

'She's got a foot in both camps!' cried another.

'Mr Bagley isn't a boss,' retorted Isobel. 'He works for the Bennysons just like us.'

'He's the manager. He's well in with Ralph Bennyson.'

There were murmurs of agreement and Nell cried, 'Don't you trust her? She's worked with us since she left school. Yes, and her mother and her granny before her worked at Bennyson's.'

The meeting swung to Isobel's favour. As she left the playing field with the other women she was patted warmly by anyone who could reach her and felt jubilant. But as she neared her home her nervousness returned. She had been so indignant about the plight of Mrs Prentice and the others, so uplifted by the women's need for stability in employment and by their brave enthusiasm that she had allowed herself to make a promise which could prove to be reckless. When she arrived home Desmond was studying books on anatomy to enable him to understand corrective corsetry.

'Something up, sis? Didn't the meeting go well?'

'It went fine. How do you know about it? Oh, the grapevine, I suppose. Does Frank know?'

'I don't think so. I said nothing. What are they going to do?'

'Oh, damn it, Desmond, I don't know what to think. They're going to strike and they've made me their spokesman.'

'A good choice.'

'But you know it puts me right in the front. What if Mr Bennyson gets rid of me?'

'The women will stick it out for you as well as the others.' The front room was empty but for them and he patted the sofa by his side. 'Sit down and tell me about it.'

She related what had happened at the meeting. 'You did the right thing,' approved Desmond. 'Those women do need someone with the gift of the gab.'

'Heavens, what a reputation I've got.'

Desmond laughed. 'You are intelligent and communicative.'

'Thanks,' said Isobel drily. 'That's better. But Desmond, what do you think Mr Bennyson will say?'

'What can he say? He's bound to listen to you. He can't sack the whole factory.'

Nell and Isobel arranged that on Mr Bennyson's next visit the women would stand by their machines as he walked through on his way out. Then Isobel would deliver her prepared speech.

Mr Bennyson, Felice and Lawrence Dane arrived two days later in the morning. They walked between the toiling women as usual and, as usual, appeared not to notice them. Upstairs they took refreshment. Felice strolled out of the office looking bored and stood by Isobel, who eventually felt obliged to stop work.

'Can I help you?' she asked coolly.

'No, thank you. I just wanted to watch. You are so skilful. I should be hopeless. In fact, I should be hopeless at anything useful.' She sounded so dismal that Isobel was startled. 'Does that surprise you, Miss Kingston?'

'I don't know. Well, yes, it does. After all your education – you must know so much that I don't.'

'Why didn't you stay on at school?' asked Felice.

'Money,' said Isobel, feeling indignant at such a question.

'But you don't have to pay to go to ordinary school!'

'No, that's true. My family needed my wages,' said Isobel resentfully.

'Oh.' Felice's face was tinged with embarrassed colour. She couldn't know how nervous Isobel was waiting for the Bennysons to finish in the office and the struggle to begin, with her in the forefront.

'It's not difficult to work a sewing machine,' she said.

'Isn't it? I would love to try.'

Felice smiled and Isobel was struck afresh by her prettiness. It was difficult to stay annoyed with a girl who still seemed to be half a child, untroubled by real life. She could no more help being her father's daughter than Isobel could help being Amos's.

'If you would like to try out the machine one day and your father gave permission I could easily find a bit of cloth for you to practise on.'

'Would she mind?' asked Felice quietly, making a gesture towards Miss Trefusis.

'She'd hardly dare if you had permission,' said Isobel drily.

The office door opened and Isobel half rose to her feet, her heart thumping. But only Lawrence Dane came out and she felt irrational irritation.

He walked across to Isobel's corner. 'What have we here?' he asked in an amused drawl. 'I didn't know you were interested in sewing, Felice.'

'I was admiring Miss Kingston's skill. She has offered to let me try my hand if I can get Father's approval.'

Lawrence raised his brows. His nose and chin seemed to Isobel to jut more prominently. 'You must be extremely optimistic if you think for one minute that you will.'

'I suppose I am.' Felice looked sad.

Isobel glared at Lawrence.

Felice drifted back to the office and Lawrence bent his head to Isobel. 'You look as if you would like to beat me, Miss Kingston.'

Isobel was confused by conflicting emotions. Her hand itched to box his ears, yet, inwardly, she responded to him. She had tried often to analyse why she felt attracted to a man who was the epitome of all she despised. He was a useless idler who, like his stepfather, seemed to regard the human flesh employed here simply as part of the sewing machines. She was glad she was about to launch into a speech which would take the whole family down a peg or two. She would be cool about it. She began to sew again, ignoring Lawrence Dane so successfully that he followed Felice back into the office.

She heard the sound of goodbyes. 'Now!' she said aloud, surprising Miss Trefusis.

'Did you speak, Miss Kingston? Miss Kingston, where are you going?'

'Downstairs,' said Isobel.

Ruby, who knew what was about to happen, kept working industriously while Miss Trefusis assumed that Isobel was going to the lavatory. She frowned. Workers were supposed to control such functions until break times.

Isobel sped downstairs and shouted loudly enough to be heard by Nell, who was on the alert for her appearance. Nell stood up and her stentorian voice rang through the machine room.

'All right, girls, let 'em have it!'

All the machines stopped working and simultaneously the women stood up.

'What's the matter?' cried Miss Jolly. 'Whatever do you think you're doing?'

Desmond hovered, looking nervous but elated.

'Something we should have done before,' replied Nell.

The visitors' footsteps could easily be heard on the flight of plain wooden steps leading down from the top floor.

157

'Get on with your work,' screeched Miss Jolly.

Mr Bennyson, halfway down, stopped. 'What's happened here? Has the power plant failed? No, I can hear it. It hasn't stopped.' He turned to Frank, who looked sick. Something unauthorised was about to happen in the factory which he was supposed to run efficiently and without trouble to his boss.

A small smile lingered about Lawrence Dane's lips. Felice was wide-eyed with astonishment.

Frank hurried past them. 'Get back to work,' he called. 'At once!'

'Wait.' Mr Bennyson held up his hand. 'Maybe the ladies wish to speak to me on something of importance.'

Isobel saw that he looked quite pleased, as if he expected some kind of compliment.

'Maybe they do,' said Lawrence, his well-modulated tones reaching every woman there. 'It is, after all, your birthday.'

Isobel stood straighter as his eyes unmistakably sought hers. He was under no illusions. He sensed revolt in the air and it amused him to confuse the issue, to trivialise something that meant so much to the waiting women. Glaring at him, she waited to allow the party to finish descending the stairs, but the Bennysons remained where they were and she was obliged to walk to the foot of the stairs and address them looking upwards. It put her at an immediate disadvantage.

'Mr Bennyson,' she began, her voice cracking. She took a deep breath. 'Mr Bennyson,' she began again. 'We, that is the machinists, held a meeting. We are asking you to reinstate Mrs Prentice.'

'Who?' Mr Bennyson looked blank. He had no memory of the incident, probably, Isobel realised, no knowledge. It needed only that to reveal to her how wide was the gulf between the workers and Ralph Bennyson.

'Mrs Prentice worked for you for years. Was sent home sick and when it was learned that her doctor had ordered her to take time to recover she was dismissed.'

'Yes?' Ralph Bennyson's face darkened and he glanced at his watch.

'We want her back.'

'You do?' He looked around him, bemused. 'There are plenty of workers here. And presumably Mr Bagley has filled the vacancy. Have you, Mr Bagley?'

'There was no need, sir. We have been a little slack recently and I saw no reason to take on another woman.'

'That's settled the matter. You heard?' He looked down at Isobel.

She said, 'That's not the way we feel about Mrs Prentice. We believe her job should be held open for her. And we have talked matters over and decided that the machinists are willing to share their jobs with their comrades who were dismissed previously. They can't get work with unemployment so high.'

'Comrades?' Mr Bennyson's eyebrows went up. Comrades. The word had a definite Communist ring to it. Communists were dangerous people who incited the masses to insurrection and violence.

Lawrence Dane had begun to look disturbed. He was probably longing to get away from the annoying situation, wanting to jump into his car and drive to his next frivolous appointment. He was doubtless wishing he had chosen another day to visit.

'I think,' he said smoothly, 'that Miss Kingston is merely speaking of her comrades in terms of friendship. Friends would be a better word than comrades, would it not, Miss Kingston?'

Isobel glared at him again, but he wasn't mocking her. He was actually trying to help.

'My comrades,' she said defiantly, 'are often the only wage-earner in their families. There is so much unemployment and they need the work. We suggest drawing up a plan whereby we could share shifts. It would cost you little more in wages.'

'Indeed!' Ralph Bennyson's silky tone in no way expressed his fury, his loathing of this upstart who defied him, and in front of the whole factory, too. 'Mr Bagley,' he said, 'I employ you, do I not, to keep order in my factory?'

'Yes, sir, of course. Get back to work,' cried Frank, clapping his thin hands. 'At once.'

The women remained standing.

Mr Bennyson descended another two steps, leaving a space between himself and the others of his party. He spoke so urbanely that it was a moment or two before the sense of his words penetrated. He looked again at his watch. 'I give you thirty seconds precisely to seat yourselves at your machines and begin work. Any woman who does not will be instantly dismissed.'

A concerted gasp went up.

'You can't do that,' said Nell loudly. 'We've got a right to strike. The unions say we've got rights.'

'There are no union rights here. And I shall have no problem in filling your places. As you yourselves have reminded me, unemployment is high.'

There was a silence which seemed to continue for ever, but a rustling movement followed, and a scraping of chair legs.

Isobel turned to see each woman sink back into her chair and pick up her work. Nell was the last. She gave Isobel a despairing look and sat down. In seconds the machines were whirring and Isobel was left abandoned at the bottom of the stairs, the Bennysons and Lawrence Dane watching her closely, a sneering, triumphant smile curving Ralph's mouth. He walked on down, ignoring Isobel so completely that she might not have been there.

As Lawrence passed he murmured, 'Brave try. Hard luck.'

Frank hurried to open the door for the Bennyson party. He said nothing to Isobel. He did not even look her way. She gave an encompassing stare round the roomful of women at their machines, not one of whom, not even Nell, met her eyes. She made her way back to the top floor.

'What happened?' asked Ruby.

'They backed down.'

'The Bennysons backed down?' squeaked Ruby.

'No. The women. My co-workers. My comrades. My friends.'

Miss Trefusis had crept to the head of the stairs and heard it all. She wrung her hands. 'You foolish girl. How could you? You have put all our jobs in jeopardy.'

'I don't think so,' said Isobel. She felt inexpressibly weary as she sank back into her chair and prepared to continue her work. 'They'll blame me.'

She had stitched only a single seam when Frank scurried in. He looked ill. 'Come with me, Miss Kingston.' He hurried into the office, asking the clerk to step outside, and beckoned Isobel to enter.

'Isobel! How could you?'

'How could I not? I was chosen as spokesman.'

'By those women! They did not stand by you.'

'I know. They're frightened. And you're behaving no better than the bosses.'

'I hope you'll still feel as high and mighty when you're unemployed. You and that brother of yours.'

'Desmond? What's it got to do with him?'

'You can't tell me he didn't know.'

'I certainly didn't tell him.'

Frank wiped away the sweat that beaded his forehead. '*I* could have been sacked. Isobel, you are both to leave Bennyson's immediately. Any money due will be sent to you.'

160

Isobel felt sick. 'That's not fair,' she managed through her dry mouth. 'I only told Mr Bennyson the truth. I did no wrong. It isn't wrong to try to help fellow human beings.' She shook off the hand that he laid on her shoulder. 'Frank, couldn't you have said something to help? You know the plight of the sacked woman. You have a home to keep up, children . . .'

'That's why I said nothing,' he replied harshly. 'You must have known I would never risk my children's future.'

'Coward!' she flashed at him. 'Coward! Britain is supposed to be the home of free speech, but men like you and Bennyson destroy that right.'

He drew back from her. 'You aren't a secret Communist, are you?'

'For God's sake, you know I'm not. I'm just a woman who's trying to earn an honest living and keep my eyes open to the needs of others.'

Frank said in softer voice, 'I realise that you live in most unsatisfactory conditions, but you are a good woman at heart.'

The insult to her background riled Isobel, all the more so because it was true. She wanted to hurl insults back at him, to call him pompous, self-satisfied, self-righteous, but her tongue seemed to be too big for her parched mouth. She turned and walked out and he didn't call her back. She collected her things, dropping her overall over the back of her chair.

'Where are you going?' asked Ruby.

'Home. They've sacked me. And Desmond.'

Miss Trefusis put her knuckles to her mouth. 'Why did you do it?'

'Someone had to speak.'

Ruby said angrily, 'She only spoke up for the women. She dared to question the bosses.'

'When was this arranged?'

'You tell her, Ruby, after I've gone. I can't bear staying here a minute longer than I must.'

Isobel turned to look through the glass walls of the office. Frank had his head well down, busying himself with papers.

She felt a lump rise in her throat. From her schooldays Bennyson's had been her only employer. She had thrown away so much. The regular income which helped her family, the self-respect of an employed person, most likely her chance of an advantageous marriage. She walked out. The machinists kept their heads down as she passed, as Frank had done. Nell alone gave her a shamefaced

161

glance. Then she was through the door and out into the street where Desmond waited for her.

Brother and sister turned towards home. As they neared their street, Isobel asked, 'What on earth are we going to tell Mum?'

'The truth,' said Desmond. 'What else can we say?' His young face was taut, his eyes deeply troubled.

'I wish I'd never agreed to speak for the others,' said Isobel passionately. 'All I've got from it is the sack, a wrecked career and no character reference. And what's worse, I've ruined your job prospects as well and you had nothing to do with it.'

'Indirectly, I did. I knew what was going to happen. I could have prevented it.'

'How? By telling the bosses? You'd never do that. I was wrong.'

'Don't blame yourself, love. I suppose I could have come to the meeting and persuaded the women not to provoke Mr Bennyson.'

'You couldn't have stopped them by that time. They were all for it.'

'Maybe. Who knows? They might have decided differently if I had raised a dissenting voice. I know they respect me. But it's no use to speculate and I won't have you blaming yourself.'

'I tried to tell Frank that none of it was your fault.'

'It makes no difference. I should still have been sacked.'

'Would you? Just for being my brother?'

'I'm positive.'

'You're sure to find another job quite soon. You're very clever.'

'So are you.'

Isobel thought: We're whistling in the dark. We'll get nowhere without references and we both know it.

'I've been so stupid,' she said.

'No. You had every right to trust the women. In spite of it all, I can't help feeling sorry for them. They face unbearable problems every day of their lives. If Ralph Bennyson had an ounce of sympathy in him he would at least have listened. Isobel, love, don't be hard on yourself. Bennyson has about as much compassion as an earthworm.'

Isobel smiled painfully. 'Is that how you see him?'

'Yes. It's about as low as you can get. Slithering along, belly scraping the ground.'

They stopped and looked at each other. Isobel said, 'Perhaps we should try for jobs before we go home.'

'In other corset factories, do you mean?'

'Yes.'

'We'd be wasting our time. Bennyson will telephone and tell them about us, probably adding a few lies.'

Isobel was aghast. 'Then what are we going to do? We must have money to give Mum. I don't know any other kind of work. And I was getting on so well.' She couldn't hide her anguish.

Desmond said angrily, 'Ralph Bennyson is a vile man.'

'Are all bosses like him?'

'Never having had another I couldn't say. I certainly hope not. I wonder if Miss Bennyson will be sorry about what's happened to us. I thought she looked a nice girl.'

'Nice?' Isobel tried to view Felice through Desmond's eyes. He was a man and Felice an attractive girl. 'Maybe she is, under all that wealth. Actually, she's always seemed very snooty until today when she suddenly asked if I'd show her how to work the sewing machine. I wonder what would have happened if we'd got that far. I might have found a quite decent person.'

'It's a pity she hadn't a different upbringing.'

' "Spare the rod and spoil the child," as Granny Shaw says.'

'I can't imagine anyone wanting to cane a delicate girl like her. She's rich but she always looks to me as if she enjoys nothing. In fact, she looks as if she needs comforting.'

Isobel was startled. 'Does she? Honestly? You surprise me.' She glanced sideways at her brother and was astonished to see how his expression had altered when he spoke of Felice. She hoped he wasn't nurturing any strong feelings towards her. Felice was as unattainable as far as he was concerned as the princess that Isobel always imagined her to resemble. Ralph Bennyson would shoot Desmond before he'd allow him near his precious daughter.

Thinking of Felice brought her thoughts to Lawrence Dane and she remembered the frisson that had run through her lately whenever she saw him. What mad sensations were insinuating themselves into her? She was as crazy as Desmond. Perhaps it was a blessing that they wouldn't see Felice Bennyson and Lawrence Dane again.

She said, 'I thought Lawrence Dane looked a bit disconcerted by what happened.'

'Did he? I didn't notice. He hates even coming to the factory. I've never thought he cared twopence about us.'

'What kind of people are they? I can't picture the lives they lead. I can only guess.'

163

'They have very different values from ours,' said Desmond. 'No doubt of that.'

Isobel cried, 'Oh, damn the bosses! Let's go now to find some kind of work before we go home?'

'Don't start swearing,' said Desmond half humorously. 'It could grow on you. Frank wouldn't care for it.'

Isobel felt like damning Frank too. Frank had done his duty. He was an honourable man who would always do his duty and he would be a good, solid provider.

'We had better make a complete confession at home,' said Desmond. 'Try to treat it lightly so as not to upset Mum.'

'It's not easy to treat the sudden stoppage of your income lightly and Mum's bound to be worried and upset.'

'I don't need you to tell me that. I just hope she's not too depressed. She has enough to put up with already.' His true feelings had got the better of him for a moment and he looked close to despair.

Isobel hated to see him so wretched. She said, 'Just lately Mum's seemed happier and more secure.'

'That's true. She's taking a pride in her appearance. She's so sweet and she'd look every bit as nice as the grandest lady if she could afford decent clothes and had freedom from worry. And if Dad . . .' He was overwhelmed by his disgust for his father.

'Not much hopes of her ever living like a lady, though she did buy a pretty hat the other day. Second-hand, it's true, but it was clean and she decorated it herself. I loved watching her put that ribbon round the crown and add the two soft pigeon feathers she picked up in the street.'

'Thank God for pigeon fanciers,' said Desmond. 'Is the hat fashionable, Isobel? I can't tell.'

'It's fashionable enough.'

Desmond smiled. 'She looks attractive in it.'

Isobel said, 'Dad will enjoy gloating over us. God, that makes me as mad as anything the Bennysons have done.'

Desmond looked grim. 'He can talk. I can't remember a time when he had a real job. Did he ever, do you think?'

'Mum hints that he was different once, a long time ago. I wonder what happened to change him.'

'Maybe she's looking back at the past through rose-coloured spectacles. People tend to do that. They forget the reality.'

164

Chapter Ten

Grace greeted Isobel and Desmond anxiously. A neighbour had run quickly to tell her the bad news, which had seeped out of the factory like oil and spread through the surrounding streets.

'Come on in,' she said. 'I've just made a pot of tea. It'll ease you.'

Isobel veered between laughter and tears. All her life Mum had used tea as a panacea for all ills. Dad went to prison, make a pot of tea, Ivor disappointed her, she made a pot of tea, and now her two most reliable children were in trouble.

She poured and handed cups to Isobel and Desmond, saying sadly, 'I wish you'd come to me first. I could have told you what would happen. I remember Ralph growing up. He was such a nasty boy. He never even looked at us women as we sewed our hearts out. He used to walk through the factory beside his father with his nose in the air. We could never understand it because old Mr Bennyson was a fine man.' Her voice grew dreamy. 'So kind and gentle. He could be tough when it was necessary, but to us girls he was like a – like a – '

'Like a father,' suggested Desmond.

Grace's face coloured and she stared down at the linoleum as if she might find a picture from the past there. 'Ralph's father had to practically command him to even wish us a merry Christmas.' She sighed. 'So now you must look for work and the unemployment figures are going up every week.'

'I'm sorry, Mum,' said Isobel. 'I wish I'd not been so rash.'

Grace said, 'Pay no heed to me. You did the right thing, love. It's Ralph Bennyson who's at fault. It's such a pity that his father didn't live to a good old age. If he had been in charge things would have been different. Mrs Prentice would have been cared for. He was understanding of people's problems.'

'That's the last thing anyone would say about his son,' said Isobel.

'We can't blame him for the work falling off,' said Desmond. 'It's happening all around us.'

165

'I know,' agreed Grace, 'but it's his fault he asks inflated prices for his corsets. He could easily cut down on his profits.'

'Doesn't he charge the same as other factories?' asked Isobel.

'On some of the cheaper lines, but on others he charges too much.'

'How do you know?'

'Sometimes I manage a walk to the shops just to see the lovely windows.'

Isobel and Desmond looked at her lovingly. 'Mum,' said Isobel, 'I never knew you did that.'

'I can't get away often. But I like to see the pretty things for sale.'

Isobel clenched her fists. If ever she had the chance she would buy her mother some of the pretty things she liked to look at. It hadn't occurred to any of them that she had even a small corner of pleasure of her own.

Grace said, 'Ralph Bennyson encourages women to believe he's selling better-quality stuff from premises run by high-minded staff, so they pay his prices.'

'It's a snob thing,' said Desmond.

'It is,' agreed Grace. 'And, of course, he's got a first-class corset-ière in Miss Trefusis. It's a pity someone doesn't give him some real competition.'

The catastrophe had loosened Grace's thoughts and Isobel saw her mother as a woman who harboured wishes and dreams. Maybe now that Desmond was tough enough to challenge his father Grace had been given a chance to flower.

'And then there's his shop in Park Row,' Grace went on. 'Women are impressed by that, too.'

'You know more than you let on,' smiled Desmond.

'Don't forget I was working in the factory until I had my babies. I was a good corsetière and learned a bit about measuring, though not like Miss Trefusis. She's an expert at the surgical stuff, but I don't suppose women's figures have changed all that much.'

Desmond said, 'They all went tube-shaped not so long ago. Now they're blossoming like women again.'

'Cheeky,' said Grace. 'Underneath it all they're still the same. Some bigger than others, of course, but all wanting to look their best.'

Isobel sipped her tea and fell into a roseate haze where she imagined setting up her own business and installing Grace in a lovely home. It had always been an ambition to work for herself. It would have to wait. She couldn't leave home while Kathy was so young.

Desmond was still discussing their future with Grace. 'Don't tell Dad yet,' he said. 'He might get into a temper.'

'*Might*,' said Grace. 'He'll be mad with anger when he hears that you've both been sacked.'

'He'll blame me,' said Isobel. 'Well, so be it.'

'That's not fair!' protested Desmond. 'Mum, why is he so down on her? She hands over most of her money, she helps round the house as much as possible, she never gives you an anxious moment – '

'Until now,' put in Isobel gloomily.

'In fact, before I went to work,' continued Desmond, 'she was the only one earning.'

Grace smoothed her hand over Desmond's hair. 'It's standing on end,' she said tenderly.

Desmond said impatiently, 'Never mind my hair, Mum. I asked you a question.'

'What was that?'

Desmond frowned. 'Why is he so unjust to Isobel? You never remonstrate with him and won't talk about it, and he's hinted more than once there's a reason for his behaviour.'

'I don't know of any special one,' said Grace. 'Perhaps it's because she was the first. When we married he was kind.'

'How long did it take for him to alter?' asked Desmond.

'That's enough of that talk,' Grace said firmly. 'He's your father and you owe him some respect.'

Isobel stayed silent, remembering. Grace had borne all her babies at home. Granny Shaw had helped during the day, leaving at the earliest opportunity, demanding that Amos took over. When Kathy was born she expected Isobel to fetch and carry for the midwife as well as keep an eye on her brothers and sister. Isobel was scared. She hadn't been allowed in the room until the new baby lay in its mother's arms, but she had heard Grace's distress during the birth and in her tender youth had suffered for her.

The war had caused a gap between the births of Olive and Kathy and it seemed as if Grace had forgotten the agonies of childbed. Or maybe she was just too tired to cope. Her cries of pain had been loud, interspersed by angry words, and she had shouted things she must have regretted.

Isobel's memories of the past became vivid. Grace was having a particularly bad time with Kathy and her moans were penetrating.

Granny Shaw had left when the midwife arrived, the other children had been taken in by neighbours, but Isobel remained in case she was needed, sitting on the top step, her head in her hands. The midwife's voice was loud after a lifetime of yelling at dozy husbands who refused even to stay to carry water or make tea.

'You're doing this far too often,' the midwife had said after a particularly bad bout of pain.

'I know, I know,' groaned Grace.

'Tell him to put it away next time. Tie a knot in it.'

'If I refused him he'd hit me. As usual. Can you imagine a man doing that?'

'I can,' the midwife said grimly. 'It didn't take me long to decide never to get married. Now, dear, it's time to push. Come on, use the pain, bear down. Push! That's a good girl.'

Isobel had heard it all. Even as a child she had seemed self-possessed and unafraid and this encouraged people, including the nurse, to see her as phlegmatically dependable. Inside she was a mass of teeming, torturing emotions. When she heard her mother crying out in her agony she wanted to kill her father. If he'd climbed the stairs right there and then she'd have pushed him back down and hoped he broke his neck.

After he'd begun his nocturnal visits to her room hatred was added to her fear, and the terrible dread that he might succeed in his vile attempts and give her a child which she would have to bear in pain and shame.

'Wake up, sis,' said Desmond. 'Mum wants help with the dinner. I'll fill the coal scuttle.'

Isobel helped her mother put the midday meal on the table and they sat down to eat. Dad was out with his pals and it was a shock to hear him slam into the house and yell for his wife.

Grace leapt to her feet, almost upsetting her dish, and hurried to the passage. 'What's happened, Amos? You're home earlier than I expected. Did you get a job?' It amazed Isobel that her mother's hope still lived. At the sound of her voice filled with eager anticipation Isobel's eyes met Desmond's.

'No, I haven't got a bloody job!' yelled Amos. 'I want my dinner. I'm going out to the lavatory and when I come back I expect my food to be on the table.'

The family hastily made room for him and Grace ladled out a large dish of stew. He stumped in, glared round at the others and sat down.

168

'Sodding stew again! Don't you ever cook anything else? I'm sick of it. Why can't we have a joint of meat? My mother always had meat on the table.'

'Perhaps she had more money than we've got,' said Grace.

'Are you getting at me over money again? I can't help it if the buggers won't give me a job.'

'Where did you try, Dad?' asked Kathy in gentle tones, trying in her childish way to help.

'What the hell business is it of yours?' yelled Amos. He stood up, crashing his chair backwards, and leaned over the table, lifting his fist over Kathy's head.

'No, Dad, please,' she managed to cry before he brought his fist down.

Desmond's young muscles acted quicker than his father's and, besides, he wasn't drunk. Before the blow landed he grabbed Amos's arm and held it in both his strong hands. Amos was too far gone in drink to care. He began to struggle. The table rocked, glasses of water were tipped into the plates of stew, the rich gravy slopped over the cloth. In the end Desmond prevailed and Amos flopped back into his chair, glaring at his son with red-rimmed eyes.

'What a bloody mess the cloth's in,' he screamed. 'Get another one.'

'There's only the other one and it's damp,' said Grace.

'My God, can't you even keep up with the washing?'

'I wash every Monday, as well you know, Amos, and I can't help the rain,' Grace said. She was trembling, her voice quavering. 'Now be a good soul, do, and eat some stew. There's no real damage done. I made plenty. Isobel, help me clear this. We'll manage without a cloth. No one will go hungry.'

Her words sent Amos into an even greater frenzy. 'Oh, so we won't go hungry. Well, that's a bloody relief. Especially for Isobel. I'd hate to see her starve. Not that it matters if the rest of us go short. Oh, no, we could all drop dead just so long as *she* don't go hungry. I'm sick of it. I've always been sick of it.'

'Shut up,' cried Grace. 'Shut up. I'm tired of you! You're a bully. A damned, dirty, stinking bully!'

Everyone stared at her, hardly able to believe that Grace had actually used such words to her husband.

Amos sat motionless. 'You swore at me,' he said disbelievingly. His voice rose. 'You swore at me, your husband.'

'Perhaps you should remember you're her husband more often,' said Desmond, 'and treat her as a man should treat his wife.'

Grace sent him an imploring look. She was already regretting her outburst.

Amos shot Desmond a vitriolic glare. Twice he tried to speak and failed. Then he picked up his plate and hurled it at the range where it smashed; the stew trickled down, hissing in the heat, and an acrid smell of burning filled the kitchen.

Kathy leaned against Isobel, tears raining down her face. 'Our mum only cleaned the range this morning, Dad,' she sobbed. 'Do you know how long the black-leading takes?'

'No, I bloody don't know how long women's work takes, and she can bloody well clean it again. And any more out of you I'll give you what for when your big brave brother isn't here to save you.'

Kathy went white and Grace said, 'No, you won't. If you touch her I'll swing for you. I swear I will.' The intense note in her voice stilled everyone.

Amos's bloodshot eyes turned on each of his family in turn before he flung out the door and up the stairs.

Grace ladled out more food, but they had lost their appetites. 'Sorry, Mum,' said Kathy. 'I can't seem to eat.'

'Run along back to school,' said Grace gently. 'By the time you come home it'll be all nice and clean again. I'll bake a chocolate cake for tea. You'll like that. Take a banana with you for playtime. You'll feel hungry by then.'

Kathy dispensed kisses all round and ran off.

'Poor kid,' said Grace.

Desmond said, 'Isobel and I must go to the labour exchange, but how can we leave you here on your own with him?'

'It's all right, love, he'll sleep for hours. I'll be fine. And so will my Kathy,' she added. 'He won't touch her. I meant what I said.'

'No, you didn't, Mum,' said Desmond soothingly. 'But you were brave to say it.'

Grace for once was not softened by her steadfast son. 'I meant it all right.' She sprang to her feet. 'I must begin on the range before the food gets even more burnt in. Desmond, fetch me the paint scraper from the shed.'

'I'll do it for you before I go out.'

She stood on tiptoe to kiss him. 'No, thanks all the same, but I can manage. You and Isbobel go and study the lie of the land.'

Felice Bennyson was sitting in her room which had been exquisitely furnished by her mother when Felice had left the nursery. Sylvia's taste was excellent and, thoughtfully, she had not done a thing without enlisting her daughter's approval.

Felice appreciated the spaciousness of her room. The heavy flock Victorian wallpaper had been stripped and the walls hung with a delicate pattern of blue and cream. The blood-red carpet had also been removed and her feet sank into soft wool of the same blue and cream shades as the paper. Her kidney-shaped dressing table was hung with a frill embroidered by Sylvia and the curtains and pelmets complemented it. Two modern easy chairs were pulled up to the glowing fire. A wardrobe took up most of one wall and Sylvia had presented her with a delicate Regency escritoire. Only the four-poster bed remained of the old furniture but this had been transformed by a good mattress and lighter hangings.

Here, in her own domain, Felice felt at home in a way that eluded her in the rest of the house. Here, Ralph only entered by invitation and here she could escape the oppressive atmosphere he and her mother created.

She stared into the flames, not seeing their brightness, unable to erase the impression she retained of Miss Kingston's face when she had so boldly spoken up for the machinists. And even less able to forget the girl's look of betrayal when she was let down.

She wished fervently that her father possessed the compassion her grandfather had used so generously, and that she had had the courage to speak out and say what she felt. Not there and then, perhaps – she could never humiliate her father in such a way – but later, in the car. Ralph had said nothing about the incident. It was as if he had already forgotten it. Felice knew little about the conditions prevailing among the working class, but lately she had begun to be curious about the crowds of ordinary people she saw around her, so many of whom looked thin and anxious, and especially about the factory women who toiled constantly in order that she and others like her could have a comfortable life. She had learned enough to understand that the Kingstons' future was likely to prove difficult. She liked Desmond Kingston's fresh-faced good looks, his open manner. He was never servile, but always polite; he was proud in the right kind of way. Lawrence had a manner of moving and speaking which stamped him as a gentleman of consequence. Desmond Kingston's way was to hold up his head, answer questions clearly and stride confidently, as if he knew exactly where he was going. What would he do now? Where would he go? It surprised her to realise that this

171

meant something to her. She shuddered to imagine her father's reaction if he discovered that she was dreaming of a common employee. No longer an employee, though. Felice's mind was suddenly taken over by Desmond's plight, his humiliation, his possible despair. She was sure he would never lay blame on his sister. How marvellous to have a brother who was dependable, loving and caring. Unexpected tears welled in her eyes.

At a tap on the door she hastily wiped her eyes and called, 'Who is there?'

'It's me, Miss Felice,' said Maud, the parlour maid. 'Dinner is served.'

Felice realised she had been sitting for over two hours, just staring, trying to sort out her confused and confusing thoughts.

Father never allowed anyone to sit at the dinner table without changing and in panic she called, 'I'm not hungry.'

There was a short silence then Maud, a long-time servant of the Bennyson household and therefore allowed a little liberty, said anxiously, 'Are you sure, Miss Felice?'

'Quite sure.'

'Are you feeling poorly?'

'No.'

'Can I bring something to your room? Something light and nourishing?'

Felice's mouth watered at the thought of food, but she could not retract. 'I told you, I'm not hungry.'

'Can I do anything for you?'

'No, thank you, Maud.'

After a brief silence the maid walked away, her tread heavier than usual, expressing her disapproval.

Felice wished that just once her father could relax his intractable rules. She had visited houses where the younger members, full of their pleasures, had dashed into dinner without changing. No one had minded. Or if they had, they had been indulgent.

She heard other footsteps approaching and sighed. Father. He knocked.

'Who is it?' she called.

'Father. May I come in?'

'Of course,' she replied, wondering what he would do if she'd said no. She never had. Her room was not entirely safe, after all.

Ralph opened the door and walked purposefully across the floor to stand over her, so that she was forced to lean back to look at him.

She hated it when he did that. 'Are you ill, my dear?'

'No. I told Maud I wasn't.'

'Then why haven't you changed? Why are you not at the table?'

'Won't you sit down, Father?'

He remained where he was. 'I asked you why you have not changed. You are not ill and you know how much I look forward to seeing you at dinner, becomingly dressed.' He stared into her unresponsive eyes and became a little jocular, which unnerved her still more. 'Don't tell me you have nothing to wear. Your wardrobe is overflowing with garments.'

'I just don't feel like eating,' she said desperately.

'That is nonsense!' His moods could change so swiftly and now he was coldly annoyed. She shrank from him and he said angrily, 'Must you cringe in that idiotic way?'

'Cringe? I am not cringing! When you stand so close I find you – '
She had been about to say intimidating.

Ralph bent and took her hand. 'My dear child, your hand is like ice. Yet you are sitting by the fire. You must be ill.' He moved at last, but only to press the bell beside her chair. He sent the parlour maid for Janet.

'Why Janet?' asked Felice.

'To assist you, of course.' He returned to an old theme. 'Why you won't have a maid of your own is beyond me.'

Felice said nothing. She had absolutely refused to have a maid, certain that Father would choose someone who would be in his pocket and report everything she did. Not that she ever did anything wrong or intended to, but the idea of someone spying upon her made her feel hysterical. For once she had argued at length and even Sylvia had joined in on her husband's side until Felice had burst into loud sobs. She'd won that time. Won? The idea was quite startling. She hadn't looked upon the incident as a battle, but if she had won then she might do so again. Ralph loathed scenes with weeping women. Felice had believed that her mother's displays of excess emotion betrayed weakness, but now she wondered if it was Sylvia's only weapon.

When Janet appeared Ralph said, 'Help Miss Felice to bed. She is unwell.' He walked to the door where he turned. 'I shall have a tray sent up.'

When he had gone Janet said, 'Come, Miss Felice, stand up, do. I can't get your frock off if you sit down.' Felice stood. 'What's the matter?' asked Janet, undoing buttons. 'Can't be your usual, it's the wrong time of the month. Do you think you've got a cold coming?'

'I'm all right,' said Felice. She hadn't meant her voice to sound so desperate.

Janet laid her dress over the chair back. 'Sit down, Miss Felice,' she said gently. She knelt to remove her shoes and stockings. Felice looked down at her and saw with a shock that Janet's hair was streaked with grey. For the first time in her life she felt awkward at having a maid, another human being, and one who was old enough to be her mother, kneel at her feet to serve her.

'Get up, Janet,' she said. 'I can manage.'

Janet looked up in surprise, then stood up. 'You're not happy, are you, love?'

It was not the kind of remark made by a servant to her young mistress, but Janet and Sylvia had known each other since childhood. In fact, Janet was probably the only confidential friend her mother possessed. What a ghastly life Sylvia led. What a ghastly, boring life she herself led. Isobel Kingston might not be the best-looking of women, she might be poor, she had been dismissed from her job, but she was brave and strong-minded and for an instant Felice thought she would like to change places with her and begin to sample life properly.

Once in bed, the fire blazing, her sheets smooth, her pillows soft, Felice relaxed. She wished she could eat in her room every day. Meals where Father dominated the atmosphere were an ordeal. A tray of food was brought – clear soup, steamed plaice with white sauce and a caramel custard. Invalid food. All light and enjoyable. She had picked up a book and was settling to read when there was yet another knock on her door.

Her stomach tightened into knots. If that was Father she thought she really would begin to scream, but when she asked who was there, to her amazement Lawrence answered.

She called and he came in. 'Ralph tells me you are ill,' he said. 'Nothing serious, I hope.'

'Only in Father's imagination.' Felice felt awkward. Since the dance she had not found Lawrence so formidable, but there was still a gulf between them.

'He is so very fond of you,' said Lawrence.

'Is he?'

'You know he is. He adores you.'

'I wish he'd send some of that adoration in Mother's direction.'

Lawrence's face closed as usual at the mention of his mother's name. Felice longed to question him, to try to understand why he blamed Sylvia for all that had happened. Why he never seemed to find Ralph at fault when he was the one who had taken her from her first husband.

She said abruptly, 'Mother loves you. Why can't you love her?'

'You know nothing,' said Lawrence, his rasping voice playing havoc with her nerves.

'Of course I don't. No one ever talks to me about the past. But I do know that it takes two to break up a marriage. You behave as if Father was the one hard done by.'

'Not exactly.' Lawrence strode to the fireplace where he stared down into the flames. His voice was level, as if he repeated a lesson learnt by heart. 'My father was the one who suffered most. My mother broke his spirit. He destroyed himself. The verdict was, "Suicide while the balance of his mind was disturbed". It should have been, "Destroyed by a heartless whoring bitch".'

Felice gasped. 'You shouldn't speak like that about my mother. I love her.'

Lawrence stared at her for a moment as if he had emerged from a trance. 'No, I beg your pardon. My language was indelicate.'

'It's not your language that bothers me. It's the awful hate you have for her. She doesn't deserve it.'

'She deserves that and more. Would you forgive someone who drove your father to kill himself?'

'The act of a coward!' snapped Felice. Lawrence turned and the expression in his eyes frightened her. 'I'm sorry, Lawrence. I spoke without thinking.'

'It's a family failing. Mother acted without thinking when she decided to leave my father and me. How can you understand? You have had a loving father who puts you first in everything. I never knew mine. And my mother didn't want to know me. She cut me completely from her life. My grandmother says that no woman who loved her child could behave in such a way.'

'But she does love you! Haven't you ever seen the way her face changes when you visit?'

'No, I have not.'

'Have you ever asked Mother why she didn't try to see you?'

'Never! And I never will. I don't want to listen to some maudlin drivel.'

Felice lay back on the pillows, eyes closed. She wished she had

175

held her tongue. The fragile, precious link which had established itself between her and Lawrence was damaged, maybe broken.

Lawrence said nothing for a while, then he crossed the room and took one of her hands in his. 'Felice, you and I are brother and sister. At least we both had the same mother. We shall never see eye to eye about her or Ralph so it would be best if we kept off the subject.'

Felice's eyes flew open and she smiled tremulously. 'Does that mean we are still friends?' she asked eagerly.

'Friends,' agreed Lawrence. 'When you feel better, how about coming out with me? Perhaps for a spin in my car.'

'Your sporty one?'

Lawrence smiled. 'You like it?'

'Oh, yes, very much. I wish Father would let me have one of my own.'

'I'm sure he will. When you're a little older.'

'I hope you're right. He treats me as if I were still a little girl.'

Lawrence said, 'Then you should not behave like one. For instance, you are not unwell this evening, are you? You are hiding from something. You should face up to things.'

Felice flushed. 'I'm not ill,' she admitted. 'It's just that sometimes I can't endure the atmosphere downstairs.' She stopped. 'I won't talk about that. Are you staying?'

He looked into her hopeful eyes and said, 'I'm afraid not. I have an engagement. What do you intend to do? I suppose you'll lie here and read.'

'No. I'll dress and go down. I'll say the food and rest has made me well. It's not so far from the truth.'

'That's the girl,' said Lawrence and bent and kissed her forehead. He was gone before Felice could respond to this unprecedented caress.

Downstairs, Lawrence had left Sylvia distraught. She fidgeted with the edge of the damask tablecloth until Ralph snapped at her. Then she kept twisting her table napkin in her thin white hands.

'Cannot you stay still for a second?' he rasped.

'I am sorry.'

'Sorry? Sorry? You are always sorry.'

'What else can I say?'

'Nothing! You never say a thing worth listening to.'

'How would you know? You are never interested in anything I have to say.'

'Can you blame me?'

The butler entered with a tray of cognac, port and a sweet liqueur which Sylvia liked and Ralph scorned. He was followed by Maud, who brought coffee. After they had gone, Sylvia poured. They went through the same ritual every time she felt strong enough to sit at the table. It should have been a pleasant family meal, but as always Ralph's attitude unnerved her so that her shaking hand spilt coffee into the saucers.

Ralph stared at his but when she offered to try again he shook his head and ostentatiously lifted his cup and waited for the drips to cease.

Sylvia sat in miserable silence. Lawrence had made one of his rare appearances at a meal. She wished he hadn't done so. He had been so excessively polite his words were like blows. As he'd said goodbye and left the room she felt he was tearing off bits of her heart and taking them with him.

Ralph said, 'I am delighted that Lawrence has gone to see his sister before he leaves. There should be friendship between them.'

'It began the night they went to the Havergills' dance.'

'Possibly. It may continue if you receive your son with some appearance of pleasure instead of looking as if you are about to die.'

'He hates me,' said Sylvia. 'I feel it so deeply.' She pressed a hand to her heart.

'Typically melodramatic.'

'I mean it.'

'You never mean anything.'

'I do! I do!'

'Try not to get overexcited or you'll bring on one of your headaches.'

'I do get headaches. I know no one believes me – '

'Including your doctor.'

'*Your* doctor. If you would allow me to see my own he would understand. I was not like this before we married.'

'So now it's my fault.'

'I don't know. I don't know whose fault it is. I have never known.' Her voice rose. 'I began to feel ill when you told me that Mrs Dane would not permit me to see Lawrence. That I must stay right out of his life until he was old enough to choose. If I had been able to visit him and he to visit me I am sure things would have been very different. He would have known how much I loved him.'

'Be quiet!' Ralph said loudly. 'I have told you never to speak of that ghastly time. And especially do not yell about these private matters like a fishwife for anyone to hear.'

'I don't know why I should not! I have been far more affected than you by the past. You have been able to see your daughter whenever you liked.'

'But not my son.'

'You have no son!'

'Exactly. And yet you grudge me my excellent relationship with Lawrence. As a mother you are about as much use as you are a wife.'

He lit a cigar.

Sylvia had gone paler than usual. She watched his movements as if she were a rabbit mesmerised by a snake. She sipped her drink and closed her eyes as the smooth liqueur slid down her throat.

Then the dining-room door opened and Felice appeared. She had put on one of her prettiest dinner frocks – chosen by Sylvia – and looked charming in rose-pink velvet.

Ralph's face changed. 'Darling, how lovely to see you. Are you well now?'

'Yes, thank you, Father. I think the food you sent up did the trick.' She was deliberately placating him and despised herself for it, but she brought a tired smile to her mother's face.

'Then I am delighted I insisted upon sending a tray to you. Sit down, my love. Would you like wine? Or a glass of your mother's liqueur?'

Felice would have preferred the latter, but she saw the tension in her mother's white face and knew that some scene had been enacted which had upset her badly. She looked worse than usual and Felice would not aggravate him further.

'I would like a very small cognac, please.'

Ralph smiled encouragingly and poured a tiny amount which Felice lifted in a toast to them both before she sipped. The fiery liquid burned her throat and she was thankful for the coffee handed her by Sylvia.

Ralph wondered fearfully if Felice had caught any of their earlier conversation. He would have to warn Sylvia yet again not to bring up the past. He must keep frightening her into submission. It was not difficult.

Amos Kingston lay on his bed fuming with impotent fury. He wished he hadn't lost his temper; it would make it more difficult to get a couple of shillings out of Grace after the sure win he'd been given had come in last. He knew that Grace hid money for bills and the only way to get some might be to use force. Her fear of running into debt made her stubborn. Lately she had become bolder and less manageable. He knew why. Desmond had actually threatened him with reprisals if he saw another bruise on his mother. Well, he and Isobel would have gone back to the factory by now.

He stamped downstairs and into the kitchen and stared to see his son and daughter. 'Factory burned down?' he snarled.

'No, Dad,' said Desmond, striving for calm. 'There's been a bit of an upheaval.'

'What the hell's that supposed to mean?'

'We've lost our jobs,' said Desmond.

Amos was goggle-eyed and the family waited for another explosion of wrath. It came. 'Lost your jobs? What the bloody hell have you done?'

'Nothing criminal,' replied Desmond unflinchingly.

Amos took a step towards his son. Desmond didn't move, but Grace gave a small cry. He turned on her. 'What's up with you?'

'Nothing. Have a cup of tea, Amos. You'll feel better.'

'To hell with your tea! That's all you've ever given me. Tea, tea, tea. It's the medicine for all evils, isn't it? No, not all! Not quite all, eh, Grace? There's some things can't be covered over with a cup of tea. So your precious daughter has lost her job. And Desmond with her! Why?'

Isobel was used to the way her father disowned her when he was annoyed. She spoke up. 'The women wanted to strike in support of one who was sacked unfairly. They asked me to be spokesman. When it came to the test they backed down and left me.'

Amos laughed loudly. 'Of course they did, you stupid bitch! What did you expect?'

'Loyalty,' said Isobel.

'Loyalty?'

'She was entitled to it, love,' said Grace.

Amos glared at her. 'You know something about loyalty, don't you?' He turned to Isobel. 'She'll tell you some time. If she don't, I will. And Desmond's sacked as well, is he? You joined in your lunatic sister's bloody-mindedness, did you?'

Isobel forestalled her brother. 'He did nothing to deserve it.'

'I might have known,' yelled Amos. He directed his vile temper at his daughter. 'You've been nothing but trouble since you were born. Before you were born, even!'

'Be quiet,' said Grace without raising her voice.

179

'Be quiet?' roared Amos. 'Don't you tell me what to do.'

He had worked himself into a deep rage and took a step towards her. Desmond stood up, but Grace waved him away. She didn't back down. 'I told you to be quiet. If you don't stop yelling I'll do for you. I swear I will! I can't stand much more.' She glanced at the table where a carving knife lay.

Desmond and Isobel stared at her. That made it twice she had threatened her husband.

He was as astonished as they were, but took refuge in returning to the attack on Isobel. 'See what you've done now? You've turned your mother against me!'

'It didn't take much doing,' cried Isobel. 'You're nothing but a pig and a bully. I hate you.'

Grace held up her hand in supplication, but Isobel went on. 'You do nothing but stir up trouble. Do you know how glad we are when you go out? Do you know how much we like it when you're in prison? We can have peace when you're inside. You'd be amazed at the peace and pleasure there is in this house when you're not here.'

Amos was open-mouthed. He turned to Grace. 'Are you going to stand there and let her talk like that to *me*?'

'You asked for it,' said Grace.

'Bloody sodding hell! You're against me. You're all against me.' He burst into tears.

Desmond and Isobel were acutely embarrassed, but Grace took her husband in her arms and said in a voice they had never heard before, 'Don't upset yourself, Amos, my love. She didn't mean it. She's upset because of losing her job. And you can't blame her for going along with her mates. You'd have done the same.'

'Would I?' Amos's sobs grew louder. Grace looked up and jerked her head towards the door and Desmond and Isobel left their parents together.

They felt they couldn't leave their mother entirely alone at the mercy of Amos, who might at any time fly into another temper, so they sat in the front room, neither able to think of anything to say. To their relief the sound of Amos's sobs died away and they could hear Grace taking him upstairs as if he were her child, talking soothingly to him. 'Rest a while,' she was murmuring. 'You'll feel better. I'll bring you some tea.'

They waited for another explosion, but all Amos said was, 'Yes, please. Some tea. Thank you.'

Desmond and Isobel were speechless. They had seen Amos in a completely different light. And their mother too. In spite of everything she really did love her husband.

Chapter Eleven

Felice and Sylvia were entertaining Lady Betty in Sylvia's small sitting room. Betty was amusing them with an account of a party she had attended.

In her laughter-filled voiced she said, 'The young sprig of a wealthy family – barely five and a half foot tall – was somehow persuaded to dance with me although I protested I couldn't do the tango. I'm bad enough at the waltz. I've very little rhythm in me at all. I trod on his feet and he tripped and tore the hem of my dress and laddered my stocking.'

'Whatever did you do?' asked Felice, her eyes alight with pleasure. What would have been to her a disaster was evidently an amusing incident to her unusual friend.

'I ripped the torn lace off my gown and put up with the ladders. The trouble was that Mother had bought me black stockings to try to make my legs look slimmer and the damage was all too obvious. She swooped on me and dragged me to the ladies' room.'

'Was she angry?' asked Sylvia. Felice glanced at her. Her voice was stronger than usual, and she looked pretty.

'Not really. Angry more with herself than me. She knows I'll never make a society belle and she shouldn't ever push me into situations which don't suit me. The maid mended my dress and found me another pair of stockings, beige this time.'

Betty looked down at her legs, substantial and muscled, ending in large feet. 'I think it's probably her last attempt to turn me into the kind of daughter she would like.'

'Is she disappointed in you?' asked Sylvia anxiously.

'Not at all, Mrs Bennyson. No need to be upset for Mama or me. I have a sister who's a pleasure for her to take out and another who has married well and I am quite content with my lot. She loves me and that's all that matters and Father likes me as I am. I'm a companion for him in his country pursuits.'

It occurred to Felice that she had forgotten what a very infectious laugh her mother had and how rarely she used it.

Betty said, 'I came really to ask Felice if she can spend a weekend with me. It'll be such fun. A house party of young people. Your brother has accepted already. Do say you'll come.' She turned to Sylvia. 'You will let her, won't you, Mrs Bennyson?'

'Delighted,' said Sylvia immediately. Felice had expected her to defer nervously to Father, but she sounded composed.

'Then that's settled. I have to make a few more calls,' said Betty, 'so I'll love you and leave you.' She got up, smoothing down her rather crumpled skirt. 'I say, Felice, why don't you come with me now? We can have a chat and catch up on our news.'

Felice jumped up eagerly, then turned to her mother. 'I won't leave you if you need me, Mother.'

Sylvia was smiling delightedly. 'Go. I insist. The air will do you good.'

Felice and Sylvia both tensed as they heard Ralph speaking to the butler. He had said he would be out until dinner. Betty looked curiously at them as they fell silent and solemn, obviously listening to the footsteps crossing the hall.

The door opened and Ralph was revealed, looking as mirthless as ever. Then he saw the visitor and advanced, smiling, towards her. 'Good afternoon, Lady Betty. How pleasant to find such a charming group waiting for me.'

'Betty has asked Felice to drive with her for a while,' said Sylvia, knowing she was safe from his wrath while Betty was present. She pushed on; 'And Felice has accepted her invitation to a house party.'

Ralph struggled to keep his equilibrium. He hated Felice to accept any invitation he had not approved first, but his gratification won. 'Splendid,' he said. 'When is it to be?'

'Next weekend,' said Betty. 'Sorry it's such short notice, but a couple of the chaps I want are regularly booked to play weekend cricket now that the season is under way – just their local village teams, don't you know, but important. One has to be careful not to break with convention and upset the villagers. We never would. Ours are such dears. Anyway, it means if we want them – and we do – we have to organise the party immediately. The local cricket competition begins the weekend after.' Betty's colour was a little higher and Felice wondered if one of the 'chaps' was special to her.

'Of course, of course,' said Ralph.

Ralph Bennyson saw Lady Betty and his daughter off, then returned to Sylvia. 'You decided to give your permission without asking me,' he stated.

'To go for a drive?' asked Sylvia. Betty's hearty presence had invested her with boldness.

'You know I do not mean that. I refer to this house party. Where is it to be?'

'As Betty issued the invitation I assume that it is in her home.'

'But you don't know?'

'She would hardly give out invitations to someone's house other than her own.'

'It is usual for parents to issue invitations.'

'I am sure they will. I think Betty was just checking that we would allow Felice to come. It must be common knowledge by now that you keep her in a straitjacket.'

Ralph went red with anger. 'What a stupid bloody thing to say. Felice has every advantage a girl can want. I care for her, even if you find it too enervating to worry about her welfare.'

'You have no right to say any such thing to me. I love my daughter enough to give her more freedom.'

'As much as you loved Lawrence, I dare say, the child you so casually left.'

Sylvia spoke in low vibrant tones which startled him. 'I did no such thing as you very well know. I longed to see him. I was desperately miserable.'

'So in the early days of our life together you were desperately miserable?'

'Yes.'

Ralph was disconcerted. 'Do you mean to tell me that after cheating on your husband and upsetting all our lives you were dissatisfied with what I provided?'

'How could I be satisfied with what you provided? Satisfied with you? With your bullying and intimidation?'

'I have never bullied you. If you fear me it's because of your own weak character. I tried to treat you well. I gave you all the luxury money could buy, furs, jewels, wonderful holidays, far more than Harry Dane could have done for you. The Danes are only moderately well-off. The only advantage I had to deny you was a full social life, and whose fault was that?'

'Yours as much as mine. And I am not acquisitive, as you like to believe. You denied me all I ever wanted, which was love. I had that in full measure with Harry. I soon became aware that you had never

185

cared for me. If I had not believed myself pregnant I think you would have abandoned me.'

Ralph said smoothly, 'I have always wondered about that convenient pregnancy. Did you really think you were having a child? Or was it a ploy? You had left Dane and without me you would have been a social outcast.'

'I feel I am one now.'

'If you had made an effort I am sure you would have been accepted back into society – and me with you.'

'And you would have carried on as if nothing had happened. As if you had not broken my life. I only ever wanted a modest home with a man I could love and respect.'

'If you had really loved Dane you would not have let me make love to you.'

'How I wish I hadn't!'

Ralph stared at her. Her voice had risen to a cry of anguish which sent shivers through him. He thought he had never really seen her properly before.

He decided upon attack. 'That must mean you wish you had never had Felice,' he said.

'Don't be stupid.'

No excuses, no explanations. Was he being wise in encouraging this new friendship between Felice and Lady Betty? It seemed to be making his wife and daughter independent.

'I shall be out for dinner,' he said flatly.

'I'll try not to shed any tears.' Sylvia picked up her embroidery and Ralph saw that her hands shook less than usual. Still, they were unsteady. She was not as self-possessed as she pretended.

That night Ralph used his key to open the door to a luxurious flat in Westbury. He never visited without phoning ahead and the woman who rose to greet him was newly bathed, her luxuriant brown hair freshly shampooed and loosely pinned. Her black eyes shone as she held out her arms.

He walked straight into them. 'God, Dulcia, you're like a breath of mountain air.'

She laughed softly. 'That sounds quite poetic. But you look harassed. Has your wife been upsetting you again? Come and sit down. Tell me about it. Or don't, just as you please. I've made cocktails.'

Ralph sank on to the deep sofa, pulling Dulcia down beside him. The discreet scent she used wafted from her, stirring him to desire.

He sipped his cocktail, a drink he scorned at home, but which seemed to go with having a mistress. He never admitted even to himself that he liked it.

Dulcia allowed him to sip and be silent. That was what was so wonderful about her. She never bothered him with stupid questions, never unloaded worries on to him, though she listened to his. If she had problems she concealed them. She accepted gifts on birthdays and anniversaries gracefully, without effusive thanks, and adored chocolate, unconcerned that her figure, always generous, was growing more ample. He found her incredibly desirable, a complete contrast to the emaciated Sylvia.

'My wife is impossible,' he said abruptly. 'I have given her everything any normal woman could want. A beautiful house, a large staff, everything.' He had told Dulcia all this before, but she listened as if for the first time. 'Today I discovered that she hates me. She told me she had never been happy with me. After throwing herself at me and breaking up her marriage she pretends that it was all my fault that she couldn't see her son growing up. Lawrence loathes her, as you know, which must say something about her. If he sensed any warmth in her, surely he would respond.'

'It can't be easy for a man to care for a mother who walked out on him and never even asked to see him.'

'Of course it can't, but she blames me.'

Ralph accepted another cocktail, then another, and sat wallowing in his sense of grievance. As the alcohol blurred his senses it decreased his anger and allowed memory to flood into his unguarded mind. He recalled the time when Sylvia had been pregnant with Felice. She had always been desperately unhappy at not being allowed to see Lawrence. Now as if her pregnancy had triggered off a much deeper anguish she longed for her son with a frightening passion. The doctors tried vainly to control her, but tortured by guilt and emotional pain she had gone into labour early and the birth of her daughter had proved protracted and extremely difficult. Afterwards she could not be calmed and a dangerous fever had attacked her.

Then the doctor told them that she could never have another child and Ralph was beside himself with rage. He had always seen himself as having a son who would take over his thriving business.

Sylvia was blinded to his despair, lost as she was in her own. She kept up her pleas to see Lawrence. 'Tell Mrs Dane I'll go down on my knees to her,' she sobbed to Ralph, 'if she'll only allow me to

187

see my son once a year on his birthday I won't ask for more. She's a kind woman. She'll understand.'

'For God's sake, calm yourself, Sylvia,' he had said, 'she refuses absolutely. You must accept it.'

'I can't, I can't,' Sylvia wailed.

Her health, both mental and emotional had deteriorated to the point where Ralph lost all patience and sent her to a nursing home where she was kept sedated and under restraint.

Ralph had continued to visit Mrs Dane, allowing her to believe he was saddened and shocked by his wife's callous attitude. Mrs Dane was astonished and disappointed when he told her that Sylvia wanted nothing more to do with Lawrence.

'It seems so unlike her,' Mrs Dane had said. 'I thought she loved him. When Harry obtained custody she was permitted to see Lawrence once a week. Of course that didn't go on for long.' Mrs Dane could say no more, she was still struggling to come to terms with Harry's suicide.

'I'm afraid Sylvia has a shallow nature,' Ralph had declared. 'She seems incapable of really loving anyone.'

'I did not think that of her. She seemed so very happy with my son.'

'I know. Believe me I regret bitterly that I allowed her to tempt me.'

'So unlike Sylvia,' Mrs Dane had breathed sorrowfully. 'Or, rather, so unlike what I believed her to be. We had some happy times together.'

Mrs Dane was strictly fair. If she ever discovered how difficult Ralph had found it to persuade Sylvia into a sexual liaison and how he had contrived it she would despise him. She might get in touch with Sylvia and his lies would be discovered. He did not want Harry Dane's son to be important to Sylvia. He could not bear the idea of her loving a boy who was not his own.

'Lawrence misses her dreadfully, Ralph. Do make one last effort to make her understand what an undesirable effect this separation is having on him. She will surely be moved.'

'I will, I promise, though I have tried every way I know to persuade her,' he lied. 'She says she has the daughter she always wanted and has cut herself off from her past with no wish to be reminded of it.'

Later he had visited Mrs Dane again. 'Sylvia simply isn't interested in seeing Lawrence,' he said. 'I think, Mrs Dane, that it would be best if we sever our connection. Lawrence will fare better without it.'

Mrs Dane and Sylvia had accepted his word. The rift he had created ensured that they never met to compare notes. He had sweated while acting as go-between, fearing that the two women might get in touch, but they had trusted him and both shrank from further torment.

When Lawrence was in his teens, a tall, athletic, fine-looking boy, Ralph, having cultivated his friendship, decided he would make a fitting heir to the Bennyson fortune. He would leave Sylvia and Felice well provided for and hopefully by then Felice would have made a suitable match.

He came back to the present with a start. He wished he could destroy his memories. Dulcia sat silently beside him, tranquil and undemanding.

He stirred and she said softly, 'Are you feeling better?' She always sensed whether his thoughts were pleasing or worrying.

'Much. How about another of your disgusting cocktails?'

She laughed, a rich laugh which bubbled from deep within her. 'You love them, you know you do. But we won't have cocktails. It's time to eat and I've chosen the wine well.'

Dulcia enjoyed cooking. It was her maid's night off and she had been busy in the kitchen. The table was laid with ceremonious care and she served him spring soup, baked sole, lamb and grilled tomatoes. Fresh fruit and a cheese savoury completed the meal and it was all complemented by perfect wines: sherry, hock, burgundy and champagne, all of which they drank judiciously. Neither wanted their later enjoyment to be impaired by overindulgence in alcohol. Dulcia sipped at Benedictine while Ralph drank a small brandy. She had eaten as much as he had. He enjoyed watching her eat; she did everything with absorbed dedication. She was a total contrast to Sylvia who picked at her food and pushed it round her plate, scarcely tasting a mouthful, and it had been years since they had shared a bed.

Ralph relaxed in the pretty sitting room and lit cigarettes for them both, then Dulcia took up her tapestry work. Making her lover wait a little longer would increase his desire. The flat was adorned on walls, cushions, stools and bell-pulls with her exquisite stitchery. This latest creation depicted a galleon in full sail and was for her daughter-in-law, who had recently presented her with a second grandson. Dulcia was a widow who had had a satisfying life with her husband, producing two sons and a daughter to whom she was devoted without showing any sign of possessiveness. They had married conformable partners who treated her with affectionate respect. Her children brought their partners and offspring to visit at stated times. Ralph envied her. She had as much solitude as she required, and plenty of money to choose how she lived. She had married young and was still in her forties. She was placidly sure of her way and had no feelings of guilt, or inhibitions.

Ralph had taken mistresses before, but they usually got greedy, either for his time or his wealth or the status of marriage, expecting him to divorce his wife. He had had his fill of marriage and paid them off. There was no danger with Dulcia. She enjoyed their sexual liaison. She liked him. That in itself was comforting to a man. Dulcia was safe.

Later they retired upstairs. Her bedroom was as neat as the rest of the apartment and the bed as comfortable as one would expect of such a dedicated hedonist.

First they climbed into the large bath together. In fact, it was so large that Ralph sometimes wondered if she'd had it installed with the idea of accommodating her lovers, an idea which gave him unexpectedly strong twinges of jealousy. Gently and slowly they soaped one another, their desire mounting. Ralph was forced to control himself with Dulcia. She dictated their pace and he was prevented from making his usual blunt approach. They dried themselves and Dulcia dabbed on perfume. Just watching where she put it gave him another thrill; knowledge of women's activity in the bathroom had been previously denied him. Then they climbed into bed, naked, and he looked down at her voluptuous body and her long loosened hair. It gave him unadulterated pleasure. In spite of being a big woman she had no unsightly bulges. Her breasts were heavy but still firm. Her white thighs and rounded stomach increased his ache. With a grunt of pleasure he leaned over her and began to plunder the box of delights so generously displayed.

Frank Bagley called. Grace was pleased. 'I told you he wouldn't let you down,' she said to Isobel.

But as soon as Isobel set eyes on him she knew she had lost him. They sat in the front room.

'I decided not to write,' he said in measured tones. 'I believe such matters should be conducted face to face.'

'What matters do you mean?'

'Don't pretend to be ignorant, Isobel, it doesn't suit you. I am

190

truly sorry that it had to come to this. I had looked forward to our marriage.'

'I never actually said I would marry you.'

'You understood as well as I did that it was my intention. I had managed to overlook the drawbacks of my connection with your father. I believed we might have been happy.'

'How condescending of you,' snapped Isobel.

'Not at all. Any man would have to give thought to having a jailbird for a father-in-law, but you are chaste and intelligent – '

'Well, thank you very much – '

' – and I decided that you would suit me. I have contemplated my present decision also. I must keep my job and if I continue to walk out with you – '

'The big bully boss might sack you, is that it?'

'There is no need to be abusive. You can hardly blame Mr Bennyson.'

'Oh, can't I? If he cared twopence for those women who slave over his machines day after day with little pay he would give them proper wages in the first place.'

'They are always paid on time.'

'So they should be, and women in similar factories get better wages.'

'Some do.'

'He doesn't employ a nurse to care for their welfare, like other, kinder men. My mother says that old Mr Bennyson was a perfect employer. He even visited the women's homes when they were sick and kept their jobs open no matter what happened.'

'Business prospects were better in those days. These are difficult times.'

'Not for the Bennysons.'

'Every man must care for himself and his family as best he can.'

'And you've decided that marrying me would be a handicap to your future? Well, let me tell you something Frank. I assumed you would propose marriage, you being such an honourable, faithful kind of man, but have you considered the possibility that I might have refused you? As a matter of fact I think I would probably have been miserable living your kind of life with a pompous, self-righteous prig like you!'

Frank pressed his lips together, then said, 'Evidently my decision does not cause you any grief. Thank you, Isobel. I need have no feeling of guilt.'

He let himself out, leaving Isobel fuming with indignation towards him and disgust at her own behaviour. She felt she'd behaved in a very petty way.

Grace came hurrying. 'Why has he gone? He didn't say goodbye to me. He always says goodbye to me.' She looked into Isobel's face. 'Oh, my love, he hasn't let you down, has he? I never thought he was a man like that.'

'He can't afford to walk out with me and expect to remain in Ralph Bennyson's good books.'

Grace was near to tears. 'Old Mr Bennyson would never have interfered in anyone's private life like that. But the women wouldn't have needed to go on strike if he'd been alive.'

Her voice broke and Isobel looked at her, catching a glimpse of something she couldn't understand. She put her arms round her mother. 'Oh, Mum, I'm sorry to give you more worry. Don't think of the Bennysons.'

'It's all right. I know you'll find work soon. I was just remembering – '

Isobel and Desmond haunted the labour exchange. They made sure they got the Bristol newspapers as soon as they appeared and read the job-offers columns. They scoured postcards in shop windows. After an abortive few weeks they relinquished hope of finding congenial employment in work they understood and lowered their expectations. It was all useless. They could not get jobs.

Amos was making himself so unbearable that neither remained in his company longer than necessary. When Isobel got work as a house-cleaner two long tram rides away Amos's sarcasm rose to new heights. 'Fancy going out as a servant. There's a comedown for you.'

'There's nothing wrong in honest toil,' said Grace gently.

He turned on her viciously. 'Honest? Who are you to talk of honest?'

'Oh, don't,' begged Grace and Amos desisted. Isobel saw his face twist with sudden grief and felt an absurd wish to comfort him.

She found more cleaning jobs and was hurrying home one damp evening when a car stopped beside her. 'Like a lift?'

She whirled round at the sound of the voice. Lawrence Dane was smiling at her from his car, which had the hood pulled up against the rain. He leant across the passenger seat and opened the door. 'It looks very wet out there.'

'Yes. The rain's so fine it seems to creep in everywhere and I've no umbrella.' Surprise had caused her to speak in her usual pleasant manner as he continued to hold the door open invitingly. 'I'll take a lift,' she agreed.

'Good, you can direct me.'

She sat in his zippy car feeling glad of the ride. Her job in the house she had just left would last only until the return of the usual general servant who was tending a sick sister. She disliked her employer, who was demanding, querulous and unkind.

'What are you doing with yourself these days?' asked Lawrence.

'I've been to work.'

'Oh, good. I knew it wouldn't be long before an excellent person like you would find something.'

'I'm a domestic servant, or rather a skivvy,' she said savagely.

'Oh?' He was taken aback. 'Why waste yourself on menial tasks?'

'Because I can't get anything else. My brother is still unemployed.' There was a silence which Isobel found uncomfortable. She need not have snapped at him. Brought up in the privileged world of money and property how could he be expected to know what the real world was like? 'I'm still searching for something which suits me better,' she said mildly.

'I'm sure a good job will turn up.'

Her temper got the better of her again. 'Will it? Perhaps you can persuade your unpleasant stepfather to take me back.'

'I would not have sacked you,' he said.

'You wouldn't?'

'You sound surprised.'

'I am. You've never shown any interest in the factory or the women.'

Lawrence was silent for a moment. 'No, that's true. I've never really seen the women as people.'

'You make that perfectly obvious.'

'I'll try to do better.' He sounded humble, but she thought she caught a satirical note.

'Do you know how long the dole queues are?' she demanded.

'Yes,' he said, sounding aggrieved. 'I do know. One has only to read the newspapers to see what is happening. I would stop the rot if I could. But you are a skilled worker and I understand that only the labouring classes are not in demand these days.'

'What a damned offensive way to speak of human beings! The labouring classes! Obviously it doesn't matter to you what a man is like inside, how honest he is, or how worthy. If he's not well educated enough to get a white-collar job you despise him.'

'Hold on! I do no such thing. It's only that from what I've read it seems a fact that the unskilled are the most easily dispensed with and find it most difficult to get work.'

Isobel knew he was right, but she'd had a hard day and was in no mood to bandy words with one of the pampered elite. Her temper rose. 'Let me out!' she demanded.

'What?' He negotiated a stationary tram.

'Let me out.'

'Don't be too hasty. I'm getting you home for free. A tram or bus will cost money. And it's raining harder than ever.'

'I shan't be using a tram or a bus. I was walking, as you might have observed if you were not so wrapped up in yourself.'

He drove on. 'I am not wrapped up in myself.' It was his turn to be angry and Isobel was glad she'd annoyed him.

'Yes you are! You have everything and my brother has nothing. Why should you drive this expensive motor car while he wears out his shoes tramping round seeking work? Why should Dad be treated as if he's scum?'

'I know your brother was a valued worker, expected to do well,' said Lawrence, 'but I gather that your father has not worked for some time. In fact, it's said that he hates the sight of work.'

'He does not! Anyway, he wasn't always that way!'

'Perhaps not. But it's the way we live now that is noticed. Your father is well known as a recidivist.'

Isobel was flooded with shame. 'How do you know he's always in and out of jail?'

'One of my relatives is a magistrate. The name of Amos Kingston often comes to his notice.'

'Why should your relative discuss my father with you?'

'No particular reason. We were discussing the world in general and the criminal classes in particular.'

'He is not a criminal. And if he is he's been driven to it.'

'Are you insinuating that someone like my stepfather has turned him from a saint into a sinner?'

'Of course not! I know he's not perfect.'

'That's an understatement.'

'What about your stepfather? Of all the greedy, overbearing, uncaring, unfair monsters – '

'Do go on,' said Lawrence. He was really mad now. 'Surely you can think up a few more adjectives.'

Isobel was seething with fury. 'Will you stop this bloody car and let me out?'

'Nice girls don't swear,' he said through gritted teeth.

She made to open the door as he was turning into the street which led to her narrow one. The door swung open and she almost fell out. He slammed his foot on the brake and grabbed her, just managing to hold on to her coat. 'You stupid idiot! Do you want to kill yourself?'

'What do you care?' she cried. The car stopped, but he maintained his clutch on her coat.

'Let me go!'

'Miss Kingston – Isobel – look, I'm sorry for losing my temper. I shouldn't have said what I did.'

He released her but she stayed where she was, slumped in her seat. 'I'm sorry too. None of it is your fault. Maybe you can change things one day. I've heard that Mr Bennyson looks upon you as his son. If you get control of the factory will you be easier on the workers? Like his father was?'

She looked at him as she spoke. His hawklike face fascinated her and there was an expression in his eyes which puzzled her as they roved over her short, sturdy body, her darned stockings, her wet shoes, her bedraggled hat.

Unbelievably Lawrence was stirred by sudden desire. She was so gallant and, in spite of her damp dishevelment, she was beautiful. Not in a conventional, boring way, but she had a beauty which came from inner strength and a powerful will. He bent over and kissed her on her lips. They were cool and delicious. He smoothed a finger over her face, enjoying her perfect complexion. Desire grew stronger.

Isobel was still for a moment. She had been terrified by a longing to kiss him back, then she pulled away, glared at him and jumped out. She was devastated by her confusion. 'Thanks for the lift,' she managed as she hurried away without looking back.

In her street a gaggle of neighbours were standing outside her house, clutching coats about themselves. They whispered together, the sort of women who gathered outside any home in the street when something dreadful had occurred. She recognised their attitude as one of relishing trouble and her heart almost stopped beating. She ran the last few yards and one of the women turned and saw her and nudged the others.

Isobel didn't ask for the explanations they would have been only too ready to give. She forgot she was soaking wet, weary and longing for a cup of tea as she hurried through the front door. There was a muffled sound of her mother speaking softly through sobs and of a soft, soothing answering voice. They came from the front room.

She had turned the door handle when Desmond put his arms round her to hold her back.

'Let me go, Desmond. What's happening? Why is Mum crying? Kathy's all right, isn't she?'

'Kathy's fine. Shocked but all right.'

'Oh my God!' Terrible scenes of horror raced through Isobel's mind. 'What does that mean?' She grasped the door handle again and again Desmond held her back.

'Will you let me go?'

'Only if you promise to come through to the kitchen. I have to explain things to you.'

She allowed herself to be guided into the kitchen.

Ivor and Olive and Kathy were seated at the table, silent for once, cups of tea half drunk and abandoned. They were white-faced, but it was Kathy who took her attention. Her red eyes and swollen face revealed that she had been weeping copiously.

As soon as she saw Isobel she leapt up and flung herself into her sister's arms, bursting into more tears.

'For God's sake,' said Olive wearily, 'don't cry again.'

'It's Dad,' cried Kathy, her eyes wide with horror.

Isobel shivered. If he had molested Kathy, if he had hurt her . . .

'Go and sit by the fire,' ordered Desmond.

'Not until you tell me what's going on.'

'Come on, Isobel,' begged Kathy, calmer now. 'You'll catch cold. Sit by the fire. I'll pour you some tea.' But the child's hands were trembling too much to handle the teapot and Olive poured.

Ivor actually rose and lifted his chair near the fire for her. His uncharacteristic behaviour was yet another sign that something awful had happened. She sank down into the chair, grateful for the warmth in spite of herself. 'Now tell me.'

She kept her eyes on Kathy as Desmond said, 'Dad's been hurt.'

Kathy wailed suddenly, 'More than hurt. He's dead.'

Isobel was unable to take in the news. 'Dead? He can't be.'

'He is, he is,' cried Kathy.

'But how? He wasn't ill.'

'He was drunk,' said Olive flatly. 'He fell down the stairs. And now we'll have to put up with God knows what and it'll be in the newspapers.'

Desmond said angrily, 'All you care about is the trouble it might put you to.'

'I shan't be going to any trouble,' said Olive. She took out a packet of cigarettes and lit one, blowing smoke over the table.

'You're not allowed to smoke at your age,' said Ivor.

'Who cares?'

'If somebody doesn't tell me what's happened I shall scream,' said Isobel.

Desmond sat on a corner of the table. Kathy shrank back into her sister's arms, hiding her face in her coat. 'We don't know exactly what happened because no one saw it,' said Desmond. 'Mum and Kathy were alone in the kitchen when they heard Dad cry out. He tumbled all the way down the stairs. Apparently he hit his head on the wall and when they ran to him he was dead.'

Isobel was stunned. She was twisted by inexplicable feelings. She had hated Amos, feared him, loathed him, but she had nursed a hope that one day they might understand each other and wipe out the past. She mourned for lost opportunities.

'Poor Mum,' she said. Mum was probably the only one who was genuinely sorry, genuinely grieving. 'I'll go and help her.'

'No,' said Desmond. 'Mrs Cooper's there.' Mrs Cooper was the local woman who helped out in emergencies. Poor women turned to her for support in nursing, childbed and laying out. She was rough but dependable and asked for little reward. 'The doctor's pronounced death, but he can't sign the certificate until the cause is found.'

'He fell down the stairs,' cried Kathy. 'That's enough, isn't it?'

'Don't be afraid, my love,' said Desmond. 'There have to be certain formalities. I suppose there will be an inquest.'

'What's that?' demanded Kathy. She was clearly terrified.

'They'll ask a few questions, then give permission for Dad to be buried.'

'What questions?' Kathy sounded hysterical.

'Don't let's talk about it now,' said Isobel gently. 'It's like Desmond says. Just formalities. Nothing to mind about.'

Dad was known to be a drunkard, thought Isobel. Why couldn't the doctor just accept that he'd drunk once too often and killed himself? Now Grace was going to be tortured again, and in public.

Chapter Twelve

Felice looked round at her room in Downside Manor and sighed with pleasure. Lady Westbury had received her with cordiality and the atmosphere in this old house was so benign that she had fallen instantly under its spell. Betty had fetched her and they had arrived in good time to join the family and the first of the guests for tea. Her suitcases had swiftly been unpacked and her clothes put away by a maid. Her bedroom was by no means as smart and immaculate as the one at home, but its faded wall-hangings, ancient furniture, scuffed and chipped in places, and the way the pictures had been hung in a haphazard mix of oils and watercolours, executed by members of the family, enchanted her. There were two by Betty, a depiction of the manor and a group of ponies in a paddock. Their anatomy was suspect but the scene was bright with sunshine. Felice smiled at it lovingly.

She stretched her arms above her head and revelled in her ease of body and mind. No more arguments with Father from today until Monday. The extent of her relief startled her. She loved him, of course she did, he was her father, but his possessiveness was suffocating.

She opened the wardrobe and contemplated the row of garments which her mother had insisted she take. Far too many in Felice's opinion and probably too fancy.

When she went downstairs Betty greeted her as warmly as if they had been parted for a week and took her on a walk through a beautiful shrubbery a hundred yards or so away from the manor.

'This is Mama's pride and joy,' said Betty. 'She hates being indoors and having to cope with menus and all the ragtag and bobtail connected with running a house. I know I'll hate it too. I shall want to spend my time in the stables. Mother likes to be there as well. She really is not cut out to be conventional. Her daily interviews with Cook and Mrs James our housekeeper are a trial to her. We kids used to have to smother our mirth when we listened and she kept losing the thread, but out here she is blissfully happy. She plans everything and Smart, the head gardener, enjoys doing what she suggests – most of the time.'

Felice smiled. 'What happens if he doesn't agree?'

Betty laughed. 'Oh, then they wrangle for hours and compromise. Both think they've had their own way.'

The more Felice learned of Betty's family the more envious she grew. Here, as in no other house she had visited, goodwill seemed to be generic, with no joy-stifling cross-currents. How marvellous to be born into a family like this.

When they arrived back at the house Lady Westbury called, 'Tea in the morning room, everybody.'

The meal was laid out with formal places for those who preferred to sit at table. Today nobody was sedate enough to want to and they helped themselves, sitting where they pleased, either in the room or outside on the terrace, arriving and departing at random. There was thinly cut bread and butter, reminding Felice with painful clarity of the way her father imposed his will even on the food her mother ate, sandwiches and cakes; there was Indian or China tea to drink and jugs of home-made lemonade. Felice was still nervous among this crowd of people, all of whom seemed to know one another, but Betty introduced her to everyone who came within easy earshot; they were open and friendly and she began to relax.

Guests kept arriving until she lost track of names. Later she retired upstairs, bathed and put on a dinner gown of pale blue organza with a low-cut neck which revealed the top of her cleavage and emphasised her trim waist. Sylvia had actually taken her shopping and supervised her as she tried on gown after gown until Sylvia was satisfied and purchased three. She had also raided her little-used jewel box and among other pretty ornaments had produced a sapphire necklace and earrings to match. All the young people Felice had seen so far had been casually smart, some still wearing tennis whites, even two girls in lounging pyjamas, and she wondered if she would be overdressed. But Sylvia had been right and she blessed her mother's knowledge of the world when she descended the wide stairway, walked into the drawing room and discovered that her gown fitted in perfectly with the formal dress of the others. She had thought hers revealing until she saw necklines cut far lower than hers and some frocks had bare backs.

Betty had been watching for her and she hurried over. 'Felice, come and meet Percival.'

Judging by her shining eyes this must be the 'special chap' Felice had speculated on. He was nothing to look at, being slight in build, about the same height as his hostess, with a face as weathered as hers and a nose which had at some time been broken. An outdoor man.

'Felice, meet Percival Morris,' said Betty, blushing slightly. 'Percival, this is my dear friend, Felice.'

Felice shook the young man's hand. His rubicund countenance turned an even deeper red while she was overcome at being described as Betty's dear friend.

'How d'you do? Happy to meet you,' said Percival. 'Any friend of Betty—'

'And I am happy to meet you,' said Felice.

They both fell silent and Betty, usually so full of chatter and charm, seemed unable to break the silence. The elegantly straight cut of her gown, which was deep bronze with more than a hint of green, muted her high colour and softened her angularity. Her eyes were a clear green, her dark red hair freshly waved and her make-up discreet. Her adornments were a simple amber necklace with earrings to match. Felice was surprised to see that Betty could look extremely attractive. But she was awkward in Percival's presence and it was a relief to them all when dinner was announced. Felice was introduced to Aubrey Whittaker, an aesthetic-looking young man who stared down his long, thin nose at her before he escorted her into the dining room.

At the table he was silent and Felice wondered what subject to broach. One of them must speak. She drank her soup and while waiting for the next course decided to make a remark about the shrubbery. She had concentrated so hard that she was startled when, before she could say anything, her partner said, 'Don't you just adore the poetry of dear Edith?'

'Edith who?' asked Felice.

He turned right round to give her a long stare. 'Edith *who*, did you say? Surely you know. Everyone knows.'

'I don't,' managed Felice, growing hot as she saw that the good-looking man opposite her was trying hard not to smile. She must appear very naive.

'*Sitwell* of course,' declaimed Aubrey. 'Heavens, where on earth have you been living?'

'In my home in Bristol,' Felice answered.

'Oh, I see. A provincial town.'

'Yes, it's where Lady Betty spends much of her time.'

201

The young man's lips drew back in a supercilious smile. 'Betty is hopelessly out of touch with the arts. Mad about horses, don't you know?'

'I know she enjoys riding.' Felice resented his criticism of Betty.

'A dreadful occupation! One gets either too hot or too cold and returns absolutely reeking of horse. She really does write some marvellous poetry.'

'Betty?'

'No, *no*, Edith Sitwell. Her work is like no other. To hear her expounding upon her subject and then to listen while she reads her latest divine creation is absolutely heavenly. I sit at her feet.'

Felice was startled. 'Do you?'

The young man looked annoyed. 'Not literally, you foolish child. Artistically.'

Felice objected to being called a child by a man who could be scarcely older than she, but servants were handing round a fish soufflé and she turned her attention to it. Aubrey Whittaker seemed to have no other subject besides Edith Sitwell and she allowed him to ramble on while she pretended to listen.

After dinner, coffee was served in the drawing room. It was rapidly growing dark, though the air was balmy and some couples strolled out into the gardens. They included Percival and Betty.

'Whitaker is a bit much, isn't he? I thought you dealt with him admirably.'

Felice turned to see the man who had controlled his amusement at the dinner table.

'Did you?' she said, deciding he had a cheek to criticise one of his fellow guests, especially to a woman he had never met before.

'Do stop pursing your lips in that displeased fashion. You remind me of my nanny.'

Felice bridled. It was hardly gratifying for a good-looking man to compare her with his nanny who was sure to have been elderly, comfortably plump and certainly bossy.

'Don't be annoyed with me. You look nothing like her,' he explained, 'except when you pucker up your lips. I'm Jeffrey Westbury, Betty's cousin on her father's side. Aubrey is also her cousin and consequently mine and therefore I feel free to criticise him.'

'I see.'

'He's not been down long from Oxford where he was one of the intelligentsia. I dare say he'll get over it. He was quite a jolly kid.'

Felice laughed.

'Now you look very pretty. I would ask you to walk in the garden with me, but we haven't known each other long and I fear it would be somewhat forward of me.'

Felice blinked at his flowery language.

'I don't usually use such high-flown phraseology,' he said apologetically. 'It's simply that whenever I get near Cousin Aubrey I seem to become infected by the bohemian bug. It will go away soon.'

Felice looked beyond the lighted room to where young people were strolling on the grass in the blue-white light of a rising moon.

'You look a little wistful. May I take you out there? I promise to behave like a thoroughgoing gentleman.' He laughed softly.

Felice looked up at him. 'Do you?'

'On my honour. Will you come?'

'Why not?'

'Why not, indeed? Do you need your wrap?'

'No thank you. It's quite a warm night.'

'Then let us away.'

Outside, Felice and Jeffrey walked in silence, she having come abruptly to her senses in the cooling night air, wondering if she was behaving in a flighty fashion. It was certain that Father would not approve. But, damn it, she was old enough to decide for herself. All the same, she got caught up in memories of her father's domination and did not notice that Jeffrey had steered her gently away from the others and that they were approaching the lake.

She looked around. 'Have they all gone in?' she asked, trying to sound casual. 'We shall be missed.'

'I think there are still a few outside. Even if there aren't, if we choose not to return yet no one will mind. Lady Westbury is a gem of a hostess. She always expects her guests to behave themselves and therefore they do.'

Felice felt reassured. She wandered along the gravel walk with him, hoping that the silver was not being scraped from the heels of her evening shoes, until they reached the lake. The moon was rising high now and its reflection rippled in the dark depths of the water. A breeze had sprung up and soughed through the young leaves of the trees. Felice shivered.

Jeffrey said, 'I knew I should have insisted on having your wrap fetched. We had better return.'

Felice felt an unexpected surge of regret. Jeffrey's face was in shadow and, unable to see him, she forgot to be nervous and remembered only that he was handsome and that his voice was soothing.

On visits to her schoolfriends' houses their brothers had sometimes kissed her, planting a boyish peck on her cheek or, if very daring, on her lips. She wondered if Jeffrey would kiss her.

He could see her face and said softly, 'If I didn't know better I would swear you were waiting for a kiss.'

'Why don't you?' she mumbled, then was aghast at her boldness.

His hands went out and slid about her waist. 'My God,' he murmured, 'you're as slender as a reed. And very lovely.'

This is film-star stuff, thought Felice, and about as real, but her heart was racing; she was caught by the magic of the moment. He pulled her close, lifted her chin with a careful finger and his mouth sank on to hers. She had expected his kiss to be different from a boy's, but she was unprepared for the total dissimilarity. He was not at all rough but she felt utterly helpless beneath the pressure of his mouth. It moved upon hers and she began to tremble.

He pulled back. 'One more kiss,' she said. She tried to sound nonchalant and sophisticated, unaware that her voice had emerged in a gasp.

Jeffrey stepped back a little and held her elbows in a firm grasp. 'You're an absolute poppet, but you shouldn't wander around in the dark with strange men.'

In an instant he had spoiled the moment for her. She felt like a foolish schoolgirl with a crush. She had once had a crush on a music master and she wanted to tell this man that it had been nothing like the way she felt now. Her inexperienced body was sending out scarcely understood signals, and she was subject to so much inner turmoil she couldn't think of a thing to say.

Her humiliation turned to anger. 'Don't bother to walk with me!' She set off over the grass which was damp with dew, quivering with impotent rage. How dare he treat her like a child! How dare he arouse turbulent sensations in her then drop her? The soft grass masked his pursuit and she was startled when he grasped her from behind and held her tight.

'Let me go, damn you!'

'Not until you've calmed down. You can't go back like this.' He spoke in such equable tones she stopped struggling. She was being ridiculous. But she imagined him telling his cousins, the other guests, everybody and anybody, about the silly little girl who had tried to act grown-up. Tears stung her eyes and ran down her cheeks. He turned her to face him and moonlight glinted on her wet face.

'My dear girl, you're crying. Oh damn it to hell! I didn't mean to upset you.'

'You haven't. It isn't you. I was upset before,' she lied.

'Truly? Who upset you?'

She pressed her lips tight together and shook her head. 'Let me go. Please.'

He took out his handkerchief and dabbed her face. 'I'm deeply sorry, Felice. I feel like a swine.'

'I told you, it has nothing to do with you!'

'I shouldn't have kissed you, but the way you looked at me . . . I thought . . .'

Felice's mind was spinning. She had blundered into a situation she was too unsophisticated to deal with.

But he didn't laugh. 'You are a dear girl,' he said, sounding as if he meant it.

'Am I? Then why wouldn't you kiss me again?'

'Because I find you very attractive.'

'Surely that's a reason for wanting to.'

'No, it isn't. Not always. Not when attraction goes side by side with innocence.'

'Oh, take me back inside,' begged Felice, shaking violently with mortification.

He took off his jacket and placed it round her shoulders. She wanted to throw it off, but its warmth penetrated and comforted her. He slipped his arm around her and steered her back to the bright lights of the house, not to the ballroom but to the open front door from where she could slip up to her bedroom and repair her face. Quickly he removed his jacket. 'Felice, I beg you, don't think badly of me.'

Felice fled from him.

The rest of the weekend passed pleasantly, except that every time Felice saw Jeffrey she blushed. But she put him out of her mind as far as possible and flirted as hard as she dared with the other men, including Aubrey. She grew heady with triumph as one after another they complimented her on her beauty, her wit, her dancing. They were flattering her, but she enjoyed it all.

Ralph came to drive her home. As they travelled he talked of the days when he had been a frequent guest at events enjoyed by Lord and Lady Westbury. Felice hardly listened as she went over the events of the weekend in her mind.

Her attention was caught when Ralph asked, 'What young men did you meet? Did any of them gain your approval?'

'I met several I liked.'

'Who were they?'

Felice caught the anxiety in her father's voice. He wanted her to marry well, by which he meant her to get a well-connected husband of good family with wealth and position.

What if she told him she had met a man who had filled her with deep yearning for some experience beyond her knowledge? Since Jeffrey's kiss she had drifted into daydreams which had taken her into the realms of sexuality. She had been taught the facts of life in a cool, impersonal manner by her mother and they had seemed bizarre. Now she was beginning to comprehend what they were really about.

'Dreaming?' said Ralph, his voice deliberately jocular.

'Sorry. You asked who I had met?'

'Yes. In particular which young men. I can still remember,' he went on, more jovial than ever, 'when I first went to balls and parties, how we boys and girls saw one another as grown-ups although we were still barely out of childhood.'

But Jeffrey still saw me as a child, thought Felice. She said, 'I met a man called Percival Morris.'

'He's a younger son,' said Ralph sharply. 'He has only a small income.'

'Has he? I don't suppose that will matter to the Westburys. They seem to have plenty. Betty's in love with him and he with her.'

Ralph signed with relief. 'Any others?'

'At dinner on Friday I sat next to an odd man called Aubrey Whittaker. He talked about poetry.'

'Would that be Lord Aubrey Whittaker?'

'I suppose so. The footmen called him "my lord".'

'He's worth cultivating. Last of his line. He's very rich. Did he show any preference?'

'He was a bore,' said Felice flatly.

'Young men frequently behave foolishly until they mature. He'll forget about poetry when he has a wife and children.'

'I like poetry,' snapped Felice.

Ralph said in the sadly reproachful voice that Felice hated, 'I would never condemn a woman for liking poetry. It is one of the gentler things of life and very suitable.'

'Not all poetry is gentle.'

'Perhaps not. Have you any other news?'

'I met Jeffrey Westbury. He was older than most of the other guests.'

'I know of him. He cuts a dashing figure though not so dashing as he thinks. Enthusiastic about all sports except when he's chasing after his latest female fancy. Plenty of money there. I hope he behaved decorously towards you.'

'Well, as long as he's got money,' said Felice acerbically.

'Money is important, my child. Never forget it.'

'Some of your factory women don't forget it, but that's because they don't ever have enough.' The words had escaped her when she hadn't even realised the women were in her mind. Her father's jaw clenched.

'There were lots of very pleasant, attractive, unattached men at the Westburys,' she hurried on. 'In fact, I gave my name to a number who want their mothers to send me invitations.'

Ralph's tenseness disappeared. 'That's a good girl.'

A good girl! He made her feel like a schoolgirl again.

Amos's family thought they had escaped with little publicity when the inquest was over without complications. Witnesses were called who gave evidence of his heavy drinking. Grace gave hers in a wavering voice. She was sorrowful and strained and was asked several times to raise her voice, but the requests were made sympathetically. Kathy waited, clutching Isobel's hand in a traplike grip. Then they were told that the court had all the statements that were needed. The verdict was 'accidental death'.

Unfortunately, news was thin that day and the inquest received publicity on the front pages. In subsequent editions there were articles by learned men and women on the evils of drink and letters from readers agreeing with this point of view. The neighbours made sure that the Kingstons received copies of everything that was printed.

Amos's death was a release for Isobel. Now she didn't have to spend hours worrying about what might happen to Kathy. Ivor and Olive were almost indifferent and even Desmond couldn't pretend to genuine sadness. Grace grieved. This was to be expected, but Kathy was distressed to such an extent she stopped eating properly and looked quite ill. She also had terrifying nightmares and her big sister had to wake her when she flung herself about and cried out in her sleep. But she refused to explain her dreams.

One night when Kathy had gone to bed Isobel spoke to her mother of her worries about her young sister.

'It's understandable,' said Grace. 'She was there when he died. She can't forget. She saw it all.'

'No one saw him fall,' said Desmond.

'No, of course not,' agreed Grace. 'She saw him lying in a heap at the bottom of the stairs with his head all twisted to one side. She saw the blood oozing from his head.'

'Don't,' begged Isobel. 'Try to forget it.'

'I never will. Never. He was my husband, no matter what anyone else thought of him.'

'I know, Mum,' said Desmond.

'No you don't! None of you knows what he really was. What awful torment he went through.'

'I know he put the rest of us through torment,' said Desmond. 'Especially you. I can't forget the way he hurt you.'

'That's my business.'

Grace had been loyal no matter how badly Amos had behaved. She had threatened to 'swing for him', but she hadn't meant it. Or had she? Fear swept over Isobel. Exactly what had happened here? Just what had Kathy seen?

She said desperately, 'Mum, you always say that Dad wasn't really bad, yet I can't remember him ever being nice. We all preferred him to be out of the house.'

'Fancy speaking ill of the dead,' cried Grace. 'And him not yet buried.'

'I'm not speaking ill of him, at least I don't mean to. I just wish I understood more. You've always told us we didn't understand him. Now that he's gone can't you tell us what made him so bad? Mum, please, I should mourn him and I can't unless you give me something to go on.'

Grace sank into a chair. 'There was something driving him. I can't speak of it. Not yet. One day I may tell you.' Tremors ran through her body, her hands shook so much she clasped them together in a vain attempt to steady them. Brother and sister glanced at one another and Isobel dropped the subject.

The funeral took place beneath a blue sky in warm sunshine. As the hearse drew away and Grace was about to step into the first of the cars, she looked up and frowned as if she resented these signs of summer on a day when she consigned her husband to the ground. They had not expected anyone other than close family and were annoyed to find that sightseers hovered by the church, staring at them, talking about them. Cigarettes were lit and Isobel even heard laughter. She stared at the coffin as it lay before the altar, picturing the small, thin body of her father lying in a nest of white satin. Tears streamed down her face. Oh, God, she implored, why? Why couldn't he love me? Why did he hate me? Why didn't I have a proper father?

Grace asked to be left alone for a few minutes by the grave and Granny Shaw marched out of the churchyard and climbed into the car.

'I can't mourn for him,' she said to Isobel who followed her. 'Your mother's far better off without him. Where did all the money come from to have such a slap-up funeral with you and Desmond unemployed and that good-for-nothing Ivor not even wanting work? And Olive clinging like a limpet to her wages.'

'From insurance. Mum always kept up to date.'

'I might have guessed. Grace was always cheerful. Well, almost always,' she added reflectively.

Isobel wanted to ask what she meant, but Kathy joined them, followed by Amos's sister Martha.

Martha said, 'He got a good send-off.' She didn't speak again and they travelled back to the small house in silence. Martha demanded to be driven home immediately and the others sat down to a tea prepared by neighbours, who also served it. They tried to lighten the atmosphere. Even at funeral parties those involved usually shook off their gloom long enough to enjoy the good food and smile and talk a little, but the Kingstons were a disappointment to them.

On her way to make more tea Isobel heard two of the helpers talking. 'It's not as if he was any good,' said one to the other. 'You'd think they'd be glad to see the back of him.'

'I'd be glad to see the back of mine,' said the second woman and they had to smother their giggles.

Then Granny Shaw lit a cigarette and the neighbours were so astonished to see an old woman smoking and practically in public they almost forgot the purpose of the party.

Ralph was annoyed. 'You have jewellery of your own. Why did you wear your mother's to the Westburys'?'

'They happened to suit my clothes,' said Felice. 'What's wrong with borrowing from my own mother?'

'There might be people who remember her jewels. She has some very valuable stuff.'

'Mother called them trinkets.'

Sylvia was listening, her embroidery in her lap. 'Naturally,' she said, 'I didn't lend her any of the important pieces.

'Why not?' demanded Ralph in a complete turnabout.

'Because,' answered Sylvia in a would-be patient tone, 'all the grand stuff is in old-fashioned settings and far too overpowering for a young girl. Felice, you were happy with my choice, weren't you?'

'Yes, Mother.' Felice felt pleasure at the newly born rapport between herself and her mother. She went to her and threw her arms around her and kissed her soft cheek.

Ralph went red with temper. 'You both know I delight in buying gifts for my daughter.'

Sylvia said languidly, 'Come now, Ralph, don't sound so aggrieved. One would think we were conspiring against you.'

Her words angered him. 'In future, Felice, if your own jewel box doesn't supply your needs, you must come to me. I shall have such pleasure in taking you to the best jeweller in Bristol and helping you choose.'

'But Father, I would prefer to make my own choices.'

'Nonsense! You're far too young to know what to buy. You must look for perfection, yes, but also pay heed to the value of gems in years to come. You must think ahead.'

Felice said, 'No one need spend a lot now that costume jewellery is so much in fashion. Women even wear wooden bangles.'

'Not my daughter!' cried Ralph. 'Before you make any more visits or even go on small outings I wish to inspect the garments you propose to wear and together we shall match the jewels.'

'That's quite unnecessary,' said Sylvia. 'Felice has taste and is happy to be guided by me. And after that fearful orange frock you bought her I couldn't blame her for not trusting you.'

'Is that so?' demanded Ralph, turning a red, furious face to Felice. 'Did you dislike the lovely frock I chose for you?'

'The colour didn't quite suit me.'

'And the material was wrong too,' said Sylvia.

'You've never said so before,' said Ralph. 'Why, if you both hated it, didn't you tell me?'

Sylvia sighed. 'Because you would have been annoyed. Because you bought it without consulting us.'

'And you would have been hurt,' said Felice.

'Oh, you care about my being hurt?'

'Father, of course I do.'

'She does care about you,' agreed Sylvia. 'That doesn't mean she has to humour you when you make a mistake.'

'A mistake!' shouted Ralph. He turned to Felice. 'You're telling me that you wore a frock you hated just because I purchased it? You would prefer your mother's guidance?' All the contempt he felt for his wife was in his tone.

Felice quailed before him and, indoctrinated by the years of his domination, felt the weakening of her will.

But Sylvia, as if sensing that her daughter was at a crossroads, interrupted. 'Why should I not guide my own child?'

'You've neglected her for years. Now that she's a young lady ready for society you begin to take an interest.'

Sylvia's eyes grew dark with anger. Felice had never seen her stand up to Ralph. It occurred to her that whereas her mother was cowed when it came to fighting for herself she was different when fighting for her child. The issue seemed trivial, but Felice saw with sudden clarity that this was a fight which needed to be won if she were ever to escape Ralph's bullying. God, that was an odd word to use about one's father. He loved her too much, that was all.

'I have never neglected my child,' said Sylvia. 'Maybe I have been prevented from doing all I might. My health has been so poor.'

'Imagination!' cried Ralph. 'You've never been really ill.'

'So you say. Yet you had me put away. Twice.'

'Put away! What an expression! I had you taken to a place of safety for your own sake. You were thought to be suicidal.'

'That is untrue.'

'It *is* true. You were a danger to yourself, a danger even, at one time, to your child.'

'Lies! All lies! You persuaded the doctors. They had no real evidence that I needed restraint.'

Ralph shrugged. 'I suppose it is too much to expect you to admit you were crazy.'

'I was not, and even if I had been I could never have hurt my child. I loved her far too much. But I have had to stand by and watch you forcing her into a mould that she doesn't fit. You've almost murdered her will and that's nearly as bad as murdering her body.'

Ralph's temper erupted. He forgot Felice's presence. 'How dare you criticise me! What filth to call me a murderer of her will. I have loved Felice as a father should, while you, who should be her first protector, have abrogated all responsibility.'

'No! I have tried for her sake to minimise the quarrels between us which would have been a hundred times worse if I had not allowed you to have your way.'

'Allowed me to have my way? You sound like a melodrama

211

queen! A role fitting for you, isn't it? You've no true feelings. After all, you abandoned your son without a moment's hesitation. Who will believe that you care twopence for your daughter? The whole world knows you never loved Lawrence.'

Sylvia went so white Felice thought she might faint. She wanted to go to her, to shield her face from Ralph so that he couldn't look upon the anguish so clearly displayed. Surely Father would realise he had gone too far. But triumph was written all over him. He was glad he had thrust so deep a wound into Sylvia. Had it always been like that? Felice's thoughts were scattering round her mind so fast she couldn't catch them and make any kind of sense of them.

Sylvia said in low, vibrant tones, 'Once and for all, Ralph, I ask you to stop perpetrating such a wicked lie about me and my son. You know I begged you to speak to Mrs Dane, that I said I'd go on my knees to her for a promise of seeing my son just once a year on his birthday. You know how I've grieved. I was ill.' She touched her handkerchief to her shaking mouth. 'You know how my sorrow has wounded me. But maybe, after all, you don't know! Maybe you really can't understand how my mistakes have made me what I am. But I won't make the same mistake again. You shall not destroy Felice as you have destroyed me. Don't let him, Felice, my darling.'

Her words brought Ralph to the horrified understanding that his daughter had been a witness to the scene. For the first time she had seen the true relationship of her parents in all its ugliness. And she had heard words he had never meant her to hear.

He turned to her. His upper lip was beaded with sweat. 'You see, my love, what I have had to put up with all these years.'

'Is it true?' stammered Felice.

'Is what true?'

'That Mother begged to see Lawrence?'

'No, it is not!'

'Liar!' cried Sylvia. 'Liar!'

Her voice rang round the room, bouncing off the furniture and the high ceilings, its echoes lingering. And the truth was in it. Felice had given Ralph all the obedience he had demanded. She had even given him her love. Perhaps she loved him still. She couldn't tell. Her mind was filled with images of a young woman on her knees imploring her husband to intercede for her. She remembered Lawrence's bitterness because his mother had abandoned him without giving him a single thought. And if Ralph had lied to Sylvia, might he not also have lied to Mrs Dane and, through her, to Lawrence?

She felt suddenly sick and ran from the room. She could hear Ralph calling her back as she slammed the door of the downstairs cloakroom and bolted it before she vomited. When the paroxysm was over she leaned her head against the cool tiles of the wall. She wished she could weep, but her tears were dammed behind a barrier of horror. She knew one thing clearly; she could not remain beneath her father's roof a day longer than she must. He was a monster.

Chapter Thirteen

The Kingstons found the manner of Amos's death left them in a profound state of shock which didn't encourage clear-sightedness.

Isobel veered between relief that he would never be a menace to her little sister and sorrow at the waste. She was worried about Grace and Kathy. It was natural that Grace should feel grief at the death of a husband she seemed to have loved in spite of all his faults, but why did Kathy still look so haunted?

'Don't worry,' Desmond said. 'It's not easy at her age to meet death in any form. Remember how she wept when her kitten got out and was killed by the bread cart?'

'I remember,' said Isobel. 'But death is natural and inevitable and she accepted that.' She took Kathy to the cinema every week, scraping together the price of two tickets; she went walking with her, carrying a picnic, sometimes persuading Grace to come with them. She went to bed early with Kathy and told her stories to help her sleep, she bought her comic magazines, she tried everything to ease Kathy's suffering and the child began to eat more. But she still had bad dreams.

Olive and Ivor appeared unmoved by their father's death, except when it came to money. They scarcely missed Amos's dole because he had hung on to it, but the sudden loss of Desmond's and Isobel's wages was a blow.

When Olive was asked for more money she screamed, 'I work damned hard for it and I'm keeping it. It's mine!'

'Selfish pig!' yelled Kathy and burst into tears.

'Now see what you've done,' cried Grace. 'As if she wasn't upset enough.'

'I can't help it if the little idiot gets upset because our horrible father pegs it.'

Kathy shrank back, crossing her arms and clutching her shoulders if they were a lifeline.

'Leave Kathy out of this,' said Desmond. 'Olive, you must help out. Mum can't buy food without cash and you still eat here.'

Olive sulked but she produced an extra half-crown a week.

Some of Isobel's cleaning jobs ended and she couldn't get more work. Desmond had no luck at all. He joined one of the hiking societies which were springing up everywhere and went on long walks, taking only bread, cheese and water with him.

'He'll lose his strength,' moaned Grace. 'A man needs more sustenance than that.'

'Bread and cheese are very good for him,' said Isobel, 'and he looks fit and well.'

Grace herself looked far from well and Kathy's vitality was slowly draining from her. Isobel lay wakeful at night, wondering how she could help. She had tried everything she knew and could only fall back upon the old adage that time would heal.

When Desmond returned from his latest hike he looked excited. 'I've had a marvellous idea. One of the fellows left his sandwiches behind. We all shared with him, but I suddenly realised there was nowhere for anyone to buy food. Today was hot for once and I finished my water and longed for a drink. Of course all the pubs were closed for the afternoon and there wasn't anywhere else. I shall set up in business on my own.'

'So will I,' said Isobel drily. 'What shall we be? I'll buy a shop and sell corsets and you open a restaurant.'

Desmond didn't laugh. 'I'm serious, sis. One of my mates told me that a few enterprising people are opening little tearooms by the side of the road. There are tons of cars these days, now that they're not so expensive, and people go driving for pleasure.'

Isobel looked at him as if he had lost his mind. 'Open a tearoom? But how? You need capital. You need a roof. You need supplies. You need – I hardly know what you need, a stove, chairs and tables – everything. It's impossible.'

'No it isn't. And I needn't begin with all those fancy things.'

'In a tearoom,' Isobel pointed out gently, 'chairs and tables and a roof are not considered fancy things.'

Desmond grinned. 'I admit I don't have much, but what I have got is a mother and sisters who can cook. I thought that if I could find a tent I could borrow stuff and you and Mum and Kathy could bake. We've still got the old Primus stove we bought when we used to go for our picnics.'

He fell silent and Isobel remembered the days when life was easier and Dad had sometimes had spells of good humour.

Desmond shook himself free of memory. 'I know a man who sells seconds china really cheap. I could do it, Isobel, I know I could.'

The way Desmond spoke made his scheme sound plausible. She thought of a snag. 'It rains in Britain. Even in summer we get showers, as you've probably noticed.'

'Of course, I've not forgotten that, but a tent should be water-proof. We could have an awning where customers could shelter from the weather yet still enjoy country air. A cup of tea and a home-made cake is just what people on a summer outing could do with. I need your help. In fact, I need the help of the whole family.'

'Olive and Ivor won't lift a finger,' said Isobel gloomily.

'I know, but you and the others will. It might take Mum and Kathy out of themselves. They're both looking very peaky.'

That was the best argument he could have used. 'They need some-thing, that's for sure. I'm so worried about them.'

'People need time to grieve. They'll gradually feel better.'

'I feel guilty for not caring more about what happened,' said Isobel. 'Whatever he was he was still my father.' She fell into a reverie. 'Desmond,' she went on abruptly, 'do you remember all the times Dad hinted that there was something odd about me?' She hesitated. 'I don't know quite how to put it but—'

'But he was more against you than the others. He kept venting his rage on you.'

'That's right. He hinted at something in Mum's past.' The memory of Amos's hot hands as they roamed over her body and his hot, foul, sickening breath assailed her like a blow. He was dead now and she must put it behind her and never let anyone know just how vile her father had been. 'Oh, well,' she said weakly, 'I suppose it was only his way. He enjoyed upsetting me.'

Grace seized upon Desmond's idea with passionate fervour. 'I'll help you any way you ask,' she said. 'It'll be lovely to have some-thing different to do.'

'Not so different,' said Desmond. 'You'll be baking a lot.'

'Yes, but fancy things, not just sausage and mash and stews. Your father loved stews. He complained about them, but he really loved them.' Her mouth quivered.

Desmond said, 'I bet Dad would be proud of us if he could see how we were coping.'

Grace smiled. 'Yes, he would. Perhaps he *can* see. His troubles are over for him. Poor man.'

Olive was smoking and reading a magazine by the kitchen fire

217

which had been lit against the cool damp after a day of rain. 'Poor man? All he did was make other people miserable.'

'You shouldn't speak ill of the dead,' said Grace.

'Why not? Dying doesn't turn them into saints.'

Desmond intervened. 'Will you give a hand at baking?'

'Yes, do, Olive,' urged Grace. 'You were good at it at school. And I remember when you were small how you loved to roll out bits of pastry and make small pies for your dolls and—'

'Can't I have a bit of peace to read?' cried Olive. 'I'd sit in the front room if it wasn't so bloody cold in there.'

'No need to swear,' said Grace.

'Dad swore all the time. You never told him off.'

Desmond glared at his sister. 'Olive obviously wants no part in it,' he said. 'Now, Mum, let's do some planning.'

Ralph fled to Dulcia, who received him in her usual placid way. 'You're so restful,' he said, leaning back on the sofa and sipping his drink. 'My home is in turmoil. Sylvia argues all the time. Felice has become impossible. It's her mother's fault. I thought for a while Felice might actually leave home though I knew she couldn't bear to leave me. And where would she go?'

'To friends?' suggested Dulcia, sinking down beside Ralph.

'Felice's only true friend, Lady Betty Westbury, has accepted a proposal of marriage and is busy preparing for her wedding, so she couldn't run there.'

Ralph finished his drink and Dulcia poured him another. He drank it slowly, thinking uneasily of his daughter. The situation was far more serious than he had painted it. Felice's suspicious anger was still hot since that terrible scene with Sylvia. She spoke to him only when it was necessary. She accepted every invitation that arrived, apparently glad to get out of the house, discussing what she should wear with her mother, leaving him out.

'She doesn't love me any more,' he wailed.

Dulcia started. 'Sylvia? But I thought you knew that.'

'Felice. My beautiful Felice. Dulcia, I want to give her everything.'

'I know. Why has she turned against you? I thought she was devoted to you and so obedient. What has happened?'

'Sylvia told her a cock-and-bull story. She blames me because Lawrence is cold towards her. He visits me, as you know. He is very fond of me, as I am of him.'

'It's a weird situation,' said Dulcia.

'Weird? What do you mean?' Ralph spoke sharply to his mistress for the first time and her heavy, unplucked eyebrows rose in displeasure.

He hastened to placate her. 'I'm sorry, darling. Sylvia gets me so rattled and there's this business with Felice – What is it you find weird?'

'I can understand your position, the divorce, Lawrence's anger with his mother. I couldn't have cut my ties with my children under any circumstances, but I don't condemn people for doing something I find puzzling. What I find really odd is the way you care for Lawrence. One would think he was your son. He isn't, is he? You didn't begin your affair with his mother much earlier than everyone supposed, did you?'

'No, but I wish I had and that Lawrence was mine. He's the son I never had,' blurted Ralph. 'The son she couldn't give me. And I must have an heir. I have so much to leave to a worthy successor. The factory, the shop, money, shares, financial interests in many things. So much.'

'But surely you will make Felice your heir. She is your only child.'

'I shall leave her amply provided for. Sylvia too if I go before her. But it takes a man to run a business like mine.'

Dulcia said, 'If you gave Felice a chance she might surprise you.'

'No, no, she wouldn't. She's not strong, you know, either physically or emotionally. I'm afraid she takes too much after her mother. She doesn't have my willpower.'

'She seems to be proving stronger than you supposed if she is able to resist you.'

Ralph controlled his terror as he remembered that Felice knew he had lied to Sylvia about Lawrence. 'She will come back to me. Sylvia will get tired of this nonsense and sink back into her usual gloom.'

'Maybe.' Dulcia laughed. 'You dislike any form of criticism, don't you?'

'I can't bear it, certainly not from you.'

'You look upon me as a refuge?'

'Yes, an adorable, uncritical, loving refuge. Do you mind?'

'Not at all. Though I don't agree with your assessment of women. We can be stronger than men when it's necessary.'

Ralph couldn't bear to spoil his visit to Dulcia by arguing with her. 'Come closer, won't you?' He slid his arm about her waist. 'I must make love to you,' he said. 'Now! In your arms I can forget my problems.'

After Grace's initial enthusiasm she was struck by doubts. 'I don't see how Desmond can have a tearoom, Isobel. And it'll have to be a fair way from town to catch the passing trade.'

She voiced her doubts to Desmond, who was patient. 'Leave it to me, Mum. I've made a start.'

'What have you done?' asked Kathy.

Her brother smiled at her. 'A fellow in the hiking club says he'll lend me a frame tent with an awning and the tent pegs and a mallet. That takes care of the premises for now.'

Ivor was listening. 'Premises? Don't make me laugh.'

'If you'd get off your lazy backside and come and see what I'm doing you might feel like helping,' said Desmond.

'Huh! There are quicker ways of making money than that.'

'What do you mean?' asked Isobel sharply.

Ivor touched the side of his nose. 'Just you wait and see. I'll surprise you all.' They watched him as he meandered out.

'He's got a new shirt and shoes,' said Grace.

'He probably gets them from a jumble sale or a second-hand clothing shop,' said Isobel. 'Remember that good blouse I bought for twopence at the church sale? Not a mark on it.'

'That's true,' said Grace, looking relieved.

Once Desmond had decided what to do his natural energetic enthusiasm took over. He canvassed his friends. One produced a large ground sheet. Several persuaded their families to lend furniture and crockery.

'If determination doesn't make this work, then nothing will,' said Isobel.

Meals in the Kingston household became very plain and simple as Grace spent money on ingredients for fancy food to sell. The activity seemed to lighten her load of grief. Kathy, too, looked better and was glad to help when she came back from school.

Isobel still worried about her. 'She should play sometimes, Mum,' she said. 'All work isn't good for any child.'

'I know. She prefers to stay at home.'

'She's taken Dad's death hard.'

Grace pounded away with her wooden spoon, reducing the margarine and sugar in the bowl to cream. Isobel watched her for a while. Her mother's face revealed the desperate misery she felt.

Isobel went out to the garden where Desmond was scrubbing the awning. Her heart expanded with love for him.

Desmond looked up. 'Hello, sis. How's the baking? I reckon we'll be on the road in a couple of days.'

'It's coming along fine. Where will you pitch your tent, oh master?'

'There's a farmer about five miles down the Bath road who says I can use a bit of his ground. For a fair rent naturally.'

'Naturally. What's a fair rent?'

'He says seven shillings a week.'

Isobel was shaken. 'It seems steep for a bit of ground. We'll have to sell a lot of cakes and scones to cover that.'

Grace had been on the borrow as well and neighbours had contributed baking tins, and containers which would keep the food fresh and clean.

When Isobel returned to the kitchen Kathy looked up and smiled, the first smile that had reached her eyes since the day of Amos's death. 'Come on, Isobel. You've got to help. I've just found another recipe in Mum's old book and I want to try it. Meringue. It's a funny word, isn't it? Have you ever tasted them. They need hardly any cooking. Mum says if we leave them on the side of the range after we've gone to bed they'll set. Then we can put things on them. Cream and chocolate and stuff. And the best of it is we only need egg whites and can use the yolks in our mashed potato. They'll do us good, she says.' Kathy was beating white of egg, her face flushed with her efforts and the heat of the fire.

Grace said worriedly, 'Do you think we ought to make savouries? The trouble is we can't use anything that won't keep. The weather's got close. I think we're in for thunder.'

'Cheese scones,' said Isobel. 'I'll get a lump of mousetrap and make them.'

The following Saturday, Desmond's friend Owen turned up at six in the morning driving a decrepit van and he and Desmond loaded up. The van seemed packed to capacity but Isobel and Kathy squeezed in and Grace waved them off, smiling, through a glint of tears.

The sun shone through the clouds like an omen of good fortune. By eight o'clock they were ready for trade. By twelve o'clock they had supplied lemonade to a passing farm labourer and a bag of cakes to a couple of schoolboys on a bike ride. Owen stayed with them. He was a cheery Welshman who rallied them when they became downhearted. 'They'll be along this afternoon,' he prophesied. 'That's when they come out for a picnic.'

'But they'll bring all their food with them,' said Kathy.

'Not they! And if they do how could they resist this lovely grub?' He munched on a buttered cheese scone and sampled a meringue. Knowing that fresh cream was impossible in the circumstances Isobel had sandwiched them with mock cream made with butter, cornflour and cocoa.

After lunch, as Owen had promised, the cars began to appear. Some shot by, but others stopped and the food began to disappear. Kathy was pink with pleasure as she carefully counted out change. Two cars even stopped on their return journey. 'It's worth travelling this road just to taste the food,' declared the plump mother who handed out chocolate meringues to her several children and seemed oblivious of the brown stains that were rapidly spreading over their faces and clothes. 'I'll tell my friends about you.' The Primus was now going constantly for washing-up water and the farmer's wife was kind enough to permit them to fill their large kettle in the yard.

At about half past three there was a lull and the vendors, weary from early rising, were sitting down to refresh themselves. 'If this goes on,' said Kathy, 'we'll have to bake every day.'

Desmond looked anxious. 'Will you mind?'

'No fear. I think it's wonderful. Fancy us owning a café.'

Desmond smiled over her head at Isobel. She turned from him as a car drew up and she saw that the driver was Lawrence Dane. She was furious. Why couldn't he have come when they had a full house and not when they were sitting amid a debris of crumbs?

Not for worlds would Isobel let him see how chagrined she felt. He climbed out of the car and looked around. Kathy jumped up and began to tidy up, sweeping the crumbs with a damp handbrush and ostentatiously plopping more used crockery and cutlery into the steaming water.

'Can I get you something?' asked Isobel, feeling embarrassed as she remembered the last time they had met. He had kissed her and she had enjoyed it.

Lawrence said, 'I say, this is very enterprising. And the food looks delicious. I'm very fond of scones.'

'Sweet or savoury?' asked Isobel coolly.

'Both.'

'Which would you like first?'

222

'Savoury, please, and lots of butter. And a cup of tea.' He munched his cheese scone without a trace of embarrassment, seated on a rather wobbly chair at an equally wobbly table because the ground was lower on one side than the other. Isobel hadn't really been aware of these imperfections before. 'Now I'll try a sweet scone. Lots of butter as before and a little jam. You do have jam, don't you?'

'Yes. My mother's own make.'

'Delicious,' he declared, wiping his mouth with his handkerchief, reminding Isobel to provide paper napkins.

Lawrence was in no hurry to leave. Desmond cleared his table while Kathy plunged her hands into the hot soda-laced water again. 'This is very enterprising of you,' Lawrence said to Desmond.

'Thanks.' Desmond was polite, but unwilling to chat to someone connected with the family who had treated him so unjustly.

'I am sorry for what happened,' said Lawrence.

'Are you?'

Lawrence persisted. 'I don't think your dismissal was fair, but I have no power in the factory.'

Desmond frowned. 'I see. Thank you.'

Kathy realised for the first time that the imposing customer with the big posh car had something to do with her beloved sister's and brother's loss of employment and left her washing-up to scowl at him.

'If you don't mind my saying so,' said Lawrence to her, 'making faces at the customers is not likely to help business along.'

Isobel glanced at Kathy and an involuntary laugh escaped her.

'Did you make the delicious food?' asked Lawrence.

'Some of it. My mother has been very busy and Kathy helped a lot.' She laid her hand on her sister's shoulder.

'How do you do, Kathy?' said Lawrence, smiling and holding out his hand. She stared at it for a moment then shyly held out hers and he shook it. 'What did you make?'

'The little currant cakes and the ones with pink icing.'

'On your own?'

'Yes.'

'How clever of you! I must try one of each, please.' He ate them with every evidence of enjoyment.

Another car stopped and disgorged another plump mother, father and three even plumper and obnoxiously noisy and ill-behaved children who pushed and shoved each other and whined for cakes.

The mother demanded rather than asked for service and when Kathy hurried to her stared at her belligerently. 'Ask the proper waitress to serve us.'

Kathy, pink-faced, retired and Isobel attended the family, who asked for a sample of everything that was left, chewed it loudly and pronounced it not as good as some they had eaten. The boy said, 'These currant cakes look like they're full of flies,' at which his family laughed uproariously. Kathy flushed and turned away. Isobel cursed them. For almost a whole day the haunted look had left Kathy's face and she had been happy.

Lawrence had been watching the performance with distaste written clearly all over him. He said distinctly, 'Could someone bring me more of those absolutely delightful small cakes? I'll have two with currants and another with the pink icing.'

The noisy family fell silent. They couldn't have helped noticing his expensive car and his cultured voice.

The mother cried, 'Arthur, the cakes are lovely. I don't know why you want to go and run them down.'

'You laughed,' said Arthur sullenly.

'Rubbish. Go and get another plateful.'

Kathy's face was alight with pleasure as she served Lawrence, and Isobel wanted to kiss him. She watched him covertly as he forced himself to eat the cakes which he hadn't wanted and had to turn away and grin when he ascertained that Kathy was well occupied then slipped a couple into his handkerchief which he stuffed into his pocket.

He asked for his bill. Kathy made it out on a sheet of their small writing pad and handed it to him. He paid her solemnly, handing her a tip. Kathy stared at it open-mouthed. She walked waveringly to her sister. 'Five shillings,' she mouthed. She made to put it into the cocoa tin standing in for a till, but Isobel stopped her. 'You've earned it, my love. Your first tip is all yours.'

Lawrence had risen to his feet when the rain which had been threatening began to fall in large, heavy drops. Then there was a flash of lightning and a crash of thunder at which the plump woman screamed. 'It's right overhead. This horrible tent is no protection. Quick, back into the car.'

Isobel was about to assure her that the tent was waterproof when it became clear that Desmond's friend had been optimistic about its ability to keep out rain. For a few moments the leaks were minor, then they increased until rain poured through almost as gushingly as outside.

The mother hurried her brood to the car crying, 'Don't pay the bill, Dad. We're all soaked. Arthur's suit'll never be the same. His best one too. Hurry up.'

Her husband reluctantly paid what was asked. 'Rotten place you've got here,' he muttered. 'I'll not recommend it to my friends.'

Isobel thought fleetingly, If they're all like you I wouldn't want you to. She hurried to put the food into containers and run with them to the old van parked in the field. That was when she discovered that its roof was also leaking. It's like a Chaplin film, she thought, or Laurel and Hardy, and began to laugh. She turned and almost collided with Lawrence who had his arms full of cake tins which he stowed away in the back of the van. Rain was streaming down his face, his hair was plastered to his head and she was equally wet. She wondered what was happening to the cakes in his pocket and giggled helplessly.

He straightened up, stared at her, then dragged her into his arms and his mouth came down on hers. She forgot the rain, the cakes, the abysmal end to the first day of their venture and kissed him back with all the strength of her passionate nature.

He broke away gasping. 'My God! How you can kiss! Isobel—'

Then Desmond appeared with the Primus stove, held gingerly because it was still hot, followed by Owen who was apologising for his leaky vehicle.

Isobel scarcely heard him. She was overcome with the realisation that Lawrence Dane's kiss had released sensations that must have been simmering for a long while.

They hurried to load the rest of the stuff, as absorbed as if life depended on haste.

Desmond thanked Lawrence fervently.

'I was glad to help,' he replied. 'I'm sorry that the rain spoilt your day. But you won't give up, will you?' He sounded genuinely concerned.

'I'll not give up,' said Desmond grimly, 'but I'll have to think about better premises.'

Lawrence said, 'By God, I admire your guts. Yours and your sisters' and your friend's. Is he unemployed too?'

'He manages to get carrier work sometimes. He gets by.'

It wasn't until then that Lawrence remembered he had left the hood of his car down. The interior was swimming with water. Normally he would have cursed. Today, it didn't seem to matter. With Desmond's help he brushed out the worst of the rain and got in. Isobel saw him grimace. He had also forgotten the cakes in his

225

pocket. He caught Isobel's smile and guessed that she had seen him hide them. He grinned, then climbed back out. 'I almost forgot. The wet canvas will be terribly heavy. I'll help with it before I go.' The three men lit cigarettes and smoked in companionable silence until the storm died, then they manhandled the tent into folds and with an immense effort packed it into the van.

Finally Lawrence left. Isobel wished she could have gone with him. She wanted to kiss him until they were both on fire. She had never felt like this with Frank. Was it love she felt for Lawrence, or desire? She was bewildered.

The creaky van smelt of damp clothing, but Kathy was still elated. 'People came. He left five shillings for a tip. The others only left pennies and not many did that,' she chattered disjointedly. 'Can I come again tomorrow, Desmond?'

'If we can do it again tomorrow,' said Desmond. He was tired and somewhat disheartened. The weather was poor and folk had a right to expect dry shelter.

'Oh, please, Desmond, it was so lovely today.'

Desmond looked at his small sister affectionately. 'We'll manage it, my love. Don't you worry about it.'

'You'll need more food, won't you?' said Kathy. 'I'll bake tonight. We'll bake together, won't we, Isobel? Was much spoilt by the rain?'

'Not too much, my sweet, and we'll certainly bake tonight.'

'Mr Dane is really nice, isn't he? He wasn't the one that made you and Desmond lose your jobs, was he?'

'No,' said Isobel firmly, 'it wasn't him.'

Kathy sighed happily.

Lawrence Dane drove home. He was soaked and uncomfortable and the sodden cakes were squashy against his hip. His car would have to be thoroughly dried out and cleaned, his tweed jacket was probably ruined and he had broken an appointment he'd made with a man who wanted to sell him the sweetest filly he'd ever handled. He knew that others were after her and he'd probably lost her, yet nothing seemed important beside the memory of the kiss in the rain. He tried to reason himself out of his euphoric state. Isobel Kingston wasn't beautiful. She was too short, too muscular, and she was altogether too damned independent. She had been a factory girl. Probably still was at heart. But other pictures presented themselves. Isobel, hard at work in the upper room. Isobel, risking her prospects to stand up for someone weaker than herself. Isobel, abandoned by the women she had trusted. Isobel, taking her dismissal proudly and diving in to help her brother. Lawrence wanted her. He wanted to hold that short, strong body in his arms, to strip her, to make love to her. He wanted her more than anything he had wanted in his life. How could he find a way to make love to her?

He arrived home and handed over his car to an astonished stable-boy to drive under cover. Then he went in and straight to his grand-mother as he had always done.

'Sorry, Gran,' he said. 'I got caught with my hood down.'

'That's not like you. Was there something wrong with it?'

'No, I just didn't put it up. I'd better change. I'm pretty wet.'

'So I see. I think your jacket may figure in the next church jumble sale. If it's good enough, that is.'

He grinned at her. Downstairs again he drank tea, but refused food. His grandmother liked to hear of his activities, not because she was a busybody – far from it – but because she loved him so much. She wondered if Sylvia ever regretted rejecting him now that she could see what a splendid young man he was. But a woman cold enough to disown her own infant must have a heart of stone.

She realised he was watching her with affectionate amusement. 'You're dreaming, Gran.'

'Sorry. My thoughts tend to wander sometimes. I think it must be old age.'

'Nonsense! You will never be old.'

Lawrence told her about the roadside tea tent and made her laugh at the ghastly family which had turned up and been drenched by the rain. He spoke of the courage of Desmond and his sisters.

She bent forward, listening intently as he explained why Ralph had dismissed Isobel and Desmond Kingston. He described the corset show as it had been told to him by Felice. And whenever he mentioned Isobel his grandmother detected a note in his voice she had never heard before. She lived much out of society but she had friends who kept her up to date. She knew he took his pleasure where it was offered, but only with experienced women. Lawrence, although he might not realise it, was attracted to this girl. She thought of all the families where he would be welcome to court a daughter, the many suitable girls who coveted his attentions, and she sighed, wondering if he had after all inherited some of his mother's irresponsibility. Thinking of Sylvia made her angry. No wonder Law-rence couldn't forgive her. Mrs Dane could never forget the small boy's bitter tears at the abrupt loss of his mother. Ralph had been so

227

understanding, carrying messages to and fro, trying to persuade Sylvia to lower her resistance, but he'd failed. Lawrence seemed to have recovered from Sylvia's cruelty, but one never knew.

Felice was finding life unbearable under her father's roof. He refused to take her seriously. He brought home gifts, showering her with precious gems and buying her quantities of the costume jewellery so much in vogue. He increased her allowance so that she could purchase clothes, concealing his annoyance when Sylvia accompanied their daughter to choose another fashionable outfit.

Sylvia's behaviour bothered Ralph. After the years of his domination she had gained courage from somewhere. He tried all his old methods of intimidating her. Only if she was weakened by a severe headache could he make an impression on her.

Felice had previously seen her mother through his eyes as a weak hypochondriac; now she appeared to regard her as someone to be cared for. He wondered if Felice confided in Sylvia. He burned with anger. He had looked forward to Felice's entry into society with pleasure, anticipating her confidences in him. She was so pretty there must be plenty of young men who desired her, though the idea of his daughter in love was a subject he turned from. It would happen one day, but far into the future. Girls were getting married later these days. He had pictured himself listening to her accounts of parties and the latest man who had fallen under her spell, but always he had imagined their shared laughter. Then one day she would tell him of some wealthy, well-born man who wished to marry her and he would give his gracious consent.

This evening he was delighted to discover that Felice was not going out. She had been staying with the Westburys, where she had been one of the bridesmaids at Betty's wedding, photographed and listed in all the society magazines. She had returned home bubbling over with the pleasure of the event, but gradually her joy had subsided, leaving her wan and listless.

The three of them sat at dinner and Ralph said, 'We shall have to do something to cheer you up, Felice.'

'Life always seems flat after a grand event. You'll soon recover,' said Sylvia.

'Trust you to trivialise her feelings,' snapped Ralph, forgetting that he had vowed to be polite to his wife while Felice was present.

'I do no such thing,' said Sylvia. Her voice was quiet but controlled; her hands were steady. Ralph fumed inwardly. Her protective attitude towards her daughter had imbued her with strength.

Sylvia said to Felice, 'Is there an outing you would like, dear? I should be happy to accompany you. Perhaps a holiday somewhere sunny. This summer is terrible. So cold and wet.'

For the first time in her life Felice saw a way of contriving to get something she craved. 'There's only one thing that would make me feel better and that's my own motor car.'

Ralph opened his mouth to make the customary protest, then closed it. A car might bring Felice close to him again, but he still hated the idea. 'I wish you wouldn't press the point,' he said. 'You may have the chauffeur any time you like.'

'It isn't the same, Father.'

'No, of course not. Well, perhaps I've been too cautious. You shall have a nice little model which will be easy to drive.'

Felice's face lit up and Ralph congratulated himself. Then she turned to Sylvia. 'Mother, will you come and help me choose?'

'Of course I will.'

Ralph waited for Felice to ask him to accompany them. Sylvia said, 'Stratton can drive us round the showrooms.'

Ralph raised his wine glass to his lips, but he didn't drink. He looked at Sylvia and hatred consumed him.

Kathy ran into the house, pink with excitement. 'There's a man outside in a *huge* van. He says he's got something for *me*. Miss Kathy Kingston the label says. It's an enormous parcel. I can't think what it can be.'

Isobel got up. If a parcel could banish that awful look in the depths of her little sister's eyes for a while she wouldn't mind if someone had sent her an elephant.

Outside, two men leaned on the van, smoking. Neighbours were peering from front doors and windows. 'A parcel for Miss Kathy Kingston,' said the older man, carefully stubbing out his cigarette and putting the stub behind his ear.

'This is it, miss,' said the younger man, jumping into the back of the van. 'If you'll just show us where to put it and sign this chit.'

'We haven't bought anything,' said Isobel.

'Can't help that,' said the older man. 'All we do is deliver parcels to the addresses on the labels.'

Isobel leapt nimbly into the van. 'It says paid.'

'That's right, miss.'

'I suppose you'd better take it in.'

229

'Shall we put it in the garden?'

'I don't know. Why the garden?'

'You ain't thinking of putting up a tent in the house, are you?'

'A tent, a tent,' squealed Kathy, jumping up and down.

Isobel and Grace watched as the men carried the heavy parcel through to the garden. The ground was damp after heavy rain and Isobel directed the men to the washhouse where they dropped their load.

'Could Miss Kathy Kingston sign?' asked the older man.

Kathy seized his pen and scribbled her signature, rendering it almost indecipherable in her haste.

She began to tear at the paper to reveal the heavy canvas of a green tent. Poles fell out and tent pegs and Kathy lifted a large mallet. 'It's got everything!'

Desmond had been to the labour exchange. When he returned he went to the washhouse and stared down in amazement. 'A tent?' He bent and fingered the material. 'It's a beauty. Only tropical rain could get through that. Where did it come from? You didn't order it, did you?' he demanded of Isobel.

'Do you think I've lost my mind? It's Kathy's.'

'Yes, it's mine,' cried Kathy.

'But how?'

'Who could have sent it?' asked Grace.

Desmond said, 'Let's try it out. My mate's inside. Owen,' he yelled. 'Come out here.'

Owen had got less and less carrier work in his dilapidated old van and he was ready to throw in his lot with the Kingstons. He and Desmond worked out the tent poles and at last it stood, clean and beautiful, in the garden. Neighbours had by now discovered that something interesting was happening at the back and had migrated to their adjoining gardens to watch the fun. They broke into a spontaneous round of applause and Desmond bowed.

Kathy was flushed, overexcited. 'Where did it come from? Who do we know who could buy a wonderful tent and send it to me?'

There was a thunderous banging on the front door. Isobel hurried to answer. Outside stood the van driver. 'You all gone deaf in there? I've been knocking. Here's a letter what I was supposed to give you.' He handed her a heavy cream envelope and left.

It was addressed to Kathy, who turned it over and over. 'Well, open it, do,' cried Grace.

Kathy slit the top and read the note aloud. 'To my new friend

Kathy. This is for your next birthday. Please do me the honour of accepting it. I look forward to visiting your tearoom again and enjoying some of your delicious cakes. Yours sincerely, Lawrence Dane.'

Chapter Fourteen

'It's from that man who likes my cakes,' cried Kathy, dancing with excitement. 'He came again the day you stayed at home to help Mum and it rained again, remember? He helped us just like last time, only he remembered to put up his car hood. What a wonderful present! Now we'll never get wet when it rains. It'll be so cosy.'

Isobel had a sudden powerful aversion to taking such a – to them – costly gift from anyone connected with Bennyson's. 'Kathy, my love, we can't take it,' she said.

There was a chorus of protest. 'Can't take it?' cried Kathy. 'Whatever do you mean?'

'Yes, what *do* you mean?' asked Grace.

'We can't take such an expensive present from a man who's nothing to us.'

'He's a friend,' said Desmond.

'The money's nothing to him,' cried Grace.

'Exactly. He's treating us as paupers, the rich man patronising the poor! We'll send the damn tent back and he can pay the carrier.'

'We'll do no such thing,' said Desmond. 'The gift isn't ours anyway, it's Kathy's. And it's for her birthday.'

Kathy let out a great sigh of relief as she sensed that Isobel was defeated.

Isobel stared round at the faces regarding her with astonished hostility. She would never make them understand. She scarcely understood herself. She was a mix of bewildering emotions. She didn't want to feel beholden to Lawrence Dane, yet the memory of that deep passionate kiss in the rain stayed with her every moment. Sometimes she longed for more; sometimes she resented it. And deep down she was grateful for the gift of the tent. She had walked to the end of the long, scrappy garden where Desmond joined her. 'I know how you feel, Isobel, but don't spoil Kathy's pleasure.'

She jerked her arm from his. 'How do you know how I feel?'

233

Desmond's eyebrows rose. 'Is there something you're not telling me?'

'If the rest of you are on his side,' she said, 'I'll have to give in. But I dislike being under an obligation to any member of the family who sacked us so unfairly.'

'But he isn't a member of the Bennyson family. He's a Dane and his father was a Dane.'

'His mother's a Bennyson.'

'Come on, Isobel, everyone knows she had Lawrence by her first husband before she married Ralph Bennyson.'

'I don't know how she could bring herself to marry such a cold-hearted creature, especially when she'd had a good man. I've heard the talk of their scandalous divorce and how her first husband killed himself out of grief. She can't be a very nice woman.'

'That has nothing to do with his gift and nothing to do with us, either. Kathy will accept it in the spirit he gave it. I can't help thinking he must be a nice chap.'

'A nice chap! Have you forgotten the snooty way he used to ignore us whenever he came to the factory?'

'I haven't forgotten, but I've seen a very different side of him since.'

'It's a pity he didn't show that side of himself to us before. He might have spoken up for us, and as Ralph Bennyson seems to think Lawrence is marvellous he'd probably have listened and we'd have kept our jobs.'

'You've no guarantee of any of that. Come on, Isobel, love, forget your feelings and congratulate Kathy.'

Isobel walked back and smiled at Kathy and said, 'Sorry, love, I was being a bit hasty. Mr Dane is very kind to have thought of you.'

Kathy's face cleared like magic. 'Thanks, Isobel. Mr Dane remembers the times we got rained out. Oh, he was so funny the day you weren't there. He rushed about with boxes of cakes and things and pretended to wipe the sweat off his face, but it was really rain. I wish he'd come more often.'

'I expect he'll be along to view the new tea tent,' said Desmond.

'I can thank him properly then. Isobel, Mum says I should write him a note, but I can't think of what to say. It's such an amazing present. Will you help me?'

'Of course I will. Do you really think he'll come again, Desmond? His first visits weren't exactly uneventful, were they? His clothes ruined and his car needing a good clean-up.'

234

'They were lovely,' cried Kathy. 'I wish he'd come again.'

So do I, thought Isobel. I wish I could see a great deal more of him. She crushed the stupid idea. Just because a rich man flirted with her she wasn't going to make the mistake of believing he was smitten. And what good did a factory girl ever get out of a rich man? Some got babies, some got money and an easy life until they were dropped. That wasn't for her.

They left the new tent up in the garden to test it. It was spacious and as smart as paint, its various metal pieces strong. And there were two struts which could be put in place to brace it against strong wind.

Desmond produced a board on which was painted in large letters, 'Kathy's Tearoom'. Kathy was pink-cheeked and wild with delight and when Isobel carried out a tray of tea and buns the child felt her cup of joy was full and for a while the lost, sad look left her eyes. Grace too smiled, but sadly, emotion keeping her cruelly imprisoned.

The new tent was put up in the field and was an immediate financial success, and they began to make a profit. Small, but enough to compensate Owen for the use of his van and leave enough over for Mum's housekeeping and small treats. Pleasure-motorists who tried valiantly to enjoy themselves outdoors even during that cold, wet summer were especially delighted to come upon a tent made cosy by the constantly burning camping stove and a warm welcome from smiling young people. Tea and sandwiches, scones and cakes vanished and the money came in. When Owen found a job in Devon and reluctantly drove off in his van, the sympathetic farmer permitted them to leave the tent up overnight, promising to keep an eye on it and allowing them to store their stuff in a barn. Between them the family raised the cash for a very tattered second-hand car which went at a snail's pace and needed water in the radiator every few miles. But they were independent and mobile.

Felice couldn't regain the old companionship with her father. Sylvia's voice echoed constantly in her head as it cried out her own terrible truth: 'Liar! Liar!'

Felice longed to know exactly what had happened to Sylvia in the past. After her outburst she had changed the subject of any conversation which touched on the emotional too nearly. Ralph was unapproachable and Felice realised for the first time that he always had been. His insistence on making himself a large part of her life, his pride in keeping her by his side had fooled her into believing that she had a warm relationship with him, but it had not been warm at all. It had been one of domination and submission. She wished sometimes that her eyes had not been opened and she missed the blinkered happiness she'd lost. She could no longer close her mind to the bitter hostility which existed between her parents and daily it pained her. And she could never forget the fact that her father had lied cruelly to her mother. Mrs Dane had never wanted the separation of mother and son. When Felice saw Lawrence she agonised over whether or not to tell him what she had learned, that his mother had always longed for him. But she found herself floundering in a quagmire of doubt. The truth might devastate him. When should truth be told and when withheld? She watched her father surreptitiously, wondering what motivated him. One afternoon when Sylvia was recovering from a headache they had just finished lunch and she watched him as he prepared an apple, the red peel coming away in a long unbroken strip, leaving the exposed juicy whiteness of the fruit. He concentrated as if nothing in the world mattered except the long red curling piece of apple peel. When he had finished he looked up and said as casually as he could, 'Your mother has not been able to take you car-hunting yet. One of her headaches . . .'

'Migraine,' supplied Felice. She had tended her mother and understood now how Sylvia suffered.

'Yes, one of her famous headaches.' Ralph glanced up in time to see the look of distaste which passed over his daughter's face. 'Poor Mother,' he said unconvincingly. 'May I be permitted to help you choose? Sometimes it takes quite a time for your mother to recover. I dare say you are anxious to have your own vehicle.'

Felice couldn't deny it.

'I think an Austin Seven would suit you. You were so happy to ride in Lady Betty's.'

Felice felt annoyed. The very last thing she wanted was to copy Betty in any way. It was such a pretentious way to behave. Betty, good-natured and wrapped up in her happiness, might not notice, but others would.

'I don't have to copy Betty.'

'No, no, of course not, but it is such an easy car to drive and manoeuvre.'

Felice, who was a little nervous at the idea of driving, said nothing.

'I may as well confess,' said Ralph jocularly. 'I have already chosen your car, an Austin Seven, and had it coloured blue, your favourite colour, I believe.'

Felice couldn't be annoyed when she was delighted to have her wish gratified. 'Thank you, Father,' she said with the first touch of animation she had shown towards him lately.

'Good. We'll pick it up from the garage.'

'I wonder if Mother will want to come with us.'

Ralph said shortly, 'Probably not. Her health is troubling her again.'

That evening Sylvia came down to dinner, looking wan and pale, and Felice gave her the news about the car. Sylvia showed no sign of resenting Ralph's action. She smiled at her daughter. 'Congratulations, Felice. A pretty little Austin Seven is perfect to begin with and won't take too much of your pin money to run.'

Ralph said aggressively, 'Naturally I shall instruct my garage to put her charges on my account. The car will cost her nothing to run.'

'Thank you, Father,' said Felice, angered by his attitude to Sylvia.

'You haven't seen much of Lady Betty lately, have you?' said Ralph.

'She's a newly married young woman,' said Sylvia.

'I was asking Felice.'

The remnants of Felice's good mood drained away. Nothing in this family could ever bring pure joy. 'Betty is happy with her husband. I saw them when they returned from their honeymoon and were visiting her parents.'

'Where do the happy couple live?'

'North Gloucestershire. Not so near now.'

'With your own car, distance will be no handicap,' said Ralph.

When dinner was over Sylvia rose from the table. 'I think I'll retire. I still feel a little unwell.'

'Will you come with us to pick up the car?' asked Felice.

'No, thank you, dear. I shan't be well enough for a while and I know you must be impatient.' She looked tired and Felice felt anxious for her. She ate so little. She moved round the house like a wraith.

The small blue car, shining, unused, waited for her and couldn't help but please Felice. She would have such fun with it and, better still, freedom. She was quick to learn how to shift gears, how to take a bend safely, how to judge distance when using the brakes, all the skills that went to prove her ability to drive alone. She wondered where to go first. A visit to the Bath shops seemed attractive. She would take Mother with her some time, but today was her own.

She had not driven far along the Bath road when she saw a large tent by an open gate leading into a field and a sign which announced it to be 'Kathy's Tearoom'. There were several cars parked on the roadside and she glanced aside as she went by, catching a glimpse of someone she recognised: Isobel Kingston, who was throwing a bowl of water into the hedge. Impulsively, inexpertly, Felice backed the car, parked crookedly half on and half off the road and went into the tent. It was busy, with people seated at small tables covered with checked cloths. A young girl was setting out cutlery for the latest customers while a man loaded cakes on to plates. She knew him too. The young factory trainee manager at Bennyson's Corset Factory. Desmond Kingston, Isobel's brother, the man whom her father had treated so badly. Shame for her father enveloped her and she decided to run before she was spotted, but her feet refused to obey her. She wanted so much to talk to the Kingstons, though she couldn't imagine what she could say or how they would react. Then Desmond Kingston turned and saw her; he smiled and gestured to an empty table.

She managed to return his smile and sat down. He came to her at once. 'How pleasant to see you, Miss Bennyson.'

'And to see you, Mr Kingston.'

'What can I get you?'

'I'd like a cup of tea and one of those delicious-looking iced cakes.'

The child who had finished tending the other tables came over. 'I can recommend them,' she said eagerly.

Desmond looked down lovingly at the girl. 'My sister, Kathy. Kathy meet Miss Bennyson, Mr Dane's sister. The small cakes are Kathy's speciality.'

'Mr Dane is a lovely, lovely man,' said Kathy. 'You can have a cake for nothing.'

'May I? And you made them? Then I'm sure I shall enjoy it all the more.' Felice wondered how Kathy and Lawrence had become friends. 'The tearoom is named after you?' she asked the child.

'Yes, we had another but it leaked and Mr Dane came and ...' Felice heard the story behind the new tent before Kathy dashed off to the kitchen.

Isobel came out from behind a small screened area with a pile of clean crockery. She smiled at Felice. How extraordinary they are,

238

thought Felice. My father destroyed their livelihood and they still make me welcome. Tears sprang to her eyes. There might be a severe shortage of money in the Kingston family, but there was no shortage of love and forgiveness. She remembered that their father had been killed in an accident. She felt she should say something, offer sympathy, but no words would come. She hadn't known him. She hardly knew them.

'Are you alone?' asked Isobel.

'I am. My father bought me a little car. An Austin Seven. He had it done in blue because I like the colour.' She stopped abruptly. How crass could you get? Here she was burbling on about her new car while the Kingstons were scraping a living as best they could at the side of the road.

She left soon afterwards. Desmond saw her to her car. 'I'm not very good at parking yet,' she said, gesturing ruefully to the Austin Seven's rear jutting out into the road.

He laughed. 'When did you learn to drive?'

'Only just. I need more practice.' She knew she could ask her father or his chauffeur, but nowadays she hated the idea of appealing to Ralph for anything.

'You'll improve, I'm sure.'

Felice looked at him searchingly. He really was a nice man. She liked his looks. Blue eyes, fair, rather floppy hair, a rugged face with a cleft in his chin. Not hero material but definitely the face of a man you could trust.

'Will I do?' he asked.

She blushed. 'I was staring, wasn't I? Sorry.'

'You can stare as much as you like, Miss Bennyson.'

'Won't you call me Felice?'

His startled look reminded her that her father would never descend to first-name terms with the proletariat. And he'd be furious if she became friends with people he had dismissed. He'd probably have apoplexy if he knew she found Desmond attractive. Damn Father!

'If I'm to call you Felice, you must call me Desmond. Will you?'

'Yes,' she said, so firmly that she made him laugh.

His teeth were white, a little crooked.

'Desmond,' she said tentatively.

'Perhaps I could help you perfect your driving.'

'How?'

'I could ride with you and give you a few tips.' He smiled wryly.

239

'Actually I've only just learned myself in an old rattletrap van belonging to a friend. I probably wouldn't help at all. Forget I asked.'

'No. I would be happy for you to drive with me. When shall I call for you?'

Desmond still looked doubtful when he said, 'If you're sure . . .?'

'I am absolutely certain. What time do you finish here?'

'Quite late, but as soon as I've driven the family home I can see you. Say about eight thirty. We'll still have an hour or so of light.'

Reluctantly Felice drove away in the direction she had come. She had lost the impetus to visit Bath. She wished she could have stayed in the tented tearoom where the sweet scent of crushed grass and wild flowers exuded an atmosphere all its own and where the workers cared for one another so deeply that the tent seemed permeated with tranquillity.

Her father was waiting for her in the drawing room where Sylvia was pouring tea. 'Where have you been?' he asked. 'Did you enjoy your first solo flight?'

'Yes, thank you. I went nowhere in particular.'

'You just cruised about, loving your car. I remember I did the same when I received my first car. The feeling of freedom, the road, all mine! I was barely eighteen at the time.'

Ralph's eyes shone and Felice wondered with sudden sadness where that eager boy had gone. She looked at her mother, very pale, gowned in a plain but expensive frock, at her father in his Savile Row suit. Both were seated on rosewood chairs. She recalled the perfumed atmosphere of the tent, the cheap furniture, the plain white crockery. Sylvia's hands betrayed a slight tremor. Her parents had quarrelled while she was out. She knew the signs.

Sylvia handed Felice a cup of tea and offered her tiny sandwiches. Felice accepted the tea but refused the food.

Ralph said, 'Why won't you eat? Are you unwell? You usually enjoy tea. You know I look forward to being with you for meals. They are oases in the desert of my day.' He laughed. 'Hark at me. I sound like a sentimental novel.'

Neither woman smiled and he frowned. 'What's the matter with you?' His question was clearly directed at Felice but Sylvia said, 'Surely she can refuse a few sandwiches without you turning it into a drama.'

Ralph glared at her but he was uneasy. Sylvia might seem crushed but the spirit which had risen in her lately was always near the

240

surface. He was not ready to relinquish any form of authority to her, especially if it pertained to Felice. They had just had a violent quarrel over the matter and although it had left her drained of energy and colour he hadn't gained the expected victory. 'Did you have something to eat while you were out?' he asked Felice. 'Now motoring has become so popular and inexpensive I have noticed that roadside tearooms are appearing.'

Felice wondered if he had had her followed. He was fanatical enough to employ someone to make sure she did not get into difficulties during her first venture alone.

In an endeavour to lighten the atmosphere she said, 'I can't fool you, can I?' Ralph looked pleased as he shook his head. 'I did stop. Not at a tearoom, well, not exactly, but at a tent. I was on the Bath road and saw this place and some cars outside. I had a delicious cake there and the people running it were so friendly.'

'What kind of people were they?' asked Sylvia.

'Oh, just ordinary,' answered Felice abruptly, losing her nerve. She was lying, too. The Kingstons couldn't be considered ordinary by any standards. Fighters, yes, survivors, but never ordinary. She recalled the sparkling eyes of the little girl, Kathy, the sturdiness of Isobel and the manly attractions of Desmond.

Ralph was instantly suspicious. 'What happened? Do you know these people? Had you met them before?'

'I have seen them before,' she said. 'Somewhere. As I said they're ordinary people. Easy to forget.' How easy it was to sink into untruths when the truth would cause a disturbance. She got up. 'I think I'll go to my room. I need to freshen up.'

'Not yet,' said Ralph. To her surprise his voice had softened and he was smiling at her with all the charm he could muster. 'I'm planning to give a dinner party soon, and I want to invite a special guest. Aubrey Whittaker called on me. I gather you and he have been seeing quite a lot of each other.'

'It's unavoidable,' said Felice coolly. 'He goes everywhere.'

'Of course he does. Lord Aubrey is bound to have plenty of invitations. Felice, my dear, you have attracted a man who can give you all you'll ever need in the world.'

'What!'

'Lord Aubrey asked if he could court you with a view to marriage.' Felice blinked. 'He asked *what*?'

'Are you so surprised?'

'Surprised? I'm astonished. Aubrey Whittaker? That numskull!

As if I'd ever consider him as a husband! And how desperately olde worlde of him to ask your permission. I feel I should be wearing a crinoline.'

'Maybe it is old-fashioned,' said Ralph, 'but he's nervous. That's better than having a brash young man who expects you to fall into his hands like a ripe fruit.'

'I've no intention of falling into his hands in any form whatsoever.'

'Don't be silly, Felice. What can you possibly have against him. He's good-looking, has a well-set-up figure, and is so rich only his accountants know how much money he has.'

'Money!' snapped Felice. 'Always money. The man is a bore. The first time I met him he went on and on about dear Edith and her poetry. I'd no idea what he meant.'

The memory of that evening returned to her vividly. The boredom she'd suffered in Aubrey Whittaker's company had been followed by the pleasure she'd experienced in Jeffrey Westbury's. Jeffrey had gone abroad soon after and she hadn't seen him since that weekend. He had treated her kindly, had opened her eyes to her latent sexuality, had shown her a new door. She kept wondering what lay beyond it. Now, in a flash, she knew. Beyond that door stood Desmond Kingston. Panic gripped her. Nothing could be more disastrous than to fall for him.

'I'm trying to talk to you,' thundered Ralph. 'Please, do me the favour of listening.'

'Sorry.' She returned to the present, which her father was turning into a nightmare.

'Lord Aubrey was speaking of Edith Sitwell,' he said.

'Yes, so I discovered.'

'I would have thought you'd welcome a cultivated man who enjoys poetry.'

'He doesn't enjoy anything,' cried Felice. 'He's just a dabbler. Last time I sat next to him at dinner – and now I realise he must have been persuading hostesses to allow us to be together – the impudence of the man – he talked of painting. He kept on and on about Arp and Ernst. I said I thought they sounded like a comedy duo but he didn't even smile, just went on about genesis and metamorphoses and mechanoid compositions.'

'What are those?' asked Sylvia.

'I don't know and I doubt if he did. He just likes the sound of his own voice. He pretends to be an intellectual. I told him to dry up,

242

but he just smiled in a kind of supercilious way and went on talking. How can you think I would consider a silly man like him as a life partner?'

'He'll get over all that when you marry him. You'll give him other things to think of. Felice, I insist on your seeing him and listening to what he has to offer you. If you don't end up attracted by the advantages which marriage with him would bring I shall be very surprised.'

'I'll never believe there are advantages in being partnered by a fool,' she cried angrily. 'If he comes to dinner I shall go out.'

'You can't do that!' said Ralph. 'It would be totally inconsistent with good manners.'

'It's totally wrong for you to give a man permission for something which was only mine to give. As for his money—'

Ralph had forced himself to cool down. 'Don't speak of money contemptuously, Felice,' he said calmly. 'I have given you everything you needed so you've never known what it was like to be without, and he can offer so much more than I. You'll be able to have exactly what you want, no matter what it is. And,' he finished triumphantly, 'as a married woman you'll be presented at court.'

'I don't care about being presented—'

'Oh, but it's a marvellous experience,' said Sylvia, surprising them both.

'Mother, I didn't think you'd be on Father's side over this!'

'I'm not.'

'You sound as if you are,' retorted Felice. 'I suppose being presented is fun, but it isn't as important as finding the right man.'

'That is supremely important, I agree.' Sylvia suddenly looked inexpressibly sad. 'Supremely important,' she repeated, looking at Ralph.

'You should know.' Ralph shot her a look of utter dislike. 'However, I'm glad you agree with me regarding Felice's future. You managed to ruin ours.'

Sylvia stood up. She had not a vestige of colour. 'Felice, dear, do come to my room later if you feel the need to talk.' She walked to the door, a shadowy figure, her soft indoor shoes making no sound, silent in her restrained movements.

Felice faced her father. 'May I go now?'

'Not until we get this matter settled. Felice, my dear, I don't want to push you into this, but you must examine the advantages before you reject such an offer.'

'You think only of the money and the society I shall keep. You don't care about me at all.'

'That simply isn't true. You have been everything to me.'

'I'm grateful for all you've done for me, but I can't obey you in this. If you persist I shall leave home.'

'Oh? And where do you imagine you will go?'

Felice thought about the question. Where would she go? She had no close relatives, no friends to confide in and little money directly under her control. She might have turned to Betty who would probably have helped had she not accompanied her husband to Scotland to visit an ancient great-aunt who had been unable to travel down for the wedding.

'I could work,' she said.

'Don't be foolish. Where could you work to make sufficient money for your needs? You couldn't earn enough to keep yourself in silk stockings.'

'I'd rather wear sackcloth than have Aubrey Whittaker pawing me about.'

'That is a very vulgar statement.'

'It's a very vulgar idea. I'll find somewhere to go, something to do if you press me.'

Ralph breathed heavily. 'If by any remote chance you decide to leave for reasons of which I don't approve I shall stop your allowance.'

'You'd go to that length?'

'I would to prevent you from making a ghastly mistake.'

A silence fell between them.

Ralph broke it by asking, 'Is there another man you prefer? If he is well born and can keep you in the luxury I want for you I'd consider him.'

Desmond Kingston's image swam into Felice's consciousness. 'There is no one,' she said.

Ralph smiled. 'I thought not. Now be sensible and start deciding what you'll wear. Look your prettiest.'

'It will be no good, Father. I shall never accept Aubrey.'

'Just get engaged to him for the time being. Wear his ring. If you decide later you don't care for him you can break the engagement.'

'What an – an obscene idea—'

'Obscene? How dare you!'

'I dare. It's my future we're talking about. My happiness. You're proposing to sell me.'

'For God's sake!'

'Yes, sell me! I'd rather never get married.'

'You've no idea what you're talking about. Marriage is an ideal state for a woman—'

'It doesn't seem to have proved one for Mother!'

Ralph reddened. 'That is none of your business. It doesn't affect my love for you.'

'Well, it affects mine for you, what little I have left.'

Both were horrified by her searing reply.

Ralph said, 'What do you want? I've done all I can to make you happy.'

'Father,' she said desperately, 'I know you've done your best for me. Don't try to marry me off. Let me work. I want so much to learn how to manage on my own.'

'It's foolish for a girl like you to earn money. Why should you?'

'I mean I want to be useful. Like the women in the factory.'

Ralph was astonished. 'Can you see yourself behind a sewing machine?'

'No, of course I can't and I wouldn't take any job which might deny employment to another woman, and anyway I think that kind of work would destroy me. Those poor women. They must go on and on however they feel. Some of them sit hunched over their machines looking as if they might collapse. They probably get no rest at home with their big families. And when they're expecting a child they slave until the very last minute. I've heard that some of them don't leave until they're actually in labour—'

'Felice! Such talk! Who has been gossiping like that to you? Who speaks to you in the factory? It couldn't be Miss Trefusis. *Was* it Miss Trefusis? I'll get rid of her.'

'Father, really, how could you? She only answered my questions straightforwardly, she's worked for Bennyson's since she left school and she must be forty at least. How would she get another job?'

'You know it's not the thing to allow her to be familiar.'

'I told you she only answered my questions. Surely it would have been discourteous for her not to. Father, please listen to me. I really do want to work at something that matters. I would like to be a welfare person.'

'A what?'

'I want to be responsible for the women's welfare in Bennyson's Corsets. See that they take rest when they need it, send them to a doctor when necessary so that they needn't suffer, employ a nurse—'

'Are you crazy? Do you know what it would all cost?'

'It's always money with you! I'm told my grandfather gave them those things and more—'

'Your grandfather was oversentimental. It cost him a great deal to be so indulgent, but it was easier then. We're in a slump, business is bad, though I don't expect you to know. It doesn't touch you.'

'How can I know anything if you keep me cocooned?'

'Forget the workers. To you they seem to live low, unattractive lives, but they're used to it.'

'That doesn't mean they wouldn't like something better.'

'You know nothing about it.'

'I know the Kingstons have no jobs and hardly any money and their father's died recently in an accident. They're having to take on any work they can get. They've even—' She stopped abruptly. She had been about to speak of the tent tearoom. She wouldn't put it past her father to try to influence someone to get it shut.

'Are you talking about that disloyal sister and brother?'

'I am and I don't think they were disloyal. Miss Kingston was trying to help women who were terrified of losing their jobs.'

'Women who abandoned her when the going turned rough,' sneered Ralph.

'They were looking for help from you. They found you unresponsive and I can't blame them for putting their families first and backing down. Some of their husbands haven't been able to find work in years and the women's wages have been the mainstay of their homes, and some have lots of children to care for. Have you no sympathy for them?'

Ralph's fury spilled over. 'Is the number of their offspring supposed to be my fault? I would have thought it was up to them to control the size of their families.'

Felice couldn't answer him. Betty had told her about Marie Stopes and the good work she was doing on contraception, but she found it far too embarrassing a subject to discuss with her father. His next words fell into the shocked silence, but he managed to speak calmly. 'The Kingstons had to go. They defied me. One cannot allow a couple of rebels to set a bad example to the others. If I hadn't dismissed them discipline could have been affected throughout the factory.'

'But Desmond didn't do a thing. He got fired because of Isobel.' She was so wound up she hadn't realised she had used their first names.

246

'Desmond? Isobel? Just how well do you know them? Exactly what's been going on?'

'Nothing. Nothing at all. I took a liking to them.'

'A liking? How? When?'

Felice was suddenly weary, but gathered her courage again. 'Father, if you won't allow me to work in the factory on a regular basis please teach me the groundwork of business. I shall need it one day.'

Ralph's brows went up. 'Oh? And why do you think that?'

'Because one day – a long time ahead, I hope – I shall own the factory, shan't I?'

Ralph said grimly. 'I have of course made proper provision in my will for you and your mother. In fact you will be very well-off, but I decided long ago to make Lawrence my heir.'

Felice felt as if she had been punched in the stomach. She had not expected to inherit the factory unconditionally – she knew she would need help – but she was her father's only child.

Ralph looked at her anxiously, 'You don't look well. Are you ill?'

'No, not ill,' she gasped. 'I'm shocked. I'm your daughter. Lawrence is no relation to you at all.'

'Surely you didn't expect me to put you in charge of a large factory.'

Felice managed a small 'Yes.'

'My dear girl! How foolish of you! A woman shouldn't dabble in commercial matters. You have no idea of what is involved in running Bennyson's.'

'I could learn.'

'No, it's far too complicated. More so because our particular business requires so many people to keep it going. The women you have such sympathy with – you don't know what they're really like. They're rough and tough. I've heard some of them using language which made even my hair curl.' He gave a rueful laugh, hoping to lighten the atmosphere, but Felice didn't respond.

'Women work nowadays in executive positions. I'm supposed to be intelligent—'

Ralph's fragile control over his temper broke. 'Felice, stop this!'

'But why? Why give what should be mine to Lawrence? I've never understood how you can treat him so well, yet behave so cruelly to Mother. She's his mother too.'

'I have never behaved cruelly to your mother. It's outrageous of you to say so. I've been strict with her, yes, I've had to be. She's

247

clumsy, hysterical, no asset at all to me—'

'She wasn't always like that. When I was small we had some lovely times together and in early photographs she looks so beautiful and serene.'

'Photographs can lie!'

'And you're familiar with lies, aren't you, Father? You certainly fooled Lawrence. She did want to see him.'

Ralph gasped. 'That simply isn't true. She's made herself believe that falsehood is truth. Whatever she thinks now she did not want Lawrence when she left her husband. She saw him a few times, but when Harry died she abandoned her son entirely to Mrs Dane, who was as shocked as I was by her indifference.'

Felice was silent. Had she been deceived by Sylvia? The echoes of that scream began to fade.

Ralph saw the doubt in her face and came to her and put an arm round her. 'Give me a kiss, darling. Do you remember when you were small how eagerly you waited for me to come home? You often stood at the gate and climbed into the car to travel the last few yards with me. You can't have forgotten.'

'No,' she said. 'I haven't. I thought you were some kind of god.'

'It makes me so happy to hear you say so.'

Felice wished devoutly she could forget everything and sink back into the comfort she'd once enjoyed. But her mind began to flood with other memories, his bullying of her mother, his domineering attitude, his callousness to any underling who opposed or displeased him. She had loved a man who didn't really exist.

'Father,' she said quietly, 'I must ask you, how can you care so much for Lawrence yet dislike his mother? You hate her, don't you?'

Ralph sidestepped her question. He looked into her eyes and said, 'Lawrence is the son I've never had.'

'That wasn't Mother's fault. Janet told me that she was very ill when I was born.'

'What! How dare she! My God, I'm learning some things about my employees.'

Felice's anger matched his. 'I once asked her why I had no brothers or sisters, that's all. I suppose you'll sack her too and leave Mother with no one to care for her.'

'Felice, please stop quarrelling with me. I can't stand it.'

'You force me to quarrel. You're not honest with me and neither is Mother. Something happened in the past. The atmosphere here is oppressive and depressing.'

'I'm sorry you should think so. I've certainly done my best. Who can do more?'

'You won't really try to sack Janet, will you?'

He frowned. 'No. Now you must promise me that on the night of the party you will be dressed in your best bib and tucker ready to greet Lord Aubrey and make him welcome. Promise me.'

Felice hesitated, but enough emotion had been spilled today without extending it further. She promised.

Chapter Fifteen

When Felice reached her bedroom her assumed calm deserted her. Her knees began to shake and she sat down heavily. Janet tapped and came in with a glass of red wine. 'Mr Bennyson sent this.'

'No thank you. I don't want it, Janet. You can take away the tray and save yourself a journey.'

Janet sighed. 'You'd best drink it. It'll do you good. Life is hard, Miss Felice, and those who aren't strong go under.'

'Like Mother, do you mean?' Felice blurted.

Janet said gently, 'Now that's no way to speak, Miss Felice.'

'You know Mother better than anyone. What was she like as a girl?'

Janet's eyes clouded and she gave Felice a searching look. 'She was one of the happiest girls on earth. Her parents loved her dearly. They engaged me as her maid when I was only a bit older than her. I loved her from the first.' Janet stopped.

'Go on,' encouraged Felice. 'No one's ever told me about Mother's early days.'

'Surely she's mentioned them to you sometimes.'

'Yes, but only in a vague way. Do tell me more.'

'It's not my place—'

'Don't say that. I want to get closer to her. Please.'

Janet sighed. 'If that's your reason – she was courted by many a good man and many were wealthy, but when Mr Harry came along she fell in love immediately and he felt the same way about her. They were married six months later. They only waited that long to "observe the proprieties" as her parents said. You can't remember your grandparents, can you, Miss Felice? Of course, you weren't much more than a child when they died.'

'I remember them more as a kindly presence than as people,' said Felice. 'Though I've never forgotten Grandma's hair. It was silver and shone.'

'She was a lovely woman up to the day she died. And Miss Sylvia takes after her. She'd still be beautiful,' Janet forgot her position in her anger, 'if she'd not been tormented until the poor soul can't think straight. She had a bubbling personality. That's the only way I can describe her. It was no wonder the men fell in love with her, but she wanted none of them. A little flirtation is as far as she went until she met Mr Harry. Her parents danced at the wedding. What a day that was! Such a suitable match. That's what people said and they were right. You'd never find two people so much in love, not if you searched the earth. Then *he* came along. That snake. He tempted her. He told her lies and made her believe them and she did one mad thing and the next I knew she'd left Mr Harry and gone off with the beast downstairs.' Janet came to herself. Her hand flew to her mouth. 'Oh, Miss Felice, I beg your pardon. I shouldn't speak like that of your father.'

'It's all right, Janet. You've only confirmed what I suspected. The one mad act was Father?'

Janet had gone pale. She twisted her hands. 'I've said too much already.'

'Come on, Janet, dear, I really do need to know. My eyes are opening at last. I'll never betray you.'

'I believe you, Miss Felice. You're as honest as your mother.'

'She is honest, isn't she?' said Felice eagerly. For so many years Father had called her mother dishonest because she'd deceived her first husband. Felice had known there were secrets. Now she wanted the truth, all of it.

'Honest as the day is long, Miss Felice. The truth is that when Mr Harry was away Mr Bennyson persuaded my dear Miss Sylvia that her husband had gone to his mistress. He even produced a photograph to prove it. My darling let that out when she was crying in my arms. He actually showed her a photograph of her husband and his so-called mistress together, she half clothed. My dear lady was such an innocent. She didn't let me see the photograph because it made *her* ashamed. What had she got to be ashamed of? Nothing. One day when I was looking for something for her in her dressing-table drawers, I came upon it hidden away at the back. It was a poor photo and I was sure it had been faked somehow. Miss Sylvia couldn't see it, but it's hard to see straight when you're suffering from shock and your eyes are full of tears. I'd been watching Mr Bennyson trying to seduce her for ages and she lost her head completely. She said she couldn't stay with her husband. I tried to per-

252

suade her to speak to Mr Harry, but she was distraught and then *he* took advantage of her. He made love to her. In her own house. What a beast he was! Sorry, Miss Felice, but you did ask.'

'My father seduced her?'

Janet bit her lip. 'Oh dear. I wish I'd never begun this.'

'But you have and now you have to finish.'

Janet said reluctantly, 'Yes, he made love to her in the home her husband had made for her. She felt so guilty that she left with Mr Bennyson that very night and went to live with him. It broke Mr Harry's heart. Well, you know the rest. Of course Mr Bennyson had to marry her.'

'Had to?'

'She thought she was expecting a baby – it was a genuine mistake – her courses stopped because of her nervous exhaustion. Of course, society expected them to marry in the circumstances, child or no child. My dear mistress only realised later that he'd not intended matters to go so far, he hadn't expected her to run from Mr Harry and had no thought of marriage. He'd just wanted an affair. Later, she realised she wasn't having a baby after all and he was like a wild beast. He said she'd trapped him. My poor Miss Sylvia. She knew she'd ruined her life. She still loved Mr Harry with all her heart. And her little son, but old Mrs Dane wouldn't hear of her seeing Lawrence and Miss Sylvia wouldn't put everyone through a sordid court case. I suppose she knew she wouldn't win anyway, the courts are hard on women who leave their husbands and children. When Mr Harry killed himself it damaged her spirit. *He* could have helped her recover, but he didn't lift a finger. In fact, he made her feel much worse with his nasty tongue.'

Janet paused and wiped her perspiring face. 'Oh, Miss Felice, you're so young. How can you understand such wild and wilful behaviour?'

'I've had to watch Mother tortured for years. My poor mother. What a terrible story.'

'Miss Felice, be very careful who you marry. It's meant to be a lifetime commitment and if you break it people can make your existence utter hell. You need to be very sure.'

'I'll take care, Janet.'

The summer drifted towards its end in the relentless rain and cold which had plagued the land that year. Kathy returned to school. She studied hard, but used her spare time cooking for the tearoom and

helping out at weekends. Customers began to dwindle with the
dying summer, preferring indoor comfort. Severe gales tore at
the tent guy ropes and blew out the stove and Desmond regretfully
had to admit that business was over for the year.

There seemed little prospect of accomplishing what he'd been
aiming at, a proper tearoom under a roof which could stay open all
year round. Their takings had helped to keep the family going
through the summer but he'd not been able to save much. They were
lucky that the farmer had become attached to them and allowed
them to store all their gear in a dry barn. On their last day, a
Saturday, they drove home feeling sad and bereft.

Kathy was particularly depressed. 'I shall miss it,' she mourned.
She began to spend her leisure time reading or listening to the
wireless and she played their records so often on the tinny gramophone that they creaked and scratched their way round. Anything, it
seemed, rather than think.

Grace mourned her husband constantly. She said often, 'He
wasn't a bad man, Isobel, not really, he just had bad luck. It drove
him to do wrong things. He often told me how sorry he was.'

Isobel thought: He wasn't sorry enough to keep his fists off you,
but she didn't say it. Grace seemed to have driven all memories of
her husband's beastliness from her mind. His drinking, his crimi-
nality and imprisonment, his violence and her bruises, his disgusting
friends, all that seemed to have left her. She talked a great deal of
the happy times they'd known. But she grew thinner by the day and
was pale and nervous. And when Kathy came home, instead of
running to Isobel her mouth stretched in a smile, she ran to her
mother and they hugged one another in what sometimes looked like
desperation.

Isobel spoke to Desmond about it. He said soothingly, 'They had a
terrible shock the day Dad died. It must be fearful to be there when
someone loses his life violently.'

Isobel feared there might be something more behind their
despair. She wanted to believe Desmond, but she began to suffer
from insomnia and when she drifted in and out of brief, unsatisfactory dozes she kept thinking that Amos was once more in her room,
hands outstretched to grab her.

She needed to exorcise his memory. Once, she asked her mother
to remind her of what had happened on the day of Amos's death,
but Grace became distraught, crying out loudly that she never
wished to talk about it, and Kathy came running. 'What's up, Mum?'

She glared at Isobel. 'Why are you upsetting her? You leave our mum alone.'

Isobel was deeply hurt at the way her beloved young sister had turned on her. 'I'm sorry,' she said to them. 'I shouldn't have brought it up.'

Kathy now shared the big bed with her mother and Isobel realised how much the warmth and companionship of her sister had satisfied a need in her to love and be loved. Kathy was still having nightmares and Isobel's sleeplessness meant she could hear the soft murmur of her mother's voice perpetually soothing her young daughter. Amos's death had locked Grace and Kathy into a unit; they needed one another. Isobel felt shut out. Kathy had deserted her, Mum was sunk in grief, Desmond was rushing round trying to find ways of making money. She felt isolated, taking any job which was offered, cleaning, scrubbing, anything to bring some money home. Life was dreary and to make matters worse she couldn't get Lawrence Dane out of her head. She told herself she was a fool to be affected by the kisses of a man who saw her only as a factory girl ripe for flirtation. She had seen him several times recently when she had been hurrying to and from work and had occasionally accepted a lift from him. His behaviour was impeccable. He had kissed her goodbye as if it were a completely natural thing to do and it had taken all her willpower not to return his kisses with passion. Were these encounters his way of softening her up so that she'd be an easy catch? If so, he had a nasty shock coming. She was her own woman.

Desmond's friend Owen returned to Bristol when his job folded. He had lived in the van and managed to save some money. He suggested that he and Desmond should pool their resources and rent small premises in West Street, Old Market.

Isobel chipped in with a little and so did Grace. Their pooled wealth came to a pitifully small amount, but they began to feel excited.

'There are already a few workmen's cafés in West Street and Old Market,' Desmond pointed out. 'Wouldn't it be better if we tried somewhere else?'

Owen shook his head. 'Working men and women know that they can get a cheap meal in that area. I thought we could undercut the others. I hoped you might have ideas on that.'

Desmond said, 'The only way to undercut is to sell food that we can make really cheap but tasty.'

Grace was animated and colour flooded her cheeks. 'There's one thing that can be done that costs almost nothing. We've practically been living on it since your dad died. Soup. Good rich soup from bones. I can get them free or for pennies from the butcher. We can buy vegetables past their best and add them in chunks. Served up with plenty of bread that we can get cheap if it's a day old, it'll be a good warming meal in winter.'

'It's a marvellous idea!' said Owen. 'But could we make enough food? There's an old gas stove on the premises, but it's only got two burners.'

'That's no problem,' said Grace. 'We'll make the soup here in the boiler.'

'The washing boiler?' asked Desmond, startled.

'Why not? I cook the Christmas puddings in it. You've never tasted soap in them, have you?'

'Great idea, Mrs Kingston,' said Owen.

Kathy was listening, looking as if she'd witnessed a miracle. She asked, 'What about puddings? People like something to finish with.'

'Rice pudding,' said Grace. 'We can make that here too. We'll get some earthenware dishes – they come cheap – and cook the rice slowly in the range overnight. It won't take much fuel to bank up the fire. Add a bit of fruit – cheap again from the barrows – or sultanas or jam or syrup, and there's a pudding for you. It'll tempt people in the middle of a hard working day. And there's bread-and-butter pudding, too. Eggs and milk don't cost a lot and we can use any stale bread there too.'

Isobel was delighted to see her mother with something to fill her time again. 'If you serve soup and pudding can it still be called a tearoom?' Kathy asked anxiously. 'Will it still be my tearoom?'

'Of course,' said Desmond. 'Owen can paint the name over the café window. He's good at painting.'

The family, even Ivor and Olive, went to see the premises in West Street. They had been empty for some time and needed a great deal of work to make them usable.

'We don't want to be too posh,' warned Owen. 'Customers who'll come here will be looking for a homely place.'

Ivor and Olive melted away as soon as they understood there was work to be done but the new place was ready in three weeks. By then the money had practically run out and the last few shillings were used to buy ingredients.

'It's great, Mrs Kingston,' said Owen. Grace had served up a meal which would be standard fare at the café. 'I'd walk a mile to get grub this good.'

256

They opened at last and there were customers from the start. In the first place they came out of curiosity, then because they relished the food. An enormous kettle was kept constantly on the boil and tea was served at all times. Kathy went back to making her scones and cakes and Isobel joined her when she could make time between her cleaning jobs, but the old sisterly comradeship was gone, destroyed by some dark emotion that was eating up the child's spirit. And Grace's first enthusiasm died, though not her willingness to help. The soup and puddings were fresh every day.

The weather turned mild and the café walls were dank and dripping with condensation and constantly had to be wiped. But the customers kept coming. Isobel looked forward with disgust to toiling away at menial jobs in other women's houses. It was not so much the work she hated, no work was demeaning, but the fact that her earnings were so poor. She thought of her ambition to open a shop of her own where women without much money could buy decently fitted corsets and attractive underwear. She visualised making hard-wearing knickers and petticoats which could be prettified by adding a bit of lace or an embroidered motif, something to raise them out of the ordinary. One day, she dreamed, she'd do it, and later sell silk garments which caressed the skin. Then she would come down to earth with a bump as she took her bucket to a kitchen sink to refill it for another stint of scrubbing.

The close weather and the work made her perspire and she was thankful to receive her money and go home to take a sponge bath. After a particularly bad day with a woman who was determined to get as much work as possible from her underpaid skivvy, Isobel felt like a limp rag. As she left the house there came a toot as a car drove up behind her and slowed. Lawrence hadn't been around recently and she'd decided he'd tired of whatever game he was playing and had tried to convince herself that she didn't care. But the pleasure that welled up in her when she knew he was there defeated her and she turned to smile at him.

He was driving a closed saloon car and held open the door for her. 'Isobel, I'm so happy to see you.'

She climbed in and sank thankfully into the leather seat.

'Aren't you going to return the compliment?' he asked.

'I'm happy to see you,' she said.

'That's not the ecstatic response I was looking for.'

'Just what have you come looking for,' she asked tetchily, 'and why don't you start the car so I can get home? I'm destroyed. That ghastly woman! I hope she loses all her money and has to do her own housework. I hope she has to skivvy for someone as beastly as herself some day.'

'My God, are you still working your fingers to the bone for ungrateful females?'

'What do you think? That Mr Bennyson has had a change of heart and begged me to return?' Lawrence checked the road before he drove away from the kerb. 'Or perhaps you thought that some long-lost relative had left me a fortune. Or maybe—'

'Mercy, for heaven's sake. No, I didn't think any of those things.'

'I don't suppose you've thought about me at all,' snapped Isobel.

He stopped the car and turned to glare at her. 'You're wrong. I've thought of you a great deal.'

'Have you? I can't think why. I'm just a sweaty menial with ruined hands who can't get a job.'

'Isobel.' He took her in his arms. She struggled against him, pushing him away, her hands on his chest. He released her and caught them, looking down at them, his eyes compassionate. 'Poor girl. They look sore.'

'It's the soda.' No matter how much she distrusted him she couldn't help enjoying his sympathy and she was annoyed with herself. 'I haven't seen you for a while,' she said acerbically. 'Have you been making up to some other girl? Someone in your own kind of society? Or maybe descending to a maid or two?'

Irritatingly, he refused to get angry. Instead he drew her hands to his lips and kissed them where they looked most sore.

He's an expert, she thought. An expert in the art of seduction, and he thinks he'll get me. He doesn't feel a damn thing for me. He's playing games. Well, I can play games too.

'Could you drive me home, please?' she asked politely.

'Of course. Why the hurry?'

'I'm needed.'

'To work some more, I suppose.' He sounded angry.

'Of course. What else would a working girl do but work?'

'You've sisters. Why can't they help?'

'They do. At least Kathy does.'

'How is little Kathy? I drove to the site of your tent and found the place abandoned. What happened to Desmond's hopes of a tearoom?'

'They've been fulfilled. That's why I have to get home, to prepare food for tomorrow.'

He slipped the car into gear and they set off again while she told him about the café.

For a while he murmured and nodded, then he said, 'You're a brick, Isobel.' He was utterly sincere and his down-to-earth compliment charmed her.

Whatever Felice was doing she couldn't get her mother's despair out of her head. Sylvia had never refused to see Lawrence. In fact, she had wanted him with a desperation which had finally turned her into a semi-invalid, an easy target for Ralph's cruelty. Felice had often come close to telling Lawrence what she had learned, but she had no evidence to support her. Felice agonised until her need to know the whole truth became unbearable and she had to act.

She drove to Mrs Dane's house outside Bristol and waited in the hall while an elderly maid took in her name. A door opened and the maid came out, giving her a searching look.

'Miss Bennyson? Please come in.'

Felice followed her into the drawing room. Mrs Dane greeted her calmly. She had courage, but she had suffered. Her shoulders were bent and her eyes wary as she regarded Felice. Her son's marriage had been broken up, he had destroyed himself. God knew what that did to a mother. Felice wished suddenly that she hadn't come. By asking for answers she would tear open old wounds.

The drawing room was comfortable. A fire blazed in the grate and was reflected in the simple, beautiful furniture. Paintings, mainly of horses and dogs, graced the walls. But it was the atmosphere that appealed most to Felice. It had a serenity that her own home so conspicuously lacked. And she was about to ask questions that might destroy that serenity. She seated herself in the armchair indicated by Mrs Dane, wishing she could excuse herself and leave.

Mrs Dane asked, 'Is something wrong, Miss Bennyson?'

A lot, thought Felice.

'How may I help you?'

Felice realised she should have prepared herself for questions. She had jumped into her car on impulse and now she was tongue-tied. Mrs Dane rang and a servant appeared with refreshments.

'Will you take coffee?' asked Mrs Dane, just as if young women turned up every day in an agitated state.

Felice accepted the coffee, but put it down without tasting it. 'Mrs Dane, I don't think I should be here, but I need help.'

'I'll do what I can.'

'Lately I've discovered something which has made me very unhappy. It's about Mother.'

Mrs Dane continued to appear serene, she still smiled, but nevertheless Felice felt a door closing to her. Desperately she said, 'My parents' marriage has not been a happy one.' She felt the barrier grow higher. 'Please listen to me. Hear me out.'

'I see no point in this conversation, but you are clearly disturbed. If I can help you I will.'

'Mother and Father have had quarrels, so many quarrels.' Felice sought for words to explain something she couldn't herself understand. 'Well, actually it's Father who starts things. He's not been kind to my mother.' Felice stopped. This was awful.

'Go on.'

'Of course I love Father, one does love one's parents, just as parents love their children.' She realised what she had said and stopped again, her face flaming. 'I know what you must be thinking. Things look bad for Mother. What she did in the past—'

Mrs Dane held up a white hand slightly knotted with rheumatism. 'You are very distressed. Perhaps it would be better if you did not continue.'

'Please, I must.' Felice began to speak hurriedly, the words tumbling out of her. 'My parents were so angry with each other one day not long ago they forgot I was there. Father accused Mother of not loving her son. But then Mother called him a liar.'

Mrs Dane's eyes were fixed on her visitor's face. 'What are you saying? What have your parents' quarrels to do with me?'

'I only know that when my mother shouted "Liar" she was telling the truth. She didn't cut Lawrence out of her life. Someone else did and she's suffered so dreadfully. She's still suffering. I've come to ask you – I've come to ask – oh, Mrs Dane, what really happened? Were you the one who separated my mother and her son?' What a monstrous thing to ask any woman. Mrs Dane would surely ring the bell and have her shown out. Thrown out, and with justification.

Mrs Dane picked up her coffee and tried to sip it, but her hand shook too much. Felice remembered how her mother's hands shook when Ralph bullied her. How could she have grown up not realising how cruel he was, how miserable Sylvia was?

'The question insults me,' said Mrs Dane coldly.

'Forgive me. Please, may I go on?'

Mrs Dane nodded, her eyes bleak. 'Mother reminded him of how she had asked him to tell you she was on her knees, begging you to

260

grant her a meeting with Lawrence, if only once a year on his birth-day. She accused Father of destroying her but said that she wouldn't allow him to destroy me. The quarrel was about me, you see. I'm sorry, I'm not telling this very well.'

Mrs Dane looked suddenly older. 'How can you possibly be sure that your mother was telling the truth? People in anger say all kinds of things they don't mean and she has been unstable for years, in a nursing home more than once.'

'When you hear the absolute truth you know it,' said Felice.

'The absolute truth,' repeated Mrs Dane. 'Can it be possible? All those years gone by. My grandson grown from babyhood to man-hood believing his mother had rejected him. I've seen his unhappi-ness, his bitterness, and prayed it wouldn't warp him. I believe it hasn't but it has left deep scars. And now you're telling me that it has all been unnecessary, that Ralph was lying when he told me that Sylvia positively didn't want her son?'

'Yes, I am.' Felice had seen the problem in fairly simple terms. Father had told lies, now the truth must come out and Sylvia and her son would be reunited and there would be a happy ending. Mrs Dane's reaction showed her there could be no simple solution. Whatever the truth was, it would cause extreme pain to everyone connected with it.

'Did he lie about me?' asked Mrs Dane.

Felice stammered, 'I don't know.'

Mrs Dane said, almost to herself, 'I allowed Ralph to act as a go-between because of the delicacy of the subject. I trusted him. I can't, I won't believe that he lied to me. Why should he? What possible object could he have had? I think you are mistaken. You are young. It is easy for the young to misread the behaviour of their elders.'

Felice shrank before the dominance of the old lady. 'Maybe I *was* mistaken,' she gasped. 'Life at home is very confusing.' She paused, horrified at the devils she might misguidedly have let loose. 'I'm sorry,' she said. 'I've made you unhappy. I could be wrong.'

Mrs Dane said, 'I remember the events of those terrible days with particular clarity. Since then Ralph has cultivated Lawrence's acquaintance and Lawrence likes him. I've been happy to see it.'

'I believe Father wanted a son. Mother could only have me. He blamed her for that too. He has made Ralph heir to his business.'

Mrs Dane looked old and strained. She picked up her coffee and managed to sip a little to ease her dry, aching throat. 'I have no doubt that you believe your story to be true, but I am equally sure

261

that you are wrong. Lawrence tells me your mother is a hypochondriac. That is an illness in itself and should be treated, but she cannot be thought reliable. Remember that she has spent time in nursing homes for the mentally afflicted.'

Felice felt like weeping. 'She's such a gentle soul. Her unhappiness has turned her into a nervous wreck. She loves Lawrence, you see. When he comes to the house she often retires to her room because she can't bear to see the loathing in his face.'

'My God. All that suffering. Ralph wouldn't, he couldn't, deliberately inflict such torment on a woman he loved.'

'I don't think he ever did love her,' said Felice. 'I don't even know if he's capable of love.'

Mrs Dane said, 'That's a dreadful thing to say. I cannot believe it. He was kind to me. When he told me about Sylvia's stubborness I was angry and he soothed me.'

Felice stared at her. She should never have come here.

Mrs Dane said slowly, 'When my son died so horribly, I hated her. My hate has grown less, I am glad to say – hate destroys those who nourish it. But she is not the innocent victim you imagine. You must try to love both your parents. By not doing so you can only create unhappiness for yourself as well as for them. Forget this fancy you have about your father. We have all accepted the truth. Now let it lie.'

Felice was defeated. Her thoughts kept jumbling about so that she couldn't pin them down. And all the evidence she could offer was the word 'Liar' shouted during a domestic quarrel. Not quite all, though. She had heard Janet's version and Janet was dependable. There was the photograph, too, but she had never seen it. And if she quoted a servant to Mrs Dane she could imagine the distasteful, disbelieving response she would get. And was Janet so reliable? She wouldn't mean to misrepresent facts, but she was immovably on Mother's side.

'Remember, Miss Bennyson, my grandson's happiness means everything to me. He has been tormented for so many years, first by his mother's desertion, then his father's.'

'But his father didn't desert him!'

'Do you know how my son died?'

'Yes, but—'

'Suicide is desertion, the most dreadful one there is. There can be no turning back after that for anyone. The guilt never releases those left behind.'

'I didn't know.'

'Pray God no one you love ever takes such a way out.'

'Surely you had nothing to feel guilty about.'

'Nevertheless I felt it, still feel it. It is inevitable.'

'Is it guilt that's turned my mother into a woman who's half afraid of her own shadow? I wish I had been kinder to her.'

Mrs Dane leaned forward. 'It all happened before you were born. You are totally innocent.'

'I'm not, I'm not!' Felice's tears flowed. 'All these years I've basked in Father's indulgence to me. Deep down I've known he treated Mother badly' – Mrs Dane held up a protesting hand, but Felice continued – 'but I wouldn't let myself think about it. In fact sometimes I even felt pretty smug about being more favoured than my mother. It makes me burn with shame now.'

'I should not be listening to this. These are private matters.'

'Let me speak, please.'

'Felice, you were a child. You could not possibly realise what was happening to your mother.'

'Maybe not then, but as I grew older I still let myself be blinded by Father. His continual supply of gifts and his overpowering love filled my world. Now I see that he felt possession rather than affection for me. At least, looking back it seems like that.'

'I am sure he does love you, Felice. Giving is the only way he knows of demonstrating it.'

'I've loved Mother, but in a weak way. Not enough to comfort her when she needed it. I let my father rule me and strike at her through me. I've been a fool and a coward, but most of all I've deliberately closed my eyes to the truth. When I was little Father was my hero. I thought he was the most marvellous man in the world. As I grew up I obeyed him automatically. Sometimes I was unhappy but didn't know why, and sometimes as I grew older it seemed as if he were more of a jailer than a father. I could see he was curt with Mother, but children believe what they're told and I was brought up to believe that Mother was useless and stupid.'

Mrs Dane said, 'Felice, my dear, dry your eyes. Put it behind you. Live your life as best you can. We all must do that. Try to understand your father's point of view. I'm sure he has problems in coming to terms with the past.'

'He seems to think most about the way he was shut out of top society. That and money. He doesn't care twopence for the people who work for him. He's a tyrant. I don't want to go on living in his house. I shall have to leave.'

Mrs Dane was startled. 'But my dear, that's unthinkable. Who will

263

care for you? And what about your mother? From what you tell me you have begun to stand up for her and this is helping her recovery.'

'I know. I'll feel more guilt, but I would make sure I saw her often. I just need a break from Father. I'd like to try to understand him, but I can't do that if I'm seeing him every day. He's a past master at manipulating people, but I believe he loves me in his own way.' She ended with a sob. 'You must think I'm a fool.'

'I think you are brave. I know it took courage to come here. Use that courage to go on with your life. And, speaking practically, if you leave home where would you go?'

'I don't know. Father says he will stop my allowance if I leave without his permission.'

Mrs Dane frowned, got up and walked over to Felice and smoothed back her tumbled hair. 'Poor child,' she said gently. 'You're paying for others' mistakes. What a tangle. Don't make it worse.'

As Felice drove her little car out of the Danes' driveway she spotted Lawrence's unmistakable Bugatti from a couple of hundred yards away. Her conversation with Mrs Dane played itself over and over in her mind and gradually she doubted her previous conviction. The horrors she had dreamed up were simply not true.

Chapter Sixteen

Lawrence spotted Felice leaving the driveway and wondered what had made her break the long silence. He went into the house, curious to hear Grandmother's explanation.

She offered none, but just smiled as he walked into the drawing room. 'I thought you'd not be home before dinner.'

'I completed my business quicker than I expected.'

'Mare no good?'

'Absolutely not. The vendor seemed surprised when I pointed out all her faults.'

'He should have known better than to try to palm off a dud buy on Lawrence Dane. Everyone knows your breeding stock is the best.'

Lawrence accepted the compliment with a grin and took the cup of tea proffered by his grandmother. She cut a slice of cake and handed it to him. He accepted it and put it down. She knew very well he never touched caraway-seed cake. She was under some kind of strain and it had to do with Felice Bennyson.

When it became obvious that he was not going to be told voluntarily why Ralph's daughter had called for the first time in her life he decided he must ask. Then Grandmother looked at him briefly with unmistakable appeal in her eyes. He was seized with anger. Hadn't the Bennysons done enough to her without Felice coming along to stir up trouble? With a tremendous effort he refrained from asking questions. He decided to discuss the stables, the weather, anything to try to lighten her mood.

When he had gone, after an unusually stilted conversation with his grandmother, Mrs Dane stared at the closed door. She knew that Lawrence had seen Felice leaving and was bursting with curiosity, which he had curbed for his grandmother's sake. Felice was anxious to reconcile the family, probably seeing a romantic picture of Lawrence clasped in Sylvia's arms while she wept for joy. She had no real

265

idea of the searing emotions she could unleash. Mrs Dane looked back at the past with eyes clouded with pity. They had all been caught up in a nightmare of deceit and passion which could never be resolved. And in the middle of this tragedy stood Felice.

Isobel had made up her mind. Somehow she was going to set up in business for herself. She would begin in their own front room. The women whom she hoped to interest as her first customers wouldn't be critical of their surroundings. She would work and save and one day the shop she dreamed of would be hers. Through her experience at Bennyson's she knew where to buy the heavy coutil pink, white and drab cloth she needed, the straps, the suspenders, the elastic and all the notions like strong hooks and eyes and laces and thread. There were the steels, too, spiral for everyday use, rigid for those whose backs needed support. All that would cost a fair bit, even for a small beginning, but there was something she could aim for, something that would give her the independence she craved. Her really huge difficulty and one she couldn't resolve lay in the purchase of the heavy sewing machine and the needles she needed. They had to be sturdy enough to sew through the durable cloth, yet precise enough to close the seams after the steels had been inserted. One day she would buy the different machines that were necessary for different operations.

She had written down everything she'd learned from Miss Trefusis and she studied her notebook at night, forcing herself to stay awake long after her tired body craved rest. She studied figures and measurements until they danced before her eyes and she was obliged to sleep, while during the day she was back with the skivvying and exhausted by the dull, hard routine and the long walks to save bus and tram fares. All that was bad enough, but it was when she tried to work out the money that her mind really blurred with the apparent hopelessness of it all. She dreamt of women's bodies, fat, angular, pretty, bent, twisted by disease and hardship, while she scurried round looking in vain for a corset to fit each one and woke sweating and unrefreshed. None of the family had money to spare. The café was doing well, but needed cash ploughed back if it was to succeed. The family was enjoying one advantage. The goodies made in the Kingstons' kitchen fed them at home as well. Olive and Ivor grumbled constantly at the boring amount of soup and bread-and-butter pudding they were eating every day, but no one took any notice of them. They were far too busy. Ivor still had no work though he didn't seem short of cash. When Grace tackled him he swore he was lucky at gambling.

'He's like his father,' muttered Grace.

Kathy was at the grammar school now and her needs were endless. The expense didn't stop at her uniform. She had to have a sports outfit and hockey stick, a swimming costume, special pencils including coloured ones, notebooks, a fountain pen, and the summer was coming when there would be tennis for which she would need a racket, white clothes and shoes. Everyone except Olive and Ivor chipped in, determined that she should never fall behind the others in material necessities. She came racing home, bursting to tell the family all about the new life she was leading and the friends she'd made. She was invited to tea to houses much grander than hers, but her nature was so generous she was only interested in their differences and showed no envy. But when the excitement of her tales was over she slipped back into the anguish which never seemed to leave her or Grace.

Isobel tried to discuss the matter with Desmond, her chief ally and helpmate, but he was too deep into developing the café business to listen with more than half an ear. 'I've told you, Isobel, they can't forget Dad's way of dying. They're both sensitive. It will take ages, maybe even years, for them to get over it. You won't do them any good by asking them questions—'

'I don't,' cried Isobel indignantly.

Desmond looked at her properly then and his face softened. 'Sorry, sis, I'm not helping you, am I, but I really mean what I say. They'll come to terms with it. It's a terrible shame that Kathy's first experience of death had to be so brutal. And Mum loved Dad in spite of everything. She's the faithful type. We can't see him from her point of view.'

Felice bathed and dressed carefully for the dinner party in a deep blue velvet dress which fell to her ankles in graceful folds and a simple gold chain and earrings. Her soft fair hair was Marcel-waved, her nails painted a pale pink. She stared at herself in the mirror. 'A lamb to the slaughter,' she said aloud, startling Janet who had been sent by Sylvia to lend a hand.

'You are a lamb,' said Janet. 'But not to the slaughter I hope.'

'I hope not, too,' said Felice fervently.

Janet knew that Lord Aubrey was about to propose marriage and thought it a good match, a nice mild young man who would treat

Miss Felice kindly and above all take her away from the tyrant Ralph, whom she had loathed more every year since the day he had wrecked Miss Sylvia's life.

'You'd better go down, Miss Felice,' she said. 'The guests are due.'

Felice lingered for a while, still gazing at herself. 'Am I pretty, Janet?'

'You're more than pretty, you're lovely.'

'I'm rather washed out. Pale face, pale hair, pale eyes – I look like something that's crawled out of an apple.'

'Miss Felice! How could you? You don't really believe that!'

'Perhaps not. It's just that the thought of tonight makes me feel dismal.' Felice's eyes caught Janet's in the mirror. Janet was a plain woman, but her eyes were gentle and kind. 'Where were you born, Janet?' she asked.

Janet smiled. 'You've asked me that before and I've told you.'

'I know, dear Janet, but please tell me again. You used to tell me stories of your childhood when I was small. I loved to hear them.'

Janet said gently, 'I was born in a cottage in Coalpit Heath not far from Bristol. Dad was a miner. We were poor, very poor.'

'Were you happy?'

'Yes. I had three brothers and five sisters. Mum was a strong woman who kept us all together. We made our own amusements and had a lot of fun. We roamed the countryside and picked flowers and fruit in season and Mum made wine and jam and pickled preserves and Dad grew onions and shallots and lots of other vegetables, and though we never had much meat we didn't miss it. You don't miss what you've never had. Mum was a thrifty soul. We never got a holiday, not a going-away holiday, but not many of our neighbours did either, so we didn't mind. We loved the local fairs and the chapel gatherings. Even when Dad and two of my brothers were killed in a pit accident my mother managed somehow. Of course it wasn't the same, it couldn't be without our dad, but she never let us mope.'

'I like to think of you in your little cottage all loving one another and –' Felice's voice broke on a sob.

'Don't cry, my baby,' said Janet as she had in nursery days. 'Everything will come all right. You'll see.' She dabbed gently at a tear and repaired the damage to Felice's make-up with a spot of powder. 'There, you look as pretty as a picture.'

Felice went downstairs reluctantly, to be greeted by her father who stood at the foot of the wide stairway. 'Darling, you look beautiful. He won't be able to resist you.'

268

Felice had stopped and smiled at him. A forced smile, but it had been there. His final words wiped it off her face. 'Father, don't throw him at me.'

'As if I would! I assure you Lord Aubrey doesn't need any throwing, he's utterly devoted to you and eager for a reply. A favourable one of course.'

Felice reached the hall. 'You haven't promised anything on my behalf, have you?'

'No, as if I would. I couldn't, could I, with such an independent little girl?'

He was deliberately thrusting her into the past, into childishness, reviving his total domination.

The doorbell rang and she hurried into the drawing room where her mother awaited her. Sylvia wore one of her diaphanous floaty gowns which gave her an ethereal appearance. She looked like a woman who had been ill for a long time and was at last making a recovery. She said quickly, 'Felice, don't let him push you into anything. A good marriage is a blessing, but a bad one is hell. Lord Aubrey sounds like a good match for you, but if you don't want it . . .'

Murray entered and announced in solemn tones, 'Lord Aubrey Whittaker, madam.'

Sylvia held out her hand and Aubrey Whittaker shook it so heartily she winced.

Then he turned to Felice. 'This is going to be the happiest night of my life.'

She was startled. He spoke as if their association was cut and dried. Exactly what had Father said to him? Then other guests entered, among them Jeffrey Westbury. He smiled at her warmly and she returned his smile. She had never forgotten his warm kisses and the way he had once rescued her from Whittaker. He'd not be able to this time.

Dinner was served and proceeded at a dignified pace. Sylvia presided with impeccable grace and Ralph with his usual urbanity.

Felice had been placed between a young man tasting society before going to university and Aubrey Whittaker, who took advantage of the young man's diffidence to monopolise her attention. Several times she made an attempt to turn from him and engage her other partner in conversation but Lord Aubrey soon outflanked her manoeuvring. From just across the table Jeffrey watched the proceedings with amusement, which irritated her.

269

In the end she succumbed and asked Lord Aubrey, 'How is your study of the painters going?'

'Splendidly. I say, fancy you remembering that I'm a keen observer of the arts.'

'You talked of nothing else last time we met.'

'Did I really? That was jolly annoying of me. You had better choose a topic this time.'

'Have you played golf lately?' she blurted.

'Golf? I don't.'

'Tennis? Oh no, you wouldn't have. It's too early in the year.'

'I went to Cannes and managed a few games of tennis there. Felice' – he bent his head towards her and said confidentially, 'I didn't play at all well because I couldn't get you out of my mind.'

Felice jumped and a piece of fish fell from her fork to the floor just as her father looked at her. His frown was quickly concealed.

'Did you see any good paintings abroad?' she asked desperately.

'Of course, I took in Paris on my way home. One can't go to France without a visit to the Louvre and as many of the other galleries as time allows.'

'Don't you make your own time? You are a man of leisure.'

'True,' he agreed happily, 'but one has obligations to hostesses.'

'Of course,' agreed Felice. He failed to notice her touch of sarcasm but Jeffrey caught it and grinned. 'Are you still enthralled by the painters you spoke of last time?' she asked.

'Who were they?'

'It doesn't really matter if you've forgotten, does it?'

Aubrey said doubtfully, 'I suppose not. I am so impressed by the Post-Impressionists, Cézanne in particular. What a genius that man was. How dreadful that he died in poverty.'

Jeffrey leaned forward. 'Cézanne didn't die in poverty,' he pointed out. 'His father was a franc millionaire and Paul inherited his wealth.'

Aubrey Whittaker's face flamed. 'I may perhaps have muddled him with someone else.'

'I think you have,' said Jeffrey, gently mocking, before turning back to his neighbour.

'Know-all,' muttered Aubrey. He looked so downcast that Felice actually felt sorry for him

'Tell me some other artists you admire,' she prompted.

'Oh, right-ho. Well, there's Mondrian and Picasso –' He looked across at Jeffrey as if to challenge him but his opposite neighbour

270

was engrossed in what a pretty redhead was telling him.

Felice ate the food placed before her as Aubrey's voice went on and on like the droning of bees on a summer's day, a sound one heard without actually listening. Fancy being married to a man who talked constantly without knowing his subject, had never known hardship and was probably too dense to recognise it if he saw it.

She waited impatiently for her mother to give the signal for the ladies to leave the men to their cigars and port. Ralph timed his intervention to the minute. Before Sylvia raised her hand he called to the servants to charge the glasses with champagne. Then he stood up.

'Ladies and gentlemen,' he said, 'I have an announcement which I am proud to make.' Felice's heart almost stopped beating as she waited. It couldn't be anything to do with her. It must be some good piece of business he had completed. It was with a sense of disbelief that she heard: 'My wife and I are most happy to announce the engagement of our beloved daughter, Felice, to Lord Aubrey Whittaker. Please join me in drinking their health.'

The guests rose. 'To Felice and Aubrey.'

Felice turned to Aubrey, who looked quite startled before he gave a delighted smile. 'You little puss,' he whispered. 'I had no idea you had accepted me. I spoke to your father – silly old-fashioned idiot that I am – and he said he was sure it would be all right but I must ask you first. I intended to later, but he must have asked you and you said yes.' He leaned towards her and kissed her cheek, which flamed with angry colour.

Her colour was taken to denote pleasure. She sat numbed, remembering Janet's words: 'You never miss what you've never had.' Oh, but she did, you did. She missed love, she craved love and surely she had never had it. Mother had lived most of her daughter's life in emotional isolation. Father had given her everything material she needed, and outward affection but no love. This announcement was simply a confirmation of his careless power. No man who truly cared for his child could have subjected her to this ordeal. She wanted to deny her father's words, to stand up and scream defiance at him, but the habits of years, the obligations of society held her fast. She even dredged up a smile for the beaming guests. Several young ladies gazed at her, envying her capture of so rich and eligible a peer. Only Sylvia looked puzzled. At least she hadn't been in on the conspiracy. Father had decided to make an all-out attack, sure that his obedient daughter would not try to wriggle away, certain that she would fall in with the inevitable.

Felice followed Sylvia and the other ladies to the drawing room where Murray and other servants brought coffee and liqueurs. There were further congratulations and Felice smiled until her muscles ached. Sylvia asked Felice if she would pour. 'After all,' she said, 'it will soon be your duty in your own home.'

A woman in a purple chiffon frock squealed, 'Yes, indeed. You will have your very own home. I will never forget how nervous I was the first time I gave a dinner party. I went into the kitchen so many times to check the food that Cook threatened to leave.'

'Was it all right?' asked a mature woman in green.

'It was. I even managed to pour the coffee without a spill.'

The conversation grew animated as each woman recalled experiences after her engagement and subsequent marriage. Felice drifted to a window seat accompanied by a couple of unmarried girls, Edna and Maisie, whom she had known since childhood. Felice hadn't been consulted about the guest list so Sylvia had no idea that she detested Edna, who dieted almost to the point of emaciation, a regime which had given her the lean face and slightly protruding eyes admired by many. She had a waspish tongue.

'You've got yourself a good catch in Aubrey Whittaker,' she said. 'All the girls have been after him. However *did* you manage to do it?' She looked Felice up and down disparagingly.

Maisie said, 'I hope you'll be very happy, Felice. I think Aubrey is a nice young man.' Maisie was plumply pretty and not very bright and her voice had a wistful note. She would probably suit Aubrey down to the ground if only he had the wit to see it. He was too full of the belief in his own importance which had been drilled into him since his birth to look at any girl properly. If he had an atom of insight he would have realised that Felice and he were incompatible.

'You'll get a solitaire ring the size of a golf ball,' said Edna. 'And lots of other jewellery.' She puckered up her forehead in a deliberate attempt to appear truly puzzled. 'Why, Felice, my dear, you're not wearing an engagement ring. Surely he isn't *mean*. I can't believe it. During his last two engagements he bought a ring straight away. One was a huge ruby, the other an emerald. And when the engagements were broken off he *didn't ask for them back*. It's worth getting a proposal out of him just for the ring.'

Maisie was shocked. 'What an unkind thing to say, Edna. I'm sure that Aubrey would never want to break off with Felice.'

'Did I say he broke the engagements? I rather think the girls got tired of him. You must admit he is a crashing bore. Whoops! Sorry,

272

Felice. I'm sure you've found hidden qualities in him.' She shrugged. 'I think I'll have another cup of coffee, and a delicious Benedictine.'

Eventually the men joined the ladies and the evening dragged to a close. Aubrey hovered about Felice like a wasp about a jampot until she wanted to scream with frustration. Then, finally, she, Ralph and Sylvia were alone.

Felice looked at her father. He smiled and actually rubbed his hands the way he did when he'd brought off a good business deal. She suddenly felt unutterably weary. She wanted above all else to sleep. 'I think I'll go straight to bed.'

'Wait, please,' said Sylvia. 'Why didn't you tell me about Lord Aubrey?'

Felice looked at her father who said, 'Well, she wasn't exactly sure when I would be making the announcement. I hope it came as a pleasant surprise.'

'Wasn't sure?' cried Sylvia. 'A surprise? Felice, had you any knowledge of what your father was going to say tonight?'

'No, Mother.'

'Ralph, it was all your idea, wasn't it?'

'Not entirely. Felice has been seeing Whittaker, he is as keen as mustard and she needs a good husband. What more could we ask for?'

'A lot,' blazed Sylvia, startling them both. 'A damn sight more! Felice, do you wish to marry that numskull Whittaker?'

Felice shook her head. Weariness was dragging at her, pulling at her limbs, tugging her body down. She ached to lie in bed, to forget this ghastly evening.

Sylvia said, her voice soft now, 'My dear girl, you need not marry a man you don't care for.'

'She can't jilt him now,' spluttered Ralph.

'She won't be jilting him. It'll be you doing the jilting, Ralph. You engineered the engagement, you can break it off.'

'I'll do no such thing. If Felice wants to make me look a fool—'

'You appear to have managed it well enough without her help,' snapped Sylvia.

Felice slipped from the room, her parents' loud voices following her into the hall. She lay in bed and wept for the years she and her mother had lost. Why couldn't Sylvia have shown more strength? Why had she allowed her daughter to grow up almost ignorant of a mother's love?

Isobel began to put her plans into action. She'd received muted

273

encouragement from the family, not because they doubted her sincerity and ability but because the task seemed impossible.

'I would love to see you succeed,' said Grace, 'but to open a small workshop and expect women to come to it when they've got all the corsets from Bennyson's to choose from seems an awful risk.'

'I'll undercut his prices.'

'When he hears about you he's bound to kick up a stink,' said Olive, 'but I suppose that's your affair.'

'Fat lot you care, Olive Kingston,' jibed Ivor.

Olive gave him a contemptuous look. 'I probably care more than you, which isn't saying much. How's Mr Dawson these days?'

Ivor flushed. 'Me and old Dawson are bosom pals, if you want to know, not that it's any business of yours.'

'Huh,' responded Olive. 'Not now it isn't, but it might be. He was no friend to Dad and he'll be no friend to you.'

Grace looked up sharply. 'What do you mean? Are you getting into trouble, Ivor?'

'Of course not. Olive's talking through her hat. All she ever thinks about is clothes and dolling herself up for her boyfriends.'

'Have you got someone special?' asked Grace.

'For heaven's sake!' cried Olive. 'Someone special? That's all you ever ask! I don't want someone special, not the sort you mean. When I marry it'll be to a man *I* think is special and that means he'll have money, lots of it, bags of it, plenty to give me.'

'Money isn't everything,' said Grace.

Olive gave a scream of mocking laughter. 'How can you say that? You've never had any. All you've ever known is pinching and scraping and coping with debt. Well, I'm not going to live like that.'

Desmond arrived in time to hear the last sentence. 'Don't speak like that to Mum,' he said. 'She's always been good to us.'

'As good as she could be, but how good was that?'

'She always does her best.'

'Her best! She's worn out with work and now you've got her cooking from morning to night. You've got no room to talk. And as for that beast she married, our dear old dad, I'm glad he's dead. I wish he'd died years ago and if you had any real feeling for Mum you'd admit you felt that way too –' She got no further. Kathy launched herself at her sister and began to pummel her, driving Olive back into the table so hard that she fell along its length.

'Kathy!' Desmond pulled her off with some difficulty. 'Let go. Stop hitting Olive.'

Olive stood up. 'You've torn my stockings, you little bitch, and I've not got another decent pair and my date tonight is used to the best.'

Grace said tremulously, 'Don't swear, Olive. Kathy, say sorry to your sister.'

'I won't! I'm not sorry!'

'Then you'll go to bed with no supper.'

'I'll starve before I say sorry to *her*.'

'Upstairs,' said Grace.

Kathy's eyes filled with tears, but she turned and walked from the room with her head high.

'Bloody savage!' said Olive. She followed Kathy upstairs and they heard her slamming about in her bedroom.

'You were a bit hard on Kathy,' said Isobel. 'She's always starving at night and she's still got homework to do.'

'I know.' Grace was utterly downcast. 'I spoke before I thought. But she shouldn't hit her sister.'

Hearing Olive marching downstairs again Desmond stood in front of her in the narrow hall.

'Let me pass,' yelled Olive.

Desmond spoke in his controlled way. 'You know Kathy's over-wrought by Dad's death. Tell her you forgive her, then she can say sorry and come down to have her supper.'

'I'll do no such thing. Let the little devil suffer.'

'You won't pass until you do.'

Olive swore under her breath. 'You can't stop me.'

'I can and I will.'

'Damn it, I'm late already. And I've had to wear these nasty lisle stockings. Oh, all right. What do I care how the rest of you manage your stupid affairs? Kathy!' she yelled. 'I forgive you.'

Kathy came running to the head of the stairs. 'Thank you, Olive,' she said in relieved tones. 'I'm sorry I hit you.'

Desmond stood aside as Olive squeezed past and through the door. They heard her high heels tapping along the pavement outside.

'What began all that?' asked Desmond.

'Isobel's going to open a corset shop,' said Kathy. 'Olive was nasty about it, then she said wicked things about Dad.' She began to sob, the tears pouring down her face. Isobel went to pull her into her arms, but Kathy evaded her and ran to her mother who held her close, soothing her hair and dabbing at her wet cheeks with a

275

corner of her apron. 'There, there, my love. Don't go upsetting yourself.'

Isobel pushed the kettle over the hob where it began to sing while she put on the tablecloth. Kathy's sobs were dying, but Isobel was near tears herself. Why did her little sister, who had always adored her, now turn from her? Of course, it was right for her to love her mother, but she and Kathy had always been special to each other.

Desmond sat down and lit a Woodbine, all he could afford and those only five at a time. He looked tired. He worked long hours and would be returning to the café for the evening shift.

Ivor was silent and brooding and when he'd gone to meet his pals Grace asked Desmond, 'Do you know of a Mr Dawson? The name sounds familiar.'

'He's a bookie,' said Desmond. 'Dad used him sometimes. He's a devil if anyone owes money they can't pay.' He didn't mention that more than once he'd had to bail Amos out to save him a beating by Dawson's bullies.

Grace was alarmed. 'Does Ivor owe him money?'

'I don't know. I hope he wouldn't be so foolish,' said Desmond, making a mental note to find out what he could. When he had rescued his father he had been earning, now he was dependent on the fluctuating takings of the café, and the thought of another member of his family falling into Dawson's clutches worried and angered him.

Lawrence Dane was troubled. His life ran as smoothly as ever, but he no longer felt entirely comfortable. He was curry-combing his latest acquisition, but even the quality of the time spent with his beloved horses was diminished. And by what? By a working-class girl with a short, sturdy figure who spent her days scrubbing and polishing for other men's wives. Yet, try as he would, he could not get her out of his mind. Their acquaintanceship was slight, their only physical contact a few kisses, yet Isobel Kingston exuded a quality that fascinated him and held him captive. She had courage; her stand against Ralph proved that. She had a tremendous will to survive and unshakeable loyalty to her family. There were times when he felt closer to the Kingstons than to his own family. If only he could analyse his feelings about Isobel he felt he would be rid of them. Without conceit he knew that any number of girls from excellent backgrounds hoped he would notice them. Yet every day, at the time he guessed Isobel would be trudging back from her dreary jobs,

276

he had the urge to drive around until he found her and could give her a lift home. Her tired face, her tumbled hair stuffed beneath a tam-o'-shanter gave him more pleasure than the prettiest debutante in a superb gown.

'Damn, damn, damn,' he said aloud, starling the groom. 'Take over here, Bill. I've remembered an engagement.'

Lawrence drove in the direction of the rows of semidetached houses where Isobel worked, and cruised around, rousing the suspicion of several housewives and at least one policeman on the beat. He knew he was behaving stupidly. She could be anywhere in the maze of streets. Then he saw her and his heart seemed to miss a beat as he realised he loved her. It was impossible, against all reason, unbelievable – she certainly would regard a declaration of love from him as incredible, but it was true. Never had he experienced the myriad sensations which assailed him at the sight of that small figure with her stiff determined back fighting the wind and drizzle which had begun to turn into driving rain.

He drove up beside her and stopped. 'Isobel.'

She looked round quickly and he could have sworn that just for an instant she had betrayed pleasure at seeing him.

'Give you a lift, ma'am,' he offered, trying to sound flippant.

She hesitated, looked at the sky, then nodded. 'Yes, please.'

He got out of the car and opened the passenger door, an action which caused her to narrow her eyes suspiciously since he usually just leaned over and pushed the door open for her. She sank into the leather seat with a sigh.

He drove away, buoyed up by the joy he felt at having her near. 'Tough day?'

'Very. Some of those snooty women treat me as if I were subhuman.' She stopped short. 'I always forget. You belong more with them than with me.'

Lawrence laughed. 'I think not. I don't belong anywhere where people are treated as subhuman.'

She laughed with him. 'What brought you to these *ordinary* streets?'

You, he wanted to yell, but he said merely, 'I had to see a man about a horse.'

'Of course, how very silly of me. People round here own lots of horses.'

Lawrence grinned and a companionable silence fell between them. Then Lawrence, unable to master his anxiety, asked, 'Will you need to do these menial tasks much longer?'

'Probably for the rest of my life,' she said drily. 'Folks in our position rarely if ever have maids.'

'You know what I mean. Will you have to work for these unspeakable women for much longer?'

'They aren't all bad, you know. Some are quite human. Only today the lady of the house gave me a bit of boiling bacon. It can go in the soup. We make gallons of soup for the new café in West Street as well as hundredweights of rice and bread-and-butter pudding absolutely stuffed with sultanas, eggs and milk and very good for a working man or woman. Haven't you visited us yet? Our cuisine is plain but palatable. Oh, but,' she couldn't resist adding, 'you don't regard yourself as a working man, do you?'

Stung by her sarcasm Lawrence said, 'I work. I supervise the home farm and groom my horses, and what's more I mucked out the stables when one of the grooms was ill.'

'Heavens!' gasped Isobel in mocking tones. 'Lawrence Dane with his hands in muck. What an amazing thought.'

In spite of his exasperation Lawrence smiled. 'Where there's muck there's brass.'

'True. At least I hope it is. Many of our patrons at the café come in very mucky but brass is still a bit thin on the ground.'

'But you're managing? You and your family?'

Isobel gave him a sideways glance. He sounded as if he really cared. 'We're managing, just about,' she said. Words which couldn't be said to an outsider trembled on her lips: I have a sister who is totally selfish and, worse, a brother who seems to be following in Dad's footsteps. God, I hope he won't land in jail. And my little sister turns from me.

Lawrence sensed her sudden distress. He laid a hand over her gloved one for a moment. There was a hole in the right thumb from which strands of darning wool were straying. It gave him an overwhelming desire to protect her and an equally strong one to stop the car, enfold her in an embrace and kiss her breathless. Women were supposed to be intuitive. Did she guess at the strength of his longings?

They arrived at the end of her street. As she turned in her seat to say goodnight he could no longer resist the urges which drove him. 'Isobel – Isobel –' He leaned towards her and took her in his arms. He scarcely knew whether he expected resistance, but she was pliable in his hands. She held up her face, clearly wanting a kiss, and his heart sang. Their lips met and met again as they clung together. Lawrence tentatively slid his tongue into her warm, soft mouth and she met it with hers and the kiss deepened. Her mouth seemed to scorch his. He lifted his head and stared into her eyes. Surely there was a message there for him? A girl like Isobel would never have permitted such a kiss unless she felt deeply for him.

She pulled away, opened the door and with a hurried goodnight fled down the street.

Chapter Seventeen

Isobel hurried from Lawrence Dane's car in a state of bewilderment. He had never kissed her that way before and his mouth on hers had inflamed her to an intensity of desire. He must have sensed her surge of need because it had encouraged his tongue to slide and dance inside her mouth. She wondered what it would feel like to have him inside her body, really inside in the most intimate way. There had been a look on his face which intrigued her, excited her, while it half scared her. The feeling she had for him made her memories of Frank look like pictures from a children's storybook.

She arrived at her front gate. There was some sort of argument going on in the house and she sighed. They were all in the front room, she could hear their voices, and she slid past the door wanting only to rest her feet in the kitchen and drink a cup of tea, but the door opened and Kathy raced out.

'Hello, Isobel,' she cried. 'I've to put the kettle on so we can all have tea. There's a lady in there.' She pointed back to the half-open door.

Isobel said, 'I'll have a cup of tea, love, while you're at it. I'll sit down where it's quiet.'

'Aren't you going in to see the lady? It's very strange her coming here.'

'Strange?'

'Yes, I think she's something to do with the factory.'

Isobel's mind filled with hopeful images of Miss Trefusis coming to beg her to return. They had decided they needed her – perhaps for another corset show – and her heart beat fast. 'I'll have my tea in the front room, Kathy,' she said.

'OK,' said Kathy, betraying her knowledge of cinema language. Lately she and Grace had visited the cinema twice a week on every change of programme, craving the power of fiction, it seemed.

Isobel pushed the door open wide and walked in. The room was full and, as she had expected, Olive and Ivor were arguing vociferously with Grace and Desmond. But what really startled her was the sight of Desmond with a protective arm around Felice Bennyson who was flushed and near to tears.

Grace turned and her pale face softened. 'Oh, there you are, Isobel. I'm sure you can find a way out.'

'A way out of what?' managed Isobel. 'Hello, Miss Bennyson.'

'Please, call me Felice. And I know you are Isobel.' Felice's soft, cultured tones were in startling contrast to the others'.

Olive cried, 'Desmond's brought *her* here without so much as a by-your-leave and now he expects her to share a bedroom with one of us.'

'Desmond doesn't have to ask for permission to bring home a friend to stay,' said Isobel calmly.

'Please, don't quarrel over me,' begged Felice. 'I couldn't think of anywhere to go except the café. My friend is abroad and I don't have any relatives near and I rushed out without any money.'

'She's been to the café a few times lately,' said Desmond with a touch of pride in his voice.

Isobel wondered why he had been so secretive about that. She knew, really. He was in love with Felice whether he realised it or not.

'And Desmond suggested . . .' Felice said.

'I suggested she should come home with me,' said Desmond. 'She needs a place to stay and I knew you and Mum would want to help her.'

The last thing Isobel wanted was to get mixed up with the vengeful Ralph Bennyson again, but Felice was clearly very distressed. The phrase 'my friend' in the singular startled her. She had supposed that a girl in Felice's walk of life would have many friends. What an odd lonely life she must lead. Isobel was burning with curiosity as to why the daughter of a wealthy family felt the need to hide herself in a household tottering on the verge of poverty.

Felice said, 'I'll leave, Mrs Kingston. I was wrong to agree to come here.'

'Kettle's boiling!' Kathy stuck her head round the door. 'And we've got some biscuits. Bought ones, not ones we made.'

The family trooped to the kitchen but Desmond lingered with Felice. He motioned Isobel to stay.

Felice said sadly, 'Desmond, it was wonderful of you to take care of me, but this won't do. I am upsetting your family. I had much better go home.' Her voice was as soft as silk and she looked at

Desmond with devotion clear in her eyes.

It could not be long before these two declared their love openly, especially if Felice stayed. Isobel's breath caught in her throat. If Desmond had conspired in any way to lure Felice from her father Ralph's revenge would be swift and cruel. He was rich enough to close down the café and anything else the Kingstons tried to open. Her business, too, could be scuppered before it began.

But Felice looked sick with misery and Isobel could not turn her back on her. She said spontaneously, 'You needn't leave. Take no notice of Olive. She can be cantankerous, but she's hardly ever here. I have a very small room and a not very wide bed but you're welcome to share it.'

The trembling tears came into Felice's eyes and ran down her cheeks. 'How kind you are. After the way my father treated you!'

'Don't cry,' said Desmond. Words of love clearly hovered on his lips, but he had the wisdom to let her recover before he opened up to her. 'We can talk later. Let's have tea.'

The family seated themselves in the overcrowded kitchen. Felice's gaze wandered to the shining black range where a cheerful fire glowed, to the wooden rack which rose on a pulley to the ceiling from which the family underwear hung to air. To the checked cloth and the cheap cups on the table, to the kitchen door from which hung coats and hats. Isobel wondered what she made of it all.

Desmond treated his guest like a piece of Dresden china, handing her biscuits and tea with polite ceremony. Olive and Ivor gave up their protests. Olive was placated by learning that Felice was to share Isobel's tiny room and Desmond slipped the avaricious Ivor half a crown.

'Did you bring any luggage at all?' asked Isobel.

'Only a little. I just grabbed a few things and ran. I didn't even drive to the café so I don't have my car. I couldn't think straight.' Felice lapsed into silence.

Desmond said, 'Her father has been telling everyone that she is engaged to be married to a man she detests. They had a fearful argument about it. He wouldn't give way, said she'd get used to the idea . . .'

'But I won't! I can't!' Felice cried.

'No one should be forced to marry unless they're in love,' said Grace quietly. 'It can bring nothing but trouble.'

She sounded inexpressibly sad and Isobel wondered sadly if she had ever truly loved her husband, even in the beginning.

'Will you go back and fetch more clothes?' asked Kathy excitedly. To her this was an adventure straight from the films. 'Beautiful heiress runs from nasty father and wicked lover'. She stared at Desmond and Isobel knew she was already picturing him in a gallant battle with the Bennysons. But he could never win. Never. For a moment she resented the girl who could bring more trouble on them.

'Won't your mum be upset?' Kathy asked, then flushed as Felice looked at her sorrowfully. 'You have got a mum, haven't you?' she blurted.

'Yes,' said Felice, 'I do have a mum.' Her voice was tender as she looked into the eager child's eyes. Here was someone who had been truly loved all her life. 'I won't let her worry about me,' she assured Kathy. 'I'd better phone her now.' She flushed again. Of course the Kingstons wouldn't have a telephone. They were for the well-off.

Desmond, who seemed imperturbable, said calmly, 'I'll take you to the nearest telephone box.'

After the two of them had left Olive said, 'I'm going out. I hope you won't regret the day you let that girl stay. From all you've told me Ralph Bennyson could play hell with our lives. He's supposed to adore his daughter, isn't he?'

'He can't possibly!' declared Kathy. 'If he did he wouldn't force her to marry someone she doesn't like.'

'She's a weak fool to run away,' said Olive. 'I'll be damned if I'd leave a house like hers just because I didn't like something my father did. I wonder who he was trying to get her to marry? I bet it was a rich man. I'll marry the first rich man who shows an interest in me.'

'What if nobody does?' asked Kathy.'

'I'll get someone. You see if I don't.'

That night Isobel and Felice lay side by side and talked for a long time. In the shielding darkness Felice felt able to unburden herself. Desmond's sister listened without comment to the ups and downs of Felice's life, occasionally patting her shoulder sympathetically. Isobel heard about the awful situation which existed between Ralph and Sylvia, about the way Ralph dominated Felice and how she had felt increasingly desperate. 'Father loves me,' she said. 'I suppose it's love, but it has made me a prisoner. I've not had a chance to make friends, not real ones, or to experience anything without my father having a hand in it.'

'Maybe he loves you too much,' said Isobel. 'Is that possible?'

'I don't know. If love makes you an unwilling prisoner, can it be called love?'

'I don't know, either. I never had any from my father.' It was the first time she had said such a thing to anyone and the truth of it struck her like a hammer blow. 'No, he didn't love me. In fact, I think he detested me and I've no idea why.'

'That's terrible. It must have been dreadful for you.'

'You and I seem to have got ourselves in a similar stew for very different reasons.' Isobel sighed. 'I wonder if we'll ever find out what love really means?'

Felice said breathlessly, 'I believe I have.'

Isobel hesitated before asking, but she needed to know. 'Can you tell me who?'

'Can't you guess?'

Isobel could, but she dared not say so.

'It's your brother. It's Desmond. He's the most kind, wonderful, loving man I've ever met. I don't mean he's made love to me or anything like that, but oh, Isobel, I want him to. I've never wanted a man to touch me before, but Desmond – he's so different.' She gave a shuddering laugh.

Isobel put an arm round her. 'Try to sleep.'

Unburdening herself had given Felice some peace of mind and she slept quickly, but Isobel lay awake for hours.

Ralph was sure Sylvia knew where his daughter was. There was a phone call which she said had come from her dressmaker, but why should she have replaced the receiver so hurriedly when he walked into the hall?

'You know where she is, don't you?' he grated through his teeth. 'You bloody well know. That was Felice on the phone, wasn't it?'

Sylvia prevaricated. 'If it was I wouldn't tell you! How dare you make our daughter a pawn in your social climbing.'

'Come into the library. I would prefer not to brawl where the servants can hear.'

Sylvia followed him and sank into one of the deep leather armchairs, gazing up at him with an assumed calmness that worried him.

'You bitch!' he rasped. 'As if I would use Felice. I've found her a good husband, a rich man against whom there has never been a breath of scandal' – Sylvia winced – 'a man who obviously adores her.'

'Aubrey Whittaker is far too conceited a fool to adore anyone except himself. You're condemning her to a life with an idiot who's swayed by every passing whim—'

'You can't know that. You've scarcely met the man.'

'Neither has Felice but clearly she doesn't want him.'

'She must get to know him properly. Naturally there can be no wedding until she realises that Whittaker is right for her. Then they can marry and life will open up to her. She'll be presented at last—'

'My God! That's all you care about. A presentation at court.'

'You had one. So did every other woman of my acquaintance. Before I got hooked by you, that is.'

Sylvia gasped. He still had the power to hurt her but this time she would be strong. Felice should have her chance of escape. Of course, she couldn't be allowed to stay with the Kingstons but she was safe there for the time being. She would set up home with her daughter. She had already begun to plan for the life they would lead and she had enough money for them both. Royalty might frown on divorce, even though it was much more common these days, but there were enough liberated people who saw no bar to happiness after breaking the marriage vow.

Ralph had been watching her like a cat with a mouse. 'Where is she?' he demanded.

'I don't know.' Well, in a way it was true. She deliberately hadn't asked Felice for the Kingstons' address. She was no good at lying.

Ralph was suddenly possessed by his ungovernable temper. He strode to his wife and dragged her to her feet. He shook her until she choked for breath, then slapped her hard across her face. Bruises appeared almost instantly on Sylvia's fine, pale skin. She pressed her lips together. She wouldn't give him the satisfaction of crying out.

'Tell me, tell me,' he yelled. 'I know she'd confide in you. You've been getting at her a lot lately behind my back, allowing her to meet people and go places without my permission.'

'Behind your back!' mocked Sylvia, through her bruised lips. A trickle of blood ran from her mouth where her teeth had bitten deep. 'Your permission?'

Ralph released her abruptly. He strode to the window and back several times like a caged beast. He is a beast, thought Sylvia, a vile beast. She was suddenly overwhelmed by thoughts of Harry Dane. 'Oh, God,' she moaned aloud. 'Oh, God,' as the memory of what she had thrown away, the havoc she had caused, struck her afresh. She had been fighting back memory for years, concealing it from herself in semi-invalidism and feminine helplessness. But she wasn't helpless. And she wasn't an invalid. At last the time had come when she must face facts and assert herself.

'You've thought of something!' said Ralph.

'Yes, I have. I thought of my husband—'

'I'm your husband! You're demented! In fact you've probably been demented for most of your life.'

'It's a pity then that you saw fit to seduce me when I was in such a state.'

'You were pretty easy to get.'

She felt sick. 'Was I? And why was that? Who persuaded me that Harry was unfaithful? Who manufactured a photograph which lied?'

For a moment Ralph was taken aback. 'So you found out,' he blustered. Then he laughed. 'Any other woman would have seen through the little ruse or laughed when they discovered I'd been playing a practical joke. I could hardly have known you would be so gullible.'

'A practical joke? Is that all it was? It backfired on you, didn't it?'

Ralph glared at her. 'I wish to God I'd never met you.'

'So do I, then I would still be with my husband.'

'I'm your husband,' he yelled again.

'No, you are not. You never were. Harry was my husband. I still think of him that way. You destroyed him, and you've tried to destroy me. And now Felice—'

'Felice? Destroy Felice? You *are* mad. Crazy in the head. I could have you put away again.'

'No.'

Ralph was brought up short by some quality in Sylvia he had never seen before.

'No! You'll never do that to me again. We're finished. I don't have to live with you and as soon as I've made arrangements I shall go.'

'You'll follow Felice, I suppose. Well, I warn you, I'll have you watched. It won't be difficult. I'll find you both no matter where you are. First I'll bring my child back where she belongs then I'll deal with you.'

'What do you intend to do with me? Have me killed off, like you did your disobedient dog?'

'With less emotion,' he said. 'But I don't need to kill you. I shall go to court and prove that you are not fit to look after her. That you have twice been detained in mental hospitals and that you are suffering another breakdown. If you try to take my daughter from me I promise you I shall use all the influence and money I've got to stop you.'

In spite of herself Sylvia shivered. Could he actually do that? 'You took my child from me,' she said in low tones. 'Does it hurt you to lose yours? Because no matter what you do you will still have lost her and through no fault of mine.'

'I assume you are referring to Lawrence when you speak of the child you lost. *You* abandoned your son. It was no doing of mine.'

'Liar,' said Sylvia. 'I always wanted him and you know it. Something happened all those years ago to separate me from Lawrence.'

'We all know that! You left your husband and abandoned your son.'

'No, there was something more. I realise that now, something you instigated. I don't know what, but I intend to find out.'

Had she imagined the flicker of fear in his eyes?

Felice was deeply interested in everything that interested Desmond and Isobel. She had been astonished by having to use an outside lavatory with no flush, by discovering that she could only bathe when a tin bath had been lifted from the shed wall and filled with water heated on the range, by the sameness of the food; but the tender humanity which linked most of this family was like a soothing draught. For the first few days she was fearful, knowing her father's ruthlessness, knowing he would bully Mother. She felt bad about that, but her mother had insisted she stayed where she was and did not communicate with Father until he was in a more reasonable frame of mind.

Felice sat in the Kingstons' kitchen and peeled vegetables willingly and learned to make puddings. Grace was surprised and pleased to find her a great help. She also tried her hand at baking and came up with some delicious lemon biscuits of the sort she'd enjoyed at home, which were added to the café menu. She wore one of Grace's coats and a shapeless gardening hat to accompany Desmond to the café and actually enjoyed putting on a floral wraparound apron and washing up in the small back room. It was not so much that she welcomed the tasks, it was being near Desmond. She could never have pictured a man so strong yet so gentle who treated her with courtesy but not overindulgence. Once, when he found some dishes not properly cleaned, he reprimanded her. She even rather liked that. In fact, she wondered how she could live without

Desmond. His eyes told her he cared, but he never said so. Would he ever? Did he see her as beyond his reach? She feared he might.

Grace and Kathy had gone to bed. Felice sensed a special link between them. It was as if each depended on the other for constant reassurance. This, for some reason, seemed to worry Isobel.

But Isobel went gallantly on with her plans for her corset business. 'I've got it all worked out,' she said. 'It'll take time to save for the cloth and the notions, but it's the sewing machine that's beating me. I've been looking through newspaper advertisements and at cards in tobacconists' windows, but there's never a machine heavy enough to take the coutil.'

Felice had quickly learned the meanings of the new words. 'I was such a fool,' she mourned. 'If I'd brought my car I could have sold it. It's nearly new and I could have got a good price for it.'

'I couldn't take money from you,' smiled Isobel. 'But you need some yourself. Could you get hold of your car?'

'No,' said Felice quickly. 'My father would tell the police it had been stolen.'

'Not if you left a note for him.'

Felice was thoughtful. 'I wonder.'

'No,' said Desmond firmly. 'She might get caught.'

'But he wouldn't hurt his own daughter!' protested Isobel. As the memory of Amos and his brutality flooded back she added miserably, 'I suppose there's no telling what an angry man can do.'

'But I want so much to help you,' said Felice.

'You're a darling girl to think so,' said Desmond.

All thoughts of money fled from Felice. He had called her a darling girl. Oh, let him love me, she prayed silently. I'll never ask for anything else.

Isobel was still tied to her routine. Out from early to late, slaving away for other women in their kitchens and laundry rooms, taking their condescension without arguing, accepting the pittance they paid because she could get nothing else. Nationwide unemployment went on rising. Desmond charged as little as he possibly could for food and still make a profit but there were plenty who couldn't afford even pence, and too often for his future prosperity he allowed some desperate job-seeking man with holes in his boots, or a frantic woman with hungry children, to creep into the steamy warmth of the café and have a free bowl of soup and a filling pudding. Felice saw all this with eyes that often filled with tears of pity for the hungry and love for Desmond.

As Isobel scrubbed and toiled she thought about her brother and Felice. Felice was deeply, truly in love with Desmond and clearly he loved her. The situation was impossible, yet it was a fact.

And there was something else. Lawrence Dane was turning up more and more often to offer her a lift home. He had studied her movements and knew roughly where she'd be on any given day. And like a fool she had begun to look for him, to hope that he would be waiting, and all her admonishments to herself failed to crush her pleasure at seeing him.

He was waiting round the corner for her tonight. 'God, you look awful,' he greeted her.

She didn't answer. She was used to his frank remarks. She slid into the deep leather seat with a sigh of pleasure. His insults on her appearance were uttered in such tender accents they were like compliments from anyone else.

'Bad day,' he commented. He didn't ask. He had pestered her until she explained exactly what she did.

She relaxed, watching his capable hands on the steering wheel. She wanted to touch them, to feel their strength. She breathed in his masculine scent of tobacco, leather, tweed and a faint impelling muskiness from his body which stirred her senses. She knew she was behaving dangerously to allow herself even this small sensual indulgence. Lawrence Dane was not for her any more than Felice was for Desmond.

'Penny for them,' said Lawrence.

'They're the same as usual. Not worth discussing.'

'You're lying to me again. I can feel the way you're thinking.'

I hope not, she thought. 'Clever, aren't you?'

'Yes, as a matter of fact I am. You're thinking you want me to stop and kiss you.'

'Is that so, you conceited oaf?'

'Yes, it is so.'

He stopped the car in a quiet road, cast a quick glance round and took her in his arms. All thought of resistance left her as he drew her close and she felt the strength of his heartbeat and his warm mouth touching hers. Her arms slid round his neck and she caught at his hair, pressing his lips closer. At first his kiss was gentle, but he couldn't control his aching longing to possess her and his tongue travelled round her lips then darted into her mouth which had

290

opened like a flower to him. They forgot time and space as their embrace grew in depth and intensity. His hand moved to her breasts and at his first touch she was galvanised with desire. Her body ached. She wanted only to know his love in its full power. Lawrence was floating on a sensual sea as his hand moved to her thighs. They were brought back abruptly to reality when they heard the muted sniggers of a couple of urchins who had their faces pressed to the window. Lawrence jerked back as if he'd been shot and Isobel's face flamed. He shoved the car into gear and drove off far too fast.

For moments they didn't speak, then Lawrence said, 'Isobel, we must go somewhere where we can be alone.'

'We can't!' she gasped. 'I don't know what possessed me back there. I was mad. Anyone could have seen us. Those boys! I feel besmirched.'

Lawrence in his anger swung the car carelessly round a tram. 'Don't say that! Don't ever feel that! Not with me.'

'Why not with you?' Tears had formed in her eyes and ran down her cheeks as the full enormity of her temptation burst upon her. She was in love with Lawrence Dane. Had been for a long time. When had it started?'

'You mean everything to me, my darling. I need you terribly.'

'Need me?' Her heart missed a beat. He hadn't said he loved her. Of course he wouldn't. Not ever. Did he honestly believe that she, Isobel Kingston, an independent woman, as proud as any woman of his class, would actually surrender her body to a man who considered himself above her?

She dried her tears and said fiercely, 'I'm sure you do.'

'You understand?'

'Oh, yes, I understand very well.'

They had reached the end of her road and he stopped and looked at her. 'You were crying. My lovely girl, I didn't mean to make you cry.'

'If I give in to you I shall shed a great many more tears.'

'No, you won't. I promise—'

'You promise? What exactly do you promise, Lawrence? I mean, what *exactly*?'

He was silent.

'A hidden love affair? Secret rendezvous? Shame and guilt?'

'I should feel neither making love to you. I care too much for you.'

'Well, I should feel both.'

He sighed. 'You've been brought up to think that sex is shaming.'

'Not at all. You have no conception of how I was brought up. How could you? You've been pampered all your life by money and people who think you're some kind of little god—'

'I have not!' His explosive anger startled her. 'You have no knowledge of what my life has been any more than I have of yours. How could you?'

'Exactly. We are poles apart.'

'We could talk about our lives. And our bodies are not poles apart.'

'Bodies are only one aspect of a relationship, and when it comes down to day-to-day living certainly not the most important one.'

'Don't tell me you're frigid. I can't accept that.'

'I tell you nothing of the kind. I have the normal instincts of a woman, but unlike you I look upon sex as a precious commodity reserved for marriage.'

The word was out and Isobel stayed quite still, wishing she had kept guard over her tongue. Now he'd think she expected marriage from him.

He said slowly, 'I'll be truthful. I'll always be truthful with you. I wasn't thinking of marriage.'

'I know. It doesn't matter.'

'But it does. I can't—'

She opened the car door. 'Let's not say any more. It would be better if you didn't give me a lift again.'

'Afraid of me?'

'A little. But more afraid of myself.'

She shut the door and ran to her house and up to her room to be alone.

Sylvia had made up her mind. She broke a luncheon engagement with her often-used excuse of a headache. She did not have one today. In fact, she felt exceptionally well and able to tackle her life as she once had done.

She decided against using their car, whose driver could be got at by Ralph, and took a tram ride then a taxi to the Dane house. A maid admitted her to the hall where she waited. Then she was shown into a cosy morning room where old Mrs Dane sat near a fire, her daintily slippered feet resting on a tapestry-covered stool. A piece of tapestry on which she had been working lay on a small Regency sewing box beside her.

She held out a hand which shook slightly. There was a wary

292

expression on her face. 'How do you do, Mrs Bennyson?'

The simple conventional greeting shook Sylvia, who had once been loved by this dignified woman. She had been put firmly in her place. Mrs Dane had aged, of course, but her eyes were as bright as Sylvia remembered. Just now, they were solemn as they regarded her.

'Won't you sit down? Here, near the fire.' The old lady rang the bell and, when her maid appeared, ordered coffee. 'It is many years since we met,' she observed.

'Yes. A long time,' blurted Sylvia. Her self-control was dissipating in the memory of how much she had wronged her former mother-in-law. The words she had come to say were imprisoned in her head.

It seemed as if Mrs Dane understood. She sat quietly awaiting the return of the maid, though her head sometimes twitched on her slender stem of a neck. She was wearing the pearl choker Harry had presented to his mother on his wedding day and the memory further undermined Sylvia.

Sylvia found the silence oppressive. 'How is Lawrence getting on with his stables?' she asked.

'Well enough. He loves his horses. I take it that he doesn't discuss them with you.'

'He never discusses anything with me,' said Sylvia, bitterness creeping into her voice.

'Did you expect him to?' asked Mrs Dane.

'I've always hoped. I still hope.'

The maid brought the coffee and a plate of small biscuits which neither woman could eat.

They sipped their coffee. Sylvia knew she must make a move. If she lost her courage now she'd leave without ever asking the questions she needed answered and her torment would be worse than before.

She put her coffee down carefully on a small occasional table and said slowly, enunciating each word as if it gave her pain to use it, 'We were good friends once.'

Mrs Dane looked at her, her brows slightly drawn. A lesser woman might have let forth a stream of accusations, but she continued to listen.

'We were good friends once,' Sylvia repeated, trying to gather her words into coherent order. 'You knew me well. You knew how much I adored Harry. Forgive me,' she said in a rush. 'Never a day passes in which I don't think of him. And I adored our son. My Lawrence. I

293

was a blind, stupid fool to believe what Ralph said about Harry, but I did, and I left that same night with him, with Ralph Bennyson. I made a terrible mistake, I knew it at once. How could I have listened to his lies and doubted my Harry?'

'What lies?' asked Mrs Dane. Sylvia clearly didn't know that Felice had been here. Mrs Dane had dismissed her stories but maybe she had been wrong to do so.

'He told me that Harry was being unfaithful to me. He produced a photograph of my dear husband in a very compromising position with a woman wearing almost no clothes.'

'What?' Mrs Dane was shaken. 'Impossible. Harry worshipped you. No other woman on earth would have tempted him, least of all one so brazen as to be photographed in such a way!'

'I know that now. I was such a gullible fool. The photograph was a montage, the woman's likeness grafted to Harry's in some way.'

'How did you find out? When?'

'After Harry – after he – died.' Sylvia choked. 'I couldn't even go to his funeral. It seemed to me that the best part of me was buried with him. My mourning got on Ralph's nerves and he yelled at me. He had never intended to marry me. I was to be a seduction and then forgotten. He married me because I thought I was pregnant. He couldn't face any more scandal. It was a false alarm, but he thought I'd done it purposely. As if I would! As if I could be so deceitful! But he still believes I tricked him. Life with him has been – difficult.'

'You poor child!' The words broke from Mrs Dane instinctively. 'Have you carried this burden alone?'

'Who could I tell? And what good would it have done? And then there was Felice. Mrs Dane, Felice has left home. I know where she's hiding, but Ralph does not.'

'Is she safe?'

'I'm sure of it.'

Mrs Dane felt she was faced with an intricate puzzle. 'How can I help you?'

'Oh, Mother Dane,' said Sylvia, in her distress falling into her old way of addressing her former mother-in-law, 'please could you tell Lawrence how much I've always loved him. I've been through hell. I loved him so much and to be forbidden to see him was torture! I understood your motives, but I feel it might help my son even now to know how much I cared.'

Mrs Dane stared at Sylvia. She recalled Felice's words. The puzzle

294

was unravelling and revealing some fearful truths. 'Forbidden to see him?' she said, struggling for calm. 'By whom?'

'By you, of course. Ralph told me you felt it best that my boy should not be tormented by memories of the past and I did understand your point of view, but it was so hard—'

'But I said no such thing! I never would!'

Sylvia stared at Mrs Dane, who gazed back in horror.

'Ralph told me,' said Mrs Dane, 'that you refused utterly to see Lawrence.'

'Oh my God,' whispered Sylvia. 'He lied to us both. It means that Lawrence has grown up thinking that I deserted him. That I cared nothing for him. No wonder he hates me. Oh, God, I knew Ralph was wicked, but this—!'

'We should have trusted each other,' said Mrs Dane. 'Why didn't we? All those years wasted.'

'My poor boy,' moaned Sylvia. 'Did he know how his father died? At the time, I mean?'

'He was little more than a toddler, but he saw what happened. His father couldn't have known that Lawrence was playing one of their favourite games. They enjoyed creeping up and surprising each other. Lawrence was hiding in Harry's study when his father pulled out a gun and shot himself. Lawrence ran to him and saw his father's head split open, his face torn, the blood spattered everywhere. It covered his hands. It appears he tried to lift his father's body.'

Sylvia gave a cry as the room began to spin round her. Then she fainted. She recovered to find herself supported in the maid's arms. Mrs Dane patted her hands and gave her brandy. Sylvia choked on the strong spirit but colour returned to her cheeks, she sat up and the maid left.

Mrs Dane sat quietly gazing at her. 'Rest yourself, my dear. You've had a dreadful shock.'

'I never imagined such horror! How could I? Lawrence must have needed me so much. Did Ralph know of his need?'

'He knew because I asked him to beg you to come to your son. I told him how much Lawrence wanted you, how he wept for you. But Ralph returned with the information that under no circumstances did you wish to be involved.'

'But why? Why?' Sylvia wailed. 'Why was he so cruel?'

Mrs Dane's lips twisted. 'I can only think he wanted revenge on you because he felt he had been trapped into marriage.'

'I laid no trap. I behaved like a damned fool. Every tenet by which

I had lived my life seemed to have vanished. I had nothing to cling to. I made mistake after mistake. But to learn now that my son wanted me, that we have been alienated because of one man's jealousy, is too much to bear. I knew Ralph was bad, but not as evil as this. I must keep Felice away from him.'

'Felice knows a little. She came to me,' said Mrs Dane. 'She tried to tell me what happened was not your fault entirely. She believes that you did not reject Lawrence. I'm afraid I thought she was imagining it. I sent her away.'

'She has left home. Oh, not because of you. Her father is trying to force her into an unsuitable marriage. Sounds like Victorian melodrama, doesn't it?' Sylvia concluded, bitter humour infecting her soft voice. 'I intend to leave Ralph and set up a home with Felice. Neither of us can stomach him any more.'

Mrs Dane looked searchingly at the woman who had broken her son's heart and pitied her.

'Mrs Dane, I know I can never atone for what I did to Harry—'

'Don't speak of it, my child. My son chose his way out. We are each of us responsible for our own actions.'

'You are kind, but it will always lie on my conscience. What can we tell Lawrence? He hates me and I love him so much. To think of the memories he has carried with him all these years! He must have the dreadful scene of his father's death forever in his mind—'

'No,' said Mrs Dane gently. 'He remembers nothing of that terrible day. I think it has been blocked from his consciousness.'

'That's a good thing,' said Sylvia. 'It is, isn't it?'

'I don't know. When he was young it seemed merciful, but now I wonder if concealing the truth from himself has not damaged him in some way. He has never had a really stable relationship and I wonder if he ever will, or if he's even capable of falling in love. I am beginning to doubt that he'll ever marry and have the children I should so much welcome.'

'It's all much more horrible than I realised,' cried Sylvia. 'What can we do?' She stared at Mrs Dane. 'What do you think we should do? You know him best.'

'I must think about it,' said Mrs Dane. 'Knowledge may ease him, or it could restore memories which might destroy his peace of mind.'

Chapter Eighteen

Sylvia left the house quietly before lunchtime. Ralph was at his golf club. Not that he'd been playing in this disastrous weather. Most likely he was deeply immersed in endless games of bridge. She sheltered beneath her umbrella as she hurried along in inadequate shoes, annoyed with herself for not thinking of brogues. As soon as she could she hailed a taxi which took her to the address Felice had given her. She sat for a moment staring at the tiny terraced house, then paid the driver and let him go. She could telephone when she wanted another. It was only as he disappeared round a bend that she realised that no house had a telephone wire.

She took a deep breath and knocked on the door. It was opened by a pleasant-faced though rather dishevelled-looking woman in a flour-sprinkled wrap-around apron. A pleasant smell of cooking wafted over her. The women stared at each other.

Then Grace Kingston smiled uncertainly and said, 'Can I help you? If you're selling something I'm a waste of your time. I've got no money to spare.' Her words were dismissive but her voice was gentle and compassionate as if she comprehended the difficulties of a saleswoman's life.

Sylvia's carefully rehearsed words of greeting went out of her head. She hadn't known what to expect. The daughter and son of the house had both worked in the factory. Before the strike they had been valued employees and she had assumed that they came from a semidetached middle-class home, but this place was almost a hovel.

'I'm Sylvia Bennyson,' she blurted. 'And you must be Mrs Kingston.'

The woman looked mystified for a few seconds before she gasped, 'Felice's mother?'

Sylvia nodded. 'She telephoned me.'

'Yes, I know,' said Grace. 'You'd better come in.' She bustled in front of her visitor. 'It's such a dreadful day again. It's awful trying to dry the washing. I've lots with a big family.'

Sylvia heard the words without appreciating their meaning. She had never even considered drying washing.

She followed her guide into a warm, spotlessly clean room which seemed to be overflowing. There was washing hanging from the ceiling and draped on wooden horses in one corner. The table was covered with dishes, and bags of flour and sugar, bread and butter and sultanas, along with bottles of milk, stood in rows along a dresser.

'How big is your family?' stammered Sylvia.

Grace looked sharply at her visitor. 'What?' Then she saw how she was looking round the kitchen in bewilderment and laughed. 'Good gracious, what can you be thinking of me? Big enough, I suppose, but not enough to eat this lot. It's for the café.'

Sylvia laughed too and the barrier between them began to crumble.

'Sit yourself down,' said Grace, lifting a tray of small biscuits from the range oven and carrying them through a far door. The biscuits gave off cinnamon-scented steam and when the scullery door opened a draught of savoury air teased Sylvia's nose.

Grace smiled. 'You can smell the soup? That's for the café, too. I make it in the boiler.'

'Do you?' Sylvia had only a sketchy idea of what a boiler looked like or what it did.

'It's my washing boiler,' explained Grace, smiling.

'But if there's soup in it how do you do your washing?' Sylvia asked, almost forgetting her purpose in coming here in her fascination with a side of life she could never have imagined.

'The washing is all finished by Monday night,' said Grace. 'Then I scrub out the boiler and it's soup, soup and more soup. You see, my son and his friend Owen run a small café in West Street, on the way to Old Market. Desmond – that's my son – used to work for Bennyson's Corset Factory and so did my girl, Isobel, but they got sacked, though they didn't deserve it, especially Desmond, and they couldn't get jobs so – ' Grace stopped abruptly, her face flaming as she remembered who she was talking to.

'It's all right,' said Sylvia gently. 'I don't have to approve all that my husband does. I don't care for the way he tried to force our daughter into a marriage which was repugnant to her. Naturally in the normal way I wouldn't speak of this outside my home, but you must already know about it since you have given Felice a haven here. I cannot thank you enough.'

'No need for thanks,' said Grace awkwardly. She turned to her mixing bowl and began to pound sugar and fat. 'You can be sure she'll come to no harm with us. Desmond looks after her well and she sleeps with Isobel, my eldest. I believe they've struck up quite a friendship. I hear them talking late at night after we've all gone to bed.'

'Do they, indeed? Then Felice has found another friend. Do you know, she has only one, who has recently married. Felice, I'm sure, would not have wished to impose upon her privacy.'

'Only one?' said Grace wonderingly. 'And your family so rich.'

'Money isn't everything,' said Sylvia.

'It feels like it is when you don't have enough,' said Grace.

Sylvia was embarrassed. She hadn't expected to like the woman so much. 'Mrs Kingston, you said that Desmond looks after Felice?'

'She goes with him to the café every day.'

'To a *café* near *Old Market*? Every day? Surely she is bored!'

'Oh, no, she works.'

'Works! She has never worked. She doesn't know how to.'

'That's not what Desmond and Owen say. In fact she is so reliable and efficient that Owen has taken to leaving the café to deliver food to folks who can't leave their shops. Felice has actually helped to increase their trade.'

'But what on earth does she do?' Sylvia finally managed.

Grace added egg and water to her mixture. 'When she's at home – that's here – she peels vegetables, potatoes mostly, for the soup, and we've taken to making Cornish pasties. They sell well. She's a dab hand at pastry.'

'Felice? A dab hand at pastry?'

'And she showed us how to make lemon biscuits. The other day she adapted the recipe to make ginger and caraway and currant and cinnamon biscuits.'

'But she's never cooked in her life! How did she know about biscuits?'

'She says she used to go to your kitchen and watch the cook. Oh, Mrs Bennyson, I hope you won't be cross with your cook. I'm sure she was only trying to make Felice happy.'

'I'm not cross. I'm amazed. But how could I have known?' Sylvia's voice had grown bitter. 'I've been hiding from the world for years because I was unhappy. How selfish I have been!' She stopped, afraid she had said too much. Mrs Kingston had a way of drawing people out.

A shadow passed over Grace's face. 'I know what you mean.

299

Some things are too difficult to face up to.'

Sylvia was taken aback. It had never occurred to her that little people living in little houses could have a life complicated by anything more than working to eat. How arrogant she had been.

Grace had taken a cloth and was lifting a tray of half-moon-shaped pastries from the oven.

'Cornish pasties,' she explained.

'Did Felice make those?'

'Not these, no.' Grace cast a half-humorous glance at her visitor. 'Last night Felice made the ones they're selling today.'

'You amaze me.'

The unmistakable smell of onions was delectable. Sylvia felt ravenous and remembered she hadn't eaten for hours. She took breakfast in her room these days, unwilling to see Ralph until she was forced to, and Janet scolded her for managing only a small piece of toast and a cup of coffee, but she never felt hungry at home. The aromas in this cluttered kitchen made her mouth water in a way she had forgotten.

Grace glanced at her. 'Perhaps you'd like to have a bit of dinner with me?'

'Dinner?' Sylvia's eyes followed the tray hungrily. Mrs Kingston was sliding a fish slice beneath each pasty and lifting it on to a cooling rack. Then she fetched a tray of uncooked pasties from the cool scullery and slid it into the range oven. Sylvia thought of the ceaseless toil of this woman's life and felt ashamed of her idleness.

'I do nothing at all,' she said abruptly.

'That's bad for you,' said Grace calmly. 'Lack of work gives you too much time to brood.' She produced two large white plates from the dresser and a pair of cheap knives and forks from a drawer. She slid a pasty on to each of the plates and put them on a corner of the table with two glasses of water.

Sylvia almost forgot her manners in her eagerness to get at the food. She sliced into the crust and savoury steam laden with flavour drifted out. She loaded her fork and began to eat. Warm delicious vegetables filled her mouth along with pastry which seemed to melt. Oh, so delicious. When she had swallowed she took another forkful, pushing the food into her mouth with an eagerness that would have delighted Janet.

'You like Cornish pasties, then?' said Grace. 'That's a recipe of my grandmother's. She was born and bred in Cornwall. Felice makes them as good as Gran used to and she was a champion cook. Won all the prizes in the local shows for cooking and preserves. It was a happy time for me when I was young. All gone now.'

She sounded so sad that Sylvia felt close to the tears that were always threatening these days, not for Mrs Kingston's lost life but for her own and Felice's. By night and day Sylvia cursed herself for her moment of madness. She and Harry would one day have had a daughter and brought her up together, gently, lovingly, without the perpetual unhappiness caused by Ralph. She shook her head and waited for the lump in her throat to disappear. This astonishing woman remained sympathetically silent, waiting for her to recover. Sylvia finished her pasty and laid down her knife and fork with a sigh. She had just eaten more food than she had even attempted for longer than she could remember and yet her stomach craved more.

Grace removed the dishes and brought a large biscuit tin. 'Here,' she said, 'you're so interested in Felice's cooking you should try these.'

Sylvia took three biscuits and again was astonished by the delicacy of the textures and flavours. 'Are these what sell so well? I'm not surprised. And to think my daughter made them! What hidden talents she must have.'

Grace poured two large cups of tea and pushed one across to Sylvia. Even the strong brew tasted right in this kitchen, even though she usually took only a small cup of coffee after lunch.

'I wonder at your not knowing that Felice could cook,' said Mrs Kingston.

'She's never had a chance to try. My husband drew the line at domestic science.'

'Well, he was wrong, wasn't he?' said Grace. Every time the memory of Ralph Bennyson was laid before her she felt her heartbeats quicken. That man had practically ruined her family. If they hadn't been brave and resourceful, where would they be today? And poor Isobel was still having to work for women who didn't appreciate her and getting very little pay when she was eating her heart out for the means to begin her own small business.

Sylvia was at last replete. She sat on in the warm kitchen, which had a soporific effect on her. Grace took the dishes away, swilled them off and left them to be washed up later. Then she began to cut slices of bread and butter.

'This is for bread-and-butter pudding,' she explained. 'The fire's died enough for it now. It's easy to make and goes a treat with the customers. I'm afraid we eat a lot of it here, and soup too. It's cheap and easy when we're all tired.'

'Doesn't Felice get bored with the same food?'

'She doesn't seem to.'

Sylvia thought of the complicated menus worked out by her cook to tempt the demanding appetites of her employers. 'Tell me, Mrs Kingston, if she cooks here in the kitchen what does she do in the café?'

'Washing-up, mostly.'

'What?'

Grace looked anxiously at her guest. 'It does her no harm.'

'I dare say not, but I just can't picture it. Is that all she does?'

'She waits at tables when she feels brave enough.'

'Brave enough? The clientele from that district must be a rough lot.'

'No. Most of them are like lambs. You don't have to be well-off to know how to behave,' said Grace with a touch of asperity.

'No, no, of course not. I wasn't implying any such thing. I'm just so astonished by Felice.' Sylvia thought of her carefully reared daughter dishing out cheap food in a cheap café. 'What did you mean when you spoke of bravery?'

'She is always frightened that someone who recognises her will give her away. She says she'd be happy to work for Desmond for ever. She's only worried in case someone runs to you and Mr Bennyson and she'll be fetched back.'

A silence fell, broken by the ticking of the kitchen clock and the slow crackle of the fire.

Grace said apologetically, 'That sounded ever so rude. I'm sorry. I didn't mean to hurt you. It's her father – ' She stopped.

'I know she's hiding from her father. He can be very strict, but he loves her, you know.'

'Does he?'

Grace sounded so sceptical that Sylvia was impelled to defend Ralph. 'He cares only for her welfare.'

'Not according to Felice,' said Grace firmly. She would not be intimidated. Felice had arrived, emotionally bruised and needing help and love, to heal the wounds inflicted by her father.

'I wish her life had turned out differently,' sighed Sylvia. 'Mrs Kingston, it is my intention to take Felice away and to set up home with her. My husband simply can't understand her feelings. And a matter has arisen which makes it imperative that I have somewhere to think undisturbed. Not long ago I would have left Felice with her father, but now I know I can't.'

Grace was laying the buttered bread cut into squares in greased pans, throwing in sultanas. 'Will Mr Bennyson allow you to set up home with her?'

'It will be a struggle, but I am sure that Felice will be on my side. She has had enough, too.'

Grace measured milk into a large basin, added sugar and eggs and began to beat the mixture thoroughly. 'From the way Felice speaks I can't see you defying your husband. She doesn't tell us everything, but it's not difficult to read between the lines. And she has told us how much of an invalid you have been.'

'I've changed. For years I've been hiding from reality. That's ended. I shall be strong. Ralph won't be allowed to bully his daughter or ruin her life – as he ruined mine.' Sylvia flushed, feeling she had gone too far, but Mrs Kingston made no comment as she began to ladle the sweet liquid over the slices of bread. Then the scent of nutmeg filled the air as she grated it on the tops of the puddings. She put a couple of bread crusts in the oven to test for heat. When they came out pale gold she murmured, 'Just right,' and lifted in the dishes.

Sylvia, in spite of her worry, was interested. Cooking actually looked quite fascinating. And to think that Felice had mastered so much of the art in so short a time.

'What do you do with the crusts you cut off?' she asked.

'Make bread pudding. That's different. It has lots of lard and fruit and is spicy and quite heavy, but it goes down a treat with men who do heavy jobs and saves us wasting anything.'

Sylvia accepted another cup of tea, even stronger because the metal pot had been standing half on the hob and kept stewing. She felt she should go home and leave Mrs Kingston in peace, but she lingered, understanding why Felice had found a place of refuge here.

'What time will Felice return?' she asked.

Grace glanced at the clock. 'Not for hours, I'm afraid. They keep the café open as long as possible, until after ten usually to catch the pub trade.'

'However does she stand up to such long hours?'

'Desmond makes her rest for part of the day. He's bought a second-hand sofa for the back room at the café and insists on her lying down for a while in the afternoon. There isn't much room, of course, just the café, the one back room and a tiny kitchen where they keep the food hot.'

'Desmond sounds most considerate. Does Felice show signs of strain?'

'She doesn't appear to, although the grinding, repetitive work is wearing. She insists she can pull her weight.'

'May I come back tonight?' asked Sylvia.

'Of course you may, but why not visit Felice at the café? I'm sure she'd welcome you.'

'Would she? Would your son?'

'Desmond takes everything in his stride?'

'He sounds marvellous,' said Sylvia abruptly. 'What does Mr Kingston do?'

Grace absorbed the shock of the question and registered the fact that Sylvia evidently didn't study the Bristol newspapers very closely. They had made quite an item of Amos's violent death. She controlled her shiver. 'He passed away not very long ago.'

'Oh, I'm so sorry. How you must miss him.'

Grace couldn't devise an answer. She missed Amos in many ways; he hadn't always been bad and they had had some pleasant times in the beginning. She was ashamed for feeling happier without him, but she couldn't help it. All she prayed was that no more harm would come because of the way he'd died. It was her constant nightmare and Kathy's too.

Sylvia said, 'You spoke of Felice sharing your daughter's bed. How kind she must be.'

'Isobel? One of the best. She was very good at her job, you know, Mrs Bennyson. She had been promoted shortly before. Now she wants to set up her own corset shop.' Grace stopped, wishing she hadn't been so open. Presumably, whatever Mrs Bennyson thought of her husband, she'd tell him of an incipient rival – if Isobel could be considered a rival. The idea was laughable, but Mr Bennyson was vindictive.

'Where will she open up?' Sylvia asked.

Grace said defiantly, 'She was thinking of our front room. It isn't used much. She would like to give the local women proper fitted garments, especially the ones that need support because of too many babies and illnesses.'

'My husband's factory makes surgical corsets.'

'Poor women can't afford to get private measurements. Isobel wants to help them.'

'I admire her enterprise.'

'Unfortunately it isn't possible yet. It's the cost, you see. She has to have a machine capable of sewing the heavy stuff.'

'Tell me more about it.'

Grace decided that Mrs Bennyson had asked purely out of interest and she talked, her hands busy. 'She's been buying material, notions like hooks and eyes, tapes, wide elastic. We club together to get them and there's quite a store put by. But the machine defeats her. We've never seen one on the second-hand market.'

'Is that all that stops her?'

'All? We're talking of a lot of money. She can only earn enough to give me her keep and have a bit over. Poor girl, she walks miles to work and back to save fares, and slaves all day cleaning up other women's messes. It's wicked when she's so clever.'

For the first time Sylvia really appreciated what the sacking of the two Kingstons meant to the family. She admired the way these courageous people fought to overcome disaster. 'How did your son afford to rent the café?'

'He began with a tea tent on the Bath road. It was a bit of a shambles at first – ' Grace explained what had happened, then stopped as she remembered that she'd need to mention Lawrence Dane. According to Desmond and Isobel he refused to have anything to do with Mrs Bennyson, who was his mother.

'You were saying – ' prompted Sylvia.

Grace kept her head down. 'Mr Lawrence Dane came to our aid with a beautiful new tent and Desmond and his partner put a downpayment of rent in advance for the café.'

'*Lawrence* bought a new tent for you? You know Lawrence? Yes, you must do.' Isobel had to curb a surge of jealousy that this woman and her family, poor as they were, had received kindness from the son who never gave his mother so much as a kind look.

Grace sensed the emotion emanating from Sylvia and grew nervous. 'I've met him,' she said, 'but he is better known to Isobel.'

'To your daughter? I don't understand. Did they become friends in the factory? No, that's not possible!'

Grace said carefully, 'From what I hear, Lawrence disliked visiting the factory because he hated to see rows of women chained to machines. That was how he put it, Isobel told me.'

'Is that what he said? I had assumed it bored him.'

'It may have. I don't know. But he intends to change things when he inherits. Though,' added Grace hurriedly, 'I'm sure he hopes that won't be for many years. He respects Mr Bennyson.'

'He looks upon my husband as a father. His own died young.'

'Yes.' The suicide had got into the newspapers in spite of all the efforts of the family to cover it up and Grace remembered that much of the blame had been laid at this woman's door.

'He and Isobel are friends. He sometimes meets her and gives her a lift home in his car.'

Sylvia was again astonished. To think that Lawrence should bother at all with this odd family was enough to amaze her. But he'd gone further. He'd given them an expensive gift and was apparently fond of the daughter.

Grace said hurriedly, 'Lawrence didn't actually give the tent to Desmond. He was very understanding. He stopped one day at the tent tearoom and took a liking to my youngest child, Kathy. She's at the grammar school' – Grace couldn't keep the pride from her voice – 'she helps her brothers and sisters in every way she can and Lawrence was impressed. The tent was a birthday gift to her.'

Sylvia tried to get her thoughts in order. Lawrence was paying attention to the eldest Kingston daughter and there had been something in Mrs Kingston's voice when she spoke of Felice and Desmond. Was this woman trying to deceive her with her cosy kitchen and her friendliness? Had she got designs on the wealthy Bennyson and Dane families? She wondered if old Mrs Dane knew that her beloved grandson was pursuing a factory girl from a common background. She watched Grace as she toiled on, still finding it difficult to tear herself from the undemanding atmosphere.

'How do I get to the café?' she finally asked.

'Take a tram to West Street. Just ask the conductor. He'll put you right. It isn't far, in fact it's within walking distance. A fairly long walk, but easy for a fit person. It's called Kathy's Tearoom.'

Grace saw Sylvia out and watched her as she walked up the street in her fashionable clothes and high heels. Hardly anyone was in sight but she knew that every curtain would be twitching.

Sylvia was put off the swaying tram by a conductor and stood amazed outside the small café. The lower part of the windows was curtained and the rest steamed up so that she couldn't see inside. The paintwork needed renewing. The menu was chalked on a board which leaned on the wall. She watched as patrons passed to and fro. There were workmen in overalls and tough boots, city clerks in lowly positions in their ill-fitting black suits and highly polished black shoes, women with small children clutching their hands, brewery

306

girls in clogs, and women in sacking aprons and mens' caps turned back to front such as Sylvia had only seen in cartoons in *Punch* magazine. And my God! a couple of dustmen in leather aprons. Surely this couldn't be the place where Felice passed her days. But the painted sign said clearly 'Kathy's Tearoom'. Then the door was held open wide for a mother to push her pram out and Sylvia caught a glimpse of Felice taking an order from one of the becapped women, smiling at her as if she were a client at the Ritz.

Just before the door swung shut Felice glanced up and saw her mother. To Sylvia's surprise she smiled even more broadly and beckoned her in. Sylvia walked through the door and was met by the same wave of savoury aromas as in the Kingstons' kitchen.

Felice called, 'Do please sit down. I'll be with you in a moment.'

She disappeared into a back room and a young man came out carrying a loaded tray. He was dressed in trousers and shirt with sleeves rolled up and a white apron. Was this Desmond, the man who figured so large in Felice's present life? He was a couple of inches under six foot, with fair hair darkened at the moment by sweat. He looked straight at her with deep blue eyes, then transferred the contents of his tray to a table round which sat a woman with four children who stared with famished eyes at the soup and the rich pasties like the one Sylvia had eaten earlier. 'There you are,' he said heartily. 'Fill up on this.' The woman offered him a single coin. It looked like a shilling and Desmond took it and handed sixpence back as he thanked her. The prices were marked clearly outside and on a wall poster inside: fourpence for a bowl of soup and a slice of bread, threepence for pudding, a penny for a cake or biscuit and a cup of tea. So his charity extended to more than her daughter. She stared at the starving woman and her children as they devoured the good food and for the first time in her life felt ashamed of being rich.

Desmond came over to her, wiped his hand on his apron and held it out to her. 'Felice said you were here. Pleased to meet you.'

'How do you do?' said Sylvia awkwardly as she shook his hand. His grip was strong and firm.

'Can I get you something? A cup of tea with a cake perhaps? Or a biscuit?'

'Tea, please,' said Sylvia.

'Coming right up.'

Felice carried out her mother's tray with two cups and saucers and sat down with her. 'Fancy seeing you here, Mother. How did you know where to come?'

'I've been to see Mrs Kingston. She told me.'

'She's marvellous, isn't she? I bet she was surrounded by cooking.'

'She was. And washing. I've been hearing about your hard work.'

'Have you? Mother, I've never been so happy.'

The incredible words were obviously sincere. Sylvia's glance wandered to Desmond, who was serving a table of four workmen. Felice eyes followed, unmistakably filled with love. Sylvia's heart missed a beat. So she was in love with the fellow. How did he feel about her? Could he possibly imagine that Ralph Bennyson would permit his daughter to have any kind of relationship with a man who had been sacked from his own factory and now ran a seedy café? And for once Sylvia wouldn't blame Ralph. There was no doubt that Felice would soon grow tired of working like a galley slave and want to come home to her comfortable existence, but she must be protected meanwhile from making a terribly mistaken connection. Sylvia questioned her own wisdom in deciding to set up a separate establishment. Ralph could deal with such matters as these better than she. She lingered in the café as the people and the talk flowed around her. Sometimes the Bristolian accents were so marked she couldn't understand what was being said. It was as if she'd entered an alien world. In a way she had. And Felice might be about to choose this world.

Felice returned to the small house weary but buoyed up by new experiences and her love for Desmond, which was growing by the hour as she worked alongside him. She believed he felt more than friendship for her but she was fearful that he would never declare himself. When they learned that Sylvia had made her own plans for Felice he said firmly that it would be the best possible thing. His eager acceptance hurt her and that night she wept.

Isobel put an arm over her. 'What's grieving you?'

'I love Desmond,' said Felice, crying the words into her pillow.

Isobel tightened her arm round the heaving shoulders.

'I thought he loved me,' wept Felice, 'but he wants me to leave.'

'No, I'm sure he doesn't, but he believes it would be best for you. Felice, he's very fond of you, but your world and his won't ever mix and he's enough sense to know it.'

'I'm willing to risk it. I'm not worried about what people think. And Desmond is far above me in every way. He's clever and brave and gentle and I couldn't help being happy with him.'

'He may never have any more money than he has now,' said Isobel.

308

'Money! I don't care about money!'

'Yet you realised very soon when you ran away how impossible life can be without it. We're all glad you came to us, but if we hadn't been there, if Mum had decided she couldn't cope with another mouth to feed, what would you have done?'

'I don't know. But you were there and your mum is the loveliest woman in the world.'

'Lovelier than your own mother?'

'I hardly know Mother. She's been badly treated by Father, but she shouldn't have been so weak. Your mother would have stood up for herself.'

Isobel fell silent and Felice sensed her pain. 'Don't you think your mother would have been strong if your father had been nasty to her?'

'He was,' said Isobel flatly, 'very nasty indeed, far worse, I'm sure, than Mr Bennyson. He almost destroyed Mum. You didn't see her before he died. It's a terrible thing to say but I don't believe one of us was sorry to see the last of Dad. When we wept it was for lost opportunities, not grief.'

Felice turned over and put her arm round Isobel's waist. 'I'm sorry. How selfish I am, thinking I'm the only one with troubles. Oh, but Isobel, I love Desmond with all my heart and soul. I really do.'

Isobel returned from work one evening to be greeted with cries of joy from Grace and Kathy. Even Ivor and Olive were grinning.

'Come and see,' shouted Kathy, running into the front room. 'See what came for you.'

Isobel followed her while the others crowded behind. In the window stood a sewing machine, heavy enough to deal with any material put through it. She stared at it, speechless.

'It came this afternoon,' said Grace. 'Oh, my love, now you can begin. You can stop those cleaning jobs. I've been telling the neighbours you'll be ready to measure them in next to no time and won't charge them the earth for new corsets.'

'How?' managed Isobel.

'There's a note,' said Grace. 'I got one too. I never thought that such a grand lady would buy it for you.'

'A grand lady?'

'Mrs Bennyson. What other grand lady has been here lately?'

In a daze Isobel took the note. It was short. Mrs Bennyson begged to be allowed to present the sewing machine by way of rendering a few thanks for their protection of her daughter, Felice.

'As if we needed thanks,' said Grace, but she was delighted.

Isobel walked to the machine and ran a finger over its smooth strong contours. She felt like weeping for joy. Here was the release from drudgery, here was her future.

She looked round the room, still dazed. 'I'll need a cutting table,' was all she could think of to say.

'I know where we can get an old dining table for five bob,' said Grace. 'I've put a shilling down-payment on it. Owen will fetch it. What else will you want?'

'Small things. A bit of carpet for the customers to stand on in their stockinged feet and somewhere they can lie down. Some of them need to, poor souls.'

'Don't worry,' cried Kathy, her eyes shining. 'We'll get it all for you.' She threw her arms round her sister's neck and Isobel kissed her, realising just how much she'd been missing Kathy's fervent caresses. She realised too that Kathy was growing tall. She could kiss her sister without standing on tiptoe. And she had a beautiful figure. One day she might model for her. And, although Grace was thin, her stomach protruded from the babies she had borne and she would get the first corset. She wrote her thanks to Mrs Bennyson.

Isobel and Kathy scrubbed the front-room floor and Grace used money she had put by to buy linoleum. Owen and Desmond painted the woodwork. The old sofa was thrown on the dustcart and Isobel put a down-payment on a new one with a firm base. A small table, a couple of chairs and a cupboard to hold the materials was about all the room could take in the way of furniture. Isobel bought second-hand curtains at a church sale and cut them to size, using the sewing machine for the first time, and re-covered an ancient screen. In an unbelievably short time she was ready and they all went from door to door leaving cards with hand-printed notices saying that Isobel's Corsets was ready for business and would open on the following Monday morning.

Monday came and she waited for customers, but doubts crowded in upon her as nobody called. She spent most of the morning ironing in the scullery for Grace.

Lunch was a gloomy affair. 'Have I made a mistake?' wondered Isobel. 'Has it all been for nothing?'

Grace tried to give her the reassurance she didn't feel. But the afternoon brought hope. Two women from a couple of streets away arrived and were shown in.

310

'My, you've got it posh,' said Mrs Kenton, the younger of the two.

'It's ever so nice,' agreed her elderly companion.

Isobel asked them to sit down and tell her what kind of corset they were looking for.

'This is my Aunty Jean,' said Mrs Kenton. 'Mrs James. She's got problems.' Mrs Kenton lowered her voice. 'Female problems.'

Isobel said sympathetically, 'What exactly is the trouble?' She thought she sounded like a doctor and the situation seemed suddenly unreal. What if she couldn't deal with Mrs James's female problems?

Mrs James leaned forward confidentially. 'I've had twelve kids,' she said. 'Never had much trouble havin' them, but since the last two I've had backache real bad. I'd be grateful if you could help. Your card said "surgical supports supplied".'

Isobel's heart beat faster as she wished her first customer hadn't been quite such a challenge. 'May I look at your back?' she asked gently.

Mrs James checked that the concealing muslin curtains were firmly in place at the window, rejected the protection of the screen and removed her lower garments, all but her voluminous knickers. 'The pain's here,' she explained, pressing one hand to her lower back. 'And here, right down in front.'

Isobel sighed with relief. The muscles had simply gone flaccid and the heavy stomach was pulling on the weakened back.

She opened her notebook. 'What I'm going to do,' she explained, 'is to give you good support for your tummy muscles. They're pulling on your back the whole time. For extra support I shall fit you with an underbelt which I'll make thigh-length. The steels will help and the laces you can tie to your own comfort.'

Both women looked impressed and Mrs Kenton leaned forward in her eagerness to hear everything. 'Do you reckon that'll stop the pain? Poor soul, she's been suffering for years.'

'She needs this special corset made just for her. Tailor-made, you might say.'

'Tailor-made,' breathed Mrs Kenton. 'Hear that, Aunty. You'll look young again.'

Isobel smiled, praying that she got this absolutely right. This could be the best advertisement she'd ever get, or the worst.

The corset was made in record time and fitted perfectly. When the laces were securely tied Mrs James began to weep. 'I can feel the pain going already. It's wonderful, Miss Kingston, I can't thank you enough. I heard that to get a special made at Bennyson's would cost me several guineas and here you are charging one pound five shillings. What a difference!'

Mrs Kenton, who had once again accompanied her aunt, said, 'We'll tell everyone about you, Miss Kingston. You're a bloomin' wonder. Could you do anything for an expectant mother? I've just found out my fourth is on the way and I always get cruel backache.'

'I certainly can,' said Isobel. 'May I measure you straight away?'

Within days Isobel had a waiting list and started to wonder how she'd manage without help. Then Ruby arrived on her doorstep.

'That pig Bennyson's given me the sack. Just because he overheard me say that Miss Bennyson had done the best thing possible running away from him.'

Isobel gave her a quizzical look. 'What did you expect? A medal?'

Ruby grinned. 'No, but honestly, he's been awful lately. An absolute bugger, shouting at Miss Trefusis till I felt sorry for the old trout, yelling at the girl they put in your place. She cries if anyone glares at her and is usually awash with tears. And the new trainee manager is just as bad. He's only sixteen and terrified of the boss.'

'You mean he weeps?'

'No, but he always looks as if he will and his nose runs.'

Isobel regarded the picture evoked with a certain irrepressible satisfaction.

'I hear you're going great guns,' said Ruby. 'I suppose you couldn't give me a job.'

'I'd like to. In fact, I need help. I can't pay as much as Bennyson's and it would be cutting at first and measuring, until I get another machine. Ruby, I've got such plans. I shall go into underwear and have my own lingerie show just like Bennyson's did. If you're willing to take less—?'

'I'm willing,' said Ruby instantly.

312

Chapter Nineteen

Ruby had no cause to regret working for Isobel. The narrow streets seemed filled with women who needed more bodily support than they could get by buying corsets over a counter. For the first time in their lives the mothers and grandmothers who had borne too many children too close together could come to a woman who really cared for them and their pain, who had patience to study their particular needs and who not only charged low prices but allowed them to pay weekly. Mrs Kenton and her aunt appeared to have told the whole district what a marvellous corset-maker they'd found; one, moreover, who was willing to call on invalid women at home and charge no more.

Isobel presented a calm front, but her new career gave her more uneasiness than she could let anyone know. She could measure and fit, but the skill lay in the exact cut, the right decision as to whether or not there should be elastic inserts, and where to place steels and laces; neither she nor Ruby had spent long in the cutting room.

After a few weeks the dreaded time came when she got it wrong and a garment intended for support squashed a woman's body, forcing the flesh down instead of giving it the uplift it needed.

'This b'aint no good!' Mrs Bryant exclaimed angrily. 'To think I been wastin' my time comin' here to get measured then you done it all wrong. I'll not pay for this.'

Seeing Isobel momentarily tongue-tied and pink-faced, and knowing that Mrs Bryant was perfectly right, Ruby jumped in. 'I'm ever so sorry, Mrs Bryant, it's all my fault. I must have measured you wrong.'

'I could've swore it was Isobel that measured me,' said Mrs Bryant. Isobel opened her mouth to confess, but was frowned into silence by Ruby. 'I must've been mistook,' said Mrs Bryant.

'Please allow me to make you a new corset,' begged Isobel.

313

'Mmm, how do I know you'll get it right next time?'

'She will,' said Ruby eagerly. 'Honest, she will.'

'And because we've put you to so much trouble you can have it half-price,' promised Isobel.

Mrs Bryant forgave her handsomely and was measured again. After she'd gone, Isobel flopped into the customer's easy chair. 'Thanks, Ruby. I shouldn't have let you take the blame, but a thousand thanks.'

'That's all right, love, I owe you plenty. Besides,' she added honestly, 'we can't afford to get a bad reputation or neither of us will make a living. Mrs Bryant knows everybody and talks all the time. She'd have ruined us. What'll you do about the new corset? Do you know where you went wrong?'

'I'm pretty sure I do. I just wish there was someone who could give me a bit of advice.'

'Miss Trefusis could. She knows the trade from beginning to end.'

'She's not likely to help,' said Isobel ruefully. 'She's had the rough edge of Mr Bennyson's tongue since I left. She must be pretty angry with me by now.'

'It's nothing to do with you, or her, for that matter. It's Felice he's angry about and he's taking it out on everyone.' Ruby chuckled. 'To think he's probably got people searching everywhere and all the time she's with you.'

'My God, yes,' said Isobel, shuddering. 'I hope he never finds out.'

'What do you care? He can't do any more to hurt you.'

'I'm not so sure. He's powerful.'

'Look, love, you only take customers that can't afford his specials. Small fry to him. He'll think you're not worth bothering with.'

'If he discovers we're hiding Felice he'll bother with us all right.'

Isobel's Corsets had been trading for two months and making a profit when Sylvia called again at the little house. She looked round the transformed front room in admiration. 'How very well you've done.'

'Thanks to your help,' said Isobel.

'I provided a little money. That's easy for me. You're the one who's done the real work. It's so cosy here. If I needed a corset this is where I should like to come.'

'Would you really, Mrs Bennyson?' asked Ruby eagerly. 'Would any of your friends?'

'They already have their arrangements, I think.'

Ruby flushed. 'Of course they have.'

'To tell you the truth,' said Sylvia awkwardly, 'I've been so much out of society I don't have many woman friends.'

'Fancy,' said Ruby, genuinely intrigued.

Isobel was afraid that Ruby, rather rough and ready as she was, was about to ask embarrassing questions and she said quickly, 'How can we help you, Mrs Bennyson?'

'It's about Felice.'

Something about Sylvia's voice made Isobel nervous. She said to Ruby, 'Be a love and go to Mum and get some tea. It's time you had a break. You can bring us a cup here.'

'She's a pleasant girl,' said Sylvia when Ruby had gone, 'but perhaps a little direct. I wonder you find her useful.'

'Oh, but I do. She suits exactly the customers who come to us.'

'Does she?' said Sylvia absently, as if she had lost interest in the subject the moment she had spoken.

'What was it you wanted to say, Mrs Bennyson?' asked Isobel gently. 'I have several customers arriving soon. They often come in groups and quite a number don't want to be screened. It seems as if watching their friends get measured gives them immense pleasure. Some of them are quite indelicate.' Isobel laughed.

Sylvia didn't laugh. Isobel didn't think she'd even heard. 'I have purchased such a pretty cottage in Stapleton, quite near the River Frome with its lovely walks. It's called a cottage but it's really quite large enough for the few servants I shall need. I'm looking forward so much to sharing it with Felice. I'm sure you can persuade her to join me.'

So, thought Isobel, I'm expected to connive in getting Felice away from her father, away from us, into her mother's care. One machine for one daughter?

Sylvia said, 'I can see how happy Felice is here with you. She may want to stay with you at least for a while, but it wouldn't do, you must see that. She needs to be among her own circle, her own friends.'

'She didn't seem very happy with them,' said Isobel, irritated at this clever division of the classes when all that Felice needed was affection.

'No,' said Sylvia sadly, 'I'm afraid she has not been truly happy for a long while. But her life will be different in future. I shan't force her to do a thing. And you will be welcome to visit.'

Isobel felt ashamed of her ungenerous reaction. 'I'll ask Felice what she wants to do,' she said.

'And persuade her she'll be best off with me?'

'I'll certainly suggest it. I can't influence her feelings.'

'No, indeed, she has had enough of that. But Miss Kingston, you and your brother have strong personalities and I feel sure that between you you can prevail upon Felice to do the proper thing. Your mother told me how you and she talk together in the night. My dear, I am so very grateful to you. You've almost driven the sadness from her eyes. Say you'll add your persuasion to mine.'

'I'll do nothing against her will,' said Isobel.

'I am satisfied with that. When the matter is put to her properly she will see the sense of what I say.' Sylvia rose. 'I'm going to see her now in the café. I shall tell her about the house. I am moving in very soon.'

'I hope you'll be very happy there,' said Isobel.

'How good you are. Not a single question about my reasons. But you probably know them. Felice will have given you a bleak picture of her home, a richly deserved one. I cannot remain beneath my husband's roof and it is obvious that Felice feels the same. But your home can only be a temporary refuge.'

After Mrs Bennyson had left Isobel thought of Desmond. His heart will break if he loses Felice, she thought. And what of Felice? She loves Desmond. But looking at everything dispassionately Mrs Bennyson was probably right and the novelty for Felice of living so differently would wear thin. If she returned to her own world she would soon forget Desmond and he would forget her in time and fix on a more suitable girl to love.

That night when Felice came home with Desmond on a late tram they went straight to the front room where Isobel was still working.

Felice looked deeply troubled. 'Mother has been to see you,' she said without preamble.

'Yes.'

'So you know what she wants?'

'I do. And having thought it over I feel she may be right. Your home is with her.'

'Don't you want me? I thought we were friends. Sisters, almost.'

It hurt Isobel to say, 'We can always be friends, Felice, but we are not sisters. Your world is so different from mine.'

Felice stared at Isobel as if she were talking a different language. 'You really believe I should go to live with my mother in the cottage in Stapleton?'

'She wants you,' said Isobel gently. 'She's your mother and she loves you.'

Desmond stood behind Felice looking stricken, but he said nothing. Isobel laid aside her work and they went to the kitchen where Grace sat near the fire sewing lace on to a corset, a refinement given out of kindness to women in whose lives the luxury of lace had seldom if ever figured.

Felice said, 'Mrs Kingston, Isobel thinks I should live with my mother. What do you think?'

Grace looked sadly at her. 'You know you are always welcome here, but I believe children should obey their parents.'

Felice whirled round to face Desmond. 'Do you agree? When Mother told us what she felt you said very little. Were you deciding to let me go? Why don't you speak? Tell me how you really feel.'

Desmond flinched beneath the barrage of angry questions. 'I can't. It's for you to decide, my—'

'My what?' demanded Felice.

'Friend,' said Desmond unhappily.

'That's not what you were thinking. My love. That was it. It was, wasn't it?'

Grace said in muffled tones, 'That's a common enough expression in Bristol.'

'Not the way Desmond would have said it to me. Oh, darling, don't tell me to go. Please, please, I beg of you.'

Her eyes shone with tears, she lifted her hands to his shoulders, hands that were no longer soft and white but stained and rough now, from her work in the café. Desmond reached up and took them in his, then, unable to resist, he bent his head and kissed each palm.

Felice burst into tears. 'You care about me, Desmond, you do.'

'I love you,' he said.

'He loves me,' cried Felice triumphantly. 'I knew it. Isobel, Mrs Kingston, Desmond loves me. Isn't it wonderful?'

Grace nodded without speaking. Isobel smiled. Felice was naive if she imagined such a love affair would be smooth.

'Say it again, Desmond. Tell me exactly how you feel,' said Felice, 'in front of witnesses.'

Desmond looked at his mother and sister and said a little self-consciously, 'I love you, very much. I – adore you.' He went pink.

'You see,' cried Felice. 'You see, Isobel, we shall be sisters after all.'

'You intend to marry?' Grace said.

317

'But of course!' Felice was jubilant. 'You know we must if we are to be together.'

Grace stood up and carefully folded her sewing in a clean cloth. 'You must think before you take the final step. You have to be sure you can cope with our kind of life.'

'But I won't have to, nor will Desmond. I have money, a great deal of it, which comes to me on my twenty-first birthday. Only a year to wait. You can wait that long for me, can't you, Desmond?'

'I didn't know you were rich. I thought you only had an allowance and that's been stopped.'

'Well, I am rich, and you needn't act as if it's a crime.'

'I don't want to sponge off my wife.'

'Oh, heavens, don't tell me you're going to turn into one of those strong silent men who stand with folded arms, on their pride because their wives have more money than they?'

'No,' said Desmond, smiling faintly at the magazine image, 'but I prefer to run my own home and give my wife a reasonable income. And I shall. I meant to keep my news as a surprise, but Owen and I have decided that the café is doing so well we can afford to rent the floor above and expand. The food upstairs will be more varied and a little more expensive. I've been in touch with a retired chef who's only too happy to earn himself a bit by cooking part-time.'

Grace lifted a protesting hand and Desmond took it in his. 'I can't ask you to do more, Mum, though I know you'd try.'

'That's wonderful!' cried Felice.

Grace said anxiously, 'Don't overreach yourself, Desmond.'

'Have faith, Mum.'

Grace smiled. 'Yes, I'll always have faith in you, my dear.'

'And I'm sure Isobel will expand her corset business too,' said Felice. 'Who knows, when my father realises how clever you both are he may give his permission for me to marry before I'm twenty-one.'

'I shall need a great deal more money than I have now to impress your father,' said Desmond. 'Besides—'

'Besides what?' asked Felice.

'However much I have I know your father won't think that I'm a suitable match for you. He wants nothing less than a lordship.'

'Now you're bringing in class again,' Felice cried.

'It has to be faced.'

'Not by me. Mrs Kingston, make him understand about love. You know, don't you? You were married. Tell him about true love.'

318

Grace went red. 'True love,' she said quietly, 'can triumph over all adversity.'

'You see,' said Felice, turning to Desmond. 'Listen to your mother.' She was too overwrought to notice the strained atmosphere her words had produced.

The kettle began to sing and Felice looked at it happily. 'That sound will always mean security to me. This little, cosy, warm room, the fire, the singing kettle, the home-made food and my dear Kingstons. This really feels like home.'

Her words defused the atmosphere and Grace stood and impulsively kissed her. Felice's face crumpled as if she was about to weep again, then she laughed shakily and embraced Grace.

She began to take a hand in preparing the meal, saying to Isobel, 'You'll expand your business soon, I just know it.'

Isobel was wondering if their association with Felice would turn out to be the downfall of Isobel's Corsets. There was no knowing what Mr Bennyson would do when he discovered the future that Felice was mapping out for herself.

'I need more money and equipment before I can move upwards,' warned Isobel. 'And more knowledge too.'

'Do you? You seem very efficient to me and all your customers are satisfied.'

Isobel let the remark go, but Desmond said, 'Is there anywhere you can train further?'

'Nowhere I can afford. Miss Trefusis would have taught me all I needed to know if I'd stayed. She is very clever.'

Grace made the tea. The table was laid with a plate of crackers and cheese, small sandwiches, a chocolate cake. Felice viewed everything greedily. Since arriving at the Kingstons' she had begun to eat well. Her face and figure had taken on healthy contours which suited her.

'Come on, everybody,' said Grace. 'Let's all sit down and talk things over. There's a lot to be decided. Felice, of course you'll be welcome here always, especially as Desmond's fiancée. I'm not saying I think a marriage between you will work, and I'm glad you have to wait a year. It will give you both time to consider.' Desmond slid his arm round Felice's waist and she responded by kissing his cheek.

'Isobel is the one who needs help at the moment. Now, for once, I have a piece of news. Miss Trefusis has become engaged to Frank Bagley.'

She glanced at Isobel who said, 'That's wonderful news. She's loved him for years and she'll be a good wife and a mother to his sons, I know she will.'

'I'm glad you're pleased. And furthermore, she will be leaving Bennyson's and I'm sure she'd be willing to give you tuition.'

'Not if it jeopardises Frank's position in the factory,' declared Isobel.

'As a matter of fact,' said Grace carefully, savouring the limelight, 'I met her out shopping today. She was on her way back from My Lady's Bower. We had a cup of tea together. It seems Mr Bennyson has been taking out his spite on her and she's sick of it, and he's been rotten to Frank, too, so when Frank was offered a job by a rival he decided to take it. It's not the first time people have tried to tempt him away, but he's always turned them down because he felt loyalty to Bennyson's. This time he's taken the job. He'll be handing his notice in any day now. She asked most kindly after Desmond and you, Isobel. She already knew about your business venture and she offered to give you any help you might need.'

Miss Trefusis, whom they now had to learn to call Rose, came round to the Kingstons' with Frank Bagley. He looked somewhat sheepish but when Isobel and the family greeted him with pleasure his stern face relaxed into a smile. 'You will have heard that Miss Trefusis has honoured me by consenting to become my wife?' were his first words after the greetings were over.

Isobel caught Desmond's eye and almost choked. She had forgotten how pompous Frank could be. What on earth had possessed her to think she might find happiness with him?

Grace made tea, the inevitable accompaniment to visitors.

Frank said, 'Isobel, I have heard of your venture and wish you well.'

'Thank you, Frank,' Isobel said demurely.

'You were dismissed from Bennyson's, unjustly in my estimation, though I cannot altogether approve of insubordination on the factory floor. I was sorry that you couldn't finish your training. Rose understands that you may come up against problems you are not equipped to handle, and with your approval, of course, she is eminently willing to assist you.'

Isobel smiled gratefully. 'Oh, Miss Trefusis – Rose – I should be so grateful.'

Frank looked as pleased as his future bride to see how valued she was.

320

So it was arranged and Rose came round to the Kingstons' almost every day and imparted her deep knowledge, demonstrating with drawings why some women needed groin-length corsets while others were comfortable with a shorter garment. She took over the measurements of a customer who had been in pain and half crippled for years through a back injury sustained in factory work. Isobel watched keenly and made notes. She saw how to fit a dorsolumbar support – strong cross-over straps at the back to give maximum ease and comfort. Rose explained the positioning of fulcrum bands which assisted weak stomach and back muscles. She taught Isobel how to decide exactly where to run the curving rows of stitches, who needed steels, why and where to insert them and where there should be elastic inserts. When a shy young woman expecting her first child arrived Rose helped to make her a garment which supported her without being too tight for health.

Over tea breaks and midday dinner Rose regaled them with stories of the past: of children who wore corsets from the age of two or younger; how the ribs of Edwardian women were restricted so cruelly that their figures remained forever deformed.

'I'm not surprised they kept swooning,' said Ruby.

'No, indeed,' said Rose, whose conversation was beginning to take on some aspects of her fiancé's style of speech. 'In fact, you need to be really careful today. If a woman's breathing is bad, say she has bronchitis or asthma and she has a bad attack and is fitted too tightly, she might even pass away.'

Isobel listened, sometimes feeling quite ill when she thought of how she had gone ahead so confidently fitting her needy customers.

Ruby was kept at home one day by a severe cold and Isobel confided to Rose her fears that some woman might be walking around in the wrong garments.

Rose frowned. 'It doesn't sound as if you've done anything terribly wrong,' she said, 'but all the same I'd like to see the ones you aren't sure of.'

'How can I do that?' asked Isobel. 'If I even hint I've made a mistake my business will collapse.'

'Send a card to the women you have doubts about telling them that Isobel's Corsets likes to follow up certain customers to make sure they are happy and comfortable. No charge, naturally.'

Isobel obeyed and half a dozen women came trotting back obediently, feeling important to be singled out for reassessment.

'My neighbour can't believe it,' said one, a Mrs Murray. 'She says she's never heard of such kindness. She's coming to you next week for her new corset and says she'll bring her sisters. There's eight of 'em so you'll be rushed off your feet.'

Rose took further measurements of Mrs Murray and examined the corset. She frowned thoughtfully and the woman asked anxiously, 'Nothing wrong, is there?'

Isobel held her breath when Rose said, 'Nothing at all, but we would feel happier if you had a couple of modifications in your garment. You have improved so much you no longer need quite the same control.'

'Well,' said Mrs Murray, 'that's wonderful. I don't have to leave this one, do I? I've got used to it and it feels comfy.'

'Not at all,' Rose assured her. 'We shall make another and charge only half-price.'

After Mrs Murray had left Isobel said, 'It's not fair to make her pay anything for my mistake.'

'I know that's how it seems to you, but you did well. The trouble is that in a while she would start feeling pain again. You have to charge her because if you start handing out free corsets you'll have people clamouring at your door complaining. Make it up to her in some way. Add a pretty brassière top with a bit of lace. She could do with support there too.'

Isobel did as Rose suggested and the customer was delighted.

By the time Rose had to cut down her tuition to prepare for her wedding, Ruby and Isobel had learned far more about the measuring, cutting and making of corsets, and their clientele was growing daily.

They were all invited to the quiet wedding. A few of Rose's relatives were there, along with Frank's mother and a couple of ancient aunts. His two sons attended the ceremony, watching with amazement as their father married a new mother. The wedding breakfast was held in Frank's house and the boys politely carried round plates of sandwiches and pastries.

The atmosphere was serene in spite of the aunts, who predicted doom for Frank and his sons. They were both hard of hearing and failed to modify their voices so their conversation was audible to all.

'No good ever came of a stepmother,' said Aunty Nellie.

'You're right, our Nellie. No good ever did. Those poor little boys. She'll frighten them to death.'

Old Mrs Bagley was frail, but she said loudly, 'That's enough, you two. Rose is a darling and I've no worries at all for my dear grandsons.' Which effectively silenced the foretellers of doom.

Lawrence turned his car into Isobel's street and stopped outside the little house. He hoped she would have time for him today. Lately he had visited often, watching her at work, hiding in the kitchen when customers arrived. Grace had felt awkward with him at first, but he was an expert at setting people at their ease and he had a very special reason for wanting to be liked. He intended to marry Isobel and was enlisting everyone possible to his cause.

Grace greeted him with a smile. 'Sit down and have a cup of something. Coffee?'

Lawrence passed no comment on the pre-sweetened bottled coffee and chicory which passed for coffee here, though normally he never took sugar.

'Plenty of customers?' he asked, gesturing towards the front room.

'Lots. More than she and Ruby can deal with sometimes. They're both working evenings as well now and Ruby gets a proper wage plus commission.'

'Isobel's a wonder.'

Grace glanced at him. She had grown fond of him. He obviously liked Isobel, though in what context he hadn't revealed. Grace wasn't worried. Isobel could look after herself. She had a strong mind and was perfectly capable of dealing with a man, even the powerful Lawrence Dane.

'How is your grandma?' she asked.

Lawrence frowned. 'I'm not sure.'

'Not sure? Why, is she ill?'

'No, she seems in good health, but something is worrying her. Twice I've tried to get at the truth, but she evades me.'

Grace said no more. She knew what it was to conceal inadmissible reality. Her mind went back abruptly to the terrible scene of Amos's death. Keeping the truth concealed was playing havoc with her nerves and with poor little Kathy's, too. She had suggested to her youngest daughter that they should confide in the others but the idea had sent Kathy into a panic.

'No, no! They'll never love us again. How could they? We have to keep our secret. You promised, Mum, we both promised never to tell.'

So Grace had subsided, confused, suppressing her sensitive feelings for Kathy's sake.

323

Isobel was busy all morning and at twelve o'clock she and Ruby staggered out longing for rest and refreshment.

'You here again?' Isobel exclaimed when she found Lawrence with his feet on the fender reading a newspaper, but Grace saw that she was delighted to find him waiting for her.

Lawrence knew it too and simply smiled at her.

Isobel washed her hands at the kitchen sink and sat down with the others to a bowl of the usual soup. Grace used different ingredients as they came into season so it never tasted quite the same. One day, said Lawrence, he would write down her recipes and put them in a book.

The next appointment wasn't until two thirty, the day was fine for once and Lawrence suggested a drive. 'The fresh air will do you good,' he said.

'He's right,' said Grace. 'You're getting pale with so much stopping indoors.'

Lawrence drove rapidly until they reached Fishponds, where they strolled on the banks of the River Frome.

'Your mother has a house somewhere near here, hasn't she?' said Isobel.

'I believe so.' His voice was icy. 'She seems to be incapable of faithfulness to a man.'

'Have you ever spoken to her about the past?'

'No, and I never will!'

'That isn't fair,' argued Isobel. 'You have no idea why she behaved as she did.'

'I know she killed my father.' His bitterness seemed to darken the day.

'That's an awful thing to say.'

'It was an awful thing to do.'

'I've only met her briefly but she didn't strike me as being happy. I feel sorry for her.'

'Her unhappiness is entirely her own fault.'

There were few walkers at this time of day and as soon as Lawrence knew they were alone he pulled her from the path into the shelter of a tree. 'Darling,' he whispered, taking her into his arms, 'I do love you.'

Isobel lifted her face for a kiss and he obliged, taking her breath away with the intensity of his demands. His hands began to rove over her body. 'You're beautiful,' he murmured. 'Lovely, sweet, brave, good – I love you so. Say you love me.'

Isobel, struggling with her ache to lie with him right here and now and make love, gasped, 'I'll say no such thing to a philanderer.'

'Don't call me names.'

'Prove you really love me.'

'I can soon do that. Put your hand here, my love, and feel the substance of my words.'

She permitted him to place her hand on his crotch, where the big hard swelling told her that he was very aroused. 'Doesn't he make you feel you'd like to relieve him?'

'You talk is if "he" was a separate entity.'

'That's how he feels a lot of the time. Whenever I'm near you he rises to greet you.'

'Idiot!'

'It's true. He makes my life most uncomfortable sometimes.'

'That's hardly my fault.'

'Whose fault is it?'

'Yours – or his. You should try telling him to behave himself.'

'It's no good. It doesn't work. Only you can assuage our hunger.'

Isobel pulled away from him. Her body was now aching with longing. She who had prided herself on self-control was becoming more helpless in the face of her desire for this man. But no man would take her who wasn't prepared to respect and honour her. She had seen too much misery caused by women yielding to impulse. As far as she could tell, Sylvia Bennyson was a case in point.

She looked at her watch, a gift from Desmond. 'Time to go back.'

'Heartless creature!' declaimed Lawrence.

'Fickle man,' she retorted.

Lawrence dropped Isobel off and drove home. He was thoughtful. He knew he would never love another woman as he did Isobel. Felice had thrown in her lot with the Kingstons and was now officially engaged, wearing her tiny single diamond ring with loving pride. Ralph was in a perpetual temper. The loss of his daughter was having a devastating effect upon him.

On a rainy Sunday when Olive and Ivor were out Grace decided to bring out the family photographs for Felice to see. Isobel was baking ready for Monday while Desmond did his accounts. Kathy stood behind her mother and Felice and looked over their shoulders at the pictures.

The three laughed together at some of the baby photos. 'Is that Desmond?' asked Felice in a would-be scandalised voice.

'Is what me?' growled Desmond.

'This youth with no clothes on,' teased Felice.

Desmond was beside them in one long stride. 'Mum, you haven't shown her that.'

Felice held the photo tantalisingly out of his reach. 'But you're adorable in your little short vest and your dear little bottom showing.' Her eyes were so full of love that Desmond bent to kiss her, a gesture which she returned enthusiastically.

Felice turned back to the scattered photographs and picked one out. 'What is this one doing here?'

Grace took it from her. 'It's Isobel when she was two.'

Felice stared down at the picture. 'I don't understand. We've got one of these in our album at home.'

'Impossible,' said Grace. She sounded breathless.

Isobel wandered over, holding her floury hands close to her apron. 'Let me see. Yes, that's me, Felice.'

'If I could get at our photos I'd show you. We do have it.'

Grace said quickly, 'You can tell it's Isobel. Look at the background. There's our apple tree and the brick wall of the shed.'

'You're right,' said Felice. She looked puzzled.

Isobel's curiosity was fully aroused. 'How can there be a photo of me in your family album, Felice?'

'But it isn't of you,' said Felice. 'I remember now – it's of my grandfather, my father's father.'

Isobel stared down at the photo of herself taken so long ago. 'Was your grandfather short and pudgy like me?'

'You're not pudgy,' declared the others.

'No, you're lovely,' said Felice, 'lovely and lovable.'

Grace stood abruptly. 'We'll put these away. I do believe it's stopped raining. We could all go for a nice walk.'

The suggestion was received without enthusiasm, all deciding that they did enough running around during the week. For the rest of the day Grace was subdued.

Late that night, when the family were about to go to bed, there was a loud knock on the front door. Desmond answered and they heard him say, 'What? What's he done? Where is he?'

Grace went white and Isobel remembered other occasions when a late-night knock meant that Dad was in more trouble with the police.

Desmond came into the kitchen followed by two policemen who

326

seemed to fill the room to overflowing.

'Shall I leave?' asked Felice.

'No,' said Desmond. 'You're a part of the family now. I would rather you knew exactly what you're letting yourself in for.'

So Felice sat and heard that Ivor had been caught with his hands in a pub till while his friends had created a diversion to deflect the manager's attention.

'Thefts have been going on for weeks and we set a trap to catch the thieves,' said the elder constable. 'I'm sorry, Mrs Kingston.'

'Not your fault,' stammered Grace through white lips. 'You've always been kind. When my Amos—' She couldn't proceed for the lump in her throat.

'Where is he?' asked Desmond.

'Down at the station. He'll be kept in a cell until morning when the magistrates will deal with him.'

'Will he go to Borstal?' asked Isobel.

'I can't say, Miss Kingston. It's up to the legal men.'

When the two men had left, Grace said vehemently, angry tears in her eyes, 'I was afraid of this. He takes after his father.'

Felice got up and put her arms round Grace. 'Don't cry, Mrs Kingston. It isn't your fault.'

'I tried to bring him up right,' sobbed Grace. 'I must have gone wrong somewhere.'

Desmond put his long arms round both of them. 'You did nothing wrong, Mum. You've been an angel.'

'Not such an angel. If you only knew—'

'Knew what?' asked Isobel. Her mother looked haunted.

Kathy was staring at Grace, her eyes large with dread. 'It's all right, Kathy,' said Grace. 'Come along, let's go to bed.' They shut everyone out and climbed the stairs, their arms around one another, while Isobel watched from below, hurt by this instant rejection.

As usual Desmond took over the role of guardian of the family. He went to the police station to get more information. 'They're keeping him in,' he told them on his return. 'The magistrates refused to allow bail.'

A moan escaped Grace. 'Did you find anything else out?'

It was Desmond's private opinion that his brother was a naturally bad lot, but he said gently, 'Dawson, the bookie, drove him to it. Ivor owes him money and if you can't pay Dawson he sends out his bully boys to beat you up. I didn't have enough to pay him off this time.'

'This time? It's happened before.'

327

Desmond, wishing he had guarded his tongue, said, 'I didn't mean Ivor.'

'Your father!' said Grace. 'You bought your father out of trouble. Oh, my dear boy, what a terrible life we've given you.'

Desmond smiled faintly. 'No, Mum, you haven't. You did your best. No one can do more.'

'How much does Ivor owe?'

'Fifty pounds.'

'How much? Fifty? We could never pay that.'

'I know, Mum.'

The news ran through the neighbourhood like wildfire. 'Like father, like son,' was the general opinion. The rest of the family was held in high esteem (except for Olive who was known as 'man-mad') but no one could resist a good gossip about a juicy scandal.

Inevitably news of the arrest reached Ralph Bennyson, who roared with rage until he realised that he could probably use Ivor Kingston's criminal behaviour to prise Felice away from them. He'd go to court if he had to. He'd hire a King's Counsel. Money was no object. He'd like to see the Kingstons try to hang on to his daughter now. He'd relish a fight, especially one which he would be sure to win and at the same time punish the Kingstons.

Chapter Twenty

Ralph began to put his plans into action. Sylvia had moved to the ridiculous house in Stapleton, but he scarcely noticed she had gone, except as an irritation removed. A private detective hired by Oates, the solicitor, had traced Felice to the Kingstons whose address was still in the factory register of Bennyson employees.

His solicitor, Mr Oates, advised him to try to win Felice over with kindly persuasion. 'So much better to have her return willingly,' he said. 'If that doesn't work we can then take another line.'

Ralph decided his first move must be to call on Felice at the Kingstons'. He arrived at the house at six o'clock when he judged that the people he considered lesser beings would be eating what they called tea. High tea! His lips twisted in disbelief at the idea that his Felice would enjoy such low standards. She was simply hiding in the easiest refuge she could find, hoping it wouldn't take him too long to rescue her. How did she amuse herself all day? Reading? Going to cinemas? Surely not spending much time talking to uneducated people with whom she had nothing in common? Grace answered the door in her wrap-around apron, wiping flour from her hands. She stared at him.

He raised his hat. 'Mrs Kingston? I have come to call upon my daughter, Miss Bennyson.'

'Felice?' Grace viewed him open-mouthed.

'May I come in? I do not wish to talk on the doorstep and I'm sure your neighbours have as much gossip about you as they need for the present.'

Grace stood back and motioned him through to the kitchen. She could hear a murmur of voices from the front room where Isobel and Ruby were busy with their latest customers. Someone laughed and Ralph raised his eyebrows. 'Is my daughter in there?'

'No, she's not,' said Grace shortly. 'If you want to talk to me you'll need to come in here. We run a business from the other room.'

'Indeed? What kind of business?'

'You came to talk about Felice?'

Ralph frowned. This woman had deliberately snubbed him. 'I am here to do more than talk. I shall be taking her home. Please fetch her for me.'

The woman left and Ralph heard voices rise and fall as Grace opened the door of the front room, went in and closed it behind her.

So she had lied. Felice was in there.

He looked round the kitchen, noting the jumble. There was not a surface free. Piles of ironing stood alongside dishes of food. The woman probably had a dozen children at least. Her sort seemed to breed like rabbits. How in hell did his gently reared child fit in here? Where did she sleep? He took pleasure in imagining her throwing herself on him in relief at his arrival. He frowned. He had to make her pay for the way she had worried him. She must be punished. Nothing like this must ever happen again.

The woman returned with someone he thought he recognised. Ah, yes, the insolent piece he'd had to sack for daring to incite the women to a strike. She should have known better than to tangle with him. He'd soon settled her hash, and her brother's, too. A fine lot of ne'er-do-wells to be hiding his child from him. One of them was in prison awaiting trail for theft and he'd heard that one daughter was little more than a tart, out all hours with men.

Isobel asked coldly, 'What can we do for you?'

'This is between your mother and me,' said Ralph.

'Anything that concerns Mum concerns her family,' said Isobel.

Ralph almost ground his teeth. He recalled his fury when this same girl had stood up to him and defied him in front of dozens of witnesses. He'd very much like to find some way of discrediting her, of hurting her. 'I wish to speak to Miss Bennyson.'

'Felice?' said Isobel carelessly. 'She isn't here.'

'Don't lie to me, young woman. I have learned that she has been living with you since she left home.'

'Hasn't she been in touch?'

'No, she has not.'

'It looks as if she doesn't want to see you,' said Isobel calmly. 'I must get back to work. I've a lot to do.'

Ralph reddened. 'If you do not tell my daughter I am here I shall return with someone who can make you.'

Grace gasped, but Isobel said, 'And who might that be?'

'The police if necessary.'

'No!' cried Grace.

'Your mother has a lively respect for the law,' said Ralph, 'unlike your brother. Ivor, isn't it? The one who's being held in custody?'

Isobel didn't flinch. She had been through scenes before where she'd had to defend herself and her family against gossip and innuendo. 'That's right,' she said.

'Have you no shame, you brazen woman?'

'Why should I? My brother is old enough to know right from wrong. He has been properly taught. It isn't my fault he didn't listen.'

'Perhaps he preferred to listen to his father. He spent his life in and out of prison, didn't he?'

Isobel glanced at Grace, who was breathing hard. 'Go into the other room, Mum.'

Grace hesitated but crept out looking cowed. Isobel hated this man for causing her mother such pain.

'Felice isn't here,' she said. 'She has a job.'

'A job? Work, do you mean?'

'Exactly.'

'What kind of work? She's not been trained to do anything beyond the usual tasks a lady performs, though I wouldn't expect you to know about that.'

'She certainly is a sweet, ladylike girl,' said Isobel, still managing to appear calm though her heart was beginning to thud with the effort of holding this man at bay.

'Where does she work?' demanded Ralph.

Isobel knew she couldn't hide the truth from him for long and Desmond would know exactly how to defend the girl he loved. 'She's in West Street in a place called Kathy's Tearoom.'

'What in hell does she do there?'

'She waits at tables and washes dishes.'

Isobel grew alarmed for Ralph Bennyson whose face went brick-red while his eyes bulged. 'What kind of place is that?'

'A workman's café,' said Isobel. 'My brother and his partner cater for men and women who can't afford posh places.' She suddenly felt weary of his bullying. 'The food is good. You should try it.'

The red turned to purple and he stamped out of the kitchen, thudded along the passage and slammed the front door behind him. Isobel was sorry she'd allowed her temper to control her. Desmond would have to bear the brunt of his rage. She wished there was a way to get to the café first.

331

Grace crept out to answer another knock on the door and Isobel heard Lawrence's voice. She dashed out to him, grabbing her coat and tam-o'-shanter. 'Quick,' she said, 'drive me to the café before he gets there.'

'What? Who? Where?' But, bewildered as he was, Lawrence knew when action was required and he hurried after Isobel, opened the passenger door of his car for her, leapt in the driver's seat and started the engine.

'To Kathy's Tearoom,' ordered Isobel.

He drove off. 'Certainly. Er, are you being pursued by bandits?'

'Sorry, but this is no laughing matter. Mr Bennyson has been here after Felice. He's on his way to the café.'

'Oh dear. How is her affair progressing?'

'It's not an affair. It's true love and she and Desmond are engaged.'

Lawrence let out a long whistle. 'And Ralph is after them?'

'Yes, and I have to warn them.'

'Desmond can take care of himself and Felice,' said Lawrence, passing a tram on the wrong side.

'Felice is such a sweet little thing and her father is so domineering.'

'You're right there.' Lawrence swore as he swerved to avoid a small boy on a bicycle who had shot out of a side street.

Isobel clung to the door strap. 'Can't you go any faster? We must get to the café first.' She saw Ralph Bennyson's large car parked outside a tobacconist's. 'Look, he's stopped. Hurry.'

'If I hurry any more I'll be pulled up for speeding and some constable will be delighted to take every detail of my life from birth onwards. And here we are.' Isobel was out of the car almost before it stopped. She raced into the café.

Felice was serving bowls of soup from a laden tray, and even in her agitation Isobel thought how much healthier she looked. And happy, too.

'Hello, Isobel,' she said. 'Are you here for lunch?'

'Where's Desmond?'

'Out. He's gone to buy more bread. We're running short.'

'Damn! Damn! Damn!'

Felice said humorously, 'You'd better come into the kitchen. You're shocking the customers.'

'They've heard worse than that.' She hurried to the kitchen, followed by Felice who was forced to ignore a demand for tea and a biscuit from a rough-looking stallholder.

Isobel said, 'Your father called on us. He's on his way here.'

'Called on you? When?'

'Not long ago. I beat him here to warn you.'

'Oh dear. I wish Desmond wasn't out. How did you get here before Father?'

Lawrence spoke from the kitchen door. 'There's a man out here who's demanding tea and a biscuit.'

'I know,' said Felice, in her agitation showing no surprise at the sudden appearance of her stepbrother. 'Father's on his way—'

'Yes, Isobel insisted on breaking the traffic laws with impunity. Is this the tea urn?' He filled an enamel mug. 'And these must be the biscuits. I can tell because they're in a box marked "Biscuits".'

'Fool,' said Isobel affectionately.

Lawrence took the order to the stallholder who growled, 'About time.'

'Sorry for the delay, sir,' said Lawrence as Ralph burst through the door yelling, 'I want to speak to Miss Bennyson.' He saw Lawrence and gaped. 'What in hell—?' Then his face darkened with anger. 'So you were in on this, too! I thought I could trust you. Where is she?' He had forgotten the customers in his anger and didn't even notice the silence that fell as these two smartly dressed men were, it seemed, about to have a quarrel. They settled back to enjoy the unexpected entertainment.

'Don't make a spectacle of us,' said Lawrence and Ralph glanced around. He looked sick as he took in the men and women who were seated round communal tables. Their soiled hands, badly cut hair, their variety of aprons from the brewer's leather to the butcher's stripes disgusted him. He stamped into the kitchen.

He saw Isobel first. 'You! How did you—? Oh, I see, Lawrence brought you.' Lawrence followed him in, crowding the small room. 'I believed I could trust you,' Ralph said again bitterly.

'You can, Ralph, but my friendship for you doesn't extend to telling tales about Felice.'

'Telling tales? What a bloody stupid reply! Felice is underage and has no idea what kind of life these people lead. Anything could happen to her.'

'What an insult,' cried Felice. 'I hope you don't think I've done something to be ashamed of.'

'Of course not,' said Ralph.

'Then why insinuate that I might have?'

333

'Just being here contaminates you.'

'It does no such thing. My new family has shown me nothing but kindness.'

'New family? These people? Have you forgotten I had to dismiss Miss Kingston for inciting the workers to go against me? And her brother too? They're simply not to be trusted.'

'And you are? What have you told Aubrey about my absence? A lie, I suppose. Where am I supposed to be? The South of France? Scotland? It's too much to hope you have told him the truth, that I will never marry him.'

'Of course I had to dissemble. Would you want him to know about this? When you return to your senses you'll see all the advantages of marriage with him. Think of the life you'd have, instead of – this.' He swept his arm around the café, almost knocking a tray of cakes to the floor.

There was a very slight quaver in his voice and Felice almost felt sorry for him. He had been a good father to her according to his own perception. She laid her hand on his arm and he looked down at it, covering it with his own. Then he jerked his hand away. 'A ring! On your engagement finger!'

'Yes, it's Desmond's. Father, we're engaged. Oh, please don't be angry. I would so much rather have your approval.'

'Where is he?'

'Out for the moment,' said Isobel.

'I didn't ask you! Felice, can't we go somewhere private? I object to conducting our affairs so publicly. This is a family matter.'

Felice said gently, 'I've told you, Father, this is my new family.'

'My God, I can't believe what I'm hearing. I have just called at the Kingstons' and was shocked to discover just how they live. How can you bear to be near such people day after day?'

Felice said coldly, 'I love them. They are good to me, gentle and kind. I have no intention of leaving them.'

'We'll see about that. I shall be visiting my solicitor.'

'You may do so,' said Felice, 'but nothing you or he can do will make any difference. Even if you force me to return I shall soon be twenty-one and free of you. Desmond will wait.'

'Oh, will he? Perhaps he doesn't know that your money is tied up in trusts over which I have sole guardianship? I am not obliged to hand it over to you when you come of age. I can hold it until you are thirty.'

'Is that so?' said Felice. 'He couldn't know because I didn't. But you must do as you think best, Father. Desmond has no intention of living off my money. As a matter of fact, he didn't even know I had any until the other day.'

'So he tells you.'

'He never lies to me.'

Ralph looked round like a cornered beast. His eyes were hard and cruel and reminded Isobel of the eyes of a stalking cat or a predatory bird. 'You are a fool if you believe him,' he snarled. 'It'll be a different matter when he knows the truth.'

Then Desmond walked in. 'Do you know two customers are waiting? Mr Bennyson! What are you doing here? Have you come to test our café?'

'Test your blasted café? Don't make me laugh. I'm here to take my daughter home.'

Desmond walked to Felice and put his arm around her waist. 'Her home is with us.'

Ralph was silent for a moment, during which the high colour drained from his face. His fury was almost tangible and his voice was ice-cold. He said, 'Tell me, Felice, will you still want to be associated with them when the story of their brother's theft is splashed all over the newspapers? And naturally the reporters will recall the days when Mr Kingston went regularly to prison. In fact, I don't know why I'm bothering to argue with you. In the circumstances no court in the land would deny me my rights over my daughter.'

'I hope you'll not go to court, but you won't force me to give up Desmond. I shall go to my mother.'

'Your mother?' All the hatred and contempt that had built within Ralph since his marriage were in his voice. 'I shall fight that, too. I shall have no hesitation in telling the world that your mother has spent long periods in nursing homes for the mentally afflicted.'

'You couldn't be so cruel, not even you.'

'Not even me? How dare you speak to me like that!'

'You don't care how you speak to Mother.'

'Your mother has gone to live in a poky place in Stapleton.'

'I know where she is, in a charming cottage near the river,' said Felice calmly.

'You shall not live with her. I won't allow it.'

'You can't stop me. She's my mother and I love her, though you've done your best to turn me against her.'

'Rubbish. You don't care for her any more than you care about this man.'

335

'You know nothing about it,' said Felice quietly.

'I know a damn sight more than you. We'll discuss it when you come home, as you most certainly will.'

'We'll see,' said Desmond.

Felice turned towards him and laid her head on his shoulder.

Ralph stared at the couple, his eyes blazing, then he marched out of the café leaving the others staring at one another.

Isobel attended to the customers while Desmond comforted Felice, then Lawrence drove her home. He stopped in his usual place at the end of the street.

'I never thought Ralph would behave so badly,' he said. 'I respected him.'

'Do you care for him?'

'No, not really. I've always felt sorry for him for having to marry my mother. I've seen him in the depths of despair at the way his life has turned out. He said he married the wrong woman because she pretended to be expecting his child.'

'Well! If that isn't just like a man! Surely having taken her from her husband he would have married her anyway. An honourable man could do nothing else. That's if you believe a seducer can be called honourable.'

'It takes two.'

'Exactly. So why blame your mother?'

'She was a married woman. Ralph was free.'

'Then he should have been courting an unmarried woman. Why go for your mother?'

'Men are like that. Some men. A woman must resist them.'

'Are you like Ralph? You've told me you love me. What you mean is that you want to make love to me. And that's where it ends. Do you think I'm easy game? That I've been with other men?'

'No,' said Lawrence, genuinely shocked. 'Of course I don't.'

'You'd like to be the first with me. Then any man I fall in love with would get damaged goods.'

'Don't, Isobel.' He hated to hear her speak that way.

They were silent for a moment.

Isobel said, 'Don't you care at all for your mother?'

'No. I suppose I did when I was small. When my father killed himself I wanted her so desperately. Grandmother tried everything to get her to come to me, but Mother refused. The cruelty of it still has the power to—' Lawrence stopped, unable to go on.

'That's terrible. She actually refused to see you?'

'So Ralph said.'

'Ralph?'

'He acted as go-between.'

'Do you mean the two women never discussed it?'

'I suppose they found it too painful and he was there, being kind and helpful.'

It didn't sound like Ralph Bennyson, thought Isobel.

'I'd rather not discuss it,' said Lawrence.

'But darling' – the endearment slipped out – 'there may be circumstances you don't know about. You may discover that your mother wasn't as bad as it sounds.'

'You called me darling.'

'Yes.'

'Am I your darling?'

Isobel hesitated. 'Yes,' she finally said. 'I think of you that way, but don't think I'll ever let you take liberties. Nothing beyond a caress.'

Lawrence looked very happy. He kissed her gently. 'Isobel, if you care for me it would make up for everything else. I've done my best to cope. I trust Grandmother's word. She's held her dislike for my mother all these years and that's so unlike her there must be something horribly wrong about Mother.'

Isobel said sadly, 'Perhaps no one knows the whole truth. Or perhaps only Ralph does.'

'Ralph? He's never mentioned the past to me.'

'Don't you find that odd? You might have thought that he'd try to help you recover from the shocks of your childhood.'

Lawrence looked so dejected that Isobel forgave him. 'How did you get acquainted with Ralph?' she asked.

Lawrence was silent for a moment. 'I can hardly remember. It happened when I was at school. I did well in my exams and he sent me a letter of congratulation. I answered him and this led to our meeting and our gradual understanding. He looks upon me as the son he can't ever have. Not by Mother anyway.'

'That must have hurt Sylvia a lot.'

'What? I suppose it did.'

Although Isobel knew she was late for an appointment she stayed where she was.

He said slowly, 'Isobel, you are making me think. Why did everyone trust Ralph?'

'Probably they were all so emotionally shattered it was easier to let him manage everything.'

337

'Surely I couldn't have been wrong all these years.'

'When did you learn how your father died?' asked Isobel gently.

'I've always known.'

'They told you?'

'I don't remember. I suppose someone must have.'

'It must have been dreadful for you. My father died in an accident. It has affected Kathy badly.'

He looked at Isobel, tracing every feature with his eyes. 'I long to kiss you.'

'Every woman in the street will be peering at us by now and Olive is already doing her bit to make our family notorious.'

'She's not as pretty as you.'

Isobel gave him a quizzical glance. 'Much as I enjoy hearing your favourable opinion I don't believe it.'

Lawrence devoured her with his eyes. 'To me you are beautiful,' he said simply.

'Thank you, Lawrence. Now I must get back to work. Heaven knows what my customers will think.'

Isobel's customers were not in the least put out by having to wait. They had been discussing the pair in the car with immense interest.

'Hello, Isobel,' said one. 'Nice boyfriend.'

'Nice car,' said the other.

'Wasn't that young Mr Dane?'

'It was. I apologise for being late.'

'Well understood, my dear.'

Lawrence drove away in a thoughtful mood. Why had he let the years slip past while such an unnatural situation had been built around him? Had he been doing his mother a terrible injustice and adding to her misery? The idea brought perspiration trickling down his upper lip.

Arriving home he parked his car and went into the house. As always grandmother knew of his return and was watching the door of her pretty drawing room, knowing that he would come to her before he did anything else. But this time he went straight past her door and up to his room. She was bothered. Something must have upset him. In her usual way she didn't interfere. When he came in later and sat down she knew at once he was deeply troubled, but still waited.

'Grandmother,' he said. 'Is there anything more about the past I should know?'

Mrs Dane forced herself to answer calmly. 'Have you been talking to someone?'

'Isobel Kingston.'

'Miss Kingston! But she knows nothing.'

'She knows as much as I do.'

'You care enough for her to tell her these things?'

'Yes. I intend to marry her.'

Mrs Dane clenched her fists in the folds of her dress. 'Is she willing?'

'That's what I'll have to discover. I haven't asked her yet.'

'She is bound to jump at your offer.'

'No, she is not the kind of woman to accept a man unless she loves him. Grandmother, you didn't answer my question about the past.'

Mrs Dane said carefully, 'Until a short while ago I knew only what Ralph told me. Then Felice Bennyson came to see me.'

Lawrence nodded. 'I saw her drive away.'

'You said nothing. She told me that she was sure Ralph had lied to me about Sylvia. That your mother always wanted you.'

Lawrence's fingers entwined in a grip that sent his knuckles white. 'Go on.'

'Felice had inadvertently been forgotten during a quarrel between her parents during which she learned, or believed she did, something quite horrifying, if it were true. I thought she had imagined what was said, or misunderstood it. Young girls often dramatise things. Then your mother called here. She didn't know that Felice had spoken to me. Sylvia was quite calm. It seemed as if she had schooled herself to speak clearly. She had need to. What she said was dreadful. We compared notes and it all dovetailed perfectly. Poor Sylvia remembers the events as clearly as if they happened yesterday and my mind is equally clear. We realised that Ralph had lied to us both. He passed false messages back and forth and because we were so distraught, especially at the time of your father's death, we believed him. Preferred to believe him.'

Mrs Dane went on to tell Lawrence exactly what had occurred when he was a child, about his mother's pleading, her despair, all of which Ralph had lied about. She spoke of her own contempt towards a mother who could behave so horribly. 'And all the time Sylvia was agonising over you and *my* apparent cruelty.'

Mrs Dane stopped speaking and Lawrence sat absolutely still. He was afraid that if he moved he would unleash the storm of fury, disgust and terrible remorse that was raging in him. At that moment he hated everyone, his grandmother for being so easily fooled, Sylvia for not forcing her way to him, and above all he felt he could kill Ralph Bennyson. Reason finally took control. He too was to blame. He had treated his mother shamefully.

Mrs Dane, who understood him so well, waited until his first fury had passed then said, 'Don't hate yourself, my dear boy. You were never to blame. I should have been braver.'

'The final responsibility lies with Bennyson. Why did he behave that way? What could he hope to gain?'

'Revenge on Sylvia. He cared nothing for our distress so long as he got his own back on her. He blamed her for everything. How could I have doubted her? I knew she was honourable and loved your father deeply.'

'You knew that?' Lawrence's voice was half strangled in his aching throat.

'Everyone did. Poor soul, she was an innocent. Her father was an honourable man and marriage to my Harry had taught her only more good about men. She didn't believe Ralph's accusations against Harry until he showed her a photograph of him with an unclothed woman.'

'My father—?'

'Your father did nothing wrong. The picture was a fake dreamed up by Ralph to get her to lower her defence and submit to his love-making.'

'Oh, my God,' groaned Lawrence. 'It seems incredible that you should all have trusted him the way you did.'

'I agree. But the incidents looked very different then, the scandal was in all the newspapers, the national ones, too. Sylvia had been a well-known debutante from an excellent family and we were all flayed by the publicity. Her parents who had adored her were dead. The few distant relatives she had distanced themselves from her. They're all dead now. How lonely Sylvia has been all these years. Ralph must have been hellish to live with, resenting her the way he did.'

'She's left him,' said Ralph. 'She has a house in Stapleton and she wants Felice to join her there.'

'And will she?'

'She may. She has to protect herself from Ralph. He's going to court because she's left home.'

'So he is still intent on making his womenfolk suffer?'

Lawrence stood up. 'I don't believe that this time he'll succeed. I'll

340

see if I can do anything to stop him.' Mrs Dane looked alarmed and he said, 'Don't worry, Grandmother, I don't intend to use force.'

'I agree that you must take action as soon as possible but we haven't discussed Miss Kingston. You said you want to marry her. Lawrence, her background, her family—'

Lawrence bent and kissed her gently. 'Don't worry, my dear. Nothing will happen quickly. Isobel won't be easily persuaded. And when you know her you'll love her.'

Ralph went to see his lawyer. 'I don't think you need worry, Mr Bennyson,' said Oates. 'When the facts are set out – Mrs Bennyson's mental state, Miss Bennyson's unsuitable lifestyle and her infatuation with Mr Kingston, the member of a discredited family – no one will doubt that she must return to you.'

Ralph went home feeling satisfied with the interview, sure that soon he would have Felice back and they would resume their original adored and adoring status. Poor little soul. She'd been so upset by her stupid mother's behaviour she was easy prey for Desmond Kingston. Once he had Felice under his control he'd look into the Kingstons' background and make every one of them suffer for what they were doing to him.

Isobel's Corsets was doing well, though not well enough to save for another machine. Isobel decided to have a small show. Her problem was where to hold it.

Desmond came to the rescue. 'We've managed to rent the floor above Kathy's Tearoom. It's been scrubbed and Owen and I will paint it.'

Isobel was delighted. Owen was to make his home in the three rooms above the café. 'He's got water and a gas stove and fire,' said Desmond, 'and he'll be comfortable and needn't pay rent. He'll be caretaker, too. With so much crime these days we need him.'

Both abruptly fell silent, remembering Ivor. He had become another statistic in the crime figures.

'Anyway, love,' said Desmond, 'the premises are yours for a couple of weeks before Owen moves in. Is that enough time?'

'It is if we work at it.'

She and Ruby washed the woodwork ready for it to be painted and Rose helped. Grace and Kathy concentrated on the ceaseless baking. Kathy was thinner and paler than ever.

'She's doing too much,' said Isobel to Grace.

341

'She's outgrowing her strength,' insisted Grace. 'It often happens at her age. She'll pick up.'

But the carefree serene girl Isobel remembered had vanished.

Isobel needed mannequins. She would herself show the garment for the short, sturdy figure; Ruby was tall with a big bosom; Rose Bagley was tall and thin and, although she didn't need a foundation garment, there were many thin women who, through a combination of constant hard work and childbearing, would feel a lot more comfortable in a custom-designed corset. Felice would model garments for the young matron and Kathy for the developing girl.

Grace couldn't be persuaded to appear. 'Never,' she declared. 'I'd faint with embarrassment. I'll come and cater for the audience, make tea and things, but you'll never get me on a – what's that thing called? – a catwalk. Never!'

'I wish you would, Mum. We can't afford professionals.'

'I wonder if one or two of your satisfied customers would oblige?'

Two were happy to help. Mrs Kenton who was plump and a Mrs Risby who was very fat indeed. 'It don't seem to make no difference what I eat,' she explained. 'I get fatter. I tried a couple of times to lose weight, but I give it up pretty quick. With twelve kids you need all the energy you've got and the nurse told me that energy comes from eatin' the right food, so I don't bother now. Mind you, the nurse goes on at me sometimes because she don't think that fish an' chips and beer's the right food, but I like it.' She was a good-natured soul who allowed Rose Bagley to measure all her billowing inches and patiently tried on the large garment which fitted her perfectly.

'I reckon this gives me a good shape,' she said. 'I wouldn't mind buyin' one. I like the way it makes me go in and out proper.'

The show went off beautifully. Every model wore her garments over a pink frilly petticoat and as only women were present they were not too shy. The women who crowded in, some carrying their youngest baby with a toddler or two by the hand, had mostly walked from home where far too much work awaited them on their return. The discreet behaviour of Bennyson's clients was not for them. They thought nothing of whistling when the models paraded, or yelling remarks, some of them quite racy, though when Kathy tripped out they were quiet, watching the progress of the pretty teenager.

When the refreshments were handed round Isobel gave a short talk on the benefits to be gained by having a 'special' made. Mrs Kenton added her recommendation and told them about her friend's backache which was very much easier. The women fell quiet and several came to Isobel and asked to be measured.

'I can't pay right away,' was a common opening statement, 'but if you could open a credit book I promise to settle in the end.'

Rose didn't altogether approve. 'We used to get quite a few bad debts at Bennyson's,' she said. She sniffed. 'Mostly from the women you'd think the most toffee-nosed.' But she sat and patiently entered names and measurements into the credit order book and the customers promised to call and pick up their garments and hand over their first payment as soon as they got some housekeeping.

As they cleared up they congratulated themselves on a success. A very old lady had lingered. Her hearing was imperfect and her wits had dulled, but her sight was still keen. She said to Isobel, 'A very nice afternoon do, Miss Bennyson.'

Isobel smiled and said kindly, 'Miss Bennyson is over there, collecting cups. I'm Isobel Kingston.'

The woman peered at her. 'You can't fool me. You're the image of old Mr Bennyson.'

Isobel watched her shuffle off, leaning heavily on her stick. The sounds around her died away as she remembered Felice's spontaneous cry when she had seen Isobel's youthful photograph. Surely two people couldn't make the same mistake, but she couldn't get her brain to accept a logical explanation. She'd have to ask Grace about it.

'Where's Mum?' she asked Ruby.

Ruby looked around. 'I don't know. She was over there a moment ago, gathering up some of the garments. She went to the lav, I think.'

Isobel went to a side room which was being converted into a cloakrom for the convenience of future customers to the café and found her mother bending over a sink, bathing her face.

'Are you all right, Mum?'

'I felt a bit giddy.'

'It was too much for you. You'd better go home. Owen can run you in his van.'

'No, thanks. I'm all right now.'

When Isobel would have remonstrated further, Grace pushed her way past quite roughly.

Isobel wondered. The old woman's thin reedy voice must have carried to Grace, who had been only a few feet away.

Her questions had to be delayed.

Olive arrived home that evening, very dishevelled, and calmly

343

announced that she was expecting a child.

Grace gasped, unable to speak.

Isobel asked, 'May we know the father's name?'

'Naturally.' Olive threw herself into a chair. 'Is there any tea? I'm parched. I've been talking for hours.'

Isobel poured her a cup of tea and she and Grace waited.

'It's Mr Dawson.'

'I thought he was married,' said Grace. 'He's at least fifty.' She sounded totally exhausted.

'Forty-eight actually. He was married but now he's divorced.'

'You want a divorced man old enough to be your father?' Grace could scarcely form her lips round the words.

'As if any of that matters!' Olive was contemptuous. 'I told you I'd have money and I shall. He's very rich—'

'Rich from tempting men to gamble,' cried Grace. 'Your father fell into his clutches and now Ivor. How can you?'

'For goodness' sake,' said Olive. 'Surely you want me to marry my baby's father.'

'I'm glad he has that much honour,' said Isobel.

'A fat lot you know, poncing around with your fancy man who'll never marry a common girl like you. But Steve's our sort.'

'He's not my sort,' declared Isobel, smarting from Olive's taunt.

'You can be as prissy as you like!' snapped Olive. 'I'm going to be rich. I'll show you!'

'Your father spent half his time in prison because of the money he owed Dawson,' said Grace, her voice breaking in a sob.

'More fool him. Steve says the punters are all fools, only the bookies end up rich. Dad was certainly a fool. Anyway, Mum, here's a bit of good news. The landlord Ivor robbed owes my Steve a lot of money and Steve's going to bribe him to drop the charges. The landlord will make up some story that he's miscounted or something.'

Grace got up. 'Lies! More lies! My whole life is one big lie. I'm too tired to talk any more. I'm going to bed.'

Olive watched her mother with a dissatisfied look on her pretty face. 'You'd think she'd be grateful to me.'

Chapter Twenty-One

Lawrence was far too disturbed by his grandmother's revelations to confront Ralph immediately. All the participants in the tragedy had suffered so long; one more day couldn't make a difference and he needed to get everything absolutely straight in his head that night. He paced his bedroom for hours, throwing his mind back to the past. The part of his life before his mother's leaving and his father's sudden death was blurred in his memory. Of course he'd been very young but surely there should have been some impression of a happy home with loving parents which is what Grandmother assured him he had enjoyed.

But it was useless trying to clear his mind. That stage of his life remained blanked out. The first thing he remembered clearly was going to live with his grandmother, who had been welcoming and deeply loving. He had been lucky to be cared for by her. Several chaps at school had been victims of divorce, staying with one or other of their parents during vacations and often used as pawns in their quarrels; or they were left at school in loneliness. Disjointed half-recollections swirled round and round in his head until he was afraid he'd go crazy. He thought of Ralph, but not for long because it made him too angry. He thought of Sylvia, but had to control himself there, too, or he'd be consumed by guilt and pity. Tomorrow he would act. Tomorrow he would see Ralph, then go to his mother.

At around three in the morning he fell into bed, his body aching with weariness, his brain too tired to take in any more. He came from the blackness of sleep into a room where the furniture seemed huge until he realised that he was small – a child whose head didn't reach the top of his father's desk. He was in Father's study. He hid beneath the desk in the deep kneehole. Father was coming soon. He'd heard him say so. To whom had he said it? Mother. Mother was sitting downstairs, busy with a charming piece of embroidery. She was tall, slender, beautiful and sweet-smelling and he loved her

345

more than anyone in the world, even Father. Then Father came into the study and they played their game of hide-and-seek.

Father sat down at his desk and exclaimed, 'Why, I do believe there is someone in the room with me!'

The child stifled his giggles.

'And, what is more, I think he's under my desk.'

A strong, gentle hand reached into the kneehole and grasped Lawrence's arm. 'Ah, ha! Pray, varlet, what are you doing here?' Father used storybook talk in their games. Sometimes he said 'forsooth' and 'gadzooks' when they were King Arthur and a Knight of the Round Table. Lawrence was helpless to prevent his giggles from escaping as the hand tickled him. 'Come forth, thou varlet,' cried Father. Lawrence laughed as he rose into his father's arms.

Father faded. Everything changed and became terrifying. Another day, overcast, the study dimly lit. Lawrence was unhappy because Mother was no longer downstairs. He knew there was evil all around him and he tried to scream, but his voice was gone; he tried to move but he was paralysed. Something terrible was about to happen and he was a total prisoner. This time he was hiding beside a large cupboard. In it, he remembered, were Father's sports things, the cricket bat with which he had made the winning run for his school team during his last term. His tennis racket, fishing rods and guns which were cared for by their one male servant.

The footsteps were there again, growing closer and closer, but instead of joy Lawrence knew only fear, a deep and agonising fear. Father entered the study and closed the door. Then the ultimate horror started. Father began to sob. Lawrence wanted to run to him, to beg him to stop. Why was he sobbing? Something about Mother. He said her name. 'Sylvia, Sylvia, why? What did I do? Oh, Sylvia.'

Lawrence heard a click. He knew it for the click of a revolver. Father had shown him his guns and said he would teach him one day how to shoot; meanwhile he was allowed to watch while they were being cleaned and oiled. There was further movement from the desk, then a long silence. Was Father waiting to surprise his son? With a gun? Lawrence wanted to jump out and surprise *him*.

So that's what he did. Suddenly released from his paralysis he leapt into view crying, 'Thou varlet – !' As he did so there was a thunderous explosion which echoed round the walls of the study, and Lawrence saw his father's face become a bloody horror and watched him fall, choking and gurgling, to the floor.

'I've killed him,' he screamed. 'I've killed Father. I shouted at him and he shot himself.'

Lawrence ran from the study as fast as he could but seemed unable to reach anyone. He could see nothing, but he heard running feet and others crying out. Those who passed him were shadows. No one seemed to see him. No one knew he had just killed his father.

Lawrence woke with a yell. He sat bolt upright in bed, streaming with sweat, half dazed, floating between childhood and manhood. Mother had gone away and never come back. He had cried for her and Grandmother had tried to comfort him, but there was no comfort. He wanted Mother, but she wouldn't come. He wanted someone to tell him he hadn't killed Father, but no one ever did.

'Mother,' he said into the darkness, still confused.

Full consciousness returned and he put on the light, staggered to his bathroom and stood, still in pyjamas, beneath a cold shower. Then he drank a long draught of water, took off his soaked pyjamas and threw them into the bath. He shivered as cool air found his damp body and he pulled on his dressing gown and got back into bed and lit a cigarette. When that was smoked he lit another, then another until the air was blue with smoke, while he finally admitted into his conscious mind the truth about the past.

He recalled how he had been in bed one night when Mother came to him. She had held him close in her arms – the memory of her scent was so clear he could smell it now – and wept over him. 'My beloved little boy, don't worry. I have to leave you for a while, but I'll come back for you. I won't be separated from you.' And she hadn't come.

But Mother had loved him all along. She wasn't evil, she never had been. She had been weak and deceived, but those were not crimes. He knew for sure now where the blame lay. Ralph. He disliked Ralph. He always had. He was a greedy, covetous, callous bastard who had tormented Sylvia almost to madness. Felice had finally recognised him for what he was and run from him. His behaviour towards those over whom he had power was vile.

But more terrible than anything was the realisation that Ralph had lied blatantly to Grandmother at a time when her heart was already breaking over the loss of her son and the treachery of his wife whom she had loved. And Ralph had cheated him out of a childhood in which he had been deprived of both parents, making his growing years bitter and unforgiving.

He was still staring into the past and smoking when a maid brought his morning tea.

She coughed. 'Goodness, Mr Lawrence, have you been smoking all night? I'll just open the window a mite.'

Lawrence watched her leave without really seeing her. The past was more concrete than the present. He drank his tea and climbed out of bed. He should feel tired but he was too overwrought. Grandmother greeted him as usual at breakfast, then frowned. There were deep dark shadows beneath his eyes. Obviously he'd had a bad night; her news had been a fearful shock.

'What are your plans for today?' she asked timorously.

'I've been thinking about them. I haven't quite decided. I shall have to speak to Ralph and explain I want nothing more from him, ever. And I must see my mother.' The word sat awkwardly on his lips.

'Yes, you must do that.'

'I wonder how she'll receive me.'

'With the deepest tenderness, I'm sure. I can't imagine how I allowed myself to be so deceived. Sylvia was such a gentle, loving woman. I should have known she could never cast you off. I blame myself.'

'Don't.' Lawrence wondered how many people were taking the blame for what Ralph had done.

He tried to eat some toast but couldn't force it down. Mrs Dane poured him more coffee. 'You don't look well, my dear. Have you slept at all?'

'Not much.'

'You've been thinking, I suppose?'

'Remembering.'

'Remembering? How much?'

'A great deal.' Lawrence wondered if he should tell her of his dreams but decided against it. It would distress her. She would be forced to recall, as he now did, the house in uproar after Father's death, filled with doctors, policemen, others who came and went. He had crept into a corner and stayed there, too terrified to tell anyone that it was all his fault. My God, all these years he'd been an emotional cripple and it was Ralph Bennyson's doing. If he'd had his mother to confide in she would have reassured him, because of course Father had shot himself before he knew his son was present. Another horror swept over Lawrence. Had his father's last view been of his son running towards him, terror on his face? He wanted to push the thought aside, but in his new-found knowledge he made himself examine it as he would in future examine everything.

He wanted, needed, to talk to someone. Isobel, of course. She'd help him. She'd know what to say. Mrs Dane had been watching

348

expressions chase across his face which now, to her relief, she saw brighten a little. He got up, kissed her and said, 'I probably won't be back for lunch.' Then he left.

Isobel was engaged in book-keeping during a rare slack period. Since the show the number of her customers had grown until now she was thinking seriously about renting larger premises as Desmond had done. The top storey of Desmond's property was going cheap, but that would pose a serious problem to women who, if they were faced with two flights of steep stairs, would turn away. She paused to consider what she had already achieved. She had bought a larger piece of carpet and gleaming on a table stood a new sewing machine which could deal with the lighter stitching. True, she had got it on the never-never, but her income was steady enough to convince the salesman that she was a safe bet. And she had been able to engage Mrs Prentice, who had been the catalyst for the threatened factory strike through which she and Desmond had lost their jobs. Poor creature, it hadn't been her fault and her problems had increased tremendously with her loss of income. She was speechless with gratitude when offered a job. The September day sent gentle, warm breezes through the open sash window, stirring the lace curtains. She heard Lawrence's car as it turned into the street. There was no mistaking its engine. She preferred him not to call during the day. Some of her customers enjoyed peeping out at him, but others, older women, were nervous to think of him walking into the house and perhaps through the wrong door.

'Tell him to go away,' hissed Isobel when Grace came in.

'You don't have any customers.'

'I told him not to call during working hours. He has to learn his lesson.'

Grace said anxiously, 'Better come, Isobel. Something's happened to him.'

'What?' Isobel stood up quickly and in that instant realised a truth she had been trying to deny. She loved him and always would. 'Is he hurt?'

'Not physically, if that's what you mean. You'd best see for yourself.'

Grace left the kitchen free and as soon as Isobel saw Lawrence she understood Grace's anxiety. Something had most definitely happened to him.

'Sit down,' she said quietly, motioning him to the easy chair.

349

He didn't sit. Instead he took her in his arms and held her close. His heart was beating frantically.

'Please, sit, my love,' begged Isobel. 'You're ill.'

'Not ill,' he gasped, thankful to be with Isobel where he could release some of the emotion which was battering at his senses. 'I'm shocked. Very shocked.'

'I see,' she said quietly. She freed herself from his clinging arms and, opening the cupboard where she kept some good brandy for any customer who might need it, poured some into a glass. 'Here, drink this.'

He gulped it down.

'Now,' said Isobel, 'can you tell me what's happened?'

He allowed himself to be persuaded into the comfortable chair and Isobel sat beside him. Grace tiptoed in as if he were an invalid, which brought a weak smile to his face. She put a tray of coffee and biscuits on the small table beside him; he thanked her, but didn't touch them.

'I went to Grandmother,' said Lawrence without preamble. 'She said that Felice had been to see her and told her that there was some discrepancy in the stories she had been told about my mother. Grandmother thought she was just an hysterical girl, but then my mother, without knowing about Felice's visit, arrived and unfolded such a vile tale of Ralph Bennyson I found it almost impossible to believe.' Lawrence went on to tell Isobel just what he had learned. His voice was flat and monotonous and she knew he was keeping himself in check with immense difficulty.

'You believe all that your mother said?'

'Yes.'

'Why?'

'What?'

'You've despised her for years, yet now you believe everything she said against the word of a man you've apparently respected.'

Lawrence was silent for a moment. 'Yes, it seems odd, but I had no strong feelings towards Ralph. In fact, I think I was unconsciously using him to revenge myself on my mother. I pretended not to see her look of appeal whenever I came to the house. I ignored her.'

'You've seen enough of life to know that everyone makes mistakes. Why couldn't you forgive her?'

'Some misguided loyalty to Ralph, I suppose. Last night I had a dream or a vision, I can't be sure which. I remembered how my

350

father died.' Lawrence told Isobel the facts briefly without going into detail. She sensed the depth of his suffering.

She took his hand in hers. 'What does Ralph Bennyson say to all this?'

'I haven't tackled him yet.'

'You've come to me first?'

'I had to.'

'Oh, Lawrence.' She bent forward and kissed him. He returned her kiss gently, without passion. 'When will you talk to him?'

'Soon. I feel more able to control myself now that I've spoken to you.'

'I wish I could come with you.'

'So do I.' Lawrence managed a weak smile. 'It would look rather odd if I arrived with you as my bodyguard.'

'Considering I'm almost a midget, I agree I wouldn't look impressive.'

'Don't denigrate yourself in any way, Isobel. I won't have it. I love you too much. Will you come for a drive with me?'

'In the middle of a working day?'

'Don't treat me lightly. I can't endure it.'

'I'm sorry.' She glanced at her timetable. Rose wasn't working today and Ruby and Mrs Prentice had plenty to do. 'All right, I can take an hour and a half.'

She sat silently by him while he drove rapidly out of the town into the countryside. He stopped by a narrow river which flowed over pebbles. Trees overhung the spot and the Indian summer sun shone warmly.

Lawrence helped her out of the car. His eyes were opaque, his voice was a monotone again. He said, 'I used to come here alone when I was a boy. I swam, and the cool water seemed to wash away my worries.'

'Had you many?'

'A lot. It isn't easy growing up believing your parents cared nothing for you.'

'You know now that was not true. And your poor father was obviously disturbed.'

'That's what the coroner said. "Suicide while the balance of his mind was disturbed." Of course I didn't know that at the time. I was still living a nightmare.'

'Poor little boy. Fancy no one realising that you needed some kind of explanation. But grown-ups often seem to underestimate the intelligence of their children, don't they? Mum didn't realise how much we understood of her life with Dad.'

'Bad, was it?'

'Terrible.' Isobel looked down at the water which flowed sweet and wholesome in its transparency. She could well imagine it soothing a child's worries with its caress. She said, 'Why don't you swim before you see Ralph? The river might work its old magic on you.'

'A good idea.' Lawrence, still half mesmerised, stripped and Isobel watched him, loving the way his muscles rippled beneath his smooth skin.

'I must remove everything,' he said. 'The magic mightn't work unless I do.'

'Go ahead.' Isobel continued to gaze as he revealed himself to her. He was beautiful in every part and suddenly she wanted to hold him and caress him. She watched him slide into the water and swim lazily upriver and she knew she wanted to be with him. Quickly she undressed, hesitated when she got to her knickers, then laughed and took them off to join him in his fantasy world. She had never swum outside a public baths, bounded by walls and guarded by attendants, but she felt no fear as she slipped into the water, gasping at its chill. Her feet didn't reach the bottom, which was much deeper than she'd expected, but she swam after him. The ripple of water sighing and gurgling over the stones that lined the banks concealed any sound of her approach and she caught up with him, dived beneath and came up in front of him and threw her arms around him.

He stared into her eyes and murmured, 'Isobel! Oh, Isobel, my love.'

They held one another close, treading water, then swam together upriver until they came to a spot where willow branches made a green curtain, shielding a place where the grass and moss made a bed. Here they climbed out, water streaming from their tingling skin.

Without a word they lay down on the soft moss. Isobel looked up at the greenery which seemed to float above them in the breeze and felt as if she were in a dream world. When Lawrence touched her she returned his caresses eagerly and they began a gentle exploration, their fingers gliding easily over each other's damp flesh which smelled of the fresh river water.

Lawrence cradled her breasts, then opened his mouth and took the nipples one by one deep into his mouth. She drew a quick breath as his tongue moved on her and her hand followed down his smooth flat belly until it reached the thick, rough hair from which his penis rose strong and vibrant. She touched it, then ran her hand up and down its length, moving the foreskin gently, not knowing how she understood just what to do. Lawrence found her lips, then his tongue wandered over her, teasing her until she thought she'd explode with desire. He lifted himself over her. For a split second the memory of Amos's disgusting contact, his stinking breath, hovered before her, then disappeared for ever, releasing her from shame. She gave herself to Lawrence without thought of past, present or future, intent only on giving and receiving ecstasy until all the power of her strong body gathered itself in stupendous sensations of joy followed by Lawrence's cries as he found his own release.

They lay quietly side by side. Then Lawrence said, 'Darling, darling Isobel. You'll have to marry me now.'

'Don't joke,' she said sadly.

'Who's joking? I mean every word.' He raised himself on his elbow and gazed into her face. 'Isobel, my only love, will you marry me?'

'You mean it. You really do mean it.' She said nothing for a full minute. 'Are you prepared to face your family and friends? They'll have no mercy on you. I'm a factory girl,' she reminded him, 'daughter and sister of jailbirds.'

'Are *you* ready to face them?'

'I care nothing for outside opinions. My only concern is with us. Of course my family may look suspiciously at one of the idle rich.'

'But they may not. Actually, the only one I care about is Grandmother and she will honour any commitment I choose. And, moreover, woman, I am not idle.'

'I'll decide that. What will your mother say? How will she feel about getting you back, then losing you again?'

'I hope she'll forgive me and be glad for me. She won't be able to resist you. I shall ask for her approval.'

'And if she or Mrs Dane object –?'

'I meant it when I said I mean to have you. If you'll have me.'

Isobel laughed softly. 'I'll let you make me an honest woman.'

'Even if your family frowns?'

Isobel said resignedly, 'As a matter of fact they've seen you as a benefactor ever since you gave Kathy the tent. And they genuinely like you, in spite of your upper-classness.'

The sun, already filtered between the leaves, was suddenly hidden behind a cloud and they shivered. Together they slid back into the river and went with the currents downstream to where their cloths lay haphazardly discarded, dressing themselves with pauses to embrace.

'We'll have to marry soon,' said Lawrence, 'or neither of us will get a thing done for thinking of the other.'

'I intend to go on working,' said Isobel. 'After marriage.'

'Expanding your business? I've no objection. Many women work nowadays. And I shall be busy making the home farm pay better and taking my stables far more seriously. And I shall invest in business.'

'What business?'

'Yours of course, darling, and possibly Desmond's.'

They beamed at one another and finished dressing. Neither had a comb so they drew their fingers through their damp, tangled hair, laughing at themselves.

Returning home they fell silent. Lawrence was facing an ordeal he didn't relish. 'But I'll have the comfort of knowing you stand with me,' he said abruptly, guessing correctly that her thoughts matched his.

Grace hurried to greet them at the gate. 'Mrs Kenton's here with her friend. Good gracious, Isobel, what on earth have you done to your hair?'

'It's got windblown,' said Isobel. 'Mrs Kenton's early.'

She watched Lawrence's car until it turned the corner, then went in to resume her responsibilities.

Lawrence drove to the pretty house in Stapleton and the maid showed him into the drawing room where Sylvia had been working on her embroidery. She stood, her delicate sewing lying on the carpet, her hand on the piano, her eyes wide. Since leaving Ralph she had filled out and got some colour in her cheeks. Even a few weeks away from Ralph was enough to begin the restoration of her beauty and tranquillity.

She greeted him gently but fearfully. And why shouldn't she when she had received nothing but callous disregard from him? Maybe she thought he'd come to persuade her to return to Ralph.

Lawrence was tongue-tied. How did you greet a mother whom you had vilified or ignored for most of your life? What could he say to make her forgive him? He had been as bad as Ralph.

Sylvia solved the problem. She must have caught his altered mood because she held out her arms and he walked into them. Neither of them spoke, both near to tears.

Again Sylvia took the lead. 'You've spoken to your grandmother?'

'Yes.'

'Come, let us sit together.'

They sat side by side on the chintz-upholstered sofa.

'Mrs Dane told you what I said? And you believe her?'

'Yes.'

'Why?'

The question had been asked by Isobel. Women had a habit of going straight to the emotional point. 'I was right to, wasn't I?'

'Of course, but you've been indoctrinated with hate for so many years I couldn't be sure that you'd listen if she spoke, let alone believe.'

'I believe. Grandmother wanted you to have your son. You wanted me. Only Ralph stood between you. I already know he's ruthless and will lie if it suits his purpose, but up to now I've ignored his faults. Every human being has faults, I told myself. Now I'm faced with the truth. And it hurts. It hurts like hell.'

Sylvia took his hand in hers. 'So like your father's hand. Well shaped, strong. I loved your father terribly, Lawrence. I never had a moment's peace after I left him. When he – died – my life altered. I believed I must be punished. I lost what little remained of my spirit. I gave in to Ralph over everything. I took all the beastliness he had to offer, I was so cowed I no longer knew how to defend myself. I didn't even want to. I suppose my weakness encouraged his bullying. I even held myself aloof from Felice, unable to show her how much I loved her because she was dominated by Ralph. We are friends now. Oh, Lawrence, I'm sorry, so deeply sorry.'

Lawrence gripped her hand. 'I'm sorry too. We know the truth now. And I needn't have been such a swine to you.'

'Ralph is a powerful man. He finds it easy to terrorise those in his power.'

'I've not been in his power and he's never terrorised me. He played upon my mistrust of you. And he hasn't got his own way with Felice. She looks fragile, yet she's so brave.'

'I fear she'll have a battle with him that she might not win.'

'She hasn't deserved the way I've treated her.'

'That makes me happy. Lawrence, in case you have lingering doubts, I have something I should like you to see.' She went to a small cupboard and drew out a photograph album. 'These are pictures of your early childhood.' She drew out a sealed envelope and handed it to him. 'Please, look at this.'

Lawrence opened the envelope and stared down at a photograph. It depicted his father, fully clothed, intimately caressing an almost naked woman. He looked up. 'Grandmother told me of this. I can see how it would deceive you. It's almost perfect.'

'But not quite, though I was too distressed to realise it until later. I thought your father was being unfaithful to me. He was away at the time and Ralph assured me he was even then with his mistress. He comforted me and overcame my resistance and I gave way to him.'

'When did you know the photo was false?'

'When Harry – your father – died. I realised that to take his own life when he loved living so meant he loved me too much to go on without me. The photograph is made up of two superimposed images. Lawrence, I've paid for my madness, believe me.'

Lawrence sat quietly beside his mother whose hands betrayed a slight tremor which he had seen many times. Almost always when he had visited the Bennyson house her hands had shaken in just such a way. God only knew what his coldness had done to her over the years.

'I'm sorry, Mother,' he said again. There were no words to express how bitterly he regretted the past.

Sylvia gave a long sigh. 'Lawrence, we can never make up for the lost years, but we can be friends now, can't we?'

'Of course. More, much more, than friends. Are you happy here?'

'So much happier, especially now you've come.'

'I shall sever all contact with Ralph,' said Lawrence.

'He has named you his heir.'

'I know. He can keep his damned factory and his money. I'll have no part of them. In any case, they should go to Felice. She could probably run the factory. Imagine her working in a tough café in West Street and living with the Kingstons and being really happy.'

'Ralph disapproves. I suppose one can't blame him.'

'She's a damn sight better off there than with such a father.'

'I know, but I'm hoping to persuade her to live here with me.'

'She's very fond of the eldest Kingston boy, Desmond,' said Lawrence cautiously.

'Yes, she wears his ring.'

'Does that shock you?'

'Nothing much shocks me now. I think she's making a mistake but I have faith enough to think she'll realise that such a connection isn't suitable.'

Lawrence stood and his mother gazed up at him. She was compassionate and forgiving. All the love which had been frustrated for so many years reached out to fill him. He bent and kissed her. Only Ralph to go now. In spite of that unpleasant prospect, this day would always rank as one of the most vital of his life.

Ralph was busy compiling a list of complaints against Sylvia to hand to his solicitor when he was told that Mr Lawrence Dane was in the drawing room. He hurried to greet him, but his smile died and the hand he'd put out dropped to his side. 'You look rather grim, Lawrence, my boy.'

'I am not your boy. I've been listening to truths about the past. My God, Ralph, how could you have behaved so badly? I still find it difficult to believe.'

'What do you mean?'

'I've been talking to Grandmother. Mother visited her.'

'Really? I'm surprised Mrs Dane received her.'

'She not only received her, she believed her.' If Lawrence had retained any doubts about Ralph's guilt they would have been dissipated in the face of a dismay too powerful to hide. 'What they say is true, isn't it? You lied to both of them. You kept me from my mother. And all for the sake of revenge.'

'For heaven's sake,' said Ralph, trying to sound jocular, 'it's long gone. I may have told a few small untruths—'

'Small untruths? A forged photograph of Father with an unclothed woman—?'

'Where did you see that?'

'Mother kept it. She showed it to me.'

'How morbid of her to hang on to it. It proves she's sick, totally unfitted to care for her daughter.'

'That's rubbish and you know it. It probably always was.'

Ralph shrugged, though he was white about the lips.

'Have you no shame at all? No regrets?'

'My regrets are for myself. I could have married anyone. In my opinion your mother was a plum ripe for the picking. If I hadn't taken her some other man would.' Lawrence clenched his fists and Ralph moved back. 'She was a very beautiful woman,' he continued hastily, 'and I wasn't the only man who coveted her. When she fell for me—' Ralph stopped as Lawrence took a step towards him. 'Yes, well, it happened years ago. I suppose I shouldn't have fooled her, but she was as much to blame as me. More so. It's up to the woman to be chaste.'

'My God, what a philosophy!'

357

'Don't tell me you've never seduced a woman?'

'I've made love, but only to women who had nothing to lose.'

'How virtuous of you.' Ralph tried again to be jocular. 'Come now, Lawrence, let's forget this nonsense. I'm going to get Felice back and I was looking to you to help me rescue her from the loathsome place she's landed in.'

'You still don't get it, do you? From now on our contact is finished and you can go to your solicitor and alter your will. I don't want your bloody factory, or your money. I never really did. I felt sorry for you because you struck me as being a lonely man. You are, aren't you? You've antagonised everyone who should be close to you. Even Felice. She may even now have the remains of a tender feeling towards you which you seem intent on destroying.'

Ralph glared at him. 'When I get her back here she'll soon realise how much she's missed me. She won't be able to stand living with that ghastly family for long, and as for working in that greasy café, it's just a game to her.'

'More than a game, Ralph. She's wearing Desmond Kingston's ring, remember?'

'I'll ruin him,' said Ralph savagely. 'I'll make him sorry he was born. And that sister of his has opened a corsetry business. I'll close it down. They'll all wish they'd never met me by the time I've done with them.'

Lawrence said coldly, 'I think they already wish that and Felice sympathises with them. Furthermore I intend to weigh in on their side. I have money enough to help them all.'

'Is that so? What do you get out of it? Of course, there's the younger sister. I hear she's nothing but a trollop. You could have her.'

Lawrence smiled. 'Olive? Oh, no. She's going to marry Steve Dawson. She'll be rich.'

'The bookie?'

'That's right.'

'My daughter really imagines I'll stand by while she becomes the sister-in-law of a bookie suspected by the police of violence towards non-payers, a man who came from the gutter?'

'That's the one,' said Lawrence cheerfully, intent now on making Ralph squirm as much as possible.

'You can't permit your sister to make such a connection. Lawrence, whatever you think of me, help me to get her away from that disgraceful bunch. Did you know there's a brother who's been arrested for theft and that the father was a recidivist?'

'I know,' said Lawrence, sounding positively buoyant, 'and none of it bothers me. As a matter of fact, the publican from whom Ivor is supposed to have stolen has decided he made a big mistake and had put the money in a drawer and forgotten it. Ivor will be freed soon and Dawson has a job waiting for him. Ivor will be in his element.'

'My God, a put-up job if ever I heard one.'

'That's slanderous.'

Ralph glared at Lawrence. 'You seem to know a hell of a lot about the family.'

'Oh, I do. I get all the news first-hand. You see, I intend to marry Isobel Kingston. I asked her today and she accepted.'

'You're joking, aren't you? Some devil's got into you. Why do you want to hurt me by trivialising such important matters?'

'No jokes, Ralph. All deadly serious.'

'You really are going to marry that Kingston woman? I wonder what Mrs Dane will say to that.'

'She's going to love Isobel.'

'She might not by the time I've finished with the family. I shall use every weapon I can find to discredit them. The papers will be full of it, I'll make sure of that. The Kingstons are a disreputable lot and you don't have enough money to stop me.'

Chapter Twenty-Two

Isobel listened to the account of Lawrence's visit to Ralph. 'He's really going to take his own wife to court?' she said incredulously. 'How can he? It'll crucify her. Imagine what the newspapers will make of it! It'll hurt Felice, too. All the past scandal will be dug up when she's just getting to know her mother properly.'

Lawrence nodded. 'I've been thinking about it ever since I spoke to him. I've come to the conclusion that it would be best all round if Felice went to live with her mother. Ralph may bluster all he pleases, but Sylvia is very different now. She'll have courage enough to stand up in court and defy him. She's very protective of her daughter.'

'You've really fallen for your mother, haven't you?'

Lawrence said softly, 'I really have. I regret having wasted so many years hating her.'

'She's never stopped loving you?'

'Not for one minute. I suppose if I hadn't been so blind I'd have realised that her kind of steadiness doesn't fit the sort of woman Ralph made her out to be.'

'I'm sure she'll be brave in court,' said Isobel, 'but all the same it won't do her nerves any good.'

'She and Felice will be forced into conflict anyway if Ralph continues with this vindictive plan to take Felice from Mother. And you have a great deal to lose, too, and Desmond. Ralph could use his money and influence to close you both down.'

'How could he?' cried Isobel scornfully. 'We're not breaking the law.'

'No, but he's powerful enough to get at Desmond's landlord. I gather the rent is paid monthly, so only a month's notice to quit need be given.'

Isobel paled. 'He couldn't!'

'I'm afraid he could. And he wouldn't hesitate to start a campaign against you. He could instigate whispers. There are plenty who would co-operate for the sake of a few pounds. And he could lower his prices to a point where you'd be helpless against him.'

'My customers get custom-made corsets,' said Isobel indignantly. 'He won't do that cheaply for them.'

'I wouldn't be too sure. And when he'd ruined you he'd abandon the women.'

'And I'd take them back again,' she said fiercely.

Laurence grinned. 'I've no doubt you would, but, darling, although you're strong, that kind of battle wouldn't do you much good and it would add to the others' misery.'

Isobel clenched her fists. 'What kind of whispers could he begin?'

'Plenty. Apart from thinking up scurrilous tales about you and Desmond, he need only draw on facts about your father, his terms of imprisonment, his untimely death.'

'Untimely, yes, but what could be made of it? Accidents happen. Dad fell down the stairs.'

'Probably because he was too drunk to save himself. Think how the newspapers would love the chance to dwell on that again. Cleverly worded hints are enough for people who enjoy scandal. And there's your sister's engagement to a notorious bookie. It would be mulled and gloated over and they'd be sure to find something to say about Ivor. And you told me that in spite of everything your mother loved your father. She'd be so hurt.'

'What can we do?' asked Isobel.

'It's a hellish problem. We'll have to think about it. Luckily we have time. A case like this will take a while to prepare and present.'

But unfortunately there were alterations and cancellations in the court lists and the case of Bennyson *versus* Bennyson suddenly arrived at the top.

The family got together in Sylvia's house to which she welcomed everyone warmly. She was especially kind to Grace, of whom she had become fond.

All the possibilities were talked over. Felice listened quietly, then said, 'Lawrence's solution is the only feasible one. I must come to live with Mother.'

Desmond looked disappointed. 'Only until we can be married,' he said. 'And need we wait for your father's permission for that? Surely your mother could give it.'

'I don't know,' said Felice, 'but I do know that Father would find out and move against us. Let's not have any more hateful battles. We can wait a few months and there's nothing to stop me getting out to see you every day.'

362

Desmond, still grumbling, agreed.

The conference ended and maids served refreshments. Isobel noticed that Grace was very pale and could eat none of the tiny delicious sandwiches and sponge cakes.

When they arrived home Kathy was waiting. 'How was school today?' asked Isobel.

'Interesting like always. What's up, Mum? Are you feeling ill?'

Grace turned to her and she and Kathy embraced before going upstairs together, shutting out Isobel so completely she had an actual physical pain in her heart as she listened to the murmur of their voices.

Later, as she laid the table for supper, Kathy came running down, saying accusingly, 'You've upset our mum. Why did you take her to that woman's house?'

At supper, Grace and Kathy were very quiet in spite of everything Isobel could do to draw them out, and whenever Kathy looked at her elder sister her smooth forehead creased in a frown. After supper Olive went to meet Dawson, and Grace, Kathy and Isobel were alone together. Isobel had no evening appointment and washed the dishes while Kathy dried. The mood grew heavier with each passing moment.

The three settled down, Kathy with her homework, Grace with her knitting, Isobel with her sketch pads, but there was no congenial atmosphere; the air sang with tension. At last Isobel threw down her pencils and asked, 'Just what's the matter with you two?'

'Nothing,' said Grace. 'We're a bit tired. You must admit our lives haven't been exactly easy lately.'

'Not since Dad's death,' said Kathy quickly, then flushed.

'Ever since this afternoon Mum's looked like death warmed up,' said Isobel, 'and you, Kathy, are obviously very upset and you weren't even at the meeting.'

'Mum told me about it. No objection, have you? I'm a big girl now.'

Kathy had never spoken so contemptuously to her sister and Isobel, try as she might, couldn't control the tears that stung her eyes. She tried to stop herself, she despised women who demanded sympathy by weeping, but Kathy saw a tear roll down her face and was dismayed.

She jumped up and put her arms round Isobel as she hadn't done for so long. 'It wasn't your fault. I'm sorry I've been so bad to you. It's just that Mum and I – Mum said – I thought—' The words dissolved as she began to sob.

Grace stared at them. 'Stop it, please, I couldn't bear to cry again. I'm sore with crying. Kathy, my love, we need to talk to someone and the best person is Isobel. She'll know what to do.'

Isobel felt deeply apprehensive as they drew close around the range fire, Kathy between her mother and sister.

Kathy controlled her weeping and said haltingly, 'The day Dad died Mum and I were here on our own. She was downstairs and I was in our bedroom, yours and mine, Isobel, as it was then. Dad came in, reeling around, really drunk. I could hear Mum trying to get him to go upstairs. I peeped out to see what was happening. He was coming up, stumbling about and dizzy, and Mum stayed behind him to make sure he didn't slip backwards. When he got to the top he started shouting at Mum, shouting and shouting.'

'I begged him to stop,' said Grace. 'I pleaded with him, but he only yelled the louder. I reminded him that the neighbours would hear, but he didn't care.'

Kathy broke in. 'He kept saying horrible things to Mum about you and somebody else.'

'Me?' said Isobel.

'Yes. I couldn't catch the other name, but Mum was ever so upset. She shook him to try to make him stop. He said he was sick of telling lies and he was going to let everyone know—'

'Know what?' asked Isobel.

'I don't know. He began to hit Mum and kick her.' By now Kathy was gabbling out her words. 'Mum couldn't stop him and I ran to help her. She had just managed to push him from her so that he stopped punching, but he was still kicking her legs. You know it's dark on the landing, but I could see he had clenched his fist and lifted it over Mum's head. He was going to give her such a punch I was afraid he'd kill her, so I had to help her.'

Kathy stopped and Isobel saw she was shaking. 'Go on, darling,' she said, needing to know, but dreading to hear the next words. 'You must tell me everything now.'

'I ran at him and hit him and he fell all the way down the stairs. I saw him bump down, bump bump bump, and his head crashed on the wall. I wasn't worried at first because he'd had other falls when he was drunk and wasn't injured, but this time – this time, he didn't get up. Mum went down to him and tried to lift him but he was all floppy. I tried to help her. In the end we had to stop.' Kathy began to sob again. 'He was dead, Isobel, and I'd killed him. I wanted to tell you, but Mum said better not. She said she'd pushed him at the same

364

time as me and we were both responsible, and if we kept a pact never to tell a soul no one need ever know. Don't be angry with us, please, we just couldn't bear the thought of going to prison. And Mum said we could be hanged for what we'd done.'

Isobel sat quite still. She was afraid that if she moved she'd vomit. Mum and Kathy had been living with this terrible, undeserved burden of guilt. No wonder they'd looked haunted.

'Do you think we should have told, Isobel?' asked Kathy. 'Should we have confessed?'

Isobel swallowed hard and put an arm round her sister and took her mother's hand. 'Confessed what? That a blind-drunk man had got himself into such a state he fell.'

'But we pushed him,' said Kathy.

'No, *I* pushed him,' insisted Grace. 'You hardly touched him.'

'I did, I did, it's no good saying it. I know what I did.'

Isobel allowed them to argue for a while. She pictured them lying in the double bed in Mum's room, whispering these things to each other over and over again, fighting off their sense of guilt, comforting and reassuring each other. And now Ralph Bennyson intended to attack them because of Felice. The details of Dad's life and death would be revived in the newspapers and the thought of it was torturing the two she loved so much.

'Someone might ask more questions in court about Amos,' said Grace.

'No, they won't,' promised Isobel. 'Why should they?' But she was by no means sure. She said slowly, 'I know this doesn't seem the time to tell you, but Lawrence and I are going to be married.'

'That's lovely,' cried Kathy, her eyes alight with pleasure. 'That's the loveliest thing that's happened. He's my favourite man. Except for Desmond. I don't like Mr Dawson at all.'

Grace said, 'So you're going to marry Lawrence. That makes it even more vital that we shouldn't let everything become public again. He'll make you a good husband, Isobel, the sort you deserve. But how will he feel about seeing our names splashed in the newspapers?'

'He knows that Ralph Bennyson is being sadistic. Would you give me permission to tell him what you've just told me? He may know what to do.'

Grace and Kathy stared wide-eyed at her.

'He'll be disgusted,' said Kathy.

'He won't want you if you tell him,' said Grace.

'He will want me, but if he rejected me because of an accident he'd be no husband for me.'

Later, when Kathy had gone to bed after giving Isobel a hug which wiped out the past months of neglect, Grace and Isobel sat alone in the kitchen. They had tugged the small chain of the gaslight gently so that they were in semi-darkness. Isobel made tea.

Then she said, 'Mum, what was Dad shouting that frightened you so much?'

'Nothing, really, just a lot of nonsense about something that happened ages ago.'

'It won't do, Mum. For years, every time Dad was in a temper he hinted at an event which had a terrible bearing on all our lives and concerned me. I think I had better know everything, don't you?'

Grace sat quietly staring into the heart of the fire. Then she sighed. 'It's your right to know, I suppose. Isobel, don't hate me. It all happened such a long time ago. I was very young. I fell in love with a married man and he with me. I allowed him to make love to me – no, I must tell the absolute truth – I wanted him to. We were so very happy on the few occasions we could meet in private. Then I discovered I was expecting. We both knew that we simply couldn't break his marriage to a good woman. Amos had loved me for a long time. I told him I was expecting a child and, God bless him, he married me, saying he'd take care of us both. My lover gave me money enough to help bring you up, because, of course, you were the child. He gave money to Granny Shaw, too, I think to keep her from making a fuss. She was thrifty enough to make sure of a comfortable old age, but Amos soon got through my share and then my lover died and I couldn't get any more help. Poor man. He meant to make provision for us, but was struck down before his time.'

'Dad was good enough to help you?' said Isobel wonderingly. 'No, he's not my dad, is he? Amos.' Her mind flashed for an instant to Amos's assaults and she realised with intense relief that although his behaviour towards her had been reprehensible it had not been incestuous and a burden she hadn't realised she'd carried so heavily was lifted.

'Are you angry with me, Isobel?' asked Grace, concerned by her silence.

'Angry? No, Mum.'

'Should I have told you before?'

366

Isobel said slowly, 'Maybe. Probably not. Until I met Lawrence I didn't understand how a woman could feel towards a man. Marriage has nothing to do with it, really.'

'Have you and Lawrence—?'

'We've made love, yes. I was so happy.'

'You do understand,' said Grace. 'Oh, thank God. Thank God.'

'And that was what Amos was shouting on the stairs? That I was someone else's daughter?'

'Yes. I couldn't bear for Kathy to hear. She's so sweet, so innocent, she couldn't possibly be expected to understand. And I didn't want anyone to point a finger at you, my good, sweet daughter. But, Isobel, I had no right to push him. Poor Amos. He thought he could cope with the problem of my child by another man; then found he couldn't. He kept picturing me making love to someone else and it drove him crazy.'

'So that's why you wouldn't consider leaving him?'

'Of course. And I did care for him. But I couldn't give him the love I gave to my lover. I suppose that's really what was driving him. Poor Amos.'

'He shouldn't have been cruel to you.'

'It was his way. I do wish he hadn't died the way he did. I've made Kathy feel guilty too.'

'You did nothing wrong. Amos was drunk. Kathy said you tried to steady him. Neither of you had any intention of harming him. It was an accident, Mum, believe me.'

'I'll try. I have to try.'

'Who was my father?' asked Isobel quietly.

'A good man. A decent man. We loved each other so much.'

'You have to answer me, Mum.'

'I know, but it will shock you. He was Mr Bennyson senior.'

'*Ralph* Bennyson's *father*?'

'Yes.'

'His father? What relation is that horrible man to me? My brother?'

'Half-brother.'

'We carry the same blood!' A sudden ghastly thought struck Isobel. 'Are Lawrence and I blood-related? He's not my brother, is he? No, he's not. He's not, is he?' In her panic she couldn't think straight.

'Of course he isn't. Lawrence's father was Harry Dane and his mother was Sylvia Dane as she was then. No wonder Felice thought she recognised your photograph. You are the image of my dear man.'

Lawrence listened quietly to Isobel as she told him how Amos had died.

When she stopped speaking he said, 'Those poor girls. To think how they've suffered. Of course it was an accident. To accuse those two innocents of anything different would be like accusing a pair of doves of starting the Great War.'

'I knew you'd understand.'

'Did you, my darling? I must kiss you for that.' His lips brushed tenderly over hers.

She put her arms around him, love mixed inextricably with gratitude. 'I love you so much, Lawrence.'

'Yet you risked losing me by confiding that awful story?'

'I couldn't see any other way. I can't think of a solution. I hope you can.'

He touched her cheek with a gentle finger. 'My God, Isobel, life's going to be wonderful with you. Absolute trust is the perfect foundation for a marriage.'

'Absolute trust. Yes.' She paused. 'There is something I must tell you about my parentage.'

Again Lawrence listened carefully. 'Your poor mother. How she's suffered.'

'You don't mind? About me, I mean? About the way I was born?'

'All I know about you, my darling, is that I love you with all my heart and nothing can ever change that. Besides, Bennyson senior was a very decent sort of man and your mother is a dear.'

'You're the most wonderful man in the world,' she said.

'How soon can you prove it again?'

'As soon as we have the time and the place.'

Ralph wanted consolation and knew where to find it. He hadn't seen Dulcia for a couple of weeks. He felt desperately angry with Desmond and Isobel Kingston, and frustrated over Felice. All his misery could be blamed on that conniving low-class pair. They were the instigators of his suffering. They had encouraged his Felice to rebel. She was so innocent, so confiding, she couldn't see what the Kingstons were really like. And they had driven Lawrence from him. He'd get them one way or another. They shouldn't thrive and prosper and continue to make a fool of him. Once he had got Felice back he knew he'd soon undermine their influence on her. She'd realise how she'd been duped and be glad of their downfall. He couldn't wait to tell Dulcia how clever he was.

She received him with her lovely smile. 'Come in, Ralph, I've been wondering where you've been.'

'I'm sorry, my dear, but when you hear what's been happening you'll understand.'

A slight frown creased her brow. 'Is this about Felice and Sylvia? You've told me most things. You've talked a lot about them lately.'

If Ralph had had any sensitivity he would have realised that Dulcia was tired of his family as a subject. He sat beside her and kissed her warmly. 'I've missed you so much. Have you dined?'

'I have. The maid will be bringing coffee. She'll add a cup for you.'

'Good. I want your approval of what I've done.' Ralph launched into the story of Felice's defection and the events following, failing to notice Dulcia's surprised glances, her increasingly dark looks. He finished and sat back complacently. 'So I shall get my daughter back and without the encumbrance of my miserable wife.'

Dulcia stubbed out her cigarette, leaving the room smelling faintly of Turkish tobacco. 'Don't you think you'll alienate Felice even more if you humiliate her in public and upset the people she cares for?'

'Cares for? The Kingstons? She's been intrigued by their strange way of living, that's all. How fed up she must be by now stuck in that cramped house without enough money, and working – can you credit it? – in a low-down café that I wouldn't be seen dead in, actually wearing a coarse apron and waiting on stallholders, butchers, even a tramp or two.'

'It's the first constructive thing she's ever done as far as I can tell.'

Ralph at last caught a whiff of her reaction. 'You aren't going to tell me you approve of her behaviour?'

'Not quite approve, no, I shouldn't want a daughter of mine to follow her example, but I should never treat my daughter as you've treated Felice. And now you've alienated Lawrence as well and intend to involve the daughter you say you love in an unsavoury court case. To get Felice from your wife will mean blackening Sylvia's character in public. I can't imagine how you'll do that since all you've ever told me is that her nerves are bad.'

'She's been in and out of nursing homes because of her mental state. Remember that?'

'You mean to throw that at her in court?'

'I'll do anything to get Felice out of her clutches. You'll see I'm right.' Ralph stood up and tried to pull Dulcia to her feet, but she braced herself. 'Let go of my hands, Ralph. I dislike being man-handled.'

'That's not what you usually say,' he protested, attempting to joke.

'It's what I say now. I think you had better leave.'

'What? Leave? Leave the room?'

'You know what I mean. Leave my house. You are no longer welcome here.'

'But why?'

'I can go along with a great deal. I don't pretend to instruct others how to behave, but I can't feel any affection for a man prepared to hurt his womenfolk so deeply.'

'Don't be cross with me, darling. Let's talk calmly. Let's enjoy ourselves. Have a drink or two and then – '

'You can drink yourself into insensibility before I shall accept the way you're behaving. I had no idea you could be so utterly lost to decency. Now go.' She touched the bell by the fireside and her maid entered.

'Show this gentleman to the door. He finds he has to leave.'

The maid, chosen for her discretion, led Ralph into the hall where she helped him into his coat and handed him his hat and gloves.

'There's something I forgot to say,' said Ralph. He pushed past the maid and hurried back to Dulcia's sitting room. She sat calmly where he had left her. She had lit another cigarette and blew smoke from her voluptuous lips. He wanted to weep when he thought of losing her beauty and her passionate love-making. She stared at him, her black eyes colder than he would have believed possible. 'Yes?'

'Dulcia, may I come back some time? When all this is over and forgotten?'

'I think not. Accept the inevitable, Ralph. You and I are finished. I was mistaken in your character.'

His affection was ousted by an explosion of anger. 'I'll see about that. I'll tell the world you take lovers.'

'Indeed?' She sent him a look of such scorn it seemed to penetrate his skin like needles.

He was fonder of her than he'd realised. 'Dulcia, darling, please don't make me go. I love you. I do, truly. I didn't mean what I said. I'll do anything for you. I've had my eye on a ruby and diamond brooch –.'

'Do you think you can buy me? Get out!'

370

'I've been buying you for a long while now,' Ralph shouted.

'You've given me a few trinkets.'

'Expensive trinkets.'

'Would you like to send me a invoice? I'll pay you for the ones I've worn and return the others.'

Ralph was defeated. She had absolutely no fear of him, and he realised he had no proof whatsoever of their intimate contact. Dulcia had seen to that.

The maid met him again in the hall and held out her hand. 'May I have your key, sir?'

Ralph felt utterly humiliated as he took the key from his pocket and handed it to the maid. She opened the door and he walked out.

For the first time in her life Felice felt secure in the love of others. Once she had trusted only in her father's love but he had proved to be false, not caring for her, simply possessing her. Her mother had genuinely loved her, but Father had ridiculed and denigrated her to the point where Felice had grown up without respect for the woman who had borne her.

Felice had moved into her mother's house, which was decorated with a delicate touch. Father's house was filled with expensive antiques from his family, most of them heavy and dark. True, her bedroom had been furnished and decorated to her taste and Felice had missed it. Then she discovered that Sylvia had made her room in the cottage into a replica, hoping that one day her daughter would visit.

Felice could weep to think how easily she might have missed knowing her mother properly. Every day away from Ralph brought an improvement in Sylvia's health and appearance.

She was still apprehensive about the immediate future. She warned Felice: 'I think there's no doubt that your father will go ahead and try to get you back and I'm horribly afraid he'll succeed.'

'Why should he? How could he? I'm a woman now.'

'I've been so unstable.'

'Not surprising,' said Felice.

'You think that now, but not so long ago you would have agreed with your father. I'm not blaming you, darling, I understand. It's easy to work on a child's imagination. The trouble is that I'm still regarded in many quarters as a half-mad creature unfit to bring you up. And when my past is read out in court, not just my illnesses but the scandal I was involved in, things will look bad for me.'

371

'He wouldn't go so far! He couldn't! He's the guilty one.'

'Not in the eyes of the law. The woman is always blamed.'

'It's insufferable! Monstrous!'

'It's a fact which must be faced.'

'Then we'll face it together. Mother, I'm twenty. Surely my opinion will count for something.'

Felice thought deeply about the threatened scandal. Father would go as far as he could. He could involve Desmond and his family because they had encouraged her wilfulness. The Kingstons would be hurt and they had been so kind to her. She talked it all over with Desmond. 'Mother and I will stand firm together,' she said.

'I know, darling, but it's only recently she's begun to test her strength.'

Felice said miserably, 'How hateful my father is. I'd do anything not to distress your family. Your mother gave me a haven when I felt utterly defeated. Oh, Desmond, what's the right thing for me to do?'

He took her in his arms. 'I love you so much.'

'And I love you and I don't want anyone to suffer on my account. I even feel a bit sorry for Father. I know he's been awful, but I can't wipe out everything we had.'

'I know, my love.'

'Can't you advise me?'

'I can see only one way out and it's a way that I loathe. Felice, you say you feel sorry for your father. Do you feel enough to go back to him, just for a while?'

Felice gasped. 'You can't want that!'

'Of course I don't, but I can't think of any other way to stop him. For all his ruthless ways he does care for you and wouldn't willingly harm you. As soon as you reach your majority we'll be married, and he won't be able to do a thing. Any court case would be irrelevant.'

Felice leaned on him. 'You're right, of course. But I'll be deceiving him, won't I?'

'I know.'

'He's cheated so many,' said Felice slowly. 'He still cheats all the time. His factory women aren't paid enough and he won't help them the way my grandfather did. He's ruthless. All the same I can't hate him completely. He is my father.'

Desmond remained silent, allowing her to work it out for herself. 'I shall go back,' she said at last. 'My birthday is in a few month's time. Who knows? By then he may even have come round to my way of thinking.'

'That could happen, I suppose.'

Felice gave him a wry smile. 'And pigs may fly.'

'Maybe they will. He does genuinely care for you.'

'In his own poor way.'

Felice called another meeting and announced her intention and the reasons for it to a stunned audience. Sylvia was the first to protest. 'You can't. He's a brute.'

'He won't be to me. I may even be able to soften him.'

Lawrence said regretfully, 'Had I remained on good terms with him I could have come to the house and kept an eye on you, Felice.'

'I'll be all right,' she assured him. 'Father loves me in his way.'

'So much so that he wants you to marry a damned half-wit,' said Desmond.

'Aubrey Whittaker isn't quite a half-wit,' said Felice, 'more of a three-quarter-wit. Anyway, he's just become engaged to a girl called Edna. I actually feel sorry for him. She's one who'll never let him go. He'll find himself married almost immediately to a positive harpy.'

'That's one problem solved then,' said Desmond callously, 'but he's sure to throw you at someone else.' His face was dark with jealous anger.

Felice took his hand. 'No one and nothing will ever part me from you, my love. And I have an idea. I have a cousin, Jeffrey Westbury. He's a philanderer if ever there was one, but he's got no designs on me. I'll ask him to pretend to be my fiancé and Father will jump at the idea. Jeffrey's very rich and always good company, and he'll certainly make my life cheerful. I'll tell him the truth, of course. I know he dislikes Father intensely, so he'll think it's a good joke.'

Desmond bridled again at the thought of even a pretend fiancé, but was soothed to a certain extent when Felice said that she was sure Jeffrey would contrive to help them meet whenever possible.

Lawrence said, 'Well done, Felice.'

'Thank you, brother.'

They smiled in understanding.

Ralph was triumphant. 'I knew you couldn't stay away from me for long. Felice, my darling, I've missed you terribly.'

'Enough to set a court case in motion against Mother? That would have hurt me.'

'I wouldn't have gone through with it.'

Felice allowed the lie to remain where it lay between them.

'I can't bear life without you,' Ralph said.

'You do look rather seedy,' said Felice.

'I feel it. I've had so many shocks lately. I've not only lost my dear daughter, but an old friend has cast me off.'

'What old friend?'

Ralph muttered, 'Oh, no one you know.' Damn his stupid tongue. He missed Dulcia so much he'd almost spoken her name. 'Lawrence doesn't call any more. Did you know?'

'Yes.'

'I've heard he fancies himself in love with that Kingston woman I sacked for disloyalty.'

'Isobel? Yes, he's very fond of her.'

Ralph veered from that tack. It was obvious that the Kingstons had brainwashed his daughter. The court case could be cancelled and he felt relieved. The idea of washing the family dirty linen in public had grown more and more distasteful to him. And he'd be cleverer now. He would wait until Felice had accepted life at home completely before he moved against the businesses run by the brother and sister. He was owed revenge for what they had done to him, especially for the way they'd used Felice to incite Sylvia to rebel. He'd been getting some odd looks from acquaintances as the fact of his wife's defection had irrevocably become known. And Isobel Kingston had taken Lawrence from him. How had they contrived all this, those two insignificant low-class factory workers? How had they managed to infiltrate his family? He still couldn't believe that Lawrence wouldn't realise he'd made a mistake and would return to him. After all, what man would be such a fool as to give up a fortune? He hadn't yet altered his will, still believing that all would be forgiven and forgotten.

He learned he was mistaken when he saw the announcement of the forthcoming wedding of Lawrence Dane and Isobel Kingston.

'Fool! Fool!' he raged. He screwed up the newspaper and hurled it to the floor. Then he picked it up, smoothed it out and read it again. Lawrence, the epitome of an English gentleman, was about to descend so far as to marry a factory girl and one, moreover, from an impossibly ill-bred family.

Felice always joined him for breakfast.

'Good morning, Father.'

'What plans have you for today, darling?' He was wary.

'I shall interview Cook, of course, and check on one or two things. Then I intend to visit Betty.'

Ralph beamed happily. Lady Betty was expecting a child and she

374

and her husband were very much in love. Ralph was delighted that Felice had such a rewarding friendship. He would have been less complacent had he known that Lady Betty was deeply sympathetic towards Felice, who found it difficult to conceal her happiness now that she and Desmond, assisted by Betty, were to meet for the first time in two weeks.

Ralph vowed that never again would anything come between him and his daughter. And he'd alter his will at once in her favour. His money must go to the right person. Lawrence, as far as he was concerned, was now an outcast.

Isobel's wedding day dawned on a fine, bright late-autumn morning. The ceremony would take place in the parish church which the Danes had always attended and there was to be a small reception at Mrs Dane's home.

Grace and Olive helped Isobel to dress. She refused to deck herself in white and chose a cream dress and a simple bouquet of pale gold spray-chrysanthemums and white and gold windflowers. She surveyed herself in the mirror and smiled ruefully. 'I fear I shall never have the tall, willowy figure of a romantic heroine. I shall remain short and somewhat dumpy all my life.'

'Probably smaller and dumpier as you get older,' suggested Olive amiably. 'And when you're pregnant, my word, it'll be a sight to see.'

'Don't be unkind,' reproved Grace, but she smiled. Olive's temper had improved considerably since her engagement and impending marriage to Dawson, whom, it seemed, she had actually grown to care for. 'You look beautiful, Isobel.'

'Yes, you do,' agreed Olive. 'Don't keep running yourself down.'

When Isobel walked up the aisle on Desmond's arm, followed by Kathy, her ecstatic bridesmaid, Lawrence turned from where he stood waiting and sent her a smile which generated the greatest joy she had yet known. His love was written clearly in his face. Behind her veil she returned the look. He couldn't see it, but soon she would be able to show him just how much she cared for him. Mentally, emotionally, physically, he was everything she could desire.

Mrs Dane watched them embrace at the conclusion of the marriage service. Isobel was not the woman she would have chosen for her grandson, but she was fond of her. She had a refreshingly honest view of life and a tremendous love for her beloved grandson. When they spoke of their future together Isobel shared his dream to build up his stables, while he encouraged her to plan ahead for her own

375

business. They would, Mrs Dane had no doubt, keep their marriage alive in spite of their different interests. She took another peep at Isobel's guests. Her machinists; a Mr and Mrs Bagley and their two young sons; Isobel's sister Olive and her fiancé; and next to them a rather sly-looking dark young fellow, Isobel's brother. Such an odd set of people. The world had changed since the war. Demarcation lines were not so irrevocably drawn between differing classes of people.

Grace sat weeping quietly with joy. All the terrors of the past years were dissipated. Between them the young people had rescued her and she could now mourn Amos sincerely without the awful sensations of guilt and fear.

Granny Shaw, in her best hat and coat, watched the ceremony with her usual calm. She liked Isobel and was pleased she'd found a good man.

Felice was there. She had told her father where she was going. He had opened his mouth to argue, then caught the look in her eyes and capitulated without a fight. Felice had changed. She was prettier than ever these days; outwardly she seemed compliant, but she had developed a tenacious will. She regularly visited her mother in spite of Ralph's initial protest and remained friends with the Kingstons. Her father was beginning to understand that he had Felice in his house in person, but not entirely in spirit.

Isobel enjoyed the reception though she ate and drank little. She then changed and Lawrence drove them away in a gleaming Rolls-Royce, Mrs Dane's generous wedding gift. Isobel turned to see the people she loved best after Lawrence waving to her happily. She sighed deeply.

'Sorry you married me?' asked Lawrence in a mock concerned tone.

'I don't think so. I'll tell you later. Sorry you married me?'

'I'll tell you later. Tonight, I think, when there won't be any distractions.'

He stopped the car in a deserted country lane and took her in his arms and kissed her, a lingering, tender kiss which promised everything. 'Isobel, I love you so much. I wish I had the words. I can only vow to spend the rest of my life proving it.'

'Just as you vowed in church.'

'Exactly.'

'The rest of your life, darling? I'll settle for that.'